THE MAGE'S SANCTUARY

THE MAGE'S SANCTUARY

S. A. CADDELL

FIND YOUR UNICORN PRESS

Title: The Mage's Sanctuary

Cover design by Maria Spada

Edited by Jennifer Sommersby

Proofread by Lawrence Editing

For every single person who's helped me on my journey to finally get this book out into the world.

You know who you are.

TRIGGER WARNING

The Mage's Sanctuary is an epic fantasy set in a parallel world to ours known as Otherworld. It contains subject matter that may be difficult for some readers, including battle and combat violence, death, poisoning, perilous situations, death of a child (implied and off-page) and animal death.

Reader discretion is advised.

CHAPTER

ONE

"I know what you're planning, Bree," Aveline whispered, her warm breath tickling Bryanna's ear. "Please, don't do this."

Bryanna sighed, keeping her eyes downcast as she straightened a crease in her embroidered day dress. Anything to not have to meet her late cousin's gaze.

She must've succumbed to sleep again. It was the only way she could've been back in the familiar chamber she'd not possessed the courage to enter in years.

Not since Aveline's death over half a decade ago.

"I'm doing what I have to, Ave," Bryanna said quietly, fidgeting on the cushioned seat in front of the dressing table, careful not to look up into the face that was so much like her own, with its prominent cheekbones, arched brows, and delicate pink lips. "For you."

"You don't have to do anything," Aveline argued, weaving Bryanna's dark-ash-brown hair into the same intricate braid they'd worn as children. "It's too dangerous."

Bryanna pressed her lips together and didn't respond. It wouldn't have made any difference. She'd decided on her path a

1

long time ago, had spent years preparing for what she was going to do, and no one was going to stop her.

Not even her cousin.

Aveline set down the heavy, gilded comb. "Bree, please—"

But with a distant tug, the dream dissolved.

Bryanna sat up, all vestiges of sleep quickly evaporating as she massaged the tender, aching bump on the top of her head. She must've bumped it in her sleep. Stifling a yawn, she glanced out the window. She and her older brother, Gawain, were no longer trundling through sparse woodlands as they'd been since first light, but jolting along a well-worn gravel path toward a smattering of small, stone-faced cottages with chimney smoke billowing in the howling wind.

She leaned against the upholstery, closing her eyes as though it would banish the haunting image of her cousin from her mind.

The dream wasn't real, she reminded herself. *Wherever Aveline's soul is, it doesn't care that you're in Sheidlow Ridge, or that you're seeking answers so that you can finally avenge her.*

Opening her eyes once more, she unfurled her aunt's rumpled letter to her father dated several weeks back and reread it for the hundredth time.

Dearest Lucan,

I hope this letter finds you in good health. Things are going well here. I've just taken in a young girl barely thirteen years old. Her mother was one of the latest Brotherhood of Sìorraidh victims. I've been trying to locate her father, but it's been difficult. Seara's mother left him years ago, and I have reason to

*believe she used her sidhe powers to make him forget about her
and their daughter's existence.*

*In response to your request, I'd love for Bryanna to join me
in Sheidlow Ridge this summer. It's been too long since I last saw
her. I was greatly heartened by her feat mentioned in your last
letter. It must've taken great courage for her to face that enraged
hobgoblin in your cellar. And to have used such a complicated
spell too! I have a feeling he won't come back for a very long
time. What more could an aunt want in her only niece?*

*Of course, it's unfortunate that she almost destroyed the first
two floors of the house in the process, though it did remind me of
when I accidentally set your wife's bridal veil on fire on your
wedding day. Do you remember how beautifully it made the
altar spark when the flames caught it? I'm glad we can laugh
about it now. Give it a few more years, and your wife might too.*

Love,

Obelia

Bryanna lowered the letter, her gray eyes falling on what she could see of her aunt's tower peeking out over the encroaching canopy of the dense forest edging the village. She'd been eager to visit Obelia from the moment she'd come across a classified scroll about the Brotherhood of Sìorraidh—the heinous brethren who'd murdered Aveline—with her aunt's name stamped on the decrepit borrower list. Bryanna knew she could learn more about the Brotherhood and how to defeat them from Obelia than anything she'd ever find on the musty, dust-riddled shelves of the Ancient Archives. Especially when she knew her aunt once sought them out too. She'd disappeared for three years, and no one knew where she'd been or what she'd seen in that unaccounted time.

"Finally, you're awake," her brother, Gawain, grumbled beside her, brushing some irksome locks of ink-black hair from his face. "I still don't know why you want to spend the summer here. After I graduated last year, I don't think I spent the same night in one place for at least a moon cycle."

Bryanna rolled her eyes. "Oh, I know. Mother was insufferable. She spent the whole summer fretting over where you'd gotten to and trying to convince Father to send sentinels after you."

He'd almost done so, too, until Gawain turned up on their doorstep, just days before he was to leave for the Avalon Institute.

Bryanna glanced out her window as their carriage came to an abrupt halt in front of an outdated clothing store. Why had they stopped?

Her quizzical gaze followed Mr. Ahearn, their coachman, as he climbed out from his perch behind the reins and crouched by one of their sleek, ethereal black steeds. They looked perfectly fine to her, if a little breathless. Though it was to be expected, seeing as they'd been traveling since the wee morning hours with only a few brief stops along the way.

Beyond him, the villagers seemed to have forgotten what they were meant to be doing as they gawked at the Tuatha steeds pulling their carriage. She supposed she shouldn't have been surprised. With their large emerald eyes glowing in the sunlight and bodies almost twice the size of regular stallions, their steeds weren't common in small, isolated villages outside Otherworld's major towns.

"I'm afraid we may be here awhile," said Mr. Ahearn when he'd finished inspecting the steeds' hooves and walked over to them. "I can't take the steeds into the forest without getting them reshod."

Bryanna suppressed a sigh, glancing longingly at her aunt's tower. After being on the thoroughfare so long, did it really matter if they waited a little longer to reshoe the steeds? "Surely they can withstand a few extra minutes?"

"I'm sorry, Ms. Nicholls, but the forest path isn't easy. Perhaps we can send a messenger—"

Gawain snorted. "These villagers wouldn't step foot near Sheidlow Tower if they knew there was leprechaun gold sitting on my aunt's doorstep for their taking." He stepped out of the carriage, nodding at a pair of villagers who didn't nod back. "Go see the farrier, Mr. Ahearn. I warn you, though, he'll charge a moon cycle's wage for his services. My sister and I will walk the rest of the way."

Bryanna stared at him. Gawain must've been under the effects of their father's nightcap if he thought she'd walk to their aunt's tower. It'd been raining on and off all day and would be again soon, judging by the heavy, dark clouds above them. Besides, she couldn't leave her belongings. She'd brought things too difficult to procure to be left behind. Things she'd need once she set off after the Brotherhood of Sìorraidh.

Mr. Ahearn's mouth tightened. "Perhaps you should wait, sir. I don't expect it'll be long."

"You've obviously never been to the farrier here, Mr. Ahearn. It'll be midnight by the time he's finished. Come on, Bree."

But Bryanna didn't move. "You go on ahead. I'll stay with Mr. Ahearn."

Gawain shrugged his broad shoulders. Bryanna wasn't sure what he'd been doing since moving to study at the Avalon Institute, but he wasn't the lean, lanky young man he'd been when he'd left Castlereagh. His linen shirt no longer hung off him, but hugged the well-defined muscles of his chest and arms. "Suit yourself."

She watched him make his way to the back compartment,

not liking the impish glint in his eyes. A moment later, he re-emerged hauling a brown leather satchel over his shoulder.

Her leather satchel.

"Bollocks," she muttered, scrambling to her feet and disembarking from the carriage. She couldn't let him take the satchel. Not when it contained her dragon-venom-tipped daggers. If he found them and told their father she had them in her possession, he'd have her back in Castlereagh faster than her mother could raise a brow at the hint of gossip.

"Put that down this instant," she ordered, joining him at the back of the carriage and lunging for the satchel in his hand.

But Gawain reacted quickly, swinging it out of her reach.

"Now, now," he said, tsking. "Is that any way to speak to your brother? Honestly, what did they teach you in those finishing classes Mother made you attend last summer?"

Bryanna opened her mouth, a scathing retort on the tip of her tongue. But before she could unleash it on Gawain, an elderly woman nearby huffed and said in a croak loud enough for Bryanna to hear, "That must be the young sorceress we keep reading 'bout in the papers. Lass looks just like that wretched Nicholls woman."

Bryanna's jaw snapped shut as she glanced around the square. They'd drawn the attention of the villagers, most of whom were staring at them with harried, narrowed eyes.

The old woman's companion curled her thin, crimson lip. "It must be. I hear she's a magic-weaver as well. And look, her lout of a nephew's back too."

A hot flush spread up Bryanna's neck, obliterating any irritation she might've harbored toward her brother. Gawain might've annoyed her more than any of her four older brothers, but that didn't mean she'd allow anyone to slight him in front of her.

She made for the women, her fists clenched at her sides.

But she hadn't taken two paces before Gawain clamped a hand around her arm, stopping her from advancing on the women. "Bree, don't," he said in an undertone.

"Come, come, ladies," said a robust man, coming out of an old gray building with a faded sign over the door, the words The Doherty Bank scarcely legible. "The lass looks harmless enough, don't she?"

The lecherous smile he gave Bryanna made her fingers itch to reach for one of her daggers.

"Hardly, Mr. Doherty." Gawain stepped forward, blocking Bryanna from his seedy view, and handed her a satchel from the carriage's storage compartment. "Let's go, Bree. We don't want to keep Aunt Obelia waiting."

Mr. Doherty's brows rose to meet the end of the measly strands crowning his receding hairline. "Surely yer not thinking of entering the forest on foot? There have been sightings of terrible creatures in the forest of late."

But Gawain adjusted the strap on his shoulder, and without another word, headed toward a narrow street lined with blacksmith workshops, copper-beater stalls, and clusters of close-knit, cruck-framed houses.

Grumbling under her breath, Bryanna hurried after him, ignoring the villagers edging away from her, fear and loathing filling their sullen, tight-lipped faces. It wasn't as though she could leave Gawain with her satchel. Not when she knew how likely he was to snoop through her things.

The trek to the forest didn't take long. Bryanna counted twenty houses before the paddocks, crops, and small farm cottages started. It made for a quaint foreground to the majestic Sheidlow Forest trees. She inhaled deeply, invigorated by the crisp, clean air, so refreshing compared to the stale, confined scents of town life, where it was difficult to escape the smell of chimney smoke or excrement of carriage-pulling animals.

They continued on until they reached a path of glistening, minute alabaster rocks that started at the forest's entrance. Bryanna frowned. She couldn't recall them from the last time she'd come to Sheidlow Ridge.

"They're called ironstones," Gawain told her, following her gaze. "They'll start glowing once night falls, lighting the way for evening visitors traveling to the Sheidlow Tower."

Darkness fell prematurely as they trudged into the forest, the dimness aided by the gloomy clouds rumbling with thunder. Before long, Bryanna's thoughts turned longingly to the furnace she could've been warming herself by while the farrier got the steeds ready for their continued journey ...

"How much longer?" she asked eventually over the rhythmic pitter-patter of rain. She didn't remember it taking so long to get to her aunt's tower. Of course, the last time she'd been there, she'd traveled in a carriage, not navigating the rutted, potholed, ironstone path on foot.

"We're almost there," Gawain assured her.

Bryanna's neck prickled, the way it always did when someone watched her. She squinted around, shaking her head to momentarily dislodge the rain coating her face, but couldn't see anything more than the shadowy outlines of swaying foliage. Yet, she couldn't shake the creeping suspicion that they weren't alone.

Goose bumps rose along her skin. She wanted to ask Gawain whether he could sense the baleful presence, too, but a voice in the back of her mind stopped her.

Urged her on.

You're nearly there.

Just a bit farther.

She kept walking, placing one aching foot in front of the other, trying to quell the gnawing unease that told her something wasn't right. She could hardly see in front of her anymore. The ironstones that should've lit their way were no longer crunching under her boots.

So much for their use.

Several times, she considered stopping to rest her fatigued legs, but each time she did, the velvety voice slipped into her mind again, willing her to press forward.

Time blurred until Bryanna couldn't tell if they'd been walking for minutes or hours. All that mattered was that they kept moving deeper toward the thick heart of the forest.

It was as though she were drifting in a mindless, dreamless sleep, content to let her thoughts wander while her body moved of its own accord. At least, until Gawain jerked back without warning, the heels of his boots crushing her toes.

"Seriously, Gawain," she cried as she lifted her foot, massaging her massacred toes through the thick hide of her boots. The dreamy haze she'd slipped into had well and truly dissipated. "Watch where you're going."

Gawain was too busy glaring down at the sword in his scabbard to register her words.

Bryanna gasped as a bolt of lightning split the sky above them, illuminating the weapon. She'd been searching for it for moon cycles, determined to bring it with her to Sheidlow Ridge and beyond, ever since learning of its rare gifts—one of which was warning its bearer of danger.

Gawain flexed his hand. "I think Father's sword burned me."

Bryanna sucked in a breath, her magic surging to her fingertips in a fierce, warm rush. If the sword had stung him, it could only mean one thing: they were not alone.

"Gawain," she whispered as the prickling on the back of her neck intensified. "Draw your sword."

Her brother must've sensed her panic because he removed the blade from its scabbard at once. For several nerve-racking seconds, they were silent, straining to hear anything besides the rumbling clouds and drumming rain. Bryanna sank a trembling hand into her pocket, wrapping her fingers around the hilt of the dragon-venom dagger she'd slipped there.

Her skin crawled at the oily, unnatural presence clinging to the air around them, so dark and unctuous, she wasn't sure how she hadn't sensed it before. Her gaze darted to the vague outlines of distorted shrubs and saplings surrounding them, trying to calm her racing heart as she bent down and grabbed two heavy branches. Pulling on her magic, she channeled some of it into the branches so that their ends blazed to life with a water-repelling flame she'd perfected years ago.

"Which way to Aunt Obelia's, Gawain?" she asked, her voice tight.

They needed to get to the tower before their pursuer descended on them.

Gawain glanced from tree to tree grimly, shaking his head. "I-I don't know."

Bryanna gritted her teeth. They couldn't continue walking around aimlessly, especially if they were being tracked by whatever unknown creature was with them. She'd heard of more than one tragic tale about travelers being lured to their death by some predatory creature.

"I'm going to perform a navigational spell."

Gawain's face creased with worry. "Are you sure?"

He might not have been a magic-weaver, but even he knew the risks involved in performing the spell she was about to cast. As a sorceress, Bryanna's magical stores were bountiful, but they weren't limitless. She wouldn't be able to keep the spell going for long. Only an ovate or mage could do that, and her skills were still years away from ascending to that level.

"I'm sure."

Bryanna raised her hands, allowing the familiar warmth of

magic to spread like wildfire in her veins. Gathering it into her fingertips, she sent it into the makeshift torches, concentrating on the image she remembered of the Sheidlow Tower. The branches blazed as the spell came to life, floating back the way they'd come.

"Let's go."

They followed the bewitched branches, moving as fast as the tangle of tree trunks and undergrowth would allow.

Bryanna could sense the creature keeping pace with them, bounding from tree to tree, always too far for them to make out more than its black, smudged silhouette. Her heart thudded against her chest. There was no doubt in her mind that it wouldn't be content to simply shadow them until they found their way back onto the ironstone path. Not after the trouble it'd gone through to lead them away from their aunt's tower.

On they went, until Bryanna could smell hearth soot in the air, mixed with the nose-wrinkling stench of freshly laid manure.

They were close.

And then she saw it.

The faint pinpricks of light that could only be the Sheidlow Tower.

Relief flooded through her. *They'd made it.*

Above them, the creature let out a deadly, ear-splitting screech, as if it, too, realized how close they were to safety. Bryanna glanced up just as giant, hooked claws descended toward her.

"Gawain, look out!" she screamed, plunging her hand into her pocket and unsheathing her dagger.

But she was too slow. White-hot pain exploded through her shoulders as the creature's claws sank deep into her flesh and wrenched her violently into the air.

"Bree!" Gawain shouted.

Fear seized Bryanna as she was lifted so high, she could no longer see the ground. Her stomach lurched with each powerful beat of the creature's wings. It was carrying her away from her aunt's tower, back toward the village.

Or worse.

Bryanna tightened her grip on the dagger still miraculously in her hand, pushing past the burning pain in her shoulders where the creature grasped her. She'd waited far too long to get to Obelia's sanctuary to let some creature carry her away without a fight. Gritting her teeth, she swung out, slicing into the creature's forearm, and felt a moment of satisfaction when it gave a pain-filled snarl. But a wave of agony quickly replaced it as its claws dug deeper into her shoulders.

They were losing height, the creature's wings unable to keep them airborne as the dragon venom's effects took hold. Bryanna twisted in its claws, biting back a sharp cry, but instead of releasing her, the creature's hold tightened.

Why wasn't it letting her go?

With the dragon venom coursing through its system, it should've been beyond agonizing for it to continue holding on to her.

Sucking in a shaky breath, Bryanna swung out again, stabbing her blade into the creature's claws.

She was rewarded with an anguished howl. The creature's grip loosened marginally, and Bryanna didn't hesitate. She gave a mighty twist, gritting her teeth against the fresh onslaught of pain—

—and went plummeting toward the ground as the creature was forced to release her.

A mangled scream tore from her throat as she poured her magic into the air beneath her, solidifying it enough to slow her fall until she found purchase on a tree limb. But the damage the creature had wrought on her shoulders wouldn't let her hold on for long before her grip failed and she continued to tumble, catching onto slick branches until she finally crashed to the ground.

"Bollocks," she growled as her ankle twisted in an odd angle that made blackness seep into the corners of her eyes. It was all she could do to stay conscious.

Gawain reached her a moment later, his face stark white in the flashing lightning. He was breathing hard, as though he'd been racing through the forest, trying to keep up with her and the creature. He took in the gushing blood streaming through the top of her dress and swore. "How badly are you hurt, Bree?"

Bryanna grimaced, fighting to control the tremors racking her body. "I'm all right."

A new bolt of lightning flooded their surroundings, making the green blood coating her blade glisten. *Wait ... green blood?*

"Gawain ..."

Gawain saw it too. "We need to get out of here."

Bryanna made to get up, but agony flooded her injured ankle, knocking the air out of her lungs far more efficiently than her earlier plunge through the trees.

"I've got you." Gawain heaved her up into his arms and raced through the forest toward their aunt's tower.

Bryanna clenched her jaw as spasms of pain shot across her shoulders and ankle with each fresh jolt his footfalls made on the uneven ground, but she didn't ask him to slow down.

Not when she knew what was behind them, gaining on them haphazardly, careening through the thick branches like an out-of-control battering ram. How it was even thinking straight with how long the dragon venom had been in its system was beyond her.

Gawain didn't stop until they cleared the last line of trees. A long, bloodcurdling screech pierced the air as he streaked past a lawn littered with wooden tables and chairs and up the four stone steps leading to the tower's portico. He'd barely reached the oak front doors when a shadow fell over them. Bryanna wrenched herself free from her brother's hold, a surge of magic tearing through her. She aimed it at the creature's sturdy chest, sending him sailing through the air.

But the being landed gracefully on his haunches. What breath remained in Bryanna's lungs was knocked out of her as he straightened. Whoever he was, he wasn't the creature who'd attacked them in the forest. Deep mahogany-brown hair dripped in curls around his chiseled, handsome face, though it was his smoky-blue eyes that drew her attention. They glinted silver in the light coming off the burning portico lanterns, as though shards of glass were nestled inside them.

His gaze swept over her face, and recognition flickered across his features, followed by something else she couldn't quite place.

Gawain reached for his sword. "You—"

Before he could finish, the soaring double doors burst open. Obelia Nicholls rushed out, her face strained with concern. "Bryanna! Gawain! Where have you been? We've been so worried."

CHAPTER

TWO

The last time Bryanna had seen her aunt, she'd been at the Sheidlow Tower, getting ready to leave, when panicked roars had come from the trees surrounding the tower. Rushing to her window, she'd seen one of her aunt's boarders propel himself onto the tower's grounds just as a solid wall of mist rose behind him, barring him and the tower from whomever he was outrunning.

Seconds later, her aunt had come charging outside, firing off words at the misty barrier that would've earned Bryanna an entire week's worth of suspension at school. At least, she'd thought it was the mist until it cleared and she got an unhindered view of the furious villagers on the other side.

"Step aside, Mistress Nicholls," Mr. Doherty had growled, standing at the forefront of the small party, his strung arrow pointed at the youth in her aunt's care. "That beast decimated several of the farmers' livestock last night."

Instead of stepping aside, though, her aunt had drawn herself up, her eyes narrowed on the arrows still pointed at her boarder. "Mr. Doherty, I will, of course, reimburse the villagers who lost their chickens. But let me be clear about one thing. If you or any of the other villagers raise your weapons against one of my boarders again, I'll turn you all into ruddy wild boars!"

From that day on, the villagers no longer pretended to be friendly or forthcoming toward Obelia or any newcomers looking for the Mage's Sanctuary. Not that Bryanna thought their estrangement was much of a loss, if how they'd treated *her* in the village was anything to go by.

"Get inside, all three of you," Obelia called over the downpour. "Mr. Ahearn and I have been expecting you for hours—" Her words died in her throat as she saw the blood staining Bryanna's day dress. "Bryanna, what happened to you?"

"Never mind that." Bryanna tugged her aunt inside, wincing as pain shot through her ankle. "We need to secure the tower. There's something dangerous in the—*no, come back!*"

The dark-haired stranger she'd mistaken for the creature had spun at her words and torn into the trees.

Bryanna stared after him. What kind of bullheaded imbecile rushed into a forest after being told there was a treacherous creature in it?

"For the love of Castlereagh, Weylin," her aunt muttered, glaring at the spot her boarder had disappeared through. She turned to the redwood squirrel perched on her shoulder. "Go after him, Tyffin. Make sure he's all right."

The squirrel nodded, scurried down her arm, and raced after the boarder.

"Get in," Obelia ordered, helping Bryanna inside and waiting for Gawain to follow before bolting the massive oak doors behind her. "You two need to tell me what happened out there."

They told her everything—how their minds had been ensnared, the creature's unnatural speed, how Bryanna had barely broken free from its grip as it carried her away. As they spoke, Bryanna studied her aunt. She'd been told by many over the years that she favored Obelia, but she'd never realized how much until that moment. Their resemblance was uncanny. They were of similar height and build, both dark-featured with high cheekbones, deep-set almond-shaped eyes, and straight noses that jutted out at the tip. They could've been the same woman, painted by two artists at different stages of her life.

"Did you get a good look at what it was?" Obelia asked when they'd finished.

"No," said Gawain. "But it was huge. It picked Bryanna up as though she were a sack of potatoes."

"It has green blood too." Bryanna pulled the dagger from her pocket and gave it to her aunt. Most of the blood had washed away, though there were still a few specks.

Obelia's eyes widened as she studied the blade. "It can't be …"

Gawain cast Obelia an ominous look. "That's what we thought. No creature in our dimension has green blood."

"Not in *our* dimension, no." She lowered the blade, her gaze narrowing on her niece. "How did you escape its clutches, Bryanna?"

"I stabbed it with the dagger," Bryanna admitted. It wasn't as though she could hide the fact when she'd handed her aunt the blade.

Gawain scoffed. "I saw how big that creature was, Bree. There's no way you could've gotten anything major with that short blade while you dangled underneath it."

"She wouldn't have needed to," Obelia murmured, studying the dagger again. "The blade's imbued with dragon venom."

"*Dragon venom?*" Gawain rounded on her, his expression darkening. "Where did you even get such a thing, Bree?"

"If you must know, at the apothecary," Bryanna lied. If word got back to her father that she'd been imbuing weapons with dangerous toxins and venoms, he'd be on the next carriage to Sheidlow Ridge. She suspected the only reason he'd agreed to let her visit Obelia at all was that he hoped his sister could dissuade her from her quest.

Not that she'd ever let that happen.

"And before you start making a fuss, if I hadn't, I'd probably be dead now."

"Well, I'm glad you had it," said Obelia, sheathing the dagger. "Come. Let's get you clean and dry. If you wake up in the morning with a cold, your mother might just make good on her threat and come to Sheidlow Ridge. I'll need to heal that ankle and those gashes for you, too, Bryanna. We don't want them to fester."

She helped Bryanna down the spacious entrance hall lined with blazing oil lamps. Several coat stands stood to their left, weighted down with more mantles, cloaks, and coats than Bryanna had seen in the Upper Castlereagh boutiques. The Mage's Sanctuary must've been near capacity, if not full. Five doors led to other chambers in the hall, though it was the familiar pair of oak and glass-paneled doors that Obelia led them through. Bryanna dimly remembered the vast kitchen they entered from the last time she'd visited.

"Sit and elevate that foot, Bryanna," said Obelia, waving them over to the empty chairs at the end of the dining table. She raised her hands and, with a twinge of magic, the water, dirt, and debris on Bryanna's dress and Gawain's breeches and tailcoat evaporated, leaving them as dry and warm as though they'd been hanging in the scorching summer sun all day. "You two must be hungry."

"Starved," said Gawain, plucking a bread roll from the kitchen bench and shoving it into his mouth.

Bryanna's gaze flickered up toward the ceiling. Only Gawain could have an appetite after the night they'd had.

"Well, lucky for you, I have just what you need." Obelia waved her hand toward the wood-burning stove where a pot was simmering merrily over a low flame.

Obelia removed her shawl and hung it on the hook beside the back door. Her movements caused the neckline of her dress to slip, revealing the *Edad* Ogham symbol imprinted on her left shoulder.

Bryanna stared at it. Unlike her aunt, whose Ogham boasted four short vertical lines that denoted her a mage, hers only featured three, marking her as a sorceress. She'd surpassed the first three magical transitions—druid, witch, and enchanter—by the time she was sixteen, a feat few ever achieved. In fact, she'd been the youngest sorceress to exist in a century, and she didn't plan to stop there. She'd been working for almost two years to become a mage, like her aunt, though it was the sixth and most powerful classification, ovate, that she craved.

"Here you are." Obelia placed two generous bowls of soup in front of them. "Eat up."

She moved behind Bryanna and placed her hands on her injured shoulders. Magic hummed over Bryanna as Obelia mended all the wounds the creature had inflicted on her.

While she worked, Bryanna glanced out the window, biting her lip as the thunderous clouds flashed. The malevolent presence she'd sensed coming off the creature wasn't there anymore, though that didn't mean it wasn't still prowling the forest beyond the tower's walls.

"You don't think the dragon venom killed the creature, do you?" she asked her aunt.

The kitchen's back door swung open before Obelia could reply, letting in a chilling gust of wind that made the flame in the wood-burning stove flicker out.

"Unlikely," Weylin said, striding into the kitchen and

shaking water out of his hair. "We would've found the creature's body if it were dead."

Bryanna heaved a silent sigh of relief.

"These were the only things out of the ordinary that we found out there," Weylin continued, dropping two limp, leathery bodies in front of them, splattering the tablecloth with mud.

Bryanna did a double-take. They weren't limp bodies at all, but her satchels, caked in layers of muck. She'd completely forgotten about them as she and Gawain had fled for the tower.

Obelia planted her hands on her hips as she gave Weylin the sort of look a mother would give her errant child. "What were you thinking, running off into the forest alone like that when we've been warned of danger close by?"

"But I wasn't alone," said Weylin, inclining his head to the squirrel on his shoulder, who puffed out his chest with an agreeable chirp.

Obelia's expression remained stony. "I mean it. Whatever was out there wasn't something we've ever encountered before."

Weylin shrugged off his cloak and hung it next to Obelia's shawl. "We could've handled it."

Tyffin chirped again, his dark gray eyes meeting Obelia's.

The spoon Bryanna had been about to bring to her lips fell from her lax fingers with a clatter. She'd just realized Tyffin wasn't an ordinary squirrel. He was Obelia's *familiar*. He *had* to be. His irises were unlike any squirrel's she'd ever seen. They were the exact shade of Obelia's, which meant they must've been bonded for quite a while. It took years for a familiar's irises to match their master's.

Tyffin's face turned more and more serious as Obelia filled him in on what happened to Bryanna and Gawain. At least, that's what Bryanna assumed they were discussing. They were communicating telepathically, through their familiar bond.

Weylin leaned back against the bench, his gaze lingering on Bryanna before moving to Gawain. Then he smirked. "Got something you want to say, Nicholls?"

"I will if you look at my sister like that again," Gawain said, a disapproving glare etched across his face.

Heat rushed over Bryanna's face. "Gawain, don't be absurd." She turned to Weylin, determinedly ignoring the way her pulse quickened when their eyes met. "I'm sorry about my brother. He doesn't know what he's saying."

"Oh, I know exactly what I'm saying," Gawain retorted.

"Anyway," she said, raising her voice to mask her brother's words. "About what happened out there ... Weylin? I'm really sorry for attacking you."

Obelia's head swiveled, abandoning her conversation with Tyffin. "You *attacked* him?"

Bryanna shifted uncomfortably in her chair. "I thought he was the creature."

Gawain's lips twitched. "Did she hurt you?"

Weylin eyed Gawain coolly. "It was nothing. I'll be upstairs if you need me, Obelia."

He placed Tyffin gently on the table and gave his head a quick scratch before striding up the staircase without a backward glance.

"Hey, you're here," said a young woman with long, fiery red hair, coming down the stairs. She was looking right at Bryanna. "Your aunt's been talking about you for weeks."

Bryanna tried to smile back, but it was difficult. The young woman's face was covered with thick strips of bright silver reptilian skin. She wasn't sure how to meet her frosty, pale-pink eyes without looking as though she were staring.

Gawain had no such reservations. "Hello, my dear red-haired friend," he said, a winning grin stretched across his lips.

Bryanna kicked him under the table, recognizing the flirtatious cadence in his voice. She'd seen too many girls get their hopes up at the slightest attention from him, only to come through crestfallen and disillusioned. She didn't want to see the boarder hurt by Gawain. After all, she was one of their aunt's patients.

"Hi, Gawain." The young woman's lips curved in a warm smile. "It's good to see you again. And it's nice to finally meet you, Bryanna. I'm Liadan Wode."

Liadan held out her hand. It bore similar fine silver streaks to those on her face.

Bryanna took it gently, ignoring how cool the streaks felt against her skin. "Nice to meet you."

"Obelia tells me you're a sorceress and that you had a minor incident with the Law Keepers about a hobgoblin in your cellar a few weeks ago?"

Gawain rounded on Obelia. "You *told* people about that?"

Obelia looked as though she'd just been thrown in front of a moving carriage. "Was I not supposed to?"

"Of course not."

"Honestly, Gawain, it wasn't that big of a deal." Bryanna turned impishly to Liadan. "It was all his fault, you see—"

"No, it wasn't."

"You're the one who opened that new barrel of mead our old hobgoblin specifically asked us not to touch. *And* you didn't leave him any treats. What did you expect? Of course he got angry and turned into his more aggressive form, which is roughly the size of a *brobinyah* ogre," she added for Liadan's benefit.

Gawain's ears turned a splotchy shade of crimson. "Yes, well, you're the one who set half the fermenting barrels of mead aflame with your *fireballs* and almost burned our house down."

Bryanna colored slightly. "It wasn't the *whole* house. Besides, the hobgoblin let you go, didn't it?"

"Only because we were engulfed by flames!"

Liadan and Obelia laughed.

"I'm glad you've come to stay, Bryanna," said Liadan when she recovered. "You're going to love it here."

Bryanna forced a smile. She didn't have any intention of loving her stay. She was there to learn all she could about the Brotherhood of Sìorraidh, and then she'd take off. *Before* her father's carriage came back for her. She wouldn't get a second chance to embark on her quest if she returned to Castlereagh. Her father would make sure of it.

"I'm sorry, everyone, but it's late," said Obelia, waving her hand so that their dishes rose and landed in the sink. "Gawain, you should speak to Mr. Ahearn before you turn in. See what time he wants to leave in the morning."

"Actually, I think we may stay a few extra days," Gawain interjected. "If that creature's still out there, I'm not going anywhere."

Bryanna's stomach clenched. She didn't want Gawain to remain at the tower, especially if her father had sent him to try to uncover what she had planned.

"Let *me* worry about the creature," said Obelia before Bryanna could object. "I can have the local Law Keepers search these parts in the morning."

Gawain rose to his feet, misgivings clouding his features. "If you're sure ..."

"We're sure," said Bryanna quickly. "Besides, don't you have that jousting tournament in a few days?"

"Well ... all right, then." He stepped around the table and gathered Bryanna in an inescapable embrace, holding on tighter when she tried pushing him away. "Bye, Bree. Try not to burn down any buildings while you're here, all right?"

"Gawain!" Bryanna growled, trying and failing to elbow him in the stomach. "Ugh! Get off!"

He let her go with a pout and turned to Liadan. "I don't understand why she's so hostile."

"Because you're obnoxious?" Bryanna suggested.

"Enough, you two," said Obelia, hiding a smile. "Gawain, go see Mr. Ahearn before the poor chap falls asleep."

Gawain heaved an exaggerated sigh. "I'm going, I'm going." He leaned down and kissed Obelia's cheek.

Bryanna watched him head up the stairs, a knot forming in her throat. She wasn't sure how long it would be before she saw him again.

Or if she ever would …

"Let's go, girls. Bryanna, your things are in your bedchamber already. I had them sent up soon after Mr. Ahearn arrived earlier this evening."

The soup in Bryanna's stomach curdled. With all the tumult, she'd forgotten about her trunks. She might've placed powerful locking enchantments on them, but someone with Obelia's aptitude for magic wouldn't have struggled long to break them. For all she knew, her aunt had already sifted through her things while she and Gawain were lost in the forest. Her only consolation was that Obelia hadn't mentioned them. She imagined that if her aunt knew exactly what she'd brought into her home, she wouldn't have been nearly as good-natured as she'd been through supper.

"Liadan, could you show Bryanna to her bedchamber, please?" Obelia asked, turning to her boarder.

"Of course."

"I'd do it myself, Bryanna, but I have to see to one of my

boarders. He's ..." Obelia's face creased with unease. "He's not doing too well."

Bryanna's brows furrowed. As far as she knew, the beings who stayed with Obelia weren't usually severely ill. "Is there anything I can do to help?"

A sad smile lifted the edge of her aunt's lips. "I'm afraid not. Now come, I'll show you where my office is and then Liadan will take you to your bedchamber."

They collected her satchels, which were still caked in mud, and followed Obelia up to the first floor.

"My office and bedchamber are here," said Obelia when they reached a narrow hallway. It was lined with candle brackets and wainscoted walls. She pointed to the door closest to her left and the one at the end of the hall. "If you need anything, just knock."

Bryanna nodded. "I will."

Obelia enveloped her in a bone-crushing hug. "It's so good to finally have you here."

Bryanna reciprocated awkwardly. It'd been a long time since she'd let anyone wrap her in their arms. Willingly, at least.

"Come on, Bryanna," said Liadan once they'd parted. "Our chambers are upstairs."

Bryanna followed her up the staircase. Just before they reached the next floor, she heard Obelia knock softly on one of the doors and enter, murmuring, "How are you feeling, Elgar?"

The rest of her words faded as Liadan led Bryanna into a vast, circular chamber lined with tall sash windows. Four alcoves stood to their immediate right, each with its own shelves, armchairs, tapestries, plush rugs, and fireplaces. On the opposite side was the main area, which boasted a massive floor-to-ceiling fireplace, countless armchairs, and a few small tables and desks.

Bryanna's attention fell on the mezzanine above them, hedged in blackthorn banisters. The shelves along the walls were filled with stacks upon stacks of volumes. She'd have to check them first thing in the morning. Perhaps she'd find the precious volumes, once part of her family library in Castlereagh, that her father had shipped off to Obelia years ago, suspecting—as Bryanna did—that they contained information on the Brotherhood of Sìorraidh.

"This is our library," Liadan told her. "Most of the boarders come here once night sets in, or if it's too cold to be outside during the day."

Despite the late hour, there were still a few boarders about. One of them, a young man with lanky black hair, pallid skin, and vein-like lines running across his forehead, looked over as they neared.

"Who's your friend, Liadan?" he asked, eyeing Bryanna keenly as he shuffled a deck of cards.

Bryanna stilled, her eyes widening as she recognized what he was. What in all of Castlereagh was her aunt doing, keeping a *neach-ithe anam* under her roof? His kind were known for feeding off other beings' life essences.

"This is Obelia's niece, Bryanna, Cayde," Liadan answered, her tone guarded. "Come on, Bryanna, we're up on the tenth floor."

Bryanna followed Liadan out of the library, waiting until there were several levels between them and Cayde before rounding on Liadan. "Why is Cayde here? I thought neach-ithe anam were dangerous."

Liadan's lips compressed into a thin line. "They are. But Obelia says Cayde's commitment to controlling his condition is paramount."

They kept going, Bryanna's legs protesting with each flight of stairs they took.

"Here we are," said Liadan when they finally made it to a

hallway that resembled the one on the second floor, save for the paintings on the walls, which depicted stunning watercolors of salamanders emerging from blue-red flames and white unicorns blending into foamy waves.

Liadan led Bryanna through a door to their left. "This bedchamber's yours. It's directly across from mine."

Bryanna walked in, taking in the small chamber. It was half the size of her one in Castlereagh but twice as cozy. Light tapestries hung from the stone walls, reminding her of the illustrations in the storybooks she and Aveline used to read together. A four-poster bed wide enough to fit two people stood to one side. Matching bedside cabinets, wardrobes, and a writing desk stood around the chamber, similar to those Bryanna would see in the traveling inns she sometimes stayed at during weekend trips away with her family.

Her trunks, valises, and the rest of her satchels were there, too, stacked against the wall.

Liadan stared at them. "That's quite a lot of things you've brought. Are you sure you aren't moving in?"

Bryanna forced a laugh. Perhaps she *had* overpacked, but she couldn't have been sure of what she'd need for her quest. She hoped that once she'd learned everything she could from Obelia, she'd have a better idea. Anything she didn't need, she'd leave behind when the time came.

"Well, I'll let you get some rest," said Liadan, stepping out of the chamber. "It's our floor's turn to cook breakfast tomorrow morning, so we need to be up early. Good night."

"Night."

Bryanna waited for her door to close before hastening to her trunks and checking the locking spells were still in place—they were. Sighing in relief, she fished out her nightgown, beyond exhausted. Thoughts of how the night could've ended resurfaced, but she pushed them away. She didn't want to think about where she and Gawain might've wound up without their father's sword or her dagger.

She pulled back her counterpane, too tired to bathe, and crawled into bed. But her head barely hit the pillow when the same prickling she'd felt in the forest returned. She bolted upright, her heart pounding against her ribcage as her gaze darted to her balcony. For a second, she thought she saw a shadow pass between the doors.

She blinked once and looked again, though, and it was gone.

THREE

Bryanna moved deeper through the leafless, gnarled trees, searching for the handsome young man she'd been following. Dusk was settling in, bringing with it a bitter chill that penetrated her fur-lined coat. Dimly, she knew they'd ventured too far into the woods, too far from the beaten path. But she didn't care. It'd been too long since they'd spent any time alone together, away from their families and friends.

"Drystan!" she called, her voice echoing in the surrounding hollows. "Drystan, where are you?"

"I thought I told you to wait in the glade," Drystan called back, his voice coming from out of sight.

Bryanna snorted, a small smile tugging at her lips as she rubbed her hands together, generating heat into her frozen fingers. "Since when do I listen?"

"Just stay where you are. You don't know what could be lurking in these trees."

Bryanna rolled her eyes. There'd been nothing in their woods for decades, save for the white stags, gold lynxes, and red-tailed hares. Sometimes Drystan worried too much—it was one of the things she loved most about him.

In the distance, barely audible, another voice called her name, one that was oddly familiar. "Drystan, I think someone's looking for us."

The crunching of gravel sounded behind her. Bryanna glanced back, expecting to see Drystan ambling toward her.

But it wasn't him.

The smile on her lips faltered, then vanished altogether as she took a hasty step back, the hairs on her arms standing on end. A creature the size of a small bear was prowling toward her, its lithe body covered in swirling silver hide.

She would've known it anywhere. She and Drystan had grown up hearing the cautionary tales of the flesh-eating questing beasts who led wanderers to their gory deaths. There hadn't been one sighted in Quarry Cliff in decades. Sometimes the townspeople told foreigners otherwise, but none of them believed such tall tales—except for Drystan. He'd always said they'd return one day.

Now one had, and it had impersonated Drystan to lure her from the safety of the wood's path.

"Why, human," it said, the perfect imitation of Drystan's voice floating from its mouth, "you seem surprised to see me."

Bryanna fumbled back another step. Images of Drystan lying somewhere, dying, made her heart constrict. "Wh- Where's Drystan?"

The creature grinned, sending chills down her spine.

Movement caught the corner of her eye. A dark figure was perched on top of a wide birch some distance away, his cloak billowing in the biting wind.

"Help me, please!" she cried.

But the figure didn't move. Instead, he leaned forward, as though he were a spectator at a street show and she and the questing beast were the entertainment.

Tears threatened behind her eyes. What was he doing?

Didn't he realize what the creature was? That she was seconds away from being shredded to pieces?

"I'm afraid no aid will be coming for you, human," the questing beast sneered, exposing bloodstained teeth as its face twisted with malicious excitement.

Bryanna spun and hurtled back the way she'd come. She wouldn't remain rooted to the spot, surrendering to the lethal, dirt-caked claws of the questing beast.

"Drystan!" she screamed, her voice echoing around the trees.

She didn't make it to the first tree before ice-cold claws dug deep into her shoulders, sending her crashing to the thistle-strewn ground. Bryanna cried out, the sound no more than a breathless gasp as the impact knocked the air out of her lungs.

"No!"

The creature flipped her onto her back, and she reacted instinctively, kicking out as hard as she could at the soft flesh below its belly. It reared back, howling with a sound similar to a pack of enraged territorial wolves.

Bryanna scrambled out from beneath the creature and raced for the carriage once more. But she'd barely taken a few paces before the questing beast hauled her onto her back, its wintry, pale-pink eyes glinting as it came bearing down on her.

A horrified scream escaped her as she squeezed her eyes shut, but it didn't block the chasm of pain that exploded as the creature's razor-sharp claws connected with her face, carving a deep, unforgiving line across her evergreen eyes.

From behind them, the real Drystan screamed her name.

"*Liadan!*"

Bryanna bolted upright, gasping.

She wrestled free of her tangled counterpane, magic buzzing at her fingertips, ready to defend her against the questing beast—

Except her eyes weren't burning because of some freshly sustained injury.

They were burning because of the blinding sunlight coming from her bedchamber's lace-covered window. The storm that had ravaged the night before had blown over, leaving a clear, innocent sky in its wake.

Bryanna let out a shaky sigh and allowed the magic tingling over her skin to retreat. She'd done it again—dream-weaved into someone's dream.

Or nightmare, more accurately.

It was something she'd been able to do since before she became a sorceress. The experience wasn't one she savored. Over the years, she'd been pulled into some terrifying nightmares. Her father's were the worst. In them, she'd witnessed herself succumbing to death at the hands of the Brotherhood of Sìorraidh countless times. Sometimes she'd be staring down at her vacant, lifeless body; other times she and her father would be hastening to find a safe route out of their family home while a figure with dead, unfeeling eyes, and a wicked leer pursued them.

"Stop!" Liadan's unmistakable sob broke through Bryanna's thoughts. "Please stop!"

She was up at once, rushing out of her bedchamber. In her groggy state, she'd completely forgotten about the creature who'd attacked her and Gawain the night before.

But when she burst into Liadan's bedchamber, she found only its distressed occupant, thrashing wildly in her sleep as she screamed, "Help me, please!"

Liadan had to still be in the throes of the nightmare she'd seen when she'd dream-weaved. She moved forward and reached out to shake the petrified young woman awake. But with a force and swiftness that Bryanna didn't expect, Liadan lashed out, striking the side of Bryanna's face and sending her sprawling into the bedside table, knocking over a tall pile of volumes.

"Aaaarrrgggghhh!" Liadan screamed on.

Bryanna blinked, the shock of being hit numbing the heat blazing along her cheekbone. Before she could pull herself up, Obelia and Tyffin hurried into the bedchamber. Bryanna sincerely hoped the others weren't far behind. It would've looked odd indeed, her nursing a black eye while Liadan screeched at the top of her lungs, "Get away from me!"

In one deft sweep, Obelia pinned Liadan's arms against the tangled sheets, her face furrowed in concentration. Magic, strong and sure, permeated the chamber as she performed a spell to calm her terrified patient. "It's all right, Liadan," she coaxed. "You're safe."

Bryanna stiffened as Liadan's eyes fluttered open. They were the same arctic-pink shade she'd seen moments before in the questing beast.

"Ooh." Liadan raised an unsteady hand to wipe her tears, struggling to catch her breath as she sat up. "That wretched questing beast. Why do I keep having the same nightmare? It's been more than a year."

"These things take time," Obelia murmured, squeezing her shoulder.

"I just wish th—" Liadan's face drained of color as she caught sight of Bryanna dabbing at her left eye. "B-Bryanna, I didn't hit you, did I?"

Bryanna dropped her hands to her sides. The last thing she wanted to do was make Liadan feel guilty for yet another thing beyond her control. "No."

Liadan's face crumpled, clearly not believing her. "I'm so sorry."

"It's fine, honestly."

Obelia rose to her full height. "Let me see that outside, Bryanna."

Bryanna let her aunt usher her out of the bedchamber, giving Liadan a small, understanding smile as she left. She followed Obelia to the hallway's window, letting her tilt her face up to the streaming light to inspect the side of her face that still felt as though it had been pressed against a burning sconce.

"It's just a bit of swelling." Obelia pressed her fingertips to Bryanna's tender cheek, healing the congealed blood around her eye. "You're lucky. The first time I caught Liadan mid-nightmare, I landed flat on my backside and couldn't sit for three days." She lowered her hand, looking at her suspiciously. "Were you using magic before?"

Bryanna stared at her, taken aback by her question until she remembered that higher-level magic-weavers, like mages and ovates, could sense when magic was used in their vicinity. As a sorceress, Bryanna could sense magic, too, though the magic-weaver had to be close for her to detect it. "I accidentally dream-weaved into Liadan's nightmare," she admitted.

Obelia clucked her tongue. "Well, we'll need to make sure that doesn't happen again. We can't have your dream-weaver abilities going wild, especially while you're stuck in proximity to so many others. You'll be sucked into a new nightmare every night."

Bryanna shuddered. Liadan's had been bad enough. She didn't want to imagine what other horrors those in her aunt's care had endured.

"We'll talk more about this later." Obelia made her way back to Liadan's chamber. "For now, I need to see to Liadan."

Bryanna returned to her bedchamber and rummaged

around in her trunks for her undergarments, a loosely fitted shirt, and breeches. Her mother had never warmed to the idea of women wearing trousers or breeches, considering them unflattering to the female figure ("That's the staple uniform of farm wenches and field workers, not those of our social class"). It was for that reason that Bryanna had two wardrobes in her bedchamber back home: the one her mother knew about, which contained all her dresses, crinolines, and overskirts, and the one concealed under her bed, which had several pairs of riding breeches, snugly cut, fitted shirts, calf-length socks, and steel-capped boots.

It was most of the latter that she'd brought with her to Sheidlow Ridge. Unlike her mother, Bryanna preferred breeches to dresses and skirts. Not only were they easier to move around in, but it meant she could walk down cobbled streets without having to worry about stray gusts of wind lifting her skirts up over her head. The fact that it warded off the squalid attentions of eligible—and ineligible—men was a bonus.

She took a quick bath and stepped out into the hallway, where Liadan was waiting for her, dressed in a loose linen blouse and long cotton skirt. Her puffy eyes flickered to Bryanna's cheek before she swallowed and glanced down at her shoes. It was hard to believe she was the same verbose young woman who'd shown Bryanna around the night before.

They headed to the kitchen in silence. Bryanna wasn't very talkative by nature, unlike her mother, who could find at least ten things to say on any topic. *Beautiful day, isn't it?* or *How did you sleep?* were usually Bryanna's customary conversation starters, but neither seemed like a sensitive option, given the circumstances.

In the kitchen, they found the back door open and curtains drawn. Soft morning sunshine glinted off the polished trestle benches, drying goblets, and cabinet doors.

Bryanna cleared her throat. "So ... what do you usually cook for breakfast?"

"Nothing too complicated." Liadan walked over to the larder and peered in. "There are a few loaves of bread and some butter left from yesterday, so we can make toast. After we milk the dun cows, of course."

Bryanna's heart gave a faint lurch. "You mean we ... ah ... actually milk them?"

Back in Castlereagh, there were markets, grocers, and butchers open daily. Bryanna had never retrieved anything from a primary source before. Just contemplating approaching a dun cow, which was at least four times her size, made her twitch.

"Yes," said Liadan. "The tower's quite self-sufficient. We produce most things ourselves. What else should we have, do you think?"

"Umm ..." Bryanna hoped Liadan wasn't about to propose they hunt down a wild boar so they could serve bacon.

"How about eggs?"

"Yes," Bryanna said in relief.

"We'll need to fetch them. Come on."

Bryanna followed her out the back door. A glistening pond twice the size of Sheidlow Square stood directly in front of them. Liadan led her past it and the dome-shaped barn and stables beside it, whose doors lay open to reveal an empty space where her family's carriage would've been stowed the night before. With the upcoming Beltane festivities, Gawain and Mr. Ahearn would've been forced to leave Sheidlow Ridge in the wee morning hours to avoid getting stuck in the clogged thoroughfares.

Liadan stopped by what looked like a miniature version of one of the thatched cottages in Sheidlow Ridge, propped up on stilts. "The eggs are in here." She picked up a wicker basket under the eave. "We need about forty. Would you rather collect them or milk the dun cows?"

Bryanna hastened to take the basket from Liadan. There was no way she was getting near a dun cow if she didn't need to. "I'll get the eggs."

"Let's meet back in the kitchen. I might be delayed a little. I need to catch a fish or two for one of the boarders."

"All right."

The smell of unaired straw and poultry accosted Bryanna as she pushed the door open and stepped inside. She'd only ever been in a henhouse once before, when she'd been on a school excursion to a local farm. The henhouse she'd visited then was very different from the one she found herself in, though. For one, there'd been eggs all over the straw-covered shelves, and for another, it'd been full of hens.

Obelia's henhouse had neither eggs nor hens. What it did have was a pair of bird-like creatures with fangs behind their beaks and striped, furry feline tails. As she watched them, one of the creatures flapped onto the floor and waddled over to her, rubbing itself against her legs, the same way her neighbor's cat would whenever it was hungry.

"Hello there," she murmured, bending to pet its soft, feathery head.

The creature leaned more heavily against her, its hefty weight making her stumble and reach for the nearest shelf—which was wet and slippery with fresh droppings.

"Eww!" Bryanna wiped her hand vigorously against the material of her breeches, trying not to gag. "Honestly—"

And then she saw them.

On the shelf the atypical bird just vacated was a nest brimming with extra-large, pale golden eggs. Bryanna moved forward at once, eager to collect what she needed and escape. But she'd barely touched one when the strange birds erupted into shrill *bawk, bawk, bawking* screeches. Their eyes were no longer a curious brown, but a bright, glowing red as they glared at her, their beaks drawn back to expose their sharp fangs.

Bryanna raced for the door, eager to put as much distance between them as she could, but in her haste, she tripped and tumbled forward onto the timber floor.

Before she could regain her footing, the vicious bird-like beasts lunged at her, pecking mercilessly at any visible morsel of flesh they could get their sharp little fangs on.

"Get off me," she cried, knocking them back with her basket. But they only dug their fangs in deeper. "Help! Liadan! Aunt Obelia!"

Footfalls pounded up the stairs and the door burst open. Weylin and a boarder she'd never seen before hurried inside. They swiftly stopped in their tracks when they saw her sprawled on the floor with the creatures. Weylin took one look at her frantic, frazzled form and his cheeks hollowed out as though he were biting them to keep from laughing.

"It's not funny!" she growled, struggling to keep the second creature at bay while the one still attached to her arm flapped its wings indignantly.

The other boarder was much more empathetic to her plight. He scooped the ferocious fiends off her and set them down on the other side of the henhouse, where they continued *bawking* resentfully until he doled out a sack of feed for them.

Weylin leaned forward, his infuriating smirk still playing on his lips, and offered Bryanna a hand up.

Bryanna didn't take it. Instead, she pushed to her feet, brushing as much hay off herself as she could. No way was she going to let someone who found amusement at her expense assist her if she could help it.

Are you all right?

The question was spoken in her head, as though a

minuscule person had crawled into her ear canal and started talking.

Bryanna?

Bryanna blinked. Her rescuer was speaking to her telepathically. It must've been him because Weylin's voice wasn't as smooth or light as the one in her mind.

"I'm fine," she said with as much dignity as she could muster, prodding the stinging scratches and fang marks covering her forearms.

I'm Bain Linton, he said, rubbing the last of the feed from his hands and shaking his glossy, mahogany-colored hair off his face. His friendly, ash-brown eyes showed more alarm and concern for Bryanna than Weylin, who still looked as though he was suppressing a laugh. *You can take the eggs now.*

Bryanna tensed. He couldn't seriously think she'd approach the small beasts again, even if they *were* now making satisfied purring noises in the back of their throats as they munched on the scratch grains.

Go on. They don't mind once they've been fed.

Bryanna would've much preferred to kneel over the side of a dun cow. But she did as he bade, acutely aware of Weylin's amused gaze on her. Squaring her shoulders, she picked up the basket she'd dropped and walked back to the nests, keeping her sights fastened on the feasting beast. She stretched out a hand and touched an egg, and when they continued to eat without complaint, picked it up and tucked it carefully into her basket.

"You're lucky it was me and not one of these little creatures last night," Weylin drawled, shaking his head in mock dismay.

Bryanna's cheeks flushed. "I said I was sorry. What are these creatures, anyway?"

"They're cockatrice crossed with tabby cat. Cute as buttons, if you don't get on their bad side." His upper lip twitched.

She might've thought it made him look endearing if she

weren't so annoyed at him. "I wasn't trying to get on their bad side."

Weylin opened his mouth to respond, but then frowned and pulled out a gold pocket watch from inside his trousers, its cover etched with an intricate tree whose roots curled in looped spirals. "I have to go. Try not to antagonize any more of your aunt's creatures if you can, Ms. Nicholls."

"I wasn't—"

But with a nod in Bain's direction, he was gone.

Bryanna watched him go, irritation and another emotion she couldn't quite place—disappointment?—pressing in on her.

Sorry about that, said Bain, shoving his hands in his pockets. *My abilities are limited to one host at a time. You won't hear me if I'm talking to someone else.*

"Are you a telepath?" she asked curiously.

No, I'm only able to project my voice into other people's minds, not hear their thoughts.

He helped Bryanna collect the rest of the eggs, then took the basket and led her back out into the refreshingly cool morning air. An enormous brindle wolfhound was waiting for them by the door, tail wagging.

This is Gelert, he said, scratching the dog behind the ears.

Bryanna patted Gelert and was rewarded with a wet, slobbery lick on her hand, which was still streaked with droppings. The wolfhound screwed up his face, gave her a great, booming bark, and padded onto Bain's other side, casting her a furtive, distrustful scowl.

Liadan should be back in the kitchen any moment. I saw her out on the pier.

"She was going to get milk too."

I did that already.

Bryanna stared at him. There weren't many people in Otherworld who'd willingly advance on a dun cow.

Bain laughed. *I grew up on my adoptive family's dairy farm. I'm used to dun cows. Has Liadan given you a tour of the grounds?*

Bryanna shook her head.

Come on, it won't take long.

He turned right, toward the paddocks several paces away. Bryanna could see dun cows, sheep, and goats munching on grass or dipping their mouths into troughs.

These are our livestock fields. You don't have to worry about feeding the animals. Obelia or I usually do that. Behind them are the wheat and barley crops. They'll be ready for harvesting in a few weeks. Obelia said you'll be here to help us this year.

Bryanna nodded, though she planned to be long gone by then. She'd seen the people in Castlereagh return home after a day working in the harvest fields, and even the sturdiest beings always looked exhausted.

The dun cows, goats, sheep, and cockatrice hybrids weren't the only animals Obelia kept. A short, stone-walled enclosure next to the livestock paddocks held a species of antlered bunny-like creatures called jackalopes and a rare breed of swine known as assal piglets, which could be painlessly slaughtered and reborn from the bones.

Bain only stopped there briefly before leading her to a tall, white picket fence.

Behind here are our vegetable patch and herb garden. We don't have time to go in there now, but you should take a walk through when you can. You'll be surprised what Obelia can grow this time of year. Just don't go into the herb garden. Your aunt's very strict about that.

He finished the tour by pointing out the well and outhouse past the courtyard trees.

Did something happen to Liadan this morning? he asked as they headed back to the kitchen.

A large, winged creature landing on the roof of a tree house at the edge of the forest saved her from answering. Bryanna had only ever seen his likeness in the illustrations of bestiaries. "Is that a wyvern?"

Bain eyed the robustly built, black-winged creature distrustfully. *His name's Finch. Obelia caught him lurking around the tower a few weeks ago. He seems to have made Sheidlow Forest his new home.*

The wyvern turned in their direction, as though he knew they were talking about him. He raised his long, scaled tail over his head and bared his teeth, emitting a low growl that carried over to them despite their distance.

Come on, said Bain, forcing Bryanna to tear her gaze away from the wyvern. *The others will be wanting breakfast soon.*

FOUR

The grandfather clock struck eight as Bryanna and Bain entered the kitchen, the soft, clear notes echoing through the tower. Bryanna loathed the sound, though she hadn't always. Once, she'd found the chimes alluring and would lie awake in bed, usually with Aveline, listening for them until the wee morning hours. But one night five years ago, as the midnight chimes sounded throughout the house, the most peculiar thing had happened. A formidable gust of wind had thrown open the windows of her bedchamber, sending volumes askew and porcelain dolls tumbling, their faces chipping and dusting the polished floor. Bryanna had clutched her counterpane, unable to shake the feeling that something bad had happened.

Something irreversible.

The next morning, she and her family had awoken to the devastating news of Aveline's demise.

Eager to escape the triggering chimes, she headed into the pantry to wait out the last of them, leaving Bain to place the eggs on the trestle bench. There, she took her time selecting a large frying pan from a tottering pile and stepped back into the main kitchen just as the final chime sounded.

Liadan was standing over the sink, grappling with a pair of sapphire salmon. What color she'd lost earlier that morning returned proudly as Bain drew her into a one-armed hug. Bryanna felt a pang of something she couldn't quite identify. Not quite envy, but close. She'd never had anyone look at her the way Bain looked at Liadan, as though she were precious and worthy of being doted on.

"Good morning, everyone," trilled a voice from the staircase.

Bryanna glanced up at the fair, golden-haired girl who'd spoken. She was some kind of faerie. A pixie, if Bryanna were to guess, what with the pair of translucent ochre wings folded behind her back.

"You must be Bryanna Nicholls," she said in a rich lilt as she made her way down the stairs. "I'm Orlagh Aubépine, and this," she inclined her head to the girl behind her, whose skin had a shimmery sheen that Bryanna had only ever seen on *sidhes*, "is Seara Grimm."

Seara?

Bryanna's gaze shifted to the second girl curiously. She'd been looking forward to meeting her from the moment she'd read her name not only in Obelia's letter, but in a feature article covering the Brotherhood of Sìorraidh weeks ago. The reported attack, which had claimed her mother's life, had caused more of a stir than usual due to its unique circumstances. There'd been three casualties instead of the customary one, and the victims had all been found propped up in the middle of a small-town square.

Seara was part of the reason why she'd been so impatient to get to Sheidlow Ridge. And it seemed the young girl had been eagerly awaiting her, too, because without warning, a subtle shift of magic—sidhe magic—descended around the two of them, cloaking them from the others.

Bryanna glanced around. Seara's spell was so seamless, no one had even realized she'd cleaved them from the others.

"I know it's a bit forward to force a private audience with you, Ms. Nicholls," Seara said apologetically as Bryanna set the frying pan on the wood-burning stove. "But I'm afraid I couldn't wait any longer. They say you're working against the Brotherhood of Sìorraidh. Is it true?"

To say Bryanna was taken aback was an understatement. She supposed she shouldn't have been surprised. If Seara was anything like her, she'd have wanted vengeance on the Brotherhood as well. She would've done her research and read the newspapers' speculations about Bryanna being on the hunt for them.

"Well?" Seara prompted, her hazel eyes boring into hers. "Are you? Because if you are, there's a lot we can learn from each other."

Bryanna hesitated. She could see vestiges of herself in Seara. The girl had lost the closest member of her family, just as she had at a similar age. But unlike Bryanna, who'd had time to grieve and steel her resolve, Seara was still reeling from the loss of her mother, still seething from the thought of those responsible being at large, reigning unpunished and untouchable. There was anger in the stiffness of her jaw, and Bryanna had seen firsthand how decisions made in anger lacked logic and sometimes even sense.

Besides, even if she'd wanted to form an alliance with Seara, the girl was still a minor. The last thing she needed was to dodge kidnapping charges while they combed Otherworld for the Brotherhood of Sìorraidh.

"I'm sorry, Seara," she said softly. "I'm not sure what you've heard, but—"

"That you've become our best hope since your ascension to sorceress," she interjected, her eyes shining with determination. "Please, I know we want the same thing. Let us help each other."

But Bryanna shook her head. She couldn't risk the younger girl unraveling everything she'd put into place to finally avenge her cousin. "I'm sorry, Seara, but I'm afraid I'm not sure what you're talking about."

Disappointment clouded Seara's features. "I see." She took a step away from her as the cloaking spell dissolved. "Let's go, Orlagh," she muttered, turning on her heels. "I'm not hungry anymore."

"Is everything all right?" Liadan asked, casting a questioning glance between her and the retreating sidhe.

Guilt churned in Bryanna's stomach as she watched Seara walk away. "Yes."

She grabbed the frying pan she'd set down and placed it on the wood-burning stove's grate. Then she poured a generous dollop of oil into the pan and set to frying the first batch of eggs. Although she'd never cooked them before, she'd watched her family's resident cook, Madam MacLead, do so many times, and it looked easy enough ...

Except, for some unfathomable reason, unlike Madam MacLead's eggs, which developed a pale film over the yolk as they cooked, hers turned a charred, brick red.

"I take it you've never fried an egg before?"

Bryanna jerked back. She'd been so focused on the eggs, she'd not realized Weylin was standing next to her, staring down at them as though she'd burned them to a crisp.

Bryanna glanced over at him, and a faint flutter she couldn't explain stirred in her stomach.

"I suppose I shouldn't be surprised," he continued, leaning a hip against the edge of the benchtop beside the wood-burning stove, his lip quirking marginally. "You being a townsgirl and all. I heard you've been raised with housemaids and butlers. Is this the first time you've seen a kitchen?"

"Of course not," she said stiffly as heat traveled up her neck.

It was just the first time she'd cooked in one, though she'd sooner collect a second batch of eggs from the cockatrice hybrids than tell him that.

"Right," he said in a tone that made it clear he didn't believe her. "I bet you cook in one all the time."

"Leave her be, Weylin," said Liadan, coming to her defense. "They look better than any eggs you've ever made before."

Weylin raised an eyebrow. "I've never made eggs."

"Oh, I know." Liadan flipped the last slice of toast before turning to him. "In fact, I don't recall you ever helping to prepare a meal."

"Not that it's any of your concern, but Bain's never asked for help." He looked to Bain for support. "Tell her, Bain."

Bain looked as though he wanted to respond, but Liadan stopped him with a warning finger. "That's not the point, Weylin. You've been here for moon cycles. You know when it's your floor's turn to cook, you help."

"Bain has all the help he needs," Weylin argued. "You're always there."

"Because *you* aren't."

Weylin heaved a great sigh. "You know what? I think I'll go to the Brodericks' for breakfast, where I'll actually be able to eat something. Even if it is porridge."

Liadan pointed toward the door. "Off with you, then. Go enjoy your porridge."

"At least I won't heave after it."

Liadan grabbed a piece of toast, but before she could throw it at him, Weylin tugged Bryanna forward, positioning her in front of him like a shield.

Bryanna's breath hitched at his unexpected touch. She'd been certain his fingers would be as calloused as his personality, but they were quite warm and surprisingly soft against her skin.

"Do something, Ms. Nicholls," he quipped, a smirk tugging at his lips. "Aren't you meant to be all-powerful?"

"I don't think I will, actually," Bryanna replied, extricating herself from his grip. She did *not* want to think about his fingers, or the lingering heat they left on her arms.

Weylin clapped a hand over his heart. "You wound me, Ms. Nicholls. After I came to your rescue?"

"*Bain* came to my rescue," she retorted. "You just stood there while I was almost pecked to death and laughed."

Liadan shook her head in dismay. "Why am I not surprised?"

Weylin rolled his eyes. "She was fine."

Bryanna scoffed and picked up the pan with her patched, deflated eggs. "I thought you were going to the Brodericks', Mr —" What *was* his surname?

"Conveil?" Weylin supplied.

"And I'd mind your manners while you're there," she added with the sweetest smile she could muster. "Or you'll get kicked out of their kitchen too."

Bryanna took over toasting bread after he left, leaving Liadan to cook the rest of the eggs.

They called breakfast fifteen minutes later. By then, most of the boarders were milling around the kitchen, sneaking slices of toast when Liadan wasn't looking. The most atypical of them was a slender young woman with long, navy-blue hair and skin so translucent, Bryanna was sure she was a sea denizen. One who lived in deep waters, judging by the thin, cloudy film covering her indigo eyes. Bryanna couldn't help but stare at her as she took the thrashing salmon from the sink and placed them on her plate, where they stilled, ogling her as though she were a flawless zooplankton.

The knife Bryanna had been using to spread butter on the last slices of toast fell from her loosened grip. The young woman had to be a *morgen*.

Her mouth dried. What in all of Castlereagh was one of her kind doing at the Mage's Sanctuary?

They were responsible for more attacks than neach-ithe anam, though it wasn't always easy to prove. The feared, seductive water spirits usually attacked seafarers on isolated, craggy coastlines or in deep ocean waters. Many of those they killed washed away and were never seen again.

"That's Iodhna," Liadan murmured, following her gaze. "Most of the boarders here think Cayde is the one to look out for, but if you ask me? It's her."

As if hearing Liadan, Iodhna turned in their direction, scowling at Liadan. Then her gaze shifted, and the scowl, if possible, turned colder as she glared at Bryanna.

Without breaking eye contact, the morgen brought one of the limp salmon to her jagged teeth. It didn't even squirm.

Bile rose in Bryanna's stomach as she forced her revolted gaze away, unable to watch as Iodhna devoured the salmon while its heart still beat between her fingers.

She glanced down at her platter of toast, no longer hungry.

Bryanna spent the rest of the morning and most of the afternoon in her bedchamber, checking that nothing was missing from her trunks—there wasn't—and searching for ideal hiding spots for her more incriminating items. She found some large places, such as the floorboards under her rug and loosened bricks behind the grate, for the weapons she'd filched from her brothers' households or purchased secretly under her neighbor's name. Her smaller items, such as her talismans, she hid in the nooks behind furniture or in the bottoms of drawers.

Her final touch was the leather-bound, hardcover volumes she'd bespelled with illusion enchantments, so that anyone flipping through their pages wouldn't see the implicating objects and phials within their hollowed pages. Of all the things she'd brought, they'd be the hardest for her to replace.

Satisfied with her work, Bryanna left her bedchamber to explore the tower. She'd read about old towers and castles all over Otherworld having hidden passages behind tapestries and fake walls that led to concealed chambers or out into the grounds. But if the Sheidlow Tower possessed any secrets to boast of, it wasn't yielding them to her. The closest she came to a mystery chamber was a short servant's stairwell off the kitchen, which led to a semi-cellar where Obelia churned butter and made cheese.

She spent most of her time in the library after that, trying to find her late grandma Kendra's volumes. She'd been sure Obelia would've kept them there. But by Beltane Eve four days later, she was forced to concede defeat. Obelia must've kept them elsewhere, away from the boarders' reach. Which made her wonder: What kind of information did they contain for her aunt not to want her boarders to find them?

That afternoon, Obelia surprised Bryanna by coming to her bedchamber. Her aunt had been so busy with her patients and the preparations for Beltane, they'd barely seen each other outside of mealtimes. Nor had they commenced the dream-weave blocking sessions Obelia had promised on her first morning.

Bryanna looked up from the marjoram leaves she was laying out to dry on the windowsill. She'd picked them on her stroll through the forest earlier that morning, to add to her growing collection of herbs she'd be taking with her when she left Sheidlow Tower.

Obelia stifled a yawn as she walked over to the volumes Bryanna had lined up on her mantel. "Your father told me you liked gathering herbs."

Bryanna tensed as her aunt picked one of the volumes and leafed through the first few pages. Just because the illusion spell was on it didn't mean what she'd stashed inside it wouldn't fall out if her aunt reached the right section. "Really?"

"It's a pastime of mine, too," Obelia said with a smile. "I've got herbs most apothecaries would kill to possess."

"Like what?" Bryanna asked, her attention glued to the pages her aunt was still flipping through.

Obelia snapped the volume shut, wiggling a brow. "Would you like to see for yourself?"

Relief and curiosity battled for dominance as Bryanna took the volume from her aunt and returned it to the shelf. "Yes."

"Follow me."

Obelia led Bryanna into the hall. Instead of leading her to the staircase, though, she headed in the opposite direction, toward the empty chamber at the end of the hall. She stopped halfway, raised her wrist, and with a flick and a prickle of magic, a polished, black ivory ladder shimmered into existence, resting securely on the edge of a trapdoor in the ceiling.

Bryanna gaped at it. It seemed the tower contained some concealed chambers after all.

"After yo—" Obelia faltered, her expression shifting as her eyes grew unfocused.

Bryanna reached for her, concern replacing curiosity at her sudden change of demeanor. "Aunt Obelia, are you all right?"

Obelia heaved a resigned sigh. "Weylin and Cayde are on the verge of a fight. Again."

Bryanna strained her ears, but the only sounds that reached her were the boarders splashing in the pond outside. "I don't hear them."

"That's because they're in the kitchen."

Bryanna stared at her aunt, her stomach sinking. Obelia must've been using some sort of surveillance spell if she could hear Weylin and Cayde with ten floors between them. What were the chances her aunt hadn't heard her dismantle half of her bedchamber when she'd looked for places to hide her covert items?

Obelia marched for the stairs, muttering under her breath. "Go on up, Bryanna. I'll be back in a minute. I need to stop them before they shatter my new porcelain set."

Bryanna nodded, working to dislodge the worry in her chest as she climbed the ladder to the musty, low-ceilinged chamber. Obelia couldn't have known about her weapons and phials, she reminded herself. If she had, she'd have confiscated them immediately. Not to mention her father would've already been there to pick her up and force her back to Castlereagh—and incarceration.

The hidden chamber, it turned out, wasn't an attic, like she'd assumed, but a larger, homier version of her aunt's office. Mismatched pieces of furniture littered the large space, covered in tea cozies, athame-carved candles, and other trinkets. Some of Bryanna's earlier anxiety evaporated as her eyes fell on the portraits hanging on the walls, depicting Obelia with various boarders from over the years. Bain, with his infectious smile, was a recurring subject.

Her gaze swept past the portraits, landing on a wall of glass cabinets to her right. They were filled with jars of dried herbs and plants submerged in briny liquid. Even from her vantage point, Bryanna recognized some of the rare plant matter on display—and others which she was fairly sure should've been extinct.

She moved toward the cabinets, any thoughts of waiting for her aunt quenched by her desire to get a closer look at her aunt's stocks. The local apothecaries would've been filled with envy if they'd known what her aunt held in her possession. But before she could reach the glass cabinets, her foot caught on something and she pitched forward with a muffled, "*Oomph!*"

Righting herself, Bryanna glared down at the wayward volume on the floor that had almost twisted her ankle, and froze. She'd seen it before ... in her late grandmother's library.

Bryanna's breath hitched. If that volume was there, the others must've been as well ...

She moved to the cedar chest closest to her, lifting the heavy lid and sifting through its contents. But there were no volumes in it, only a pile of old cloaks. She moved on to the next one, then the next, until at last, she found what she was looking for.

Her hands shook as she rifled through the volumes, reading their titles. *Cryptotaxonomy: Classifications of Supernatural Beings*, *The Comprehensive Bestiary of Olympus, Otherworld, and Other Realms*, and *Magical Solutions of the Fifth Century*. Some of the other titles, though, were impossible to read. They were written in another language. Possibly Atlantean, her late grandmother's native tongue, though she couldn't be sure.

At the very bottom of the chest was a booklet unlike the others. Small and thin, it looked pliable, as if it'd been handled often. Bryanna picked it up and leafed through the pages, her brows rising as she scanned the list of place names written throughout the booklet. Each one matched the towns and villages she'd written in her own notebook at the bottom of her trunk.

Gridlet's Pass
Hagslea
Hope Valley
Samisbury
Lancien

They were places where the last Brotherhood of Sìorraidh victims had been found.

Bryanna sat back, stunned. Why was her aunt tracking the Brotherhood of Sìorraidh when she'd given up her vengeance years ago?

The sound of ruffling skirts at the bottom of the ladder made her jump. She shoved the volumes under her skirt, pulled the chest closed, and dived into the nearest winged chair just as Obelia reached the landing.

"So many stairs," her aunt puffed, wiping her brow with the back of her hand. "I got to them right before Weylin sent the first pewter goblet flying. Tyffin's keeping an eye on them for me."

"Why *is* Weylin here?" Bryanna asked, despite herself. Not that she'd seen him much since her first breakfast. The majority of the time that she had, he'd either been dozing in one of the library armchairs or returning from one of his solitary hunts in the forest, usually with a forest critter in tow for Obelia to roast in the oven for supper.

Not that she'd been keeping track of him.

Obelia lowered herself into the winged chair opposite her. "Weylin's here as a favor to a friend. He's been temporarily banished from his village. I can't say more without breaking patient-healer privileges."

"But I thought you just said he wasn't a patient," said Bryanna slyly.

Obelia laughed. "Oh, you're quick! You get that from our

side of the family. Speaking of family, your father tells me you've been working at the apothecary with Lady Auberagh for the last few years. How is she?"

The thought of the tetchy old woman she'd known her whole life made Bryanna smile. Lady Auberagh was the one who'd helped her when she'd made the painful initial transition from a thaumaturge—someone with the capability to develop magical abilities—to a druid, the first level a magic-weaver could reach. While her mother had paced back and forth in the hallway, refusing to believe her daughter was the newest magic-weaver to emerge from the prolific Nicholls lineage, it had been Lady Auberagh who'd held Bryanna against her chest and whispered, "You'll have the power to make a difference to all of Otherworld and beyond soon. Just keep fighting."

It'd been Bryanna's only coherent thought, the thing that anchored her: the knowledge that if she pulled through, she'd become a potent rival to the Brotherhood of Sìorraidh.

After her transition, Lady Auberagh was the one who'd trained her in magic. It'd been only natural for Bryanna to work at her apothecary when she'd been old enough—she'd been there every other day, anyway. Mostly to train, but also because she'd found Lady Auberagh's secret cache of classified volumes on the Brotherhood of Sìorraidh. She'd ducked into the chamber at the back of the store whenever her mentor wasn't looking and spent hours flipping through the leather-bound pages for information.

At least until Lady Auberagh caught her.

The elderly apothecary had been beyond furious, lecturing Bryanna for what felt like hours on the values of self-control and privacy, before making her promise not to tell anyone about what she kept in her back chamber. Not that Bryanna would've told anyone. Her father wouldn't have let her see Lady

Auberagh again if he'd known, and who would've trained her then?

"Lady Auberagh's well," Bryanna told her aunt. "She's always comparing my blunders to the antics you used to pull when you worked with her at the Castlereagh Healer Hospital."

Obelia's eyes twinkled. "Does she?"

Bryanna nodded, letting out a nervous breath and watching Obelia closely as she continued, "She talks about Fillian sometimes too."

The tired smile slipped from Obelia's face. "You know about Fillian?"

Bryanna nodded again.

Fillian Conveil had been her aunt's betrothed. His name had cropped up repeatedly during Bryanna's research. He'd been infamous for his expeditions tracking the Brotherhood of Sìorraidh and had died at the foot of Mount Ygerna on his final voyage. Although he wasn't technically a Brotherhood of Sìorraidh victim, the companion he'd been traveling with, Delen Instone, had been—and he was found four days later in Castlereagh, floating prone under the docks.

"He's the reason you left Castlereagh, right? When you ... disappeared?"

It was as though a shadow had clamped over her aunt's features, extinguishing the warmth that usually radiated from her. "Staying in Castlereagh after his funeral wasn't exactly an option."

Bryanna leaned forward. "Why not—"

But Obelia jumped to her feet. "We should join the others. I believe they've begun celebrating Beltane early."

As if on cue, raucous laughter carried through the narrow windows, followed by low whistles.

Bryanna pressed her lips together. The boarders had been drinking since luncheon, growing louder by the hour, and her aunt hadn't felt the need to intervene until that moment? If she didn't know better, she would've thought her aunt was using their boisterous behavior as an excuse to end their conversation.

Bryanna stood, tucked the volumes into the waistband of her skirt when her aunt wasn't looking, and followed her downstairs, her disappointment palpable. She'd really hoped her aunt would have given her a few tidbits about her past.

Only when they reached the kitchen did she realize Obelia had given her a tidbit, however unintentionally.

Staying in Castlereagh after his funeral wasn't exactly an option.

What had she meant by that? That it had been too painful to remain there, surrounded by the memory of Fillian? Or had something much more sinister happened?

CHAPTER

FIVE

Bryanna was still mulling over Obelia's words an hour later as she sat at one of the courtyard tables with several of her aunt's boarders. Most of them were playing a game called Five, where they went around the table counting. Anyone who landed on a multiple of five would have to drink from their goblets of the Sheidlow Tower's home-brewed spiced mead.

Eventually, Bryanna excused herself and ventured off to the well beyond the courtyard to splash her face with water. She'd nursed her own goblet of the sweet, sharp-edged mead, and it was starting to make her head spin. She wanted to be clear-minded, just in case Obelia became more talkative as the night wore on. Not that she thought she would be. She'd been watching her aunt bustle about the courtyard all afternoon, lost in the monotonous motion of playing hostess.

"I think you're supposed to drink that," a languid voice drawled behind Bryanna as she patted her face with the back of her sleeves.

Bryanna turned with an uncomfortable jolt. Cayde, the neach-ithe anam, was leaning against a tree, his brown-

58

speckled eyes—the only lively part of his otherwise weathered features—resting on her.

A subtle calm settled over Bryanna. The sort that came when she awoke to find there was still time before she needed to get out of bed.

"What are you doing here?" she asked, the words heavy on her mead-addled tongue.

Cayde shrugged. "The others prefer it when I don't join them in the courtyard."

Bryanna's face softened. She knew what it was like to be ostracized by her peers. The Nicholls family might've been one of the most prominent in Otherworld, but at Castlereagh Grammar, no one had been keen to befriend her. Not when Grear Winterton, an unpleasant girl in her class, turned on anyone who talked to her.

"You shouldn't have to hide from them," she said, her voice gentle. "You've just as much right to be here as they do."

Cayde gave her a faint smile. "If only the others thought that way. Speaking of which, why aren't you with them?"

Bryanna's eyes narrowed at his question. It was the kind of thing her mother would ask anytime she found her hiding from her snobbish classmates in the ballrooms she was forced to attend. She took a step away from him as, somewhere in the depths of her mind, she remembered that neach-ithe anams could manipulate the thoughts and feelings of their victims, forcing a supernaturally induced tranquility that made it easier to keep their prey complacent. She reached for her magic, sending it over her mind to check for any foreign forces—and, sure enough, sensed a subtle presence that could only be Cayde's influence.

Her magic flared as though of its own accord, and she latched onto it, gathering it in her palms before sending it careening into the neach-ithe anam and pinning him to the closest tree.

Immediately, the sense of calm that had descended over her dissipated as though a heavy blanket had slipped off her shoulders, leaving another emotion surging in its wake—rage.

"Did you just use your thrall on me?" Bryanna snarled, advancing on Cayde. Gone was any apprehension she'd harbored when she'd first seen him. Her body thrummed with fury.

"I'm sorry," he managed as alarm flashed across his face. "I just wanted to make you comfortable."

"We're all entitled to our feelings," she growled. "No one should take that away from us. *No one.*"

It was no longer Cayde she was seeing, but the countless Brotherhood of Sìorraidh victims who'd been stripped of their minds against their will.

Victims like Aveline.

"You're right," he said, his muscles straining against her magical restraints. "I shouldn't have done it. I wasn't thinking."

She twisted her hand, pressing him further against the tree, and stepped forward until they were eye to eye. "If you ever do that to me again, I'll make sure it's the last thing you ever do."

"I won't," he replied, consternation heavy in his tone.

Bryanna deliberated another moment before releasing her magic and letting Cayde drop. It wasn't as though she could keep him pressed to the tree the whole night. Well, she probably could've, but she didn't think her aunt would've approved.

"Blimey," Cayde said, one hand pressed to his chest as he righted himself. "I haven't felt that shocked since I woke up in my open casket."

"Why were you in an open casket in the first place?" Bryanna asked before she could stop herself.

"Because my healer thought I'd died," he replied. "Which I had, technically. From faerie-stroke."

Bryanna thawed slightly. More than half the patients she'd seen at the apothecary she'd worked at were family members of faerie-stroke patients, desperate to find a cure for their loved ones. It was common enough that every person in Otherworld was either affected by the sickness or knew someone who was. "I'm sorry."

"Don't be. I'm stronger for it." He chuckled. "Do you get it? Because I'm a neach-ithe anam now?"

Bryanna's lips tugged up.

"Signs of a sense of humor," he said approvingly. "I thought there was one in there somewhere."

Bryanna crossed her arms. "How did you end up here?"

"Well, where I come from, my kind are feared. Before me, there'd been two other neach-ithe anam, and they'd both been killed right out of the casket. When I came to and realized what I'd become, I knew I couldn't let anyone learn I'd been reanimated. So I snuck past the funeral guards and hid in my parents' wardrobe, figuring they'd take me somewhere safe once they found me, you know? But when they discovered what I'd become, my father gave me two choices: run away or turn myself in."

"That's awful," Bryanna whispered. Her parents hadn't always been around when she and her brothers had grown up, but they would've never abandoned them in such a heartless way.

"I spent a year in the wilderness, trying to control my feelers." Cayde pointed to the veiny center of his forehead, where the feelers his kind used to siphon their victims' life essence rested. "I didn't have any money, and no one was willing to give me free passage to the larger towns, where others like me lurked. Eventually, I heard about the Mage's

Sanctuary and decided to come here. I made the mistake of approaching the Sheidlow Ridge villagers first. They chased me into the forest with pitchforks."

Bryanna snorted. "Sounds about right."

He smirked. "You should hear what happened next. I got to the tower, and a murder of crows descended on me."

Bryanna had seen crows flying around Sheidlow Tower. They belonged to Nisienne, Obelia's resident banshee.

"What happened?" she asked.

"Well, I didn't know they were Nisienne's ..."

Bryanna's hand flew to her mouth. "Tell me you didn't."

He gave her a sheepish look. "Just three."

Bryanna's shoulders quivered in silent laughter.

"Why are you laughing? It was terrible." He shook his head in mock dismay. "Nisienne started keening. The sound she makes when she senses death in her vicinity is inescapable. Like grinding metal pressed right against your ear—"

"I hope I'm not ruining the moment," Weylin drawled, coming up behind them.

Bryanna jumped. She'd been so focused on Cayde, she'd not realized they were no longer alone.

Weylin stepped in front of Bryanna, blocking her from Cayde's view. "You should be in the courtyard, Garnet. It's your turn to cook."

Cayde's jaw clenched so hard that the ridges of his cheeks became even more prominent against his pale skin. "I'll be there in a minute."

"You need to get there now," Weylin said tightly, shifting to keep himself between her and Cayde as she edged around him.

If he was looking to aggravate the neach-ithe anam by keeping her out of his view, it was working. Cayde's expression darkened.

"I'm not going to hurt her," he said through clenched teeth.

"You're a neach-ithe anam," Weylin pointed out, as if that was more than enough to warrant his skepticism.

"Obelia trusts me."

"Well, I don't."

The look Cayde sent Weylin was just shy of malicious. "Yes, well, you don't trust anyone, do you?"

"What's that supposed to mean?" Weylin asked, the muscles along his back flexing.

"Only that I'd feel the same way, had *my* ex run off with one of my frien—"

Before he could finish, Weylin's fist snaked out lightning-fast, connecting with the side of Cayde's face.

"Weylin—" But whatever Bryanna was about to say got lodged in her throat as two dark, tentacle-like feelers burst from Cayde's forehead.

She took an involuntary step back, pulling on the back of Weylin's shirt to tug him away from Cayde. But Weylin disentangled himself from her grip in one fluid motion and knocked her out of the way just as the neach-ithe anam reached him and clamped his hands around his throat, his feelers seeking purchase on the center of Weylin's forehead.

"Cayde!" Bryanna shouted, her voice cracking as horror washed over her. She propelled herself forward, but before she could get to them, Weylin's knee came up, sinking into Cayde's stomach with a sickening thud.

Cayde's grip on Weylin's throat loosened, but only for a moment. Then he grabbed the front of Weylin's shirt and pulled him to the ground, catching his jaw with a punch that echoed through the trees.

"Stop!"

Bryanna hurried forward, intent on wedging herself between them, but they moved so fast, they were nothing more than a blur of flashing limbs. Panic clawed at her throat. She needed to stop them before one of them got seriously injured—or killed. Weylin more so than Cayde. He might've been fast, but he was no match for Cayde's primitive instincts. She reached for her magic, but before she could gather it in her palms, a burst of magic crackled through the air, sending Weylin and Cayde flying apart.

"I've had it with you two," Obelia cried as she strode toward them, her expression thunderous. "This needs to end. Now."

Bryanna's legs nearly gave way with relief.

Weylin pushed to his feet and scowled at Obelia, as though she were an unfair mother who'd taken his sibling's side instead of his. "He started it."

"I don't care who started," Obelia retorted with a withering look. "Both of you know better."

Cayde's gaze flickered to Bryanna, guilt replacing the animalistic rage that had contorted his features moments before. "I'm sorry, Obelia," he said, retracting his feelers into his weathered forehead. "I was just defen—"

"Say you were just defending yourself, and I'm going to—"

Before he could say any more, Tyffin launched himself from an overhanging branch, landing on Weylin's shoulder, and dug his sharp claws into his flesh.

"Ow!"

"Let's go, Cayde," said Obelia, her tone steely as she directed him toward the others, shooting Weylin a disapproving glare.

Weylin kept his gaze trained on the neach-ithe anam, rubbing at his throat where Cayde had gripped him. Only when they were completely out of sight did he turn back to Bryanna. His hands came around each side of her cheeks, tilting her head up so that she was forced to look at him.

"What are you doing?" Bryanna asked, her breath catching at his unexpected touch.

Instead of responding, Weylin's eyes bored into hers with

an intensity that made her pulse quicken. Her gaze dropped to his lips. For one disorienting moment, she thought he might close the distance between them, and despite the fact that they'd barely spent more than a few minutes together, she wasn't completely opposed to the idea.

But then he angled her head to the left, and the right, and Bryanna realized what he was doing: checking to see if she was under Cayde's compulsion. She wrenched herself free, flushing deeply at her own foolishness. "I'm not under his influence."

His voice, when he spoke, was granite hard. "I had to see if you were daft enough to stay alone with someone like him."

Bryanna bristled. And to think, for a second there, she'd actually contemplated letting him kiss her. What had she been thinking? "He can't help what he is."

"Exactly. Which is why you need to stay away from beings like that, not dally with them."

Bryanna gaped at him. Surely he didn't believe she'd harbored anything but polite intentions toward Cayde? He was one of her aunt's boarders, for the love of Castlereagh.

"You're unbelievable," she growled. "I wasn't *dallying*. I was *talking* to him."

"That's not what it looked like," he gritted out, his hands balling into tight fists at his sides.

"You're incorrigible!"

"That's a big word," he said, his eyes flashing the same way they had the night they'd met. "I don't think I've ever heard it spoken out loud before."

"Then perhaps it's time you expanded your vocabulary," she said tartly before spinning on her heels and marching toward the courtyard.

"Keep away from him, Ms. Nicholls," Weylin called after her.

"Don't tell me what to do, Mr. Conveil," she shot back and stormed off, her skin still tingling where his hand had been.

By the time Bryanna returned to the courtyard, Liadan and Bain were back from running an errand for Obelia in the village. They sat with a couple who looked too old to be boarders. The man, who appeared to be in his mid-twenties, was dark-haired and stocky, giving Bryanna the impression that he spent his days lifting hay bales. The woman, in contrast, was small and fair, with an engorged belly that was deep in its final trimester of pregnancy.

"Bryanna, come meet Valentine and Deagon Broderick," Liadan called when she saw her. "They live in Sheidlow Ridge."

Bryanna tried to hide her surprise as she reached them. She hadn't thought any of the villagers would dare be caught anywhere near Obelia or her tower.

Deagon grinned. "'Tis great ter finally meet yeh, Ms. Nicholls. The villagers haven't been able ter talk 'bout anyone else fer days."

Bryanna's heart sank. "Really?"

Valentine threw her husband an exasperated look. "He's exaggerating," she said in an accent similar to that of the southern dwellers. "It's lovely to meet you, Ms. Nicholls."

"Valentine used to be a boarder," Liadan told her. "She wedded Deagon a few years ago."

"Villagers didn't take too kindly ter it," said Deagon, dropping a kiss on his wife's head. "Not that I was ever looked at too kindly, even as a wee lad. Spent more time here than I did at me own ma's house. And I'm not exaggerating. Yer visit has caused almost as much of a stir as the latest Brotherhood of Sìorraidh attack in Wilde Meadows."

Bryanna's stomach turned, and this time it had nothing to do with the mead. "There's been another attack?"

How was it the first time she was hearing about it? Back in Castlereagh, a Brotherhood of Sìorraidh attack caused so much hubbub that the streets became congested with neighbors, families, and friends congregating to share the terrible news.

"It was in the papers this morn," Deagon informed her. "The victim was a man in his seventies. Older than usual. Travelers found his body by one of the main canals—"

"Come, come, ladies and gents," said Obelia, joining them. Her gaze lingered on Liadan, who'd gone pale. "It's Beltane. Let's not talk about the Brotherhood of Sìorraidh tonight."

"Of course, Obelia," said Deagon meekly, and he steered the subject onto the states of their crops.

Bryanna tried to focus on what he was saying, but all she could do was think about the attack. Deagon had said Wilde Meadows. That was one of the villages she, Gawain, and Mr. Ahearn had stopped at to rest the Tuatha steeds on their way to Sheidlow Ridge just days before. Had the Brotherhood of Sìorraidh been there already, hiding in plain sight?

And why had Obelia stopped them from talking about the Brotherhood? Sure, they were celebrating Beltane, but was there another reason? Was Obelia trying to keep word of any new attacks from her, the way her parents and brothers had done for years?

She dismissed the thought at once. Her aunt couldn't have known about the attack yet, surely. Not when she'd been around the tower all day, rushing between sessions to make sure everything was ready for the Beltane festivities.

Bryanna had been hoping her aunt would be more forthcoming about the Brotherhood of Sìorraidh, but if she was going to continue to avoid any mention of them, then Bryanna couldn't remain at the tower much longer. Not when doing so would only cause her to waste time she could be spending tracking down the brotherhood and making them pay for what they'd done.

What they'd continue to do if she didn't find a way to stop them.

If Obelia wouldn't help her, then perhaps she needed to find people who'd help her get the information she sought.

Perhaps she'd been too hasty in knocking back Seara's offer of alliance. At the time, she'd been sure her aunt would help her, that she wouldn't need to ally herself with anyone else. But if Obelia really was trying to keep anything related to the Brotherhood of Sìorraidh from her, then she needed to take matters into her own hands.

"Mind if I sit here?" she asked once she'd located Seara and Orlagh at one of the courtyard tables.

Seara gave her a noncommittal shrug without looking up from her plate of venison. "Suit yourself."

Bryanna lowered herself onto the bench beside her, glancing around to make sure no one was listening before whispering, "Are you still looking for an ally?"

The forkful of venison Seara was guiding to her mouth stopped in midair. She rounded on Bryanna, her eyes lighting up as though the sun had taken residence there, and nodded.

Bryanna released a sigh of relief. "Good."

Neither dared to say more. Not when Orlagh was already looking between them suspiciously.

And she wasn't the only one.

From the other side of the courtyard, shadowed by the trees, was Weylin. Bryanna could feel his eyes trained on her and the disapproval emanating from him, as though he knew what they were talking about.

She threw a glare squarely in his direction, knowing he'd see it, before turning back to Seara.

They spent the rest of the night eating and drinking with the others, listening to Orlagh regale them with the extensive journey she'd be undertaking the next morning for the faerie kingdom of Gorias.

Deagon was a born entertainer, and by the time Obelia carried out the cherry pudding she'd made as a surprise farewell dessert for Orlagh, he stood before them like a bard, telling them story after story about the Sheidlow Ridge villagers that had his captive audience clutching their sides with laughter.

As midnight advanced, the volume in the courtyard rose in anticipation. Bryanna's smile faded as she remembered another Beltane night she'd enjoyed just as much when she'd been a girl of eleven. Aveline and Gawain had been with her, and they'd snuck away from their parents to follow Lady Auberagh's small coven of magic-weavers so they could watch them perform the Belfire rite, away from the masses.

Her mother had found them the second they'd returned to the Castlereagh Gate and dragged them home by the ears amid roars of drunken laughter. Despite that, though, Bryanna had never regretted sneaking away. Not when Aveline had enjoyed it so much—her last Belfire rite.

"Happy Beltane!" everyone chorused as the midnight chimes rang.

"Happy Beltane," Bryanna echoed, forcing a smile.

She was relieved when Obelia stood, drawing her boarders' attention.

"It's time for the Belfire rite," she said, raising her voice so they could all hear her. "But before that, I want to say a few words. Beltane is an important sabbat. Tonight, we celebrate the birth of one season and the demise of another. Summer brings forth more reaping and nourishment for the year ahead. It's a time when our minds rejuvenate and our souls replenish in the vibrant colors that emerge with the season. That is why, to celebrate, magic-weavers all over Otherworld conjure a Belfire rite to honor the occasion."

Around the bonfire, a fervent energy stirred. It was almost palpable, like it had been all those years ago as Bryanna, Aveline, and Gawain had hidden in the bushes awaiting Lady Auberagh's ritual. Bryanna hadn't seen a Belfire rite since that night, and as the ripples of anticipation coursed through her company, the desire to perform it seized her.

"Are you sure?" Obelia asked when Bryanna approached her and told her what she wanted to do. "It takes a substantial amount of magic."

"I know." It had taken Lady Auberagh's entire coven to perform the rite, but most of them had been druids or witches at most. As a sorceress, Bryanna knew she could do it alone.

A crease appeared between Obelia's brows before she nodded and turned back to the others. "It appears I'm in for a treat. Bryanna has volunteered to perform the Belfire rite this year."

Excited whispers erupted at her announcement, though Bryanna noticed Weylin's gaze dart to Obelia, as though expecting her to intervene and stop her from performing the rite by herself.

Bryanna squared her shoulders. He might've thought she couldn't do it, but she was about to prove him wrong.

"It's been decades since I've been privy to such a sight from the sidelines," Obelia continued as though she hadn't seen the sharp look Weylin shot at her. She sat down, leaving Bryanna with the undivided attention of those in the courtyard. So many eager faces stared back at her that her resolve wavered. She took a slow, deep breath, letting her magic unfurl. It tingled as it left her fingertips, invisible tendrils penetrating the sweltering hot bonfire in their center.

Her audience fell silent, mesmerized, as the fire rose with a hiss, as though she'd poured a flagon of mead into the blaze. Higher and higher the fire soared, feeding off her magic as if she were a forge pumping air into a blacksmith's furnace until the flames reached the top of the ancient trees.

Bryanna drew on a little more magic, sweat beading on her brow. The spell was taking a lot out of her. But she persevered, splintering the tip of the bright, orange pillar so that small pieces drooped down into heavy, leaflike petals, making it look as though they were nestled under a blazing marigold.

Obelia's expression shifted to surprise as the onlookers oohed and aahed, as if she couldn't believe the power Bryanna could wield. There was another expression there too. One Bryanna wasn't expecting: pride.

Her chest swelled. No one in her family had ever understood her magical side. They'd been too busy trying to mold her into the perfect, dutiful daughter who attended grand balls and excelled at superfluous conversations.

Breathing hard, Bryanna let her burning flower linger for a moment before releasing her hold.

Around her, the boarders and Brodericks erupted in cheers and whistles as the marigold rose into the starry night sky. Even Weylin looked quietly impressed, try as he might to hide it behind the grim set of his mouth. Their gazes met across the Belfire, and his jaw tightened, as though he was fighting some inner battle. His eyes, though, darkened in a way that made Bryanna's pulse quicken.

She took a dizzying bow, letting the boarders' euphoria sweep over her.

She wasn't sure if it was just her imagination, but in the din that followed, she could have sworn she heard Aveline's cheers among them.

CHAPTER

SIX

In the nights following Beltane, Bryanna's dreams centered on the hidden chamber above her. Sometimes she dreamed she was reading one of her late grandma Kendra's old volumes; other times she was unearthing sketches of grotesquely shaped creatures from loose floorboards. The dreams left her with a nagging feeling, as though there was something on her aunt's uppermost floor that she needed to find.

When Bryanna tried to access the chamber, however, she found herself unable to summon the trapdoor. She tried every spell she could think of, but Obelia's wards were so complex that even propping a ladder against the window ledges didn't work.

"It's not just Obelia's wards," Seara mused one morning, after Bryanna had enlisted her help. "There's an ancient seal barring us as well."

Bryanna could sense it too. The magic didn't feel human, sidhe, or fae in origin, but something more.

Something *olde*.

"Why don't you just ask Obelia to let you in?" Seara

suggested. "Tell her you want a closer look at her herbs or something."

But Bryanna shook her head. Even if Obelia let her in, she wouldn't leave her alone. Not when she suspected the true reason for her being at the Sheidlow Tower.

Things had become rather strained between them since Beltane. Her aunt had been avoiding her, using the excuse of the unusual influx of boarders to delay any further meetings, though Bryanna could sense she was still keeping tabs on her via her surveillance spell. Not to mention Tyffin kept appearing behind every door, window, and tree she passed, looking as disgruntled about trailing her as Bryanna felt.

"What are you two doing?" Liadan asked behind them.

Bryanna and Seara tensed. They'd been so focused on the conundrum of getting into the chamber above them, they hadn't heard Liadan emerge from her bedchamber.

Without missing a beat, Seara brandished a white parchment envelope from her back pocket. "Orlagh wrote to us. Finally." She skipped down the hall and handed it to Liadan. "It arrived earlier this morning. Just in time too. Obelia was ready to send out a search party if we didn't hear from her soon."

They set off for the library, their usual morning haunt before breakfast. Bain was already there, sitting in his customary spot in front of the piano, playing a soft, soothing composition. He looked up as they entered, and gave Liadan a small smile before returning his attention to the keys.

"I was thinking," Liadan said as they made for him, "we should visit Orlagh after Lammas. My family and I are going to Coral Cove. Why don't you join us, Seara, and we can stop by Gorias?"

"Coral Cove?" Iodhna repeated with disdain from where she was preening in front of a hanging, full-length, distressed mirror. "I was there last year visiting family until I got arrested for taking a boy who didn't have the strength to swim."

Bryanna's stomach clenched. There'd been a report almost a year back about an eight-year-old child discovered among the foamy waves of Coral Cove. From what she could remember, he'd been found with a contented smile on his lips and sparkling, blue-green scales on his palms—just like the ones on Iodhna's neck.

"Oh, Iodhna," said Liadan, her voice laced with dread. "Please tell me that little boy who drowned in Coral Cove last year wasn't because of you."

Iodhna shrugged. "His original fate would've been much worse."

Bile rose in Bryanna's throat, coupled with a fury that left her shaking from head to toe. How was Iodhna not rotting in some dank, infested cell awaiting the gallows?

"You found a struggling child out of his depth in the water and didn't think of swimming him back to shore?" Weylin asked from his secluded armchair, contempt barely contained in his tight features.

Around the chamber, others, too, stared at the morgen in varying shades of horror and revulsion.

Bryanna's gaze met Weylin's, and something unspoken passed between them—a shared disgust that dissolved whatever tension had lingered from the night before.

The morgen straightened, flicking her long hair over one slender shoulder. "I didn't even consider it."

Bryanna tore her gaze from Weylin's to glare at her. "You should be ashamed of yourself."

Iodhna speared her with a look filled with venom. "It is you land-dwellers who should be ashamed. Our waters are polluted because of your kind. Our numbers decline every year because of your greed."

Bryanna balled her hands beneath the material of her skirts. She wasn't ignorant of the seafarers who plundered and spoiled the underwater territories surrounding Otherworld. "That doesn't make it all right for you to attack innocent children."

Iodhna's eyes flashed. "He would've grown up contributing to the destruction of homes like mine."

Bryanna, said Bain gently as she opened her mouth to argue. *Be careful with Iodhna. She's been raised to hate our kind.*

Bryanna spun on her heels and headed for the staircase. She needed to get out of there before she did something she'd regret, like wipe the smug look off Iodhna's translucent face with her fist.

She didn't stop until she'd made it outside, but the crisp morning air did little to calm her. Not when her mind kept replaying the relish on Iodhna's face as she'd talked about the boy she'd killed.

The more she thought about it, the less she wanted to remain at the tower. What was the point, when her aunt didn't seem inclined to divulge what she knew, anyway? There were other ways to get the answers she sought. Perhaps it was time to take a leaf out of her aunt's book and set off on her own.

It wouldn't take her long to pack her weapons, volumes, and what clothes she could travel comfortably in. The other things could stay behind. She didn't have any use for crinolines or ribbons where she was going, and she'd easily be able to purchase supplies and lodging with the savings she'd brought.

The first few moon cycles wouldn't be easy. Once word reached her father that she'd left Sheidlow Ridge, every steed that could be spared would be sent after her. She'd need to seek refuge somewhere no one would think to find her. Abandoned buildings, hidden caves, old tree houses—those were the sorts of places she was thinking of. Hopefully, after those initial weeks passed, her father's sentinels would dissipate and she'd be able to go wherever she needed.

"Bryanna!"

Bryanna almost lost her footing as she turned in the direction of the ironstone path and saw Obelia astride a palomino stealth steed. The lithe creature had definitely not been in the stables the last time Bryanna had been there. In fact, she'd only ever seen one at a traveling circus before. With their hooves made of air, they left no tracks, nor did they make any sound. They were the ideal companions for those wishing to remain untraceable, like Bryanna did once she left Sheidlow Tower ...

"You have a letter," said Obelia, guiding the steed over to her and handing her an envelope with the Nicholls' family crest —the letter N surrounded by a great black steed on a shield.

Bryanna took it wordlessly and broke the seal, unfolding the parchment. Gawain's neat handwriting filled the page.

Dearest younger sister,

A very happy Beltane from all of us in Castlereagh. Everyone's good here. I can tell you're thinking about us from the overwhelming lack of letters we've been receiving from you.

I met a lovely young woman on Beltane Eve. She was very forthcoming. I missed the Beltane rite in the main square because of her, but to be honest, I didn't mind. Grear, her name was. She had red hair that reached her waist and a tongue that could do more than talk. You might know her. I think you shoved her through a class chamber window once.

Did you hear about the attack in Wilde Meadows? I hope you aren't getting any ideas. Mother and Father have been unbearable. Father, especially. He thinks you're going to get it into your head to go chasing after the Brotherhood of Sìorraidh.

I told him he's being ridiculous. You'll probably be shut up in Aunt Obelia's library for a few weeks yet.

I know Sheidlow Tower is always busy, but if you could take a few moments and write to our parents, my nerves would be forever indebted to you.

Your brother,

Gawain

P.S. Stay away from Weylin Conveil. He's not to be trusted.

Bryanna sighed and tucked Gawain's letter into her skirt pocket. Sometimes her brother was too overprotective. Besides, it wasn't as though Weylin had done anything untoward. He was barely around half the time, too busy with whatever he got up to in the forest.

"Has something happened?" Obelia asked, peering at her closely.

Bryanna met her aunt's gaze unflinchingly. "Oh, only that I've just found out you're harboring a child murderer."

Obelia dropped her satchel, her eyes wide with shock. "How did you—" She broke off, glancing toward the clothesline, where Seara's dark head had just ducked behind a load of washing. "Follow me. This isn't a conversation to have out in the open."

Bryanna was so far past the point of caring that she could've had the conversation center stage in the Sheidlow Square. But she followed her aunt, seizing the satchel Obelia had dropped and stuffing the newspaper peeking out under its flap into the back of her skirt when her aunt wasn't looking. If Obelia wouldn't share any information on the Brotherhood of Sìorraidh, she'd get it herself.

"How did you find out?" asked Obelia once they'd reached the stables and she'd dismounted.

"Iodhna was bragging about it in the library," Bryanna

ground out. "You'd think it was the proudest moment of her life. Why is she even here? You're risking our lives by keeping her around."

Obelia arched a brow. "You mustn't think too highly of me if you believe I don't have precautions in place for my most volatile boarders. Besides, you're risking just as much by being on the warpath against the Brotherhood."

Bryanna's shoulders stiffened. "I'd never risk anyone's life."

Obelia unbuckled the steed's saddle and tugged him toward a spare stall. "Not intentionally, no. But the moment the Brotherhood learns you're hunting them, anyone you're connected to is in danger. Your friends. Your *family*."

Some of Bryanna's anger subsided. She'd never considered how her actions would affect her family. At least not beyond them trying to haul her back to Castlereagh by any means necessary. "Is that what they did to you? Go after someone you cared about?"

Obelia's expression turned stony. "They tried. Believe me, I understand your thirst for vengeance. What happened to Aveline—"

"Shouldn't remain unpunished!"

A shadow crossed Obelia's features. "I know. But—"

"Don't tell me I need to let it go," Bryanna bit out, clenching her hands into fists. "You haven't. I saw your booklet. You're still tracking them."

Obelia pursed her lips. "I should've guessed you'd ferret around in those cedar chests," she muttered, tugging the reins from around the stealth steed's neck. "But it's not what you think, Bryanna. I track them because I sleep easier knowing they're nowhere near me or my boarders."

"You're lying," Bryanna said flatly, her voice hard.

Obelia slid the stall gate closed with enough force to make the metal hinges groan. "You don't know what you're up against, Bryanna. Going after the Brotherhood of Sìorraidh isn't as simple as you think. You have to be willing to live as a nomad, follow every lead without a moment's hesitation—"

"I could do that," Bryanna interjected.

Her aunt's brows rose. "Could you? Live for weeks on end without the comforts of traveling inns and well-stocked grocers? I've been watching you, Bryanna. You can't even milk a dun cow or gut a hare."

Bryanna crossed her arms over her chest. "I could if I had to."

"Say you could master those basics, that's only half the danger," Obelia continued. "Otherworld isn't as safe or civilized as Upper Castlereagh."

Bryanna snorted, remembering the last ball she'd attended where her fellow peers had spread such vicious rumors that it had ended a fellow attendee's betrothal before the canapes had stopped being served. "People aren't as civil in Upper Castlereagh as you might think, Aunt Obelia."

Obelia's face softened, as though she too had experienced their society's malice. "I know why you're here, Bryanna. And I'd try to dissuade you, but something tells me I wouldn't succeed."

"You wouldn't," Bryanna said at once.

"Then you need to show me that you're ready to learn what I know."

Bryanna squared her shoulders. "How?"

"Work for me. As it happens, I'm short-staffed." Obelia rubbed the back of her neck. "Actually, I'm my only staff. If you can show me you truly are willing to do what's necessary, I'll tell you everything I discovered after leaving Castlereagh."

"Fine." There was no way she could turn down Obelia's offer, even *if* it meant being stuck in the tower with the callous morgen. "What would you need me to do?"

"Various things." Obelia wiped her hands on her skirts. "You can start by coming with me."

Bryanna followed her aunt back toward the tower. "Where are we going?"

"To see your first patient."

Obelia led Bryanna to the only chamber she didn't occupy on the second floor, where the boarder named Elgar lived. Bryanna wouldn't have known he was there had she not seen her aunt visit him on her first night. He'd never come down for meals or joined the others in the library once evening fell.

As soon as Obelia opened the door, the scents of burning eucalyptus oil and candlewick accosted Bryanna's nostrils. She stepped into the chamber, blinking as her eyes adjusted to the dimness. Bloodstones—deep green stones that could heal superficial wounds and slow poisons and illnesses—hung from the coffered ceiling like large-scale crib mobiles, reminding her of the hospices she sometimes visited with Lady Auberagh.

Whoever Elgar was, he had to be sick.

Very sick.

Obelia directed Bryanna closer to the elegantly chiseled bed where a pale, blue-tinged boy no older than fifteen lay, propped up on four pillows. Bryanna almost gasped as she took in his mop of fine white-blond hair and dark lips that stood in stark contrast to his pale skin. She knew exactly what he was, even though she'd never seen his kind with her own eyes before—a *Tuatha Dé Danann*. His kind were so powerful, they'd been the ones who'd cleaved their world from the parallel one that now existed without magic.

"Elgar, I want you to meet my niece, Bryanna," said Obelia, walking around to the side of the bed.

Elgar inclined his head in Bryanna's direction. "How do you do, Ms. Nicholls?" he said, his voice raspy.

Obelia turned to Bryanna. "What I'm about to tell you must remain in this chamber."

Bryanna nodded. She'd been working with patients for years. She knew about patient-healer confidentiality.

Obelia took a slow breath before meeting Bryanna's gaze solemnly. "Elgar has been cursed with mortality."

Bryanna stared at her aunt, her jaw slackening. She wasn't sure what she'd been expecting, but it certainly wasn't that. "*Mortality?*"

Elgar smiled faintly at the incredulous look on her face. "I am afraid so. A couple of years ago, I became among the unlucky few of my kind whose lives have been linked to one clinging to an immortal existence."

The blood drained from Bryanna's face. "Do you mean … the Brotherhood of Sìorraidh?"

"Yes."

Bryanna's mouth went dry. Over the years, she'd come up with hundreds of different theories for how the Brotherhood had endured for so many centuries, but she never would've guessed what Elgar had just disclosed. "Are you saying the Brotherhood has been stealing their immortality from the Tuatha Dé Danann?"

"Yes," said Obelia. "We believe—"

Elgar gasped suddenly, as though he'd been plunged into a barrel of ice water.

Then he stopped breathing.

For one horrifying second, Bryanna thought he'd died. She lunged forward, pressing her hands to his ribs, ready to start compressions. But before she could, he moved again, his face a mask of silent agony.

She rounded on her aunt. "What's happening to him?"

"It's the Brotherhood of Sìorraidh," Obelia said grimly, hovering over Elgar as well. "They're striking again."

Bryanna's whole body went numb. "Are you saying his seizure is being brought on because the Brotherhood of Sìorraidh is attacking?"

"That's right."

Bryanna's stomach twisted, watching Elgar writhe with a helplessness that left her trembling with rage. "Aunt Obelia, we have to fetch the Law Keepers—"

"No," said Obelia, her tone sharp. "No one can know about Elgar."

Bryanna whirled to face her. Had her aunt lost her senses? "Aunt Obelia, listen to me. If the Law Keepers knew the Brotherhood of Sìorraidh was connected to the Tuatha Dé Danann, they could bring an end to their reign."

"At what cost?" Obelia countered. "If anyone discovered Elgar's connection to the Brotherhood, they'd kill him to destroy whoever is tethered to him. One innocent life sacrificed in exchange for the death of one in their ranks. We can't let that happen."

Bryanna dug her nails into her palms. Although she could understand her aunt's unwillingness to hand Elgar over to the authorities if it meant risking his life, she couldn't bear the idea of letting the Brotherhood get away with yet another murder. "But ... we can't do nothing."

"Believe me, Bryanna, I'm not doing nothing." Obelia moved forward, wiping the sweat from Elgar's glistening forehead. Whatever had caused the seizure had run its course, leaving him spent and unconscious.

Bryanna swallowed the tightness in her throat. "And what *are* you doing?"

"Keeping him strong until I can figure out how to sever the connection he has to the Brotherhood." Obelia retrieved a small, round phial from her pocket. "I need you to administer one tablespoon of this to him every eight hours."

Bryanna took the phial from her aunt wordlessly, her gaze lingering on Elgar's pale face.

"Now come along," Obelia said, tucking the blankets over Elgar's frail frame before moving away. "I have a few more errands I need you to manage for me."

Bryanna's new chores kept her busy for the rest of the evening. On top of her rounds with Elgar, Obelia put her in charge of laundry, pickling and preserving early summer vegetables, gathering eggs from the cockatrice hybrids who still hadn't fully forgiven her, mucking out the stables, and preparing bedchambers for new boarders. Pickling and preserving was the worst. The cold-pressed oil left her hands stained a sickly dark green and her fingers reeking of garlic no matter how many times she washed them.

By the time Bryanna finished, she was too tired to do more than sit on the window seat in the library, pretending to read a volume Liadan had recommended so she didn't have to speak to anyone. Thoughts she'd been pushing away all afternoon surged back as she watched the branches sway and nocturnal creatures stir. She couldn't stop wondering who the Brotherhood of Sìorraidh had attacked, and if it had been someone's parent or sibling. Or worse, a child like Aveline, whose possession couldn't have advanced their reign in any way.

Slowly, the boarders retired one by one until only Weylin remained. Bryanna glanced sidelong at him over the rim of her volume, and her heart skipped a beat as she found his gaze locked on her.

"Isn't it past your bedtime, Ms. Nicholls?" he asked, his low voice brushing over her like a caress.

"I could ask you the same thing," she replied.

"I couldn't sleep," he said, propping his feet on the ottoman.

"I know what that's like," Bryanna said quietly.

Weylin's face clouded over. "Is that so?"

Bryanna lifted her chin, irritation quickly overriding any kinship they might've established earlier that morning after Iodhna's confession. "I'm not the conceited socialite you think I am."

He raised a brow. "You don't know what sort of person I think you are, Ms. Nicholls."

"Why don't you tell me then?"

Weylin deliberated a moment, his lips pressing into a thin line before finally replying, "Someone who's out of their depth."

Bryanna straightened, her eyes narrowing. "What's that supposed to mean?"

"Why are you really here?" he countered.

Bryanna's stomach clenched. From the way he was looking at her, she'd almost believe he knew the real reason why she was there. "To spend time with my aunt."

He leaned back in his armchair and drummed his fingers against its edges. "Somehow, I don't believe that."

"Why else would I be here?" she shot back.

Silence stretched between them, charged with an anticipation she couldn't explain, before Weylin finally said, "You tell me, Ms. Nicholls."

Bryanna turned back to the window and didn't respond.

A new being had ventured onto the Sheidlow Tower's grounds while she'd been distracted by Weylin. Bryanna pressed her face against the cool glass, struggling to comprehend what she was seeing as she stared at the white, steed-like creature. An ethereal glow pulsed off him, as though he were a full moon condensed into equine form.

"I don't believe it," she murmured, unable to look away from the silver-coned horn protruding from his forehead.

Weylin sprang to her side, standing so close that Bryanna could feel the warmth radiating from him. As if sensing them, the unicorn lifted his head. He glanced at Weylin fleetingly before turning to Bryanna. As their eyes met, the strangest feeling came over her, as if a ghost had stepped through her and left behind a cold, foreign impression on her psyche.

The unicorn shook out his mane as though the same odd sensation had come over him. He took a final swig of water, the sharp point of his horn rippling the pond's surface, and galloped back into the forest.

"Well," said Weylin, staring at the spot where the unicorn had disappeared. "There's a sight you only see once in a lifetime."

Bryanna could only nod. Seeing a unicorn was so rare that it was considered a powerful omen.

An omen of hope.

For the first time since she'd arrived at the Sheidlow Tower, Bryanna felt as though she was in the right place.

SEVEN

"She's mine! You can't take her from me!"

Weylin's shout rang in Bryanna's mind as she jerked awake, her heart slamming against her chest.

Taking a deep breath, she relinquished the magic humming over her skin, willing the vestiges of Weylin's nightmare to loosen their grip on her. She could still see the narrow, musty wooden cell he'd been locked in, still feel the anger and desperation that had coursed through him—and through her, by default.

It wasn't too much of a stretch to guess who Weylin had been referring to when he'd yelled, "She's mine!" Who else could it have been but the ex who'd broken his heart? The thought of Weylin still longing for her left a sour taste in her mouth. Which was ridiculous. She didn't even like the brooding boarder.

Bryanna shoved away her covers and set her feet onto the cool floorboards. There was no way she'd be getting back to sleep. She padded over to the window and drew the curtains wide, letting the early dawn glow wash over her skin. It was lucky that she and some of the other boarders were going berry picking that morning. She really needed the distraction —from Weylin, from the lack of headway she was making on the volumes she'd taken from Obelia's cedar chests, and from Elgar's slow recovery from the Brotherhood of Sìorraidh attack. Obelia had been keeping her busy, brewing potions and the like, but that had only kept her hands occupied, not her mind.

A knock sounded at the door, tearing her from her spiraling thoughts. "Bryanna?" Liadan's voice came from the hallway. "Are you awake?"

"Yes," she replied, moving away from the window.

"I thought you might be. How would you feel about leaving earlier?"

Bryanna reached for her breeches and boots at once. Putting some distance between herself and the tower—and a certain elusive, enigmatic boarder—was exactly what she needed.

"I'll be right out."

It took Bryanna and the boarders a while to find bushes that hadn't been picked clean by the villagers brave enough to venture into the forest, though Bryanna didn't mind. The task of finding berries, as well as the fresh air and time away from the tower's confines, helped quiet her mind from what she'd seen in Weylin's nightmare, though the unease still lingered.

At around midday, a distant chant carried on the breeze, close to where she and Liadan were picking berries. Bryanna couldn't pinpoint the language, though it sounded like an old form of Gaelic.

"It must be Founder's Day," Liadan mused, turning toward the slivers of the ancient Sheidlow Ruins they could just see between the trees. "The villagers did this last year too."

Bryanna craned her neck to get a better view of the field beyond the trees. "Did what, exactly?"

"Performed a ritual to appease the angry spirits of Sheidlow Ridge's founding family," came a husky, masculine reply before Liadan could respond.

Bryanna and Liadan jumped back with muffled cries of surprise. They'd been so focused on the crowd, they hadn't noticed Weylin standing several trees away from them. Bryanna's pulse picked up at the sight of him, her gaze lingering on the dark shadows that lined his eyes, reminding her of the nightmare he'd suffered from.

"I see," she said, recovering and glancing over at the villagers standing around the outskirts of the ruins, tying garlands of tiny, white-petaled alyssums along the fence posts as they chanted. "I'd gotten the impression the villagers weren't fond of magic or magic-weavers. Yet, they're performing their own ritual?"

Not that it was an actual ritual. There wasn't a hint of magic in the air.

"It's an annual tradition," Liadan told her.

"Theirs is a dark tale," Weylin said, leaning casually against the trunk of a tree. "They say that the Sheidlow Tower has been haunted since the day Lord Sheidlow, his young wife, and their newborn son were murdered behind its walls, several centuries back."

Bryanna almost dropped her sack of berries. "Murdered?"

He nodded. "They say it was all Lord Sheidlow's half-brother's doing. The tower fell into his possession after they died. According to the legends, the two brothers loathed each other. When the tower went to him, he turned it into a ghastly gaol with hangings and beheadings there every twelfth hour."

The hairs on Bryanna's arms rose. "You're jesting."

"Afraid not. It was only open for a moon cycle or so, mind

you. One morning, the villagers woke to find the guards and prisoners stampeding out of Sheidlow Forest, shouting about ghosts and impenetrable misty walls."

Bryanna frowned. She'd seen a white, shimmering wall rise around the Sheidlow Tower years ago, when the villagers attacked Lochiel. She'd always thought it had been Obelia's doing, to save her boarder from the villagers' arrows. It had never occurred to her that it might've been something much more supernatural …

"It's rumored Lord Sheidlow's half-brother was never seen again after the tower was vacated," Liadan added. "Some say he went into hiding, others that Lord Sheidlow returned to the living long enough to take his brother to the Underworld, body and all. They say the Sheidlow Tower's cursed. Time was, no one could inhabit it after the Sheidlows. Anyone who tried would wake to find their furnishings and trinkets tossed out the windows. At least until your aunt came to stay almost two decades ago."

Footfalls sounded behind them. Bryanna turned, half expecting a villager to have stumbled upon them, but it was Seara, tugging her burlap sack behind her. "There you are. We weren't sure where you'd gone. Nisienne wants to leave. It's almost luncheon."

They rejoined the others and headed back to the tower companionably. Bryanna wasn't sure if it was the weight of their burlap sacks, but their trek back seemed to take much longer than the way to the village's edge. Though that might've been because of how uncharacteristically quiet Weylin had become as he walked beside her, one of her burlap sacks hanging over his shoulder. Bryanna couldn't help but sneak glances at him.

As if he could sense her attention on him, Weylin raised a brow. "Something bothering you, Ms. Nicholls?"

"Just wondering what you're doing here," she replied honestly.

The smile that almost tugged at his lips sent Bryanna's pulse rising. "Why, I'm here to make sure you don't get yourself into any trouble, of course."

Bryanna rolled her eyes. "You saw what I can do on Beltane. Trust me, I can handle a little trouble."

"That's what you think," he muttered under his breath.

When they finally arrived at the Sheidlow Tower, they found a brace of steeds harnessed to a hefty green traveling wagon.

"Who do you suppose is here?" she asked. Visitors' Day wasn't until the following week.

Weylin took one look at the wagon and gave a long-winded sigh. "My family."

Bryanna's heart skipped a beat. What was Weylin's family doing there? Had his banishment been lifted?

"Brace yourself, Ms. Nicholls," he said, bitterness laced in his voice. "You might just meet Otherworld's last natural faoladh chieftain today."

It took Bryanna a moment to register his words. "Wait ... your father's a *chieftain*?"

She hadn't even known he was a faoladh, much less the son of such a powerful member of his tribe. She supposed he was tall for a human, but most faoladhs had wider mouths to fit their extra sets of canines when they morphed between their human and semi-lupine forms.

From what she knew of faoladhs, the chieftain's offspring were critical to their tribe. The banishment of one was rare. How, then, had Weylin gotten himself banished?

"I'll see you later, Ms. Nicholls," Weylin said, his fingers brushing Bryanna's as he handed her back her satchel, sending her skin tingling.

Bryanna glanced at the traveling wagon just as the curtain shifted. A cool pair of eyes settled on her, sending the hairs on the back of her neck standing on end. Fighting the impulse to shiver, she turned and followed the others inside.

In the entrance hall, they found Iodhna in front of the large, oval-shaped mirror, smearing the excrement of a water snail across her thin, navy lips. She was wearing her most provocative dress yet. Long and ink-black, with slits that ran so high up her thighs, it would've frayed the village women's nerves.

Bryanna's grip on her burlap sack tightened. Iodhna had been trying to get Weylin's attention ever since he'd reproached her for the Coral Cove incident. She hadn't succeeded in gaining his favor yet, though that didn't mean she wouldn't.

Bryanna tore her gaze away from Iodhna. Why did she care so much if Weylin found himself drawn to the insipid, heartless morgen?

In the kitchen, they found Bain deboning chickens. Solo, as usual. At their entrance, he wiped his hands on a damp tea towel and grabbed a large lattice hamper from the pantry for them to unload their pickings.

"Need any help?" Bryanna asked as Bain took the burlap sack from her.

Sure, he said. *Thanks.*

She and Liadan went about setting the table, adding extra places for Weylin and his family, though they needn't have bothered. The Conveils didn't join them for luncheon. They remained in the visitors' parlor, with Weylin's and his father's voices carrying as they argued in Faoladhian.

By six o'clock that evening, the Conveils had still not left the visitors' parlor. In that time, Bryanna had washed, dried, and folded four piles of linen, as well as run what felt like a hundred other errands for her aunt.

And she still wasn't done.

She rolled her shoulders, easing the ache between them, then headed to her aunt's office to see what else needed to be done.

Obelia was already there, sitting in front of a mahogany desk, strewn with volumes, letters, quills, and inkpots. She looked up as Bryanna entered, rubbing her temples as though to chase away a persistent migraine.

"What is it, Aunt Obelia?" Bryanna asked at once, noticing the worry lines around her eyes. Had something happened to Elgar? He'd been fine the last time she'd administered his tonic.

Obelia waved her concern away. "Nothing. I just performed a spell on Bain to help his telepathic range, but ... I don't know, something felt off. Anyway, I'm glad you're here. There's something I'd like you to do."

Bryanna suppressed a groan. She barely got any time to herself as it was.

Obelia laughed. "Don't worry, you'll like this task."

Bryanna pulled out one of the ornate, floral-patterned chairs in front of her aunt's desk, but Obelia stopped her before she could sit.

"Oh, no, don't use that. They're for representatives of the Department of National Health. Not comfortable at all."

She led her instead to two newer, cushioned wing chairs near the window, facing each other over a doily-covered tea table.

"I thought we'd finally start on blocking those dream-weaver skills of yours," she said, lowering herself into the seat in front of her. "I've got time to guide you through it now. What do you say?"

Bryanna hesitated. She knew all about guiding. It was a common magical tool used among magic-weavers. Faster and more efficient than other modes of learning, it allowed the mentor full access to the novice's consciousness. From there, the mentor could use the novice's body to cast a new spell, allowing the novice to familiarize themselves with the feeling of it, making it easier for them to perform it independently.

Lady Auberagh had tried guiding her once, and it had been disastrous. Bryanna had felt herself losing control of her physical form and panicked. It had brought to mind how Aveline must've felt when the Brotherhood of Sìorraidh had ensnared her body. She'd pushed Lady Auberagh out of her mind with such force that the older woman had collapsed. Since then, they'd trained using volumes and corporeal demonstrations only.

"What's wrong?" Obelia asked, sensing Bryanna's reluctance.

Bryanna shrugged. "I just prefer learning magic through volumes. If you have one that can help, I'll make sure to practice by our next session."

"Don't be silly, it'll just take a minute."

"No."

The word came out harder than Bryanna intended. She immediately regretted her tone. Obelia didn't know why she was so averse to being guided. Though the long, searching look her aunt bestowed on her made her think otherwise.

"Bryanna," her aunt said carefully, "did you know that on the day Aveline went missing, your father sent me an express letter?"

Bryanna shifted uncomfortably. "No."

"He said you were meant to meet Aveline in the courtyard once school was out, but she never showed up. You came home and locked yourself in your bedchamber. As soon as I read that, I suspected something amiss. Your father wrote about you and your brothers so often, I knew you wouldn't have returned to your house without searching every corner of

Castlereagh for Aveline first, possibly bullying Gawain into helping you."

Sweat trickled down Bryanna's spine despite the relatively cool chamber.

"You lied that day, didn't you? You did see Aveline?"

Bryanna couldn't answer. There was a knot at the back of her throat that only got worse the longer Obelia waited for her reply. She didn't want to admit what she'd seen that day: Aveline standing alone in the dark alleyway, her expression unrecognizable as she stared blankly back at her.

Obelia leaned forward and took her hands. "It's all right, Bryanna. It wasn't Aveline anymore, was it?"

Bryanna turned her blurry gaze to the window, unable to meet her aunt's eyes as she shook her head.

"Did it speak to you?"

She nodded.

"What did it say?"

Bryanna's throat unclogged sufficiently for her to reply, "It asked me who I was."

"And ... did you tell it?"

"No." She'd heard enough about the Brotherhood of Sìorraidh, even at that age, to understand what had happened to Aveline. "I gave it a fake name ... told it I was a classmate ... and then I ran."

She'd never been able to reconcile with herself since that day. Every time she thought back to that awful afternoon, she was reminded that Aveline's last memory of her was of her running away in the pivotal moments when she'd been scared, defenseless, and dying.

It was why Bryanna could never set aside her vengeance or bring herself to meet Aveline's gaze in her dreams. She was afraid to see the betrayal there, or worse, those same cold, dank eyes staring back at her.

Obelia's arms wrapped around Bryanna, pulling her close. "You couldn't have done anything for her," she said softly as the tears Bryanna had never allowed anyone to see spilled down her cheeks.

"I could've stayed with her," Bryanna choked out.

"No. She wouldn't have wanted that."

A scraping sound at Obelia's door made them break apart. "That's Tyffin." Her aunt wiped at her misted eyes. "The Conveils are leaving. I'll be right back."

Bryanna stared out the window as her aunt left the chamber, watching without really seeing as a burly, bearded man emerged from the tower, closely followed by a curly, dark-haired little girl. An older woman about Obelia's age followed, an arm linked around Weylin's. They exchanged hushed words, Weylin's clipped, the woman's soft, placating.

Bryanna stood. Her aunt would be back within minutes, and she didn't want to be there when she did. She was done talking about what had happened on that accursed day. It was bad enough that she relived those last few hours of Aveline's life over and over in her mind. She didn't need to talk about it with her aunt.

Besides, she'd already said more than she should have.

She headed downstairs, wiping away any residual tear marks on her cheeks with the edge of her sleeve. Obelia wouldn't dare interrogate her further if she were surrounded by her boarders.

She'd just reached the kitchen when the front doors slammed with such force that the windows rattled. A few seconds later, Weylin marched into the kitchen, Obelia practically running to keep up with him.

"Weylin—"

"Obelia," he warned, his eyes turning a stormy, flashing

blue, revealing the pain and fury Bryanna had glimpsed in his nightmare. "Please. Don't."

"You just need to give it time—"

"If that were true, why does the mere mention of my cousin's name still make you flinch?"

Obelia's face turned to steel. For the first time, Bryanna saw the Obelia Nicholls who'd left Castlereagh behind with determination in her eyes and bloodlust in her heart. "Go get some fresh air," she said. "Come back when you've calmed down."

Before Weylin could argue, Bain stepped between them and towed him out the back door.

A deafening silence descended upon their departure.

Bryanna couldn't take her gaze off her aunt as she poured herself some water, gripping the goblet so stiffly that her knuckles turned white. For years, she'd been incapable of comprehending how her aunt could leave Castlereagh and forge a new life for herself, letting go of her vengeance. But thanks to Weylin, she understood. Obelia hadn't gotten over Fillian's loss. She'd left Castlereagh because she hadn't been able to bear the agonizing reminders of him and the life they'd started but never finished together. For Bryanna, having those reminders was like fuel that fed her resolve.

But for others, like her aunt, those reminders only brought pain.

EIGHT

Can you hear me?

"Yes."

What about now?

"Yes."

Now?

"Yes."

It was worse than being stuck in a carriage with her two little nephews.

Bryanna, Bain, and Obelia were barricaded in her aunt's office. They had been from the moment the rising sun had turned the navy, speckled night sky into a canvas of light fuchsia, vivid lilacs, and arctic blues. Obelia hadn't been able to fit Bain into her tight schedule any other time that day, and it had become imperative that Bain's new telepathic sessions begin immediately after most of the boarders had retired to bed the evening before with migraines.

It turned out the spell Obelia had cast on Bain the previous afternoon to amplify his telepathic projection had backfired. Rather than making it possible for him to converse with two hosts simultaneously, everyone in his vicinity could hear him.

No one had been able to hold a conversation or keep their train of thought with Bain's voice constantly reverberating in their minds.

"Darned unicorn magic," Obelia muttered as she flipped through yet another volume of spells, trying to find something that would work on Bain.

Bryanna stared at her, stunned. "What do unicorns have to do with anything?"

It's how I lost my voice, Bain explained. *I spooked one when I was nine and he somehow stripped me of my ability to speak out loud.*

"Oh." Bryanna hadn't known such a thing could happen. It surprised her almost as much as learning that Bain was a druid, as she'd discovered when they'd started their session. She could usually tell when another magic-weaver was in proximity to her, yet she barely felt any magic coming from him.

This is ridiculous. Bain fell back into his wing chair. *What am I going to do? I won't be able to walk into Sheidlow Square without the villagers falling over each other in fright.*

Bryanna bit her lip. Even in Castlereagh, where some of the oddest beings in existence lived, Bain's telepathic range would've turned heads.

"Don't worry, Bain," said Obelia bracingly. "You'll have control over this soon."

Bain sighed heavily. *I've spent the last nine years trying to get people to hear me. Now that they can, I just want to go back to the way it was.*

Obelia cast a reproachful look his way. "Don't be daft, Bain. This is better than I'd hoped for you."

The office door burst open and Iodhna marched into the chamber, fury radiating off her.

"Obelia, what is this I'm hearing of a new Brotherhood of

Sìorraidh attack?" she demanded, tossing a newspaper onto the floor at their feet.

"What are you talking about?" Bryanna asked at once. They'd been waiting for news of the latest Brotherhood attack since Elgar's episode.

The morgen sent her a cool glower. "Apparently, there was an attack in Wilde Meadows on Beltane."

Bryanna's whole body went lax. For a moment, she'd thought they'd finally learn who'd been compromised.

Obelia stifled a sigh before turning to Bain. "Perhaps we should leave it here for now. We can pick up again in a day or two."

Bain nodded and stood. Bryanna followed suit, but she was barely out of her seat when her aunt's voice stopped her.

"Hold on, Bryanna. I want a word."

Bryanna halted in her tracks. She had a feeling her aunt wanted to revisit their conversation about Aveline from the night before. A conversation Bryanna had no desire to resume. She still didn't know why she'd told her aunt about what she'd done that horrible day so many years ago.

Iodhna pivoted so that she had her back to Bryanna, commanding her aunt's full attention. "I insist that you contact my father and have him take me home at once."

Obelia's face tightened with impatience. "You know I can't do that. You're staying under my jurisdiction until the end of your sentence, as per the land- and water-dwellers statutory agreement. Nothing short of an all-encompassing evacuation of the Sheidlow Ridge area will change that."

Shock rippled through Bryanna. She'd assumed the morgen had come to the Mage's Sanctuary by choice, not under duress.

"But I'm in great peril while I remain in Sheidlow Ridge," Iodhna snapped, tossing her long, navy hair behind her shoulder.

"The last attack was six hours away, Iodhna," Obelia returned calmly. "Much closer to your underwater home than here."

There was silence. Bryanna suspected Obelia was standing on the opposite end of a frigid, resentful glower.

"You can't keep me here," Iodhna hissed, malice dripping from her every word. "I'll find a way to get out of here. Not a single being can stop me. Not even you."

A chill ran down Bryanna's spine as the morgen spun on her barnacle-crusted heels and stalked off down the hall. There was no doubt in her mind that Iodhna would sacrifice whoever she had to in order to leave the tower. And yet, there her aunt was, keeping her around, knowing that she could turn against any of them at any point.

"That Iodhna tries my patience," Obelia muttered, lowering herself back in her chair. "Every day there's a new excuse to leave the Sheidlow Tower. My favorite was when she told me the pond water was too sweet for her. You should've seen her face when I told her I'd specifically drained the pond and refilled it with the saltwater from her permanent residence."

If she thought Bryanna would find humor in that, she was deeply mistaken. "Why is Iodhna serving her sentence here? Isn't there anywhere else she can be sent? You're supposed to be running a sanctuary for the supernaturally challenged, not housing murderous delinquents."

"It's complicated," Obelia said in that tone Bryanna was getting all too familiar with. The one that meant she wouldn't be getting answers. She picked up a large pile of unopened letters on her desk and dropped them beside Bryanna. "Here. I need you to draft a few responses."

Bryanna stared at the letters, her trepidation that they'd pick up from the previous night's conversation dissipating in indignation. "Wha—More chores?"

"It is what you signed up for," Obelia pointed out.

"In exchange for you giving me insight into the Brotherhood of Sìorraidh," Bryanna returned. "That hasn't happened yet."

"A sparrow must learn to fly before it can leave the nest."

Bryanna clenched her teeth. She was beginning to regret not going through with her original plan to leave the Sheidlow Tower and figure things out on her own.

She snatched one of the letters and read it.

Dear Mistress Nicholls,

Thank you for responding to our last letter. Since then, our young nephew, Miles, has been in quite some pain. He tried to take a salamander from our fireplace. Do you have any advice on what we can do to heal him?

Sincerely yours,

Mrs. Baker-Smith

Bryanna frowned. Why had someone written to her aunt about treatment advice they should've gone to their local apothecary for? The remedy was quite simple—massage salamander blood onto the wound. Most families didn't need to consult a healer or apothecary to know that.

She leafed through a few other letters, finding more of the same.

"You answer all of these?" she asked incredulously, staring at her aunt. Clearly, the only reason people were writing to her was for the pleasure and privilege of receiving a response.

Obelia nodded. "I receive payment for each reply. Funds aren't always easy to come by. Between you and me, Esta MacLeary, the Department of National Health auditor who was here last week, is behind it."

"What makes you think that?" Bryanna asked, pushing the letters aside.

Obelia's face tightened. "We were friends once. Our acquaintance came to a bitter end some time ago and I'm afraid she still hasn't forgiven me for what transpired between us."

"Why, what happened?"

"Something that's long since passed," Obelia said evasively.

Bryanna gritted her teeth. She should've known better than to expect a straight answer. She riffled through several more letters until she came upon a most peculiar one, written in an unfamiliar script. Or rather, she thought it was unfamiliar until she recognized some of the characters. They were the same ones as those in her late grandma Kendra's volumes.

"Is this Atlantean?" she asked, showing her aunt the letter.

Obelia took it with a frown. "No. It's witchscript, a form of code that was once used by magic-weavers—"

"—to record potent spells," Bryanna finished for her. She'd heard of witchscript. She'd just never come across it before. "What's it say?"

Obelia skimmed the page. "It's an invitation to join a coven in Kaysville."

Instead of returning the letter to the pile, though, Obelia pocketed it.

Bryanna's eyes narrowed, certain her aunt was lying. But she pushed her suspicions aside. There was something she wanted much more than answers about why her aunt was receiving letters written in ancient magical code. "Can you teach me how to read witchscript?"

She'd been trying to decipher her grandmother's old volumes for days, using an Atlantean dictionary she'd found in her aunt's library. At least now she knew why she'd failed to decipher a single word. The volumes weren't written in Atlantean at all.

Obelia glanced at her suspiciously. "Why would you want to learn?"

Bryanna shrugged. "Because it's a skill worth knowing."

It was also the only way she'd be able to read her late grandmother's volumes.

Obelia deliberated a moment, her eyes meeting Tyffin's. Bryanna suspected they were having one of their private, telepathic conversations.

Finally, Obelia flicked her wrist at a cabinet to Bryanna's left. It sprang open, revealing a series of drawers. With a click, as though a key were being twisted in a lock, the bottom drawer slid open, showcasing a medium-sized scroll with iron handles. It floated to Bryanna and landed on her lap, where it unfurled to reveal a chart of different witchscript symbols and their corresponding letters.

"You can start by memorizing this scroll. In your spare time, mind you. There's a lot to do today."

Bryanna didn't get time to start on her aunt's mail until the end of the week. She'd tried to settle in the library first, but the noise-canceling alcoves were all occupied. The boarders had barricaded themselves in there to keep Bain's telepathic voice from penetrating their minds. Instead, she opted for the kitchen, spreading the letters over the dining table and skimming them briefly.

The majority were ailment remedy requests or appointment inquiries, which were easy to reply to, if time-consuming. She started with the latter, putting the miscellaneous ones to the side so she could confer with Obelia before writing responses.

"There is a library, you know?" Iodhna drawled, sauntering into the kitchen for her cooking shift later that afternoon.

"I do," Bryanna said without looking up from the healing balm recipe she was drafting. She was afraid that if she did, she'd launch something at her. Like the sharp quill she was using.

"Bryanna," Cayde said warmly, a genuine smile warming his brown-speckled eyes as he stepped into the kitchen, carrying a bucket of writhing trout. "I rarely see you anymore."

"You have my aunt to thank for that," Bryanna told him. "She's been filling my every waking hour with chores."

"Hmm, maybe I'll have a word with her," he said pensively.

"That would be nice."

"Yes ... I need someone to clean my bedchamber."

Bryanna laughed. "Hilarious."

Cayde winked and followed Iodhna over to the workbench.

Bryanna returned to the letters, doing her best to ignore Iodhna as she moved around the kitchen, banging cupboard doors shut and clanging pots and pans together. If she didn't know better, she might've thought Iodhna was doing it on purpose, to force her to move along to another chamber. Bryanna stayed put, though. She would not be driven out by the ruthless morgen.

Cayde joined her with two goblets a few minutes later. "I thought you might like some refreshment." He slid one of the goblets toward her. "This one's yours, unless you want to try some of mine? It has the essence of the dun cow I slaughtered earlier. With Obelia's permission, of course."

Bryanna scrunched up her nose. "I'll stick to the essence-free one, thanks."

He sighed dramatically. "I thought you might."

Bryanna took the goblet and swallowed a mouthful, shuddering as the bitter, tangy taste hit her tongue. "What is this, poison?" she joked.

"Some sort of summer concoction the boarders have been

working on for the upcoming solstice," he said, taking a seat beside her. "So, do you have someone waiting for you back in Castler—"

Crash!

They both whipped around. The morgen stood rooted to the spot in the middle of the kitchen, a frying pan at her feet oozing oil onto the flagstone floor. Her wide eyes were covered in a cloudy film as she cowered at something no one else could see.

Bryanna lowered her goblet, the hairs along her arms rising as she turned to Cayde. "What's wrong with her?"

He shot to his feet, his face tight as he looked at Iodhna. "I think she's having another one of her premonitions."

Bryanna tensed. She'd forgotten morgens had an aptitude for visions. "Should we get my aunt—"

Before she could finish her sentence, Obelia came barreling down the staircase and grasped the morgen by the shoulders. "Iodhna, what are you seeing?"

"Them," Iodhna whispered, the tremble in her voice a stark contrast to her usual aloof tone. "I see them."

Bryanna didn't need to ask to know who she was talking about. Even the water-dwellers feared the Brotherhood of Sìorraidh.

"Can you tell me where you are?" Obelia asked in a soft, measured tone.

Iodhna gritted her teeth, as though she didn't want to answer. "I don't know."

"Can you describe it?" Obelia prompted. "Anything at all."

Iodhna swallowed hard. "I've never seen a place like it. The land is smooth and ... rocky."

"Anything else?"

Iodhna's eyes swiveled, as though something else was fighting for her attention. "There are ... purple shrubs growing between the cracks … and there's a waterfall too." She clapped her hands to her ears. "It's so loud."

Bryanna's breath hitched. Iodhna might've never seen such a place, but *she* had—plenty of times. Her family owned a country residence several hours from Castlereagh, where wild lavender bloomed each summer over slates of smooth rock.

Faylinn.

It took Bryanna only moments to gather what she needed. With Obelia and Tyffin busy calming a hysterical Iodhna, her chance to leave Sheidlow Ridge without their interference would never be more convenient. Guilt nagged at the back of her mind at what she was about to do, but she tamped it down. She couldn't stay in Sheidlow Ridge. Not when she knew where the next attack would be.

Her pockets filled with concealment crystals, holster weighed down with dragon-venom daggers, and her traveling cloak brimming with gold coins, she was ready. All she needed was a steed.

And she knew exactly which one she wanted.

No one stopped her on her way to the stables. Most of the boarders were too busy buzzing over Iodhna's premonition to notice Bryanna sneak away.

She went straight to Obelia's stealth steed. The lithe, agile creature stilled as she reached for his saddle, sending her a reproachful look, as though he knew she shouldn't be there.

He neighed in warning as Bryanna unlatched his stall's gate, abandoning the carrot he'd been chewing on.

"Shhh," she cooed.

But he just neighed louder, forcing her to retrace her steps before he alerted her aunt.

"Fine," she hissed. "You're not the only steed in these stables."

The one in the next stall was much more accommodating. Tawny in color, its girth was identical to the stealth steed. It was easily placated with the sugar cones she found in a crate next to the water trough, too. Bryanna tied the saddle around its flanks and pulled herself onto its back. Gripping the reins, she dug her heels into the steed's sides. They took off at a gallop, out of the stables and into the trees. Bryanna steered the steed away from the ironstone path. It would be harder for Obelia to track her on the uncultivated forest ground.

They wove between the trees, toward the village, with surprising ease. Her steed seemed to know the way without much steering, as though he was familiar with the surrounding forest. Her heart hammered against her ribcage with each stride away from the tower, half-expecting her aunt to come galloping behind them. But somehow, they reached the main thoroughfare without pursuit.

Bryanna inhaled deeply, fighting the urge to laugh even as her stomach clenched uncomfortably. She hadn't thought she'd be able to hoodwink her aunt and Tyffin and escape the confines of the tower. Not when her aunt constantly had the surveillance spell active. How many times had she imagined striking out on her own? And finally, after years of careful preparation, she was doing it. She was setting out to get her vengeance and no one could stop her—

"What are you doing, Ms. Nicholls?"

Bryanna's heart sank as her steed came to a sudden halt. She would've flown right over the beast's head if her feet hadn't caught in the stirrups.

Standing in the middle of the thoroughfare, legs spread and arms crossed, was Weylin, looking at her as though she'd just told an unamusing joke.

"What are *you* doing here?" she managed.

In a few large strides, he stood in front of her, the steed's bridle clenched in his hands. "I could ask you the same thing."

Bryanna tried to yank the bridle out of his grip, but he held firm. "Let go of my aunt's steed this instant."

"This isn't your aunt's steed," Weylin said as the traitorous creature dipped its head, rubbing its cheek against Weylin's shoulder. "It's mine."

Heat rose over Bryanna like a sudden fever. Of all the steeds she could've chosen, she'd had to choose his. "You'll get him back. I won't be long."

"Her," he corrected. "Epona's female."

"That's what I meant—"

Without warning, Weylin swung himself onto the saddle behind her.

For a moment, Bryanna forgot why she was on the steed in the first place. Her pulse spiked as the warmth of his inner thighs pressed against the back of her legs. What was wrong with her? Why was she noticing the pine-and-fresh-linen scent wafting from him when he could very well be the reason she didn't make it to Faylinn in time?

"What are you doing?" Bryanna managed as he swept the reins from her hands. She tried to haul them back, but it was no use. Weylin's strength far surpassed hers. "Get off! This is highly improper!"

Weylin snorted. "Says the lass who stole my steed."

"Borrowed," she interjected.

He gave a soft whistle, and Epona responded immediately, turning them back toward the Sheidlow Tower.

"No." Bryanna redoubled her efforts to take back the reins from Weylin. She couldn't let him take her back to the tower. Her aunt would make sure she wouldn't get a second chance to get to Faylinn before the Brotherhood of Sìorraidh attacked.

"Will you desist?" Weylin gritted out, the deep rumble of his voice thick with irritation. "Where were you hoping to go in such a hurry, anyway?"

"Nowhere. Now let go."

But Weylin's grip remained steadfast, keeping her firmly in place in front of him. "Not until you tell me where you were going."

"I told you, I was going for a leisurely ride."

"With this?" He reached into her cloak pocket and pulled out the dragon-venom dagger she'd stowed there.

Ice slid down Bryanna's spine. How had he known that was there? "Put that back before you cut one of us with it."

Though it would serve him right if he nicked himself.

Weylin leaned forward, tucking the dagger back into its hiding place. "If I didn't know better, Ms. Nicholls, I would've thought you were trying to leave."

Bryanna huffed. "What is it to you if I was?"

"Well, I'd miss your delightful company, for one."

Bryanna scoffed. "In order to do that, you'd have to be around more, instead of spending your afternoons napping or wandering around the forest."

"I had no idea you were so attuned to my movements, Ms. Nicholls."

"I'm not," Bryanna said as a sharp cramp seized her abdomen. "I just haven't failed to notice how you leave Bain to attend to your chores. Would it really be so difficult to show up when it's your floor's turn to cook?"

Epona jolted on the uneven path, pushing her back against Weylin's chest. His arms came around her waist instinctively, holding her steady. Warmth flooded Bryanna's cheeks at his touch. No one besides her family had ever been this close to her.

"And just who do you think hunts the game that Bain and everyone else prepares to fill your belly, Ms. Nicholls?"

Bryanna fumbled to come up with an adequate response, ignoring another cramp gripping her stomach. Sure, she'd seen Weylin return with his hunt several times, but it had never occurred to her that it was part of his contribution to the tower.

"Well, it still would be nice if you helped Bain every once in a while," she muttered, yanking once more on the reins. But even one-handed, Weylin's grip was too tight for Bryanna to wrench it free.

"You know, Ms. Nicholls, if you wanted me around more, all you had to do was ask."

"Ughh. You are even more obnoxious than my brother."

"I think that might just be the most offensive thing you could've said to me," he drawled, amusement rumbling in his voice.

Before she could respond, another tug came from her stomach, sharper than the last, as though millions of minuscule hands were squeezing her insides. She doubled over, her teeth grinding as she stifled a moan. Had she eaten something that disagreed with her?

Weylin stiffened, all vestiges of humor evaporating as he placed the hand on her waist up to her forehead. It was cool to the touch and almost welcoming against her blazing face. "Ms. Nicholls?"

Bryanna groaned as a new spasm twisted her insides, the pain so intense that she could barely form a coherent thought, much less answer Weylin. Her lips were becoming thick and heavy, her throat so dry, she couldn't breathe without coughing up a thin, metallic-tasting fluid.

"Bryanna!" he said urgently, his voice imbued with a concern that bordered on panic. "What's wrong?"

Her limbs were so heavy, she could barely move. Black swirls closed in around her. She blinked, trying to clear them away, but it was no use.

What was happening to her?

She clutched Weylin's arm weakly, her fingers trembling, but couldn't manage any words. Not with how hard the contents of her stomach were heaving.

"Bryanna, talk to me," Weylin cried, his ashen face coming into view as he turned her around to look at him.

But Bryanna couldn't answer. She stared up at the dazzling lights of the canopy, conscious only of the forest's embrace as it beckoned her into oblivion.

NINE

Bryanna knew she was back in her bedchamber at the Sheidlow Tower. She knew that Obelia was standing over her, forcing a lumpy concoction that tasted like rotten cabbage and minced liver between her puffy lips. But she was swimming in and out of view, competing with what could only be a hallucination. Because even in her befuddled state, Bryanna knew she couldn't be lying in bed and simultaneously pressed against a narrow cave wall, staring at a curtain of rushing water.

On the other side of the cascade, standing on the edge of a silver and purple bank, was an array of vile creatures, each more perilous than the last. Some she recognized vaguely from bestiaries: winged trolls, wyverns, ogres. But there were others Bryanna had never seen before. Creatures under thick black robes with hollow, emaciated bodies and deformed figures that reminded her of undead, reanimated corpses.

"Please," whimpered a young woman in their midst, her gaze glued to a lanky, olive-skinned man. "Please, let me go."

The man chuckled, causing the hair on Bryanna's nape to stand on end. It was a sound she'd heard once before ... as she'd run from Aveline in that narrow, accursed alleyway five years ago.

He let out a cruel, calculated laugh. "Let you go, my dear? But I haven't let anyone go for over a thousand years."

The creatures chortled, the sound so cold that it sent shivers coursing down Bryanna's spine. She moved closer to the water, crawling over the uneven, jutted floor, mindless of the hands trying to hold her back.

"Bryanna, you need to relax," a husky, familiar voice urged from her bedchamber.

"I'll join you," the woman cried, tears running down her cheeks. "Please. I have coin."

"Oh, I know." The man took a step forward until his face came into unhindered view.

Bryanna gasped. She'd seen him before. He'd been at the Sheidlow Tower years ago, as one of Obelia's boarders.

Lochiel.

Except it wasn't him.

Not anymore.

"Keep watching," said a grainy voice beside her.

Bryanna jerked back. A woman clad in a tattered black robe that dwarfed her cadaverous form was crouched at her side, her limp, unkempt hair draping down her sharp, bony face.

"Who—"

But the woman seized a clump of Bryanna's hair and forced her gaze back to the scene on the bank.

"I know you won't ever understand," Lochiel crooned to the weeping woman. "But this is necessary."

The woman shook her head, a jumble of pleas spilling from her lips. But they had no effect on him as he strutted forward, his face turning slack.

The woman screamed, thrashing against the two winged trolls holding her still as Lochiel's body slumped to the ground, leaving in its place a pallid, skeletal creature with long limbs and a hunched, sickly body. Bryanna would've screamed, too, if the breath hadn't been stolen from her lungs.

She watched, helpless, as the wispy creature pitched forward and disappeared inside the woman's body.

Sound melted away as though it'd been leeched from existence. Even the water lapping against the bank became inaudible as Bryanna and the assortment of dark creatures stared fixedly at the motionless woman. Bryanna wanted to tear her gaze away, but some morbid pull forced her to watch on, compelled to see what would become of the woman.

A sour taste coated her mouth as the woman moved, tilting her head to the left and to the right as though stretching a crick in her neck. Pale hands came up, wiping away the tears that had stopped flowing down her cheeks.

Then she laughed, the sound chilling Bryanna to the bone.

Bryanna fell back as the water and cave receded, the creature's laughter ringing in her ears.

"It's all right, Bryanna," her aunt coaxed as her bedchamber came into clear view. "Calm down."

But Bryanna couldn't calm down. Not after what she'd seen. She latched onto the collar of her aunt's blouse, her heart lurching in her chest. Someone needed to know what had happened to Lochiel and the woman. "Aunt Obelia—"

But her aunt's white-starched fabric shifted in Bryanna's hand, turning grimy and coarse. She scrambled back, a scream lodged in her throat as the ghastly black-robed woman from the cave materialized in front of her.

"Did you see it?" she rasped.

"Get away from me!" Bryanna screamed, trying to put as much distance between them as she could.

But the woman clamped Bryanna's arms, digging her nails into her flesh. "Enough of that, girl. Did you see it?"

"Let me go!"

The woman only gripped her tighter, shaking Bryanna so hard that her teeth rattled. "If you weren't my last hope …"

A damp handkerchief came over Bryanna's nose, the scent of sedative potion filling her nostrils.

"No!" Bryanna cried.

"Obelia, wait," a voice that she was pretty sure was Weylin's came from her side, snatching the cloth her aunt had pressed to her face.

"I have to calm her down, Weylin," her aunt insisted.

"Just wait." Weylin's hand gripped Bryanna's shoulder, turning her to face him. "Bryanna, listen to me. What you're seeing isn't real."

"Yes, it is!" she yelled. "Don't you see her?"

Obelia's hand came down once more, clamping the cloth over her nose again.

"No!" Bryanna lunged toward Weylin as her vision swam. "Please! She's … trying … to …"

But the potion's effects were too strong, and blackness overtook her.

TEN

"I'm not denying that your niece is a powerful magic-weaver, Obelia," Weylin's low, husky voice came from Bryanna's left when she awoke again. "But she's young."

Bryanna grimaced, her throat and stomach burning as though she'd swallowed a pint of acid. The rest of her body wasn't faring much better. Every muscle ached, as though she'd been beaten by a flock of cockatrice hybrids. She was back in her bedchamber, judging by the familiar feel of the mattress beneath her. Though how she'd gotten there was beyond her. The last thing she remembered was being in the forest, astride Weylin's steed as he'd turned her back around, toward the tower ...

"You're not much older than her, Weylin," came her aunt's equally soft response.

"Yes, but there aren't any rumors circulating about me being on the Brotherhood's tail." He sank onto the edge of her bed. "She could still have a normal life."

"Bryanna's too much like me to let go of her vengeance," Obelia replied quietly. "When someone is taken from you the way that her cousin was from her ... the way your cousin was from me ..."

Bryanna fought against the sleepy haze wrapped around her mind. She hadn't known Weylin's cousin had been taken by the Brotherhood of Sìorraidh ... unless her aunt meant Fillian. His surname had been Conveil, just like Weylin's ...

"I know," Weylin said with unexpected gentleness. He sounded weary, as though he'd been forced to grow too soon. "But you need to help her try. This isn't a life for her."

"You've met my niece, Weylin," Obelia said pointedly. "She won't listen to me. Not about this."

Weylin sighed. "Then she's going to get herself killed."

Bryanna shifted as a wave of nausea engulfed her, ending their conversation. Which was just as well. Bryanna didn't want to hear how neither of them believed she could vanquish the Brotherhood.

Weylin was at her side at once. "Try not to move," he said. "You'll make yourself sick."

"I know," Bryanna groaned, pulling her counterpane to just below her chin. "What are you doing here?"

Weylin stood, the gleam of the flickering oil lamp dancing over the dark shadows lingering under his eyes. "Oh, you know ... I was bored and thought I'd check in on the stubborn, reckless young sorceress who almost died in my arms."

Bryanna closed her eyes as the memory of what had felt like swirls of molten lava sloshing the lining of her stomach returned to her.

"You have no idea how lucky it was that I was there to stop you from leaving Sheidlow Ridge," he said, disapproval etched between his brows. "You would've been on the other side of the village and beyond our help otherwise. What were you thinking, taking off without telling anyone?"

Bryanna squirmed and looked away. She'd known she'd be

reprimanded for fleeing the tower, but never had she thought it would be Weylin doing it.

"Weylin, why don't you go and get some rest?" Obelia said, her concerned gaze raking over Bryanna's flushed cheeks before moving to Weylin. "You've barely left my niece's side since you brought her back."

Bryanna glanced over at Weylin, certain she'd heard her aunt wrong. Because surely he hadn't remained by her bedside since she'd fallen so violently ill. But then she noticed that he wore the same clothes that he'd been in when he'd stopped her on the edge of the forest.

Warmth bloomed in the center of her chest, though it was quickly followed by confusion. Why would Weylin have remained with her?

"Don't let it go to your head, Ms. Nicholls," he said, as though he'd read the direction of her thoughts. "I was just making sure you didn't die on us. It wouldn't do the sanctuary any good if Obelia's own niece were to perish while in her care, after all."

The warmth in her chest cooled faster than a glass of iced water.

"I'll be downstairs," he said to Obelia.

Bryanna stared after him as he walked out the door, a strange reluctance knotting in her chest. She wasn't sure why, but she didn't want him to leave.

"So," Obelia said, setting Tyffin down from his perch on her shoulder and moving her hands to rest at her hips. "Do you want to tell me how you were poisoned with basilisk venom?"

"Basilisk?" Bryanna croaked, the word scraping painfully up her raw, blistered throat. "Are you certain?"

"Yes," said Obelia, her features set. "You're fortunate Weylin was nearby when the venom's effects took hold. *And* that I had an emergency batch of antidote. You wouldn't have made it to the closest apothecary."

Bryanna shuddered. She'd heard of enough basilisk venom victims to know her aunt wasn't exaggerating. "How long was I out?"

"About five days."

Bryanna's mouth fell open. "*Five days?*"

Obelia nodded, her fingers brushing Tyffin's soft fur. "I don't suppose you could tell me what happened? You were in quite a state when Weylin carried you into the tower."

Unbidden, the memory of a cold, cruel laugh resurfaced. "I think I was hallucinating," she said slowly as the image of what she'd seen crept back to her with a sickening jolt. "I saw your old boarder, Lochiel. He jumped into a woman's body. Literally."

Obelia cast Tyffin an uneasy look. "What do you mean?"

"He was the leader of the Brotherhood of Sìorraidh ... until he wasn't ..." Bryanna shook her head. She sounded absurd even to herself. "I must've been really delirious."

"Basilisk poisoning does bring about hallucinations," her aunt said. "I'd ask what you were doing so close to the village, but I think I can guess." She threw Bryanna a quelling glare. "You're lucky you're bedridden. I had to write to your parents about what happened."

Bryanna stiffened, her stomach clenching worse than it had when she'd been in the throes of her poisoning. "You what?"

"Oh, don't look at me like that. You almost died. I didn't have a choice."

Bryanna let her head fall back against the pillow, her mouth set in a grim line.

"Relax," said Obelia. "Your father's agreed to let me keep you a few extra weeks until you're fully recovered. Which reminds me, your mother sent you this." Obelia handed her a rose-scented letter. The smell made Bryanna's stomach roil. She unfolded it, dreading what she'd find written there.

My dearest daughter,

What is this I hear about you being ill? I've written to your aunt and you're to come home as soon as you're able. I don't know what we were thinking, sending you off to that irresponsible aunt of yours. I told your father how bad an idea it was. And I was right. Not even a moon cycle and you've already taken ill.

Stay in bed and keep away from those frightful sicklings your aunt insists on caring for. The last thing I want is for you to catch whatever it is they've got.

Love,

Your worried-sick mother

"She sent me one too," Obelia said once Bryanna finished reading. "Mine had lots of underlined words and capital letters. I don't think she's too happy with me."

Bryanna placed the letter on her bedside table and leaned back against her headboard.

"I know you're still recovering, Bryanna, but we need to get to the bottom of how you were poisoned. Did you eat or drink anything unusual that day? Perhaps something in the forest while you were picking berries?"

Bryanna shook her head. The only thing she'd ingested that the others hadn't was the concoction Cayde gave her, and she didn't think he would've poisoned her. If he'd wanted to attack her, he wouldn't have needed basilisk venom. He had his own preternatural abilities that would've sated him much more completely.

Iodhna, on the other hand …

She'd seen the way the morgen watched her, as though she was a predator sizing up her next intended victim. "Could it have been Iodhna?"

Obelia shook her head. "None of my boarders could've acquired such a substance in this area."

But that wasn't entirely true …

Bryanna glanced at the volumes on her mantelpiece, where she'd concealed the phials and talismans she'd traveled with, and her stomach sank.

They were no longer in the same order she'd left them.

She sat back up, ignoring the nausea climbing up her throat.

Someone had been in her bedchamber.

They'd made an effort to conceal their intrusion, but there were telltale signs all over her chamber. Her trunks weren't crammed at the bottom of her wardrobe anymore, the bedsheet at the end of her bed was untucked, and the collection of perfumes on her dresser was empty.

"What is it?" asked Obelia at once, catching the alarm on Bryanna's face.

Bryanna swallowed, hissing at the pain it caused down her throat. "I brought some basilisk venom with me."

Obelia sprang to her feet. "For the love of Castlereagh, Bryanna. Where did you store it?"

Bryanna raised a quivering finger in the mantel's direction.

Obelia flicked her hand and a bout of magic crackled through the air. The volumes soared across the chamber, landing on Bryanna's bed with a thud.

Bryanna reached for one, but Obelia caught her wrist before she could touch it.

"Don't. If someone handled them, their scent might still be on there."

She cast a second spell over the volumes, turning the covers transparent and revealing the hollow cavities where Bryanna's phials, powders, and talismans had once been. Whoever had taken them hadn't even left the small collection of dried herbs she'd been pressing for remedial use over the last few weeks.

Bryanna's head spun. Who could've snuck into her bedchamber?

"No magical signatures," her aunt muttered. "Whoever broke in doesn't possess magic."

"They must have," Bryanna argued. "How else were they able to break the illusion spells I had on these volumes?"

"I have no idea." Obelia ran a hand through her hair, loosening her dignified bun. "What else did you have stashed in here, Bryanna? Answer honestly. I already know about the dragon-venom daggers."

Bryanna clenched her teeth. Had Weylin tattled to get back at her? But then she saw the belt she'd had around her waist on top of her dresser, the daggers resting securely in their holsters.

She considered lying, but had a feeling it wouldn't be of any use. Her aunt would dismantle every bit of her chamber if she had to, and she'd be in even more trouble if that happened. Better to be honest, especially when the things she'd brought could be used against the other boarders the way they had her. Besides, they needed to figure out what else was missing and who'd taken it—before it was too late.

Biting her lip, Bryanna pointed to the loose floorboard and secret compartment behind the hearth. Obelia waved her hand once more, and the weapons and other artifacts Bryanna had painstakingly hidden floated out from their concealed locations. Her aunt's face darkened as she studied the things she'd brought, exchanging words with Tyffin through their bond. Somehow, Bryanna didn't think Obelia was praising her skills at imbuing weapons.

"Are you going to tell my parents?" Bryanna asked in a small voice when the last of her things had been collected.

Obelia made a derisive sound at the back of her throat. "What, and get another condescending letter from your mother?" She hoisted the weapons into her arms. "Get some rest. We'll have words about this once you're better."

Obelia extinguished her oil lamp.

"Oh, and Bryanna? If you ever go missing again, forget your father's wrath. You'll have mine to contend with when I find you. And I *will* find you. Long before anyone else does."

Bryanna didn't doubt her for one moment.

Obelia kept Bryanna restricted to her floor for the rest of the week. Not as a punishment, she assured her, but because they couldn't risk her catching an infection that would deter her recovery. Bryanna didn't mind the isolation. She barely possessed the energy to walk to the privy, much less descend nine flights of stairs. Not to mention the smell that sometimes wafted up from the kitchen made her stomach want to revolt.

As she stabilized, she found herself having to stave off sleep. Each time she succumbed to slumber, she'd have the strangest dreams, filled with the grimy, black-robed woman from her hallucination. She'd see her in the corner of bright, crowded ballrooms or paces behind her in the Sheidlow Forest, repeating some *olde* tongue Bryanna didn't understand over and over.

Another week passed before Obelia cleared her for company. Her first official visitor was Seara. The moment the younger girl stepped into her bedchamber, she launched herself onto Bryanna's bed. "What really happened to you?" she asked without preamble. "You know I don't believe that nonsense your aunt's been sprouting about you having some contagious stomach bug."

Bryanna hesitated. Seara was not going to like the truth.

In fact, no sooner had she told her about what she'd almost succeeded in doing than Seara huffed. "I can't believe you almost left Sheidlow Ridge without me. What were you thinking?"

Bryanna tucked a loose tendril of hair behind Seara's ear. "I didn't want you getting hurt."

"That's not up to you," Seara growled, stamping her foot. "Next time you get a lead, tell me. Otherwise, you can forget us being allies."

Liadan and Bain visited Bryanna, too, though they didn't stay long. Bain was overseeing the harvest, which was well underway.

"He gets a bit obsessive when it comes to this time of year," Liadan told her. "He grew up on a farm. Thinks he knows everything there is to know about harvesting."

I do *know everything*, Bain quipped, earning himself a playful swat on the arm.

Cayde, too, tried to see her. Bryanna heard his voice in her hallway one afternoon, but he never made it to her bedchamber. Someone with a deep, husky voice stopped him several paces from her door. She'd been half-asleep when it happened, but was pretty sure it'd been Weylin. Either that, or she'd dreamed the entire thing. It made more sense than Weylin standing guard outside her hallway, keeping Cayde away from her.

To keep herself awake—and fend off boredom—Bryanna memorized the witchscript scroll Obelia gave her. She was getting so good at recognizing the different symbols that she'd been able to decipher the contents of one of her late grandmother's volumes. To her disappointment, there wasn't anything about the Brotherhood in it.

When she wasn't reading or entertaining visitors, Bryanna spent her time planning how to regain what she'd lost. The herbs and other plant samples could be easily restocked at any apothecary in Otherworld. The weapons were what worried her. It'd taken her years to amass her collection, as well as most of the coins she'd earned working for Lady Auberagh.

One morning, Obelia handed Bryanna an old leather volume with browned, desiccated edges. By then, Bryanna was sufficiently skilled in witchscript to decipher its title: *Self-Protection and the Ancient Magical Arts*. She took it eagerly, but her enthusiasm waned the more pages she flipped. The volume was filled with the most gruesome spells she'd ever seen: dislocating limbs, rupturing internal organs, slicing unhealable gashes ...

She looked up at her aunt, appalled. "This is dark magic."

"Technically, it's *ancient* magic," countered Obelia.

Bryanna slid the volume away from her. She'd embarked on her quest more than willing to endure pain, torture, even death. But she'd never considered wielding dark magic. That was the weapon the Brotherhood of Sìorraidh used, and for her to use it, too, made her feel tainted, less commendable for what she was trying to do.

"Let me ask you something, Bryanna. Would you consider a spell that cuts firewood to be dark magic?"

"Of course not," Bryanna said at once.

"And yet, if you were to use the same spell on something living, you would?"

"Yes."

Obelia quirked a brow. "But it's the same spell."

"Yes ... no, there's a difference."

"No, there isn't. It's the intention that's dark. You've been asking me to train you for weeks. Here I am, doing just that—against my better judgment, I might add—and you're refusing?"

Bryanna folded her arms across her chest. "I'm not practicing dark magic."

"Ancient magic. And this sort of magic is important for you to understand. What better way to fight against it than by learning how to wield it?"

Bryanna clenched her teeth. "There has to be another way."

"So find it." Obelia picked up the volume and placed it in Bryanna's lap once more. "In the meantime, arm yourself with your last resort."

"I don't see any harm in what your aunt's trying to teach you," Elgar said a week later.

Obelia had finally reinstated some of Bryanna's chores, including administering Elgar's tonic. She'd been anxious to see him again, especially when she'd learned he'd had another episode at around the same time as her poisoning.

It hadn't taken him long to notice Bryanna's preoccupation and, after much prodding on his part, she'd told him about Obelia's dark magic volume.

"As a magic-weaver, your weapon is your magic, just like a soldier's is a sword or mace. Take me, for example. I've always possessed an affinity for archery." He indicated his chest of drawers, where an immaculate bow and quiver of arrows lay. "But that doesn't mean I wasn't trained in other weapons. Every soldier is. That's all Obelia wants to do—give you another weapon to add to your disposal, just in case you ever find yourself needing it."

Bryanna had to admit Elgar's argument was compelling.

Although undesirable, there were advantages to familiarizing herself with dark magic.

Elgar yawned. "You should join the others. Besides, I have a feeling I'll be asleep within minutes."

"I don't mind staying."

But he'd dozed off before Bryanna finished smoothing his bedcovers.

Traditionally, on the summer solstice, a feast of freshly harvested fruits and vegetables was served. As it was Bain and Weylin's turn to cook that night, Bain didn't disappoint. He'd started early, applying his artistic flair to every fruit and vegetable platter he designed. The finished products looked so appealing that even Iodhna, who usually refused to eat anything but fish, loaded her plate.

Bryanna and the boarders sat in the courtyard, enjoying the dwindling summer breeze and the fruits—literally—of their labor, relishing the respite from the harvest. They'd had a grueling couple of days in the vegetable patches, picking and preserving anything that wouldn't be consumed before the end of the summer. Bryanna had helped with the preserving at first, but she'd had to excuse herself after the smell of overripe, diced tomatoes threatened to overcome her still-sensitive stomach.

They spent the evening in good spirits, chatting comfortably, until three young men bounded up the courtyard, astride sturdy dappled steeds. Bryanna was on guard at once. Their leader was heavyset and looked like a professional white-stag wrestler, with the trademark extra set of canines every full-blooded faoladh had. Behind him rode a younger man who looked like a shorter, darker version of him, and a tall, lean one with sleek golden hair tied at the back of his head.

Weylin, who'd been uncharacteristically quiet and unobtrusive the last few days, shook his head wryly when he saw them and jumped to the ground from the tree bough he'd been perched on.

"There he is, boys!" their leader shouted, striding toward Weylin. Halfway to him, though, he made a deliberate and excessive show of stopping when he saw the honey cake on Bryanna's plate and swooped down, grabbing it with grubby, calloused fingers.

"Hey!" Bryanna protested.

"Hey, lass," he said through a mouthful of cake. "Are you having a good night?"

"Watch yourself with that one, Niall," Weylin called, his light tone a stark contrast to the sudden tension in his body. "If you're not careful, she'll have you on your arse in a few seconds flat."

Niall raised his brows. "You think so?"

Weylin's gaze flicked to Bryanna before returning to Niall. "If you don't believe me, suit yourself. I've missed watching you get your ego bruised."

Niall laughed as Weylin bridged the space between them. "You always did like your little brunettes."

Bryanna wasn't sure if she was imagining it, but she thought Weylin's cheeks flushed.

"Speaking of brunettes," said the shortest faoladh, stepping forward. "Tavia and her new husband had a little girl two nights ago—with your gray-blue eyes and dark head of hair."

Bryanna wouldn't have been more shocked if the Brotherhood of Sìorraidh had just descended on them.

Weylin was a *father*?

Around her, the courtyard had slid into a void of silence.

"Lochie," said the other faoladh quietly. "This isn't the place."

"Come off it, Whyatt. It's not like Weylin didn't know she was coming."

Whyatt stepped forward, his expression grim as he met Weylin's gaze. "She's a healthy baby. She'll grow up strong, a member of your father's tribe."

Weylin made a derisive sound at the back of his throat.

Something in Bryanna's chest constricted as she looked at him, as though she could feel the turmoil he was trying to hide from the others.

It's not like Weylin didn't know she was coming.

Lochie's words reverberated in her mind. Was that why the Conveils had come unannounced? Why Weylin had been so livid when they'd left? Had he asked his father to lift the banishment so he could be there when his daughter was born, and been denied?

"Cousin," said Niall, a nasty gleam in his eyes as he spotted Cayde. "You didn't tell us there was a neach-ithe anam here."

Bryanna stood up, glaring at the faoladh. If he was looking to start any trouble where Cayde was concerned, he'd have to go through her first.

Several boarders stood, too, creating a loose perimeter around Cayde. Bryanna wasn't sure whether she or the neach-ithe anam was more surprised.

If you have a problem with Cayde being here, you can leave, Bain said coolly.

Niall moved lightning-quick, appearing in front of Bain so fast that Bryanna barely saw it with her own eyes, and practically pressed his face into Bain's. "Is that right?"

To his credit, Bain remained rooted to the spot, unflinching despite the faoladh looming over him.

"Niall," Weylin said in a low voice. "Knock it off."

But Niall grabbed the front of Bain's shirt and shoved him as though he were nothing more than a coat stand. Unfamiliar with such strength or violence, Bain went sailing into one of the tables.

"Bain!" Liadan screamed.

Gelert charged at once, his jaw clamping around Niall's leg. But with a powerful kick, the wolfhound rolled to the ground.

Something inside Bryanna snapped. She didn't care who they were. No one would harm her friends on her watch and get away with it. She drew on her magic, sending it slamming into the faoladh, and he went crashing back several paces.

Niall righted himself at once, his eyes turning to slits. "No one attacks me and gets away with it. Not even you, lass."

But before he could advance on her, Weylin stepped forward, standing between them. "I mean it, Niall," he said sharply. "Not here."

Bryanna bristled, a confinement spell she'd picked up from her late grandmother's volumes tingling at her fingertips. "Step aside, Weylin, I can handle him."

But Niall was no longer paying her any attention. He'd caught sight of Iodhna behind them, and his eyes glazed over.

Bryanna turned, her heart sinking as she caught sight of the little rivers flowing out from the depths of the flagon in her hand.

"Iodhna, no!" she cried as the rivulets shot straight up Niall's and the other faoladhs' nostrils.

"Release them!" Weylin shouted, fury vibrating in his every word as the faoladhs remained perfectly composed, staring dreamily at the morgen, whose face was twisted with malicious intent. "Now!"

Iodhna raised a hairless brow. "You saw what they did. Violent, the whole lot of them. They deserve this."

The shortest faoladh nodded, heedless of the water filling his lungs.

Goose bumps rose over Bryanna's body at the complete control she had over them. Iodhna didn't even look like the power she was wielding to keep them in her thrall was affecting her. "That doesn't mean you drown them! Release them right now!"

Where was Obelia? Hadn't she heard the commotion happening in the courtyard?

Iodhna rolled her eyes. "This is what I get for trying to help you land-dwellers."

The streams of water splashed to the ground, harmless once more.

Immediately, the faoladhs dropped to the ground, choking and gasping as they coughed up water.

Niall was the first to recover. "That was the last thing you'll ever do!" he barked, making for Iodhna, his expression murderous. But before he could reach her, magic sliced through the air, throwing him against a tree trunk.

Bryanna turned at the familiar magic, her relief palpable. Obelia stood beside Bain's injured form, breathing hard through her flared nostrils. "Leave," she snarled, her gaze fixed on Niall. "You are never to set foot on my grounds again. Is that clear?"

Niall struggled against his restraints. "Who the f—" He gave a shout of pain as Obelia twisted her wrist.

"Is. That. Clear?"

Bryanna's mouth went dry. She'd never seen her aunt so livid. She was shaking, her eyes practically popping from their sockets.

"Yes," Niall gasped.

"Let him go, Obelia," said Weylin softly, leaving Bryanna's side to stand in front of her aunt.

He said something Bryanna couldn't hear, and the fury on Obelia's face dulled. She let out a shaky breath and released

Niall. He landed on his hands and knees, directly over the spot where Gelert had relieved himself earlier that night.

"I'll see them back to the village," said Weylin, gripping Obelia's arm for a fleeting moment before turning to his unwelcome visitors.

Bryanna watched as he led the other faoladhs toward the front of the tower, leaving her and the boarders with nothing but the aftershocks of their short company.

CHAPTER

ELEVEN

Weylin didn't return that night.

Or the next morning.

Bryanna strained her ears for the sound of hooves coming from the ironstone path, but when any did, it was never Weylin. By the end of luncheon, she was anxious that something had happened to him. She could barely focus on the cough and cold syrups her aunt had set her to brewing. Her mind kept conjuring images of him lying on the forest floor near the village, dying from basilisk poisoning, or being ensnared by the green-blooded creature that had attacked her and Gawain the night they'd arrived.

By midafternoon, she couldn't take it anymore. She dampened the fire in the grate and left the small apothecary workstation above the barn, setting off for the herb garden, where her aunt would likely be. Someone needed to make sure Weylin was all right. After all, hadn't he remained by her side while she'd been recovering from her poisoning?

Sure enough, she found her with Seara, weeding a rare and expensive vine that Bryanna recognized as ayahuasca. Obelia had been using it in her tonics for Elgar. Bryanna had already seen the difference it made in the short time she'd been administering it.

"Aunt Obelia, have you heard from Weylin?" she asked when she reached them.

"Not yet." Obelia leaned back on her knees and raised a hand to shield her eyes from the blazing sun. "But don't worry, this isn't the first time he's been gone for a few hours."

"But it's been *more* than a few hours."

Why wasn't her aunt taking Weylin's disappearance seriously? Had she forgotten that the last time she'd been in the forest, a creature they still hadn't identified had attacked *her*? Or that someone or something had slipped into her bedchamber, undetected, and tried to kill her with her own belongings?

Obelia lowered her hand. "If he's not back by nightfall, I'll send Tyffin to search for him."

Bryanna clenched her jaw. "Can't you send him now?"

Tyffin lay curled up against Obelia's skirts, but at Bryanna's words, he shut his eyes, feigning sleep.

"I'm sure he's fine." Obelia handed Bryanna her weeding apparatus. "Why don't you help Seara with the last of the weeds while I check on the beehives?"

Bryanna gritted her teeth. She didn't want to weed herbs. She wanted to go after Weylin.

"Don't worry," Seara said once Obelia left, taking Tyffin with her. "Weylin knows how to defend himself."

"Yes, but we don't know what's out there."

Or close by, she thought privately. Ever since her poisoning, she'd felt ill at ease around the tower, as though she were constantly being watched.

"Have you had any other thoughts about who poisoned you?" Seara asked as though sensing her morose thoughts.

Bryanna shook her head. They'd been trying to figure out who could've done it for weeks. "I still think it was Iodhna."

Seara added more prickly weeds to her mounting pile before speaking again. "I don't know … I was thinking … what if it was someone working for the Brotherhood of Sìorraidh? I mean, it happened just as you were trying to get to Faylinn, where Iodhna prophesied the new attack to be. That can't be a coincidence."

Bryanna went still. "You think someone's spying on me?"

"I think they spy on all of us," Seara replied grimly, wiping her dirt-riddled hands on her shirt. "I mean, it's no secret Obelia disappeared to go after them all those years ago. They're probably still watching her and anyone she associates with. The same thing happened with my mother and the Boltons. They never kept it a secret that they were searching for a way to end the Brotherhood."

Bryanna's mouth fell open. "You never told me your mother was seeking the Brotherhood."

She'd been trying to wheedle information out of Seara for weeks, though the sidhe had remained tight-lipped, especially after Bryanna had tried to leave Sheidlow Ridge without her.

"Well, she was. And she wasn't alone. A few days before she and the Boltons died, I went downstairs and found strangers in our kitchen. My mother's cloaking spell was up, so I couldn't hear what they were saying, but I could tell they were worried. The next day, my mother sent me away. That was the last time I ever saw her."

The hair at the back of Bryanna's nape stiffened. "She knew she was going to be attacked?"

Seara nodded. "I think the Brithlean League warned her."

"The *what*?"

"The Brithlean League. They're an activist group working against the Brotherhood of Sìorraidh. I think they—"

But Bryanna never found out what Seara was going to say next as, around them, the same thick, misty wall that had appeared when the villagers had chased Obelia's boarder years ago rose high above them, enclosing the tower.

Bryanna leaped to her feet, her breath catching as the massive wyvern that had been residing on the outskirts of the Sheidlow Tower glided toward them, his triple-set of sharp, jagged teeth bared.

"Get back!" Bryanna yelled, pulling Seara behind her

The creature landed in front of them with a ground-shaking thud and raised its thick, barbed tail over its head, its venomous spike pointing straight at Bryanna. Its slitted eyes fused to her with an unsettling hunger, as though it was starved and she was the only meal it wanted.

Bryanna reached for her magic, her heart pounding against her chest, but before she could so much as think of a spell to use against him, Seara shouted, "Get away from us!" and unleashed a complex spell that connected with the wyvern's face, sending his head snapping back.

"Seara, no!"

But it was too late.

The wyvern roared, the sound vibrating down Bryanna's spine as he righted himself. She dived, forcing Seara down with her just as a volley of spikes flew out the end of its tail. They barreled over their heads like deadly bolts unlatching from a crossbow, lodging into the wooden fence behind them with an ominous crunch.

"Stay down," Bryanna cried, jumping to her feet, the organ-rupturing spell from her aunt's volumes burning at her fingertips. She no longer cared about the spell's nature. Her thoughts were singularly bent on protecting Seara by whatever means necessary.

A husky, rumbling bay sounded from close by. Bryanna

forgot how to breathe as a tall, sinewy being with a rich-mahogany coat vaulted the white picket fence. He had the head, shoulders, and hind legs of a wolf, a burly, humanlike chest, and arms that ended in thick, clawed fingernails.

A faoladh.

The being pulled Bryanna behind him and faced their predator, a low growl emitting from deep within his chest.

"Finch!" Obelia shouted, racing toward them. "What do you think you're doing?"

The wyvern roared again, sending thick, cloudy spittle flying out of his formidable jowls as his slitted, baleful eyes locked on Bryanna. He moved forward, unfurling his immense black wings, and Bryanna knew without a doubt that she was his quarry.

She raised her hands, blocking the fear that threatened at the edge of her mind.

She could *not* give in to it.

But before she could unleash her curse, Obelia drew her arms wide and cast a spell so powerful, Bryanna's whole body thrummed with the strength of it. A growl of fury exploded from the wyvern's lips as the spell crashed into him with such force that he was sent sailing into the air, straight for the misty wall.

Before he reached it, though, his wings expanded, fighting Obelia's spell.

Bryanna's hand shot out, magic surging forth from her palm. It hit him squarely in the chest, propelling him against the misty wall, which parted long enough for him to soar past before sealing once more, barring him from the tower.

Bryanna sagged forward, her legs quaking so hard that she thought they'd give way at any moment.

She watched, unable to tear her gaze away, as the faoladh shifted. Before her eyes, his snout flattened and claws retreated until they were harmless, stubby fingernails. Thick fur receded under sun-kissed skin, revealing the face of the young man who'd been making her heart race for weeks.

"Weylin?" she whispered, relief catching in her throat.

How was it that he was always around when she found herself facing danger?

Weylin's smoky-blue eyes met hers. "You should have run."

"We didn't have time," she replied, trying to keep her hands from trembling. "He just came at us."

"At *you*," he corrected, turning to face Obelia. "That wyvern was after your niece. If I hadn't gotten here in time, he'd be halfway across Otherworld with her right now."

A shiver ran down Bryanna's spine. The wyvern had never given her more than a distant scowl. Surely if he'd been biding his time to kidnap her, he'd have done it when she'd been alone.

Obelia opened her mouth to reply, but before she could, the wooden gate to the herb garden swung open, and Deagon stepped through it, a wooden post clutched in his hand.

Bryanna stared at him. His skin was covered with angry, purpling lumps. "What happened to you?"

Deagon waved her concern away. "'Tis nothing. Weylin's lads are a rowdy bunch, tha's all."

"*They* did this to you?" she asked, aghast, her gaze swiveling to Weylin.

"No, some o' the lads at the tavern las' night who thought Weylin was being too forward with Mrs. Olwen's granddaughter."

Something contracted in Bryanna's midsection. She shouldn't have been surprised that Weylin and his friends had spent the entire night courting young women, really. She'd grown up with four older brothers. She knew exactly what young men were like, particularly under the influence of mead and raucous friends.

"It was the other way round, actually," Weylin muttered, picking up the weeding tool she'd dropped. "I guess some young women can't resist my charms."

Bryanna snorted, though some of the tension that had gripped her belly eased. "Or your modesty."

Weylin shrugged. "That, too."

Bryanna wiped her hands on her skirt. "You took your time getting back," she said, changing the subject. "We weren't sure where you were when you didn't return last night. My aunt was ready to send Tyffin out after you."

A slow smile curved Weylin's lips. "Really? You were that worried about me?"

"Not me, my aunt," Bryanna lied.

His smile widened as his gaze flicked to Obelia, who was too busy healing a gash on Seara's arm to pay them any mind. "Right."

"What took you so long to get back? Did you go back to your village to try to see your daughter?"

Weylin's face clouded over. "Not that I wouldn't have, if I could, but I'm currently banished from my tribe. I thought you knew that."

Bryanna swallowed, tucking a stray lock of hair behind her ear. "I'd heard. I just thought, given the circumstances—"

"You don't know my father," he said darkly. "I doubt I'd be getting the happy news that I can return to Dalvin's Pound any time soon."

"Speaking of news," said Deagon, unearthing a wadded newspaper from his satchel and handing it to Obelia, "Lochiel Blackburn's dead. Some trekkers found him in the Faylinn Forest. The Brotherhood of Sìorraidh got him."

Bryanna could hardly pull in a lungful of air. How was it possible that the first Brotherhood of Sìorraidh victim to come to light since her poisoning was the very same man she'd seen in her venom-addled hallucination?

Obelia must've been thinking the same thing because her face tightened.

"He's the tenth ex-boarder ter be taken by the Brotherhood this year," Deagon continued.

"Wait—the Brotherhood has taken *ten* ex-boarders?" she asked, her voice rising.

"Coincidence," said Obelia quickly. "I hope you aren't scaring your poor wife with this, Deagon. She must be close to giving birth by now. The last thing she needs to worry about is those wretched creatures descending on your doorstep."

"Of course not. But yeh have ter admit, 'tis strange. Ten of the seventeen victims this year were once boarders. Don't yeh think it's a wee bit more than coincidence?" Deagon caught sight of Seara and glanced away, shamefaced. "I'm sorry, Seara. I shouldn't have brought this up in front of yeh. I know yer mother was one of them."

A muscle jumped in Seara's cheek. "Why not? I'm not a child."

Deagon glanced uncomfortably over at the ironstone path. The misty wall had dissipated without any of them realizing. Wherever the wyvern was, he was no longer around the tower. "I should go. The baby'll be coming any day now. Just … think about what I said, Obelia."

Obelia nodded and headed back to the tower.

"I'll see you later," Bryanna murmured to Seara and rushed after her aunt. There was something she knew about the latest Brotherhood attacks, and she wasn't going to rest until she knew what it was.

As soon as she and her aunt were up in the hidden chamber and closed off from the rest of the tower, Bryanna turned to her.

"Why didn't you tell me the Brotherhood of Sìorraidh is killing ex-boarders?"

Obelia sank heavily into one of the mismatched chairs. "Because I didn't want to believe it myself." She rubbed the back of her neck, looking years older. "Do you remember me telling you the Brotherhood of Sìorraidh has ways of getting to those we care about?"

Bryanna nodded, taking a seat in front of her aunt. "You think they're going after boarders to get to you?"

A pained look crossed Obelia's features. "The thought has crossed my mind. Perhaps it's time for you to leave Sheidlow Ridge."

Bryanna jumped to her feet. Her aunt had to be mad if she thought she was leaving the tower, especially if what she suspected was true. "I'm not going anywhere."

"I don't want you caught up in any of this."

"I don't care! If you send me away, I'll just come back. All the ovates in Otherworld couldn't stop me." Bryanna met her aunt's gaze unflinchingly. "Besides, I need you to train me in ancient magic."

Obelia's brow arched. "I thought you didn't want to learn by my methods."

"Yes, well ... after facing that wyvern, I've changed my mind. I think it's time I learned more powerful spells. The kind that would have an effect on creatures like the wyvern."

She finally understood what her aunt had meant when she'd told her she wasn't ready to face the Brotherhood of Sìorraidh. The mainstream spells she'd mastered over the years wouldn't be enough against their dark foes. A more aggressive form of magic was needed. The type that, had she not so blatantly refused when Obelia had offered it, would've given her a fighting chance against the wyvern.

Not that she was under any illusion that ancient magic

would be enough against the Brotherhood. What they needed was help. The kind the Brithlean League could provide …

Seara had said they were activists fighting against the Brotherhood of Sìorraidh. Surely they'd help if they knew Obelia and her boarders—past and present—were being targeted?

"Have you heard of the Brithlean League?" Bryanna asked.

Surprise flickered in Obelia's eyes. "I have," she said slowly. "How did *you* hear about the League?"

Bryanna shrugged. "They've come up in conversation before. How do *you* know about them?"

Obelia shifted in her seat, glancing at Tyffin. "They approached me at Fillian's wake many years ago. At first, I thought they wanted to offer condolences, but then they told me how highly Fillian had thought of me and how he'd always hoped I'd join the League."

Bryanna's eyes bulged. "Wait, Fillian knew about the League?"

"Oh, more than knew," said Obelia with a hint of bitterness. "He was one of them. I should've guessed, really. He was always disappearing for days or weeks on end and returning with injuries he refused to explain."

Obelia was quiet for a moment, twiddling the ornate ring on the fourth digit of her left hand. "The people who approached me had the gall to call it an honor to be asked to join the League. But I didn't see it that way. As far as I was concerned, the League was the reason Fillian had been killed. So I set off on my own instead. They said Fillian had wanted me to join the ranks of those trying to end the Brotherhood, so that was exactly what I did."

Bryanna leaned forward. "Where did you go?"

"To Mount Ygerna, where Fillian's body had been found. One of Fillian's closest friends, a faoladh named Alec Marrock, came with me. For two years, we traveled around Otherworld, disguised as nomads, tracking the Brotherhood of Sìorraidh. Then one day, their trail disappeared, and we realized we were no longer tracking them—they were tracking us."

Bryanna's breath hitched. "They were *what*?"

"I can hardly believe I'm still here when I think back to those days. Alec thought our best chance was to disappear. He knew a place where we'd be safe. But I knew that if I went with him, the Brotherhood would seek my family to draw me out. All four of your brothers had been born by then, and I couldn't have their lives on my conscience. So I led the Brotherhood as far from Castlereagh as I could and prepared to meet them on my own.

"I had everything planned. I hid in an alleyway, and when the man who'd been compromised sauntered out of the local tavern, I was ready. I had my blade at his throat, poised to end his life. But before I could, I was teleported away."

Bryanna gasped. "*Teleported?*"

Obelia nodded. "By an ovate named Andraste Oona. She told me she'd seen me in one of her visions, fighting in the final battle against the Brotherhood, and that I'd have a pivotal role to play one day. If she hadn't intervened that night, it probably would've led to my demise. I wasn't happy about it at the time, I can tell you. But she offered to protect our family and teach me things I couldn't learn anywhere else. Things I'd need if I wanted a fighting chance against the Brotherhood."

"She helped you become a mage, didn't she?" Bryanna asked.

Obelia nodded. "Eventually, I decided to rejoin society. I needed a new purpose, a new life that would fulfill me in a way I hadn't felt fulfilled since losing Fillian. I've been at the Sheidlow Tower, running my sanctuary, ever since."

Bryanna sat back in her wing chair, unable to take her eyes

off her aunt. She'd always wondered why her aunt hadn't moved back to Castlereagh after she'd resurfaced from her failed quest. Though she supposed she wouldn't have, either, now that she knew what she did. The loss of her betrothed, of not being able to avenge him, would've made it impossible for her aunt to resume her life back home.

"Did the Brotherhood ever track you after that night?" she asked after a moment.

"No. I suppose they felt I was no longer a threat to them ... though I'm not so sure that's the case anymore."

A chill Bryanna couldn't explain slid down her spine.

Somehow, she didn't think so either.

TWELVE

"I don't understand why you won't send Iodhna somewhere else," Bryanna grumbled a week later as she and her aunt neared the Sheidlow Ridge Square, each lugging a hefty bundle of wheat over their shoulders. "Just this morning, I overheard her try to convince Cayde that it's in his nature to stalk and lure his prey, to give in to his natural predator instincts. It's like she wants him to become a monster."

Obelia sighed, shielding her eyes from the brilliant summer sunlight beating down on them. "You know why I can't send her away. I'm bound by the land- and water-dweller statutory agreement to keep her here."

"Even though she's so dangerous?" Bryanna pressed. "I still think she's the one who poisoned me a few weeks ago—"

"We've been through this already. Iodhna couldn't have snuck into your chambers without our knowledge. I have Tyffin watching her every move. And when did you hear her speaking with Cayde?"

"This morning."

Her aunt had finally set more time aside to help her delve

into ancient magic, as well as practice the surveillance spell. The latter had proved most difficult, though that might've been because they were in an eleven-story building teeming with inhabitants. She didn't know how Obelia remained under it consistently when *she* couldn't last a few minutes without getting migraines.

The spell did come with its advantages, though.

She'd been using it to spy on Iodhna, mostly because she was hoping to catch her mid-premonition again.

"I don't trust her," Bryanna said, shifting the weight of the bundle on her shoulder. "Why did you even agree to take her in?"

Obelia sighed. "You haven't been talking to Weylin, have you? He's been badgering me about the same thing for weeks now."

"Well, when it comes to Iodhna, he's not wrong," said Bryanna, coming to his defense. "If we're not careful, she'll turn him against all of us."

"Cayde's too clever to let that happen," Obelia said, her expression darkening with irritation. "Now, tell me how are those dream-weaver blocking spells going?"

Bryanna pursed her lips. She did *not* want to stop talking about Iodhna. Not until she could make her aunt see sense so she'd hand the morgen back to the authorities. "Fine."

They walked the rest of the way in silence.

When they reached the square, it was buzzing with villagers wending their way through a harvest market. Bryanna would've loved to inspect some of the stalls—she needed to replenish what had been stolen from her—but her bundle kept her from doing so. Instead, she followed her aunt to the other side of the square and onto a narrow lane lined with clusters of cruck-framed houses, ignoring the disdainful looks the villagers sent their way.

The watermill was situated at the end of the lane, its front lawn crowded by wagons crammed with large sacks of flour. Farmers and harvest hands bustled about, shouting orders at one another as they carried bundles of wheat over to the side of the building.

Inside, the deafening sound of grinding stones and coursing torrents of water was inescapable, like being stuck behind a cascading waterfall. A handful of villagers sat on rickety chairs, waiting for their sacks of freshly ground flour. When they saw Obelia and Bryanna, their chary eyes followed them all the way to the counter, where the miller, a stout, graying man with an overgrown chin and thick mane of hair, looked at their bundles.

"Not even worth putting through the mill fer the flour yeh'll get from it," he grunted, but motioned for his assistant nonetheless, who put their wheat into a deep tub and carried it away.

"Will it be long?" asked Obelia.

"Yeh picked yerself the wrong morn, Mistress Nicholls. I have at least an hour's worth of orders before yers."

Obelia rolled her eyes. "You always do. Come, Bryanna."

They chose seats at the very back of the dim, dank waiting area so the others couldn't stare at them. But every time Bryanna looked up, at least three villagers were feigning cricked necks so they could glare their way.

Obelia took out a leather binder from her satchel and started calculating finances, checking her gold pocket watch every few minutes. Bryanna wasn't sure why. If anything happened while they were gone, Tyffin would've informed Obelia immediately through their telepathic link.

"I'll be right back," said Obelia eventually, snapping her pocket watch shut.

Bryanna nodded, glaring daggers at the miller. She'd watched villagers who'd placed their orders after them get called up to collect their flour. Each time it happened, he'd look in their direction and smirk. Bryanna had half a mind to storm up to him and demand their wheat back.

She sat up, eager to watch her aunt give the miller the verbal dressing down he deserved. But Obelia didn't stop at his counter. She strode past it and walked out the side door.

Five minutes passed without Obelia returning.

Then ten.

Bryanna chewed on her bottom lip, ignoring the remaining villagers glowering at her. Why wasn't her aunt back yet? Surely it didn't take that long to use the privy?

Darker thoughts slithered into her mind. What if her aunt was lying helpless on the floor, basilisk venom swelling her throat, the way Bryanna had been less than a moon cycle ago? Or if whoever had poisoned her had come for her aunt …

She was out of her seat before she could finish the thought. Several villagers tutted at her abrupt departure, but she paid them no mind, rushing out the side door and back out into the dry heat. She sprinted up the hilltop, where the public privy stood, her heart heavy with dread, but halfway there, she spotted her aunt some distance from it, talking to a tall, broad-shouldered man near the forest's edge. Even from her distance, she could see he was heavily armed, with daggers strapped to the holster at his waist and a bow slung over his shoulder.

They exchanged a few more low words before he glanced around furtively and handed Obelia a small package. His gaze stalled when he caught sight of Bryanna, recognition flickering across his face. Then he looked back at her aunt, muttering something to her before stepping into the shadows of the trees and out of sight.

"Who was that?" Bryanna asked when Obelia joined her, her gaze lingering on the spot where the man had disappeared. "And what did he give you?"

"Always eavesdropping, you are," her aunt muttered. "Let's just say it's something that I can't get easily through the mainstream channels."

"Like … something illegal?"

"If I told you it would help Elgar's situation, would it matter?" her aunt returned, tugging her around and back toward the watermill.

"I suppose not," Bryanna admitted quietly.

They stepped back inside to find their meager sack of flour waiting for them.

The miller cleared his throat. "That'll be twenty shillings, Mistress Nicholls."

Bryanna's whole body vibrated with outrage. His asking price was more than twice that of the villagers who'd hauled several large sacks out to their wagons.

"You know, Aunt Obelia," she said, fighting to keep her voice from quivering as Obelia paid him, "my father has invented a mill that's becoming quite popular in Castlereagh. It can fit into the corner of any barn and grind wheat into flour within minutes. By this time next year, watermills will be quite obsolete, even in remote little villages like Sheidlow Ridge."

Obelia's lip twitched. She knew very well that her father had never invented such a thing. "Isn't the price of one of these devices the same as a single visit to the watermill?"

"Only because it's so new to the market. Soon, even the poorest villagers will be able to afford one."

The miller blanched.

***

Bryanna and Obelia barely made it onto the dirt road back to Sheidlow Square before bursting into peals of laughter.

"Did you see his face?" Bryanna gasped, tears running down her cheeks. "He looked like he was going to wet himself."

They doubled over, clutching their sides. Bryanna couldn't remember the last time she'd laughed so hard. She supposed she shouldn't have found their little jest so amusing, but the miller had really brought it on himself, keeping them waiting so long and overcharging them to boot.

The market stalls had closed for the day by the time they reached the square. Tarps covered the merchandise, keeping the sun and pickpockets away while the merchants enjoyed some refreshments before they packed up and rode out to the next town. Bryanna had to curb her disappointment. With the wheat out of her hands, she'd been hoping to peruse the stall keeper's wares.

"Obelia!" came a shout from the other side of the square.

Deagon was waving at them, standing under The Doherty Bank's eave.

Obelia made for him at once. "What are you doing here, Deagon?"

Deagon's eyes were feverish with delight and exhaustion. "I have a son!" he blurted, and his entire face lit up.

Obelia clapped a hand to her mouth. "But that's wonderful news."

"Congratulations," said Bryanna, grinning. "When was he born?"

Deagon consulted his gold pocket watch with shaky fingers. "Three hours and twenty-seven minutes ago. We called him Reith. Yeh have ter come past before yeh head back ter the tower."

"Oh, why not?" said Obelia with a smile. "We've got some time."

The Brodericks' cottage was several paddocks away from the Sheidlow Ruins. It was a small, quaint house with a little vegetable patch to the side, a hen pen, and a small field of wheat. Deagon opened his front door and ushered them into a narrow, oil-lamp-lit hallway. Four tiny quarters divided the house—two bedchambers, a privy, and a kitchen. Its entirety could've fit in Bryanna's bedchamber back in Castlereagh.

"Vallie?" Deagon called, leading them toward the kitchen. "I know the midwife said Reith is a healthy li'l boy, but I've brought us the greatest healer in Otherworld fer a second opinion."

Valentine glanced over from the frayed couch she was half-sitting, half-lying on, looking tired but happy. "Obelia, Bryanna," she said warmly. "Come in, come in."

Bryanna stepped into the kitchen and almost lost her footing. Weylin stood by the small, round dining table, holding a tiny baby against his chest. She hadn't been able to picture him with a child, yet as she watched him tapping the back of the Brodericks' newborn, something in her chest tightened.

"Oh, Bryanna, look," Obelia said breathlessly beside her. "Isn't he the sweetest thing?"

It took Bryanna a moment to realize her aunt was talking about Reith and not Weylin. "Yes," she replied, her voice raspy as she forced her focus to the infant. "He's adorable."

"You can hold him if you want," Valentine offered, her eyes twinkling. "Let Bryanna hold him, Weylin."

Weylin tensed, holding the baby closer. For a second, Bryanna thought he was going to refuse. But then he walked over and tentatively lowered Reith into her arms.

"You need to support his head," he said gruffly.

"I know." Bryanna threaded her arms under Reith's blue one-piece. "I have two little nephews back home."

Still, Weylin didn't let him go straight away. Bryanna glanced over at him hesitantly and caught the raw pain and longing cross his face, as though it weren't the Brodericks' newborn between them, but his own infant child.

"I've got him," Bryanna said softly.

They stood awkwardly, Bryanna's face flaming, distinctly aware of the five pairs of eyes on them and the hard ridges of Weylin's torso pressed against her arms. Finally, he patted Reith's head and disentangled himself.

Reith opened his small, watery brown eyes and looked up at Bryanna. He seemed to feel she was safe enough, lowered his lids, and fell fast asleep, his tiny lips puckered in a little *O*.

While Deagon bustled about the old-fashioned hearth, making tea, Obelia performed a range of spells on Reith before confirming his clean bill of health. By then, a plate of fresh scones had been served, and they whiled away the time chatting about the new member of the Broderick family and the remarkable feats he'd achieved in his short few hours of life.

"We'd best be off," Obelia announced eventually. "I don't want to leave my boarders too much longer, in case they get into a new casket of mead."

"That, and we shouldn't be keeping a certain boarder unattended much longer," Weylin said with a cool note no one could miss.

The look Obelia threw him was equally cool. "Let's go."

They headed off, Obelia and Weylin feigning interest in the hens waddling about the Brodericks' yard so they didn't have to talk to each other. Bryanna glanced between them, recalling Obelia's admission about Weylin's disapproval over Iodhna's continued stay.

She searched for something to say to defuse their tension, but idle chatter had never been one of her strong suits.

They were halfway to the tower when a strange shadow of pain flashed in Bryanna's limbs. She stopped abruptly, twisting in the direction of the trees to their right as the sensation faded.

"What is it?" Weylin asked.

Bryanna wasn't sure how, but every fiber of her being told her that whatever she'd sensed, it had come from deeper in the woods. "I think there's something in the trees."

"Stay here," Weylin ordered.

Before Obelia or Bryanna could object, he bounded off into the trees.

"Weylin!" Bryanna rushed after him. She couldn't leave him in the forest on his own, especially when she knew the dangers that lurked there, out of sight.

Dangers like the green-blooded creature who'd attacked her the first night she'd arrived.

"Bryanna, wait!" Obelia shouted behind her.

But Bryanna kept moving, jumping over low ferns and bristly bushes, avoiding the gigantic, moss-covered trees in her bid to keep up with Weylin. He was much faster than her, though, and before long, she was relying on the crunching of his footfalls to judge which direction he was moving in. But soon, those faded too, absorbed by the dense trees, bushes, and forest ferns.

She stopped short, her breaths coming in quick, shallow gasps.

There was something exceedingly strange about the copse of trees she was in. As she'd been running, the natural sounds surrounding her had been like a companion, humming around her. But those sounds had ceased, leaving an ominous void in their wake.

Anxiety tugged at her stomach as she felt in her pockets for the dragon-venom daggers before remembering her aunt had confiscated them. Something had seized the attention of the other woodland creatures. She scanned the trees, half expecting to sense the dark, unctuous presence she'd felt the night the green-blooded creature had tried to abduct her.

But it wasn't there.

Before she could reach for her magic, a hand clamped over her mouth, pulling her backward.

Bryanna's stomach jerked involuntarily as her spine collided with a hard, solid frame. She opened her mouth, a mangled scream halfway up her throat, but then the smell of pine infiltrated her nostrils.

"Shhh," Weylin hissed against her ear, the heat of his breath sending goose bumps over her skin.

From around the trunk came the sound of hooves beating on the leaf-scattered ground. Whatever was on the other side of the tree was massive.

She took a deep breath, trying to calm her frayed nerves. If it was the green-blooded creature on the other side of the trees, they needed to get away from it. Even injured, it would be able to ensnare their minds, and if it did, they'd both be dead—

But then a frustrated, pain-filled neigh reached her.

Bryanna stiffened. Whatever was on the other side of the trees was definitely *not* the green-blooded creature.

She made to peek around the tree trunk, but Weylin snatched her back.

"Don't," he whispered, his voice a low rasp against her ear.

"Whatever is there needs our help," she returned, pulling herself free of his grip.

She peered around the trunk, her breath hitching as she caught sight of the pure-white mane and smooth silver horn protruding from the large equine figure's forehead.

It was the same unicorn they'd seen weeks back by the pond at the Sheidlow Tower. His front leg was twice the size of the others. Dried blood caked his flanks, some of it a deep red, but some ... some was dark green.

The same color as the blood that had been on her dagger the night she'd stabbed the creature in the forest.

Bryanna made for the unicorn. She'd never been able to stay away from a creature in need.

"Ms. Nicholls, what are you doing?" Weylin growled, grabbing her arm and stopping her from getting any closer. "He could seriously injure you."

"I'll be fine."

Weylin snorted. "I'm sure that's what Bain thought before he approached *his* unicorn. Look what happened to him."

"I have to help him," Bryanna said as the unicorn's jet-black eyes fastened on her. Just like the first time, the strangest sensation passed over her as their gazes met, as though a ghost had stepped through her.

Weylin muttered an oath and released her. "If you get hurt …"

"I won't."

He followed her as she took slow, measured steps toward the unicorn. The creature remained still, waiting for her to approach him before leaning forward and allowing Bryanna to run her fingers through his soft, silky mane.

"I'm going to heal you," Bryanna whispered, stroking the bridge of his nose.

"I didn't know you were a healer," Weylin grumbled.

Bryanna ignored him. She'd never healed a unicorn before, though she'd assisted her father's steed master when their Tuatha steeds sustained injuries in the past. How different could healing him be?

She crouched, placing her hand lightly on the unicorn's injured leg. Closing her eyes, she let her magic pool to the surface, conjuring a perfunctory healing spell to assess the extent of his injuries. She detected several areas that needed attention, the worst being the cannon bone in his front leg. It had been shattered in a few places, likely days before, judging by the swelling around it.

She prioritized the injured front leg first, reducing the swelling and inflammation. It needed to go down before she could reset the bone. Once she was done, she maneuvered the fragments back into place and melded them together, reinforcing them so they wouldn't splinter once he put weight on his leg.

Then she moved to the gashes on his flanks, weaving his skin back together. As she worked, she couldn't help but wonder how he'd sustained his injuries. Unicorns were one of the fastest creatures in Otherworld. It was rare for them to get into a skirmish, and when they did, they were rarely beaten.

It took several more minutes before Bryanna finished and stepped away, light-headed from the amount of magic she'd expelled. The unicorn lowered his leg gingerly, pawing at the ground before putting his full weight on it. Then, he let out a soft neigh and trotted over to the bush behind them, returning with one of her old, spare pillowcases secured between his teeth.

Bryanna's jaw dropped. How had he gotten hold of it?

Had he wrestled it from the green-blooded creature who'd tried to kidnap her? But if that was the case, how had it surpassed her aunt's sensors and gotten into her chambers to steal her things?

Taking the pillowcase from him, she drew it open, her hands still numb from shock. The phials of potions and poisons that had been taken from her bedchamber were gone. All that remained were a few shards of glass, fused together by dried potion remnants.

"What's in there?" Weylin asked, leaning forward to peer over her shoulder.

Bryanna bunched it shut before he could see what was inside. She could just imagine how he'd react if he knew she'd brought the very substance that had been used to poison her into the tower.

"Thank you," she said softly to the unicorn.

The being touched his horn to Bryanna's forehead gently, gave one final soft neigh, and galloped back into the encroaching trees.

"Well," said Weylin, his gaze fixed on the retreating unicorn, "perhaps you aren't completely useless, Ms. Nicholls."

Bryanna had to fight a smile. "If I didn't know better, Mr. Conveil, I'd think you'd just paid me a compliment."

Weylin smirked, his gaze catching hers. "Let's not get carried away."

For a moment, neither of them could look away. It was as though some greater force was keeping their gazes locked. An overwhelming thrill bloomed in the pit of Bryanna's stomach, combined with a needling pull she'd never felt before.

Her gaze lowered to his lips, wondering if they'd feel as warm and soft as they looked. The thought sent a wave of anticipation and excitement coursing through her.

Weylin drew closer, his eyes darkening to a deep shade of blue that reminded her of the ocean before a storm. The kind she could easily get swept away in and not care if she ever surfaced. His hand came up, but before he could touch her, Obelia rushed into the clearing.

Weylin stepped back, breaking the inexplicable hold that had come over them, his brows furrowing as though whatever had passed between them had caught him as off guard as it had Bryanna.

"The two of you—and I—are going—to have words—running off like that," Obelia puffed, bending at the waist and wheezing. "The second—I get—my breath—back."

THIRTEEN

Bryanna had a dream that night. She was dressed in an ivory gown made of pearls and fine silk that fell in soft, luscious folds, its train trailing behind her. The traditional bridal Ogham symbols of prosperity and fertility were embroidered along the dress, a smooth, shiny porcelain that shimmered as it caught the sunlight.

She walked down the ironstone path toward Weylin, who stood at the landing of the Sheidlow Tower's portico, surrounded by white lilies. He was dressed in black patterned trousers and a matching tailcoat. A polished, bejeweled sword gleamed in a scabbard at his side. In his hand was a dark top hat, which he was twiddling between his fingers.

Bryanna's heart swelled with an emotion she couldn't quite understand. She picked up her pace, eager to reach him. But as she neared, he began to change. His hair darkened to midnight black, the stubble that usually dusted his face turned into a short, freshly shaven beard, and his wide shoulders rounded and narrowed until he was no longer Weylin, but Fillian Conveil.

He descended the steps with a confident gait and held out

his hand to Obelia, who'd been sitting in the front row. Together, they strode off toward the trees. At the edge of the forest, Fillian stopped and dropped a long, lingering kiss on Obelia's lips before walking down the ironstone path and out of sight.

Obelia's fingers trailed over her mouth, tracing where his lips had met hers. Turmoil darkened her slate-gray eyes. She stared at the spot where Fillian had disappeared, uncertainty clouding her face as if she didn't know whether to follow her lost lover or return to the Sheidlow Tower.

"Bryanna," an urgent voice hissed in her ear, waking her before she could see what her aunt chose.

Bryanna squinted up at the bright oil lamp hovering above her face, all vestiges of sleep falling away as her eyes adjusted to its soft flame. Obelia loomed over her, still dressed in the same blouse and long, navy skirt she'd worn that evening.

"Aunt Obelia?" she rasped, sitting up.

Disastrous scenarios chased each other in Bryanna's sleep-addled mind, each more dire than the last. Had one of the boarders been poisoned? Or had Elgar suffered another episode? Obelia had only told her last night that he was getting so strong, he'd be able to leave his chambers every once in a while soon.

"I need you to come downstairs," Obelia whispered. "There are people who want to see you."

Bryanna pushed her counterpane aside and stumbled to her feet. "Who'd want to see me right now?"

She had a few acquaintances back in Castlereagh, but none who'd travel to Sheidlow Ridge to visit her in the middle of the night.

"Hurry, please," was her aunt's only reply. She took the oil lamp and left Bryanna to change out of her nightgown in the dark.

Bryanna pulled on the fitted button-down shirt, breeches, and boots she'd worn the night before, stumbling in the pale light emanating from the full moon outside her window.

Once she was ready, they headed downstairs. But instead of leading her toward the visitors' parlor, Obelia walked to the built-in window seat and pulled off the cushions one by one, revealing a set of concealment Ogham symbols carved into the oak timber.

Bryanna watched on, puzzled, as Obelia pressed her palm to each one in turn, chanting under her breath until the symbols flickered and vanished. As the window seat melted away, she found herself staring at a narrow stone staircase.

Obelia picked up the oil lamp and held it aloft. "Follow me."

"Wait," Bryanna whispered, pulling at her aunt's sleeve. "What's going on, Aunt Obelia?"

But Obelia ignored her and started down the narrow, uneven, winding steps. Bryanna sighed and followed.

At the base of the steps was a vast, high-ceilinged underground cellar. Sconces burned in every corner, illuminating stone walls lined with crooked shelves weighed down by ancient tomes and old, bloodstained, dented weapons, arranged in a way that reminded Bryanna of precious artifacts encased behind glass in museums.

In the center of the cellar was a sphere-shaped sparring area with a lengthy table at the far end, occupied by five bleary-eyed individuals. On the left were a grouchy-looking elf and an elderly sidhe who didn't look like she'd smiled in a long time. They'd been exchanging hushed words, but stopped at the sight of Bryanna. Beside them sat a middle-aged, goat-like being with long antlers protruding from his temples—a *bocanach*.

The tall, stocky man next to the latter rose as Bryanna and Obelia neared them. Bryanna almost tripped over her feet. He was the man who'd been outside the watermill with her aunt.

"I've seen you before—" she started, but then caught sight of the stern, stringy-haired older woman at the end of the table. "Lady Auberagh?" she spluttered, gawping at her old mentor. "What are you doing here?"

"Just because most eighty-year-old codgers think they're too old to travel doesn't mean I believe such nonsense," said Lady Auberagh in her customary brisk tone. "It's nice of you to finally get here. I see your habit of keeping people waiting hasn't changed."

"Leave the girl be," said the tall, stocky man, adjusting the tweed flat cap on his head. He walked over to Bryanna and shook her hand. "I'm Alec Marrock, Ms. Nicholls. We've been wanting to meet you for some time."

"Alec?" Bryanna glanced at Obelia as she recognized the name. "Are you the one who left Castlereagh with my aunt?"

Alec's smile faltered, something unreadable crossing his face as his gaze darted to Obelia briefly. "Heard of me, have you?"

"Another time, Alec," Lady Auberagh cut in. "We didn't drag our young sorceress out of bed to massage your ego. Now, girl, surely you know why we're here?"

Bryanna shook her head, at a complete loss for their impromptu appearance.

Lady Auberagh clucked her tongue. "We're here on behalf of the Brithlean League, aren't we?"

Bryanna might've thought her old mentor was jesting, except she'd never heard her jest in her life. "But ... you can't be ..." There was no way Lady Auberagh, of all people, was a member of the Brithlean League. Her old mentor couldn't bear mention of the Brotherhood of Sìorraidh without flinching.

"It's true, Bryanna," said Obelia gently. "We're all with the League."

Bryanna rounded on her aunt, stunned. "I don't

understand. You said you hadn't joined the League when they approached you."

"I hadn't," said Obelia. "I joined a few years later."

"The League has been watching you for years," Lady Auberagh told Bryanna. "Particularly when we realized how serious you were about your vendetta against the Brotherhood. Why do you think I trained you?"

Bryanna stared at Lady Auberagh. "But then ... why wasn't I inducted years ago?"

"We don't just induct people into the Brithlean League because they want to bring about the Brotherhood of Sìorraidh's end, girl. Our selections follow more rigid measures. Besides," she added, a shadow of discomfort crossing her features, "several members opposed your induction."

Bryanna's hands curled into fists at her sides. "I'm the youngest sorceress in our century," she said, an edge in her voice. "Why would anyone oppose me? I'm just as dedicated to ending the Brotherhood as anyone else in your League, if not more so."

"That's what we said," Obelia assured her. "And after much deliberation, the League has decided to offer you initiation. If you're willing to join."

"Of course she is," Lady Auberagh said, as though joining the League didn't warrant thinking about. "Tell her about the trial, Alec."

"Think of it as a rite of passage," Alec said, stepping forward. "Everyone needs to pass in order to be inducted."

"And if I fail?" Bryanna asked, though she was pretty sure she already knew the answer.

"You'll lose all recollection of being here."

Dread pooled in Bryanna's stomach. She couldn't afford to forget being there. Not when the Brithlean League was everything she'd been hoping to find since embarking on her quest. They could answer questions she hadn't been able to get any other way.

"We've been debating what we wanted to see from you," Alec continued. "We know you have an aptitude for creating unique weaponry, if the items your aunt brought down from your bedchamber a few weeks ago are any indication."

Bryanna's gaze snapped to her aunt, her mouth agape. She thought she'd gotten rid of them.

"But we also know your magic is very powerful for someone your age, so it's been decided that your trial will focus on that."

"And ... what would you need me to do?" Bryanna asked. She hoped the trial wouldn't be anything like the ones undertaken in folktales. Those usually involved difficult tests that relied on more than skill to pass.

"To prove your abilities by incapacitating one of our members."

Bryanna didn't like the sound of that. She'd never been comfortable using magic against another being.

"Who would I need to combat?" she asked, glancing at Obelia and Lady Auberagh. If he told her she'd have to duel either of them, she didn't think she'd be able to go through with the trial. Not when using magic against either of them went against her every instinct.

Alec ran a hand through his long, hazel hair, tying it back at his nape. "Me."

Bryanna almost keeled over. Alec was twice her size and one of the burliest men she'd ever seen. All it would take was his fist to touch her, and they'd be carting her to the nearest healer hospital.

If she didn't know better, she might've thought her trial was being set at a much more rigorous caliber, to ensure she wouldn't pass.

Bryanna gritted her teeth. If that were the case, they'd be

in for a very unpleasant surprise. It wasn't in her nature to back down from anything thrown her way. Not when the cost was losing information she was willing to sacrifice her life for.

"When would this trial take place?" she asked, lifting her chin.

"Now, of course," said Lady Auberagh briskly. "The Brithlean League needs to see that you can defend yourself at a moment's notice."

Bryanna balked. They wouldn't give her time to prepare?

She glanced at the remaining League members still seated at the table. Only the middle-aged bocanach smiled back. The elf and sidhe drummed their fingers against the wooden surface, checking the time on the pocket watch beside them.

Obelia squeezed her shoulder. "You'll do fine. Just pretend you're facing that hobgoblin in your cellar again."

Bryanna didn't miss the looks of unease she and Lady Auberagh exchanged as they joined the others at the long table. It wasn't the sign of confidence she'd hoped to glean from them.

Alec cleared his throat, drawing her attention back to him. "Initiates may select a weapon of choice, if they wish." He inclined his head towards the armory.

Bryanna hesitated. She'd never been too skilled with weapons. Her brothers tried teaching her when she was younger, but it'd never been one of her favorite pastimes. Perhaps because they used to double over laughing every time she lost her footing.

"What will you be using?" she asked.

Alec smiled crookedly. "I won't be needing a physical weapon."

Bryanna's gaze fell on his enormous biceps, evident despite his loose white shirt. "Right."

She glanced at the weapons once more. How long had it been since she'd used a bow and arrow? Three years?

She frowned at the other weapons, but there was nothing there that she'd be able to wield adequately, especially when she wouldn't be given time to practice. There was only one thing she could confidently rely on, and it wasn't anything being stored in the armory. She pulled on her magic, letting it hum around her.

"I won't be needing a physical weapon either," she said.

Alec's lips tugged up. In humor or respect, Bryanna wasn't sure.

He led her to the center of the sparring ground, directly in front of the Brithlean League members. Bryanna didn't look in their direction. She needed to concentrate on Alec and forget about them if she was going to stand a chance of passing the trial.

"Initiates make the first move," said Alec, crouching low like a wolf. "Don't hold back, Ms. Nicholls."

Bryanna swallowed hard, trying to silence the little voice in her head telling her that beating Alec was impossible. That the Brithlean League chose him on purpose, to make sure she didn't join their ranks.

For several tense seconds, they stared at each other, Alec's impenetrable gaze taking in her every move. Bryanna couldn't sense any magic radiating from him, yet she got the impression he wasn't the least bit concerned about facing a magic-weaver. It made her wonder how he was going to defend himself.

She supposed she was about to find out. Magic tingled at her fingertips, as eager for the trial to be over as she was. The sooner she passed, the sooner she could learn everything she needed to defeat the Brotherhood of Sìorraidh. With that driving thought in mind, she raised her hand, mustered up her courage, and sent a gust of hurricane wind at Alec.

An ordinary man might've tumbled to the floor with the force of her spell, but Alec moved fast, the same way Weylin had the night she'd thrown him into the air. He landed on his feet, a grin splitting across his lips.

His face elongated into lupine features, hair sprouting from his every pore as his hands curved into claw-like fists. Bryanna took several hasty steps back, an intense cold sweeping over her.

How had she forgotten her aunt telling her that he was a *faoladh*?

Her mind raced. How in all of Castlereagh was she supposed to get the upper hand against Alec? She wouldn't stand a chance against him in physical combat. Not with his strength and agility.

Bryanna barely had time to send a second volley in Alec's direction as he sprang for her in one swift, fluid movement. She threw a third and fourth volley in quick succession, keeping him at bay while she tried to figure out how to incapacitate him.

She searched the area around them frantically, her heart pounding against her ears, desperate for something she could use against him. Her gaze fell on the short fence surrounding the sparring area, and she raised her hands, letting her magic pour out of her palms, and uprooted a section from the ground, pitching it straight at Alec.

His hands came up instinctively, catching the fence easily.

Bryanna had been expecting him to, though. She pulled on a little more magic and channeled it into the fence, increasing its weight until Alec's knees buckled under its bulk and the fence fell over him, pinning him to the ground.

Bryanna bolted for the armory. She needed something stronger to keep him restrained. The fence wouldn't keep him down for long. Perhaps there'd be some chains she could wrap around him—

Clang.

Bryanna spun as the fence clattered to the floor. Another volley tingled at her fingertips as Alec launched himself at her, but he was too close. Thinking fast, she hurled the volley at the loose ground between them.

There was a resounding *crack* as the compressed dirt floor exploded, filling the cellar with a thick cloud of dust and debris.

Alec skidded to a halt, coughing and gasping for air. Unlike her, he hadn't squeezed his eyes shut or taken a deep breath before the dust had enveloped them, leaving him at the mercy of the minute, grainy dirt particles that had been kicked up into the air.

Bryanna moved, taking advantage of Alec's incapacitated state by putting some much-needed distance between them. She wasn't sure how much time it would take for Alec to recover, though she didn't think it would take long. Already, the dust was settling, reinstating the visibility she'd sent asunder. She scrambled for the armory once more, but before she'd taken more than a few paces, Alec slammed into her, sending them both crashing to the ground. His maw was so close, Bryanna could feel the heat of his breath on her cheek.

A cold wave of panic broke over her. Was this how she would be defeated?

No.

Bryanna reared her head back, the way she'd seen her brothers do when they wrestled each other on the drawing chamber rug, and with all the force she could muster, sent her forehead crashing into Alec's jaw. Pain erupted around her skull, as though she'd hit it against a brick wall.

Alec's head whipped back with a muffled yip. He let her go, his clawed hands clapping over his mouth. A few drops of blood landed on Bryanna's face, but she wiped them away and sent a new volley into Alec, launching him off her. Before he could regroup, she threw herself onto him, wrapped her arms around his neck, and squeezed, cutting off his air supply.

Alec growled and tried to wrench free, but Bryanna tightened her grip, her muscles burning from the strain of keeping her hold. His clawed fingers dug into her skin, but she sent a burst of magic into his arm, forcing his grip to loosen.

With a frustrated yip, he slumped forward. Beneath her hands, his body shrank, the thick, coarse hair vanishing until he'd completely shed his faoladh skin.

Bryanna's hold slackened, hesitation creeping in now that he'd shifted back to his human form.

But it was the wrong thing to do.

Sensing her weakness, Alec flipped, taking her with him. Bryanna hit the floor hard, the impact knocking the air from her lungs. Alec's substantial weight landed on top of her once more. Heaving for breath, Bryanna searched for something, *anything*, to keep him from knocking her unconscious or however they disqualified those who failed the trial.

Her eyes fell on the flaming chandelier above them. Before she could lose her nerve, she raised her hand, unleashing a severing spell at the chain keeping the chandelier secured.

It snapped, sending the imposing light fixture straight for them.

Gasps filled the cellar as the Brithlean League members sprang out of their chairs. Alec reacted at once, jumping to his haunches to catch the chandelier, just as Bryanna knew he would.

She dived, narrowly missing the chandelier as it crashed to the ground, trapping Alec beneath it in the same way the fence had. Unlike the fence, though, the chandelier's frame was white-hot, thanks to its brightly burning sconces.

"Yield!" Alec cried.

Obelia's magic imbued the air at once, lifting the chandelier off him.

Bryanna staggered back, her chest heaving as a deep-seated euphoria enveloped her. Pain that she hadn't registered when she'd been deep in the throes of her fight with Alec came crashing down on her with a vengeance, but it paled into insignificance as relief and exhilaration engulfed her.

Behind her, the table burst into applause. Lady Auberagh clapped the loudest, beaming with pride.

Bryanna leaned forward, resting her hands on her knees, letting out a shaky, disbelieving laugh.

She'd done it.

She'd passed the trial.

She was a member of the Brithlean League.

CHAPTER

FOURTEEN

Bryanna had barely caught her breath when the bocanach joined her side, a friendly grin lighting his features. "Congratulations, Ms. Nicholls," he said, patting her shoulder. "It's been a while since I've been left on the edge of my seat from witnessing a trial."

Bryanna stood up straighter, despite her aching muscles. "Thank you."

"Allow me to formally introduce myself, Ms. Nicholls—"

"Bryanna, please," Bryanna interjected.

"I'm Eremon, one of the Brithlean League's scouts. You won't see me in Sheidlow Ridge a lot, but I couldn't miss witnessing your induction. I was really rooting for you to win, if only to knock Alec down a peg or two."

Alec rolled his eyes. "Thanks, Eremon."

"I have to say, I didn't expect a young lady of your social standing to wrestle like a street urchin," he continued as Obelia joined them, beaming.

"Aye, neither did I," Alec quipped, his fingers tracing the edge of his mouth, where his lip had split.

"Honestly, Alec, I think you critically underestimated my niece," Obelia chided, raising a hand and healing the welts on his arms.

Alec's lips curled in a wry expression. "I might've done."

"Perhaps now *certain* members will refrain from interfering where our young sorceress is concerned," Lady Auberagh said, directing a disapproving glare at the other panel members, who were gathering their belongings.

Bryanna couldn't help but notice that they looked rather grim as they headed toward a bookcase that had been pushed away from the cellar's stone wall, revealing a hidden passage.

"Don't pay them any mind, Ms. Nicholls," the bocanach said, following her line of vision. "They will come around."

"Some sooner than others," Alec muttered.

"Why do so many oppose my induction?" Bryanna asked. She'd more than proved she was worthy of being counted as one of their own by beating Alec against the odds.

"That doesn't matter anymore," said Lady Auberagh, though she continued to glare at the bookshelf the others had retreated behind. "All that matters is that you passed and showed them all how wrong they were to doubt you. You should be proud. We haven't had many recruits of your age pass the trial. And those who did ought to be reminded of just how difficult going through one is," she added with a piercing look in Alec's direction.

"I'm sure they will see just how capable our young sorceress is soon enough, Lady Auberagh," Alec muttered.

"I'd best be off," Eremon said with a wink in Bryanna's direction. "It's a pleasure to have you among us, Ms. Nich— Bryanna."

"Thanks, Eremon."

While Obelia and Alec walked the bocanach to the secret

exit, Bryanna turned to Lady Auberagh. "I still can't believe you didn't tell me you were in the League," she said quietly, staring down at her shorter mentor. "We worked together for *years*."

"I couldn't," Lady Auberagh maintained. "If anyone got wind that I'd told you, they would've kicked me out of the League and taken all recollection of my being part of it to boot. Who would've put your name forward then, hmm?"

Bryanna crossed her arms, wincing as pain shot through her triceps. She could feel a lump forming already. She must've sustained the injury when Alec had thrown her to the ground, right as he'd been poised to end her hopes of induction.

"You still could've told me *something*," she muttered. "I almost wasn't prepared for the trial tonight."

"Of course you were prepared," said Lady Auberagh, her eyes narrowed in exasperation. "You don't think I would've let you go to your aunt's if I didn't know you were ready for whatever they threw at you?"

"Was I?" Bryanna shook her head. "I almost didn't make it. You could've trained me better instead of focusing on those mundane, everyday spells."

"Mastering those everyday spells was what got you here," Lady Auberagh countered. "How else do you think you became a sorceress at such a young age? Besides, it wasn't your magic that got you through tonight, girl. It was your wit. Now, do you want to keep arguing about this, or do you have better questions to ask?"

Bryanna gritted her teeth. Her old mentor was right, she did have more burning questions than why she'd never so much as hinted about the League. "Eremon said he's a scout for the League. What role does the League have for me?"

"That will be decided after your initial training," Obelia said, joining her once more with Alec.

"I'm going to be trained?" Bryanna asked. "In what?"

"Everything," said Alec. "It's the only way we'll know where you can best serve the League. Most of our members become sentinels or scouts, like Eremon or me, but others have more specialized skills. Lady Auberagh, for example, is our potions mistress and healer. And your aunt is our Head of Training and Recruitment here at headquarters—"

"Did you just say 'headquarters'?" Bryanna interrupted, staring at him as though she'd heard wrong.

Because why in all of Castlereagh would the League's *headquarters* be in the middle of a forest on the edge of Otherworld?

"Aye," Alec said with a nod. "We have other gathering quarters, of course, but Sheidlow Ridge is our home base. It's where we can conduct our affairs without the peering eyes of unwanted onlookers. The passage the others left through leads to the edge of the forest near the watermill."

Bryanna nodded. "That's where I saw you the other day. But it's not the most convenient, is it? It's not like you can come up to the kitchen to speak to my aunt whenever you have urgent business she needs to attend to."

"Ah, that's where these pocket watches come in," Obelia said, taking an ornate golden timepiece with an engraved evergreen tree from her inner pocket. "We use these to communicate." She handed it to Bryanna. It was relatively cool in her palm, despite it having been in her aunt's pocket the whole time. "This one's yours. If it vibrates, it means someone in the vicinity is in need. And if it ever burns hot, then you can be sure trouble is nigh and that you need to report for duty."

Bryanna stared at it, her chest swelling with emotion. Holding the pocket watch—*her* pocket watch—made what she'd achieved that night all the more real. "Can I trigger it?"

"Of course," her aunt said, pulling out her own watch from

her skirt. "Just tap the face twice, like this—" Obelia tapped the glass casing with the tip of her index finger.

Immediately, the pocket watch in Bryanna's hand quivered. She clasped her fingers around it before it could clatter to the floor.

"—and if you wanted to sound the alarm, just squeeze it like so and ..."

Bryanna hissed as the pocket watch became scorchingly hot to the touch and dropped it to the floor, where it glistened innocently below the blazing flame of the chandelier.

"Does that happen often?" she asked. "That it burns like that?"

"No, it's only happened a few times," her aunt answered, exchanging a troubled look with Alec. "Mostly, it's when one of our members has been found by the Brotherhood."

Bryanna's stomach dropped. "I see."

She couldn't imagine what the Brotherhood would do to someone who was actively fighting against them.

Except that wasn't completely true.

Hadn't they taken Seara's mother and her friends—all of whom she was certain had been members of the League—been viciously murdered and left in the center of a town square for all to see the destruction they could reap on anyone who dared to stand against them?

"You can still back out, if you want, Bryanna," Obelia said softly.

But Bryanna shook her head. She'd known what she was getting into when she'd left Castlereagh. And as afraid as she was of the Brotherhood coming after her before she was ready to face them, it was nothing compared to the regret she'd feel if she rejected the League and everything she could gain from them.

"Then we need to talk about your training," said Alec,

stepping forward. "Tomorrow, if it's safe for you to get down here, we will start training."

Bryanna gaped at him. "*You're* training me? I thought you said you were a sentinel."

"I am," he conceded. "I'm also in charge of training new recruits in hand-to-hand combat, if they're in this area. I'll be taking you for weapons and physical training. Your aunt will train you for everything else—"

Before he could say any more, the telltale crunching of gravel came from the ironstone path, making them all tense.

Bryanna's brows furrowed. Who'd be traveling to the Sheidlow Tower at such an early hour?

"Go," said Alec, inclining his head toward the uneven stone staircase. "We'll talk more soon."

But Bryanna dug her heels in. She didn't want to leave yet. There were too many questions she needed answers to. Besides, there were still hours before the sun would rise. No one would notice she wasn't in bed. She could spend a few more hours down in the cellar, asking Alec and Lady Auberagh questions before the rest of the tower roused themselves from their beds.

Obelia wouldn't hear of it, though. "You can't stay down here, Bryanna. I need to reseal the entrance into the cellar, and depending on who it is, I may not be able to open it again for a while."

"So tell the others I've left Sheidlow Ridge for a few days," Bryanna argued. She could use at least that long just to read the ancient tomes on the far bookshelves ...

Obelia pursed her lips. "The majority of your training will be happening with me, and we *can't* start that if you're down here and I'm up there." She jabbed a finger toward the ceiling. "So if you would like to start training with me as soon as possible, you're going to have to follow me right now. Make your choice: are you going to stay down here with Alec, or are you coming up with me?"

Bryanna bunched her fists at her sides. Her aunt knew as well as she did that she couldn't refuse her training, even if it meant she could spend hours devouring the resources they'd amassed in the cellar. "Fine," she gritted out. "But I'm coming back tomorrow night. I don't care if I have to find the secret entrance near the watermill in order to do so."

She marched up the stairs, bracing a hand against the rough stone wall as she did. Her legs felt weak, as though she'd run a lap of the village. It seemed her body was reeling from everything that had transpired since she'd left her bedchamber with Obelia as much as her mind was.

Back in the kitchen, she waited for Obelia to emerge and wave her hand so that the timber seat reappeared, the Ogham carvings intact once more.

"When will we start our training?" she asked her aunt, following her down the entrance hall.

"Let's discuss that tomorrow," Obelia replied, smoothing the hair on top of her head. It had become disheveled sometime during Bryanna's trial. "Right now, I have to see to our new arrivals."

They'd reached the front doors by then. Obelia drew them open as a hooded figure disembarked from a blue, double-story carriage pulled by what looked like five large, ethereal steeds made of stardust. Seven sentries shadowed the figure as he approached them, their faces obscured by visors that gleamed gold in the lamplight.

To Bryanna's surprise, Obelia bent into a curtsy. "Prince Resli."

Prince?

Bryanna couldn't help but stare at the regal figure.

Was he one of the royal faeries? He couldn't be. Their kind

rarely associated with other beings in Otherworld, preferring to remain among themselves. They had little need beyond their secluded kingdoms, most of them holding more power than the ovates.

"I hope I haven't woken you, mistress," he said, stepping into the entrance hall.

He had a distinct accent Bryanna had heard before, though she couldn't recall from where. At least not until he removed his hood, exposing blue-tinged skin and light blond hair styled in a long, smooth braid.

He was another Tuatha Dé Danann.

In fact, he looked like a younger, healthier version of Elgar.

"You haven't woken me at all," said Obelia. "I was just in the kitchen with my niece. Bryanna, meet Prince Resli."

"Your Majesty," said Bryanna, channeling her mother for the first time in her life as she bent into her own curtsy.

Some of the tension eased from the Tuatha's face as his gaze settled on her. "Elgar has written about you, Ms. Nicholls. He says you've spent time with him over the last few weeks. I'm very grateful. My brother has remained stubborn throughout his illness. He won't let many members of our family visit. I'm glad he has people looking in on him."

"It's no bother, Your Majesty," Bryanna replied, trying to hide her shock. Why hadn't anyone told her Elgar was royal? "I quite enjoy my time with him."

Sorrow flashed across Prince Resli's face. "As do I."

Bryanna's chest constricted as she took in the young, defeated Tuatha, no longer seeing a young prince before her, but a boy trying doggedly to remain strong with the impending demise of his brother.

"Come, Prince Resli," said Obelia, leading him toward the staircase. "You can sit with your brother until he wakes."

Bryanna accompanied them to the second floor but didn't

follow them into Elgar's chamber. She was thoroughly exhausted. All she wanted to do was crawl back into bed so she could process everything that had happened.

But when she opened her door, she found Seara sitting on her bed.

"Well?" she demanded as her cloaking spell descended over Bryanna. "Tell me *everything*."

FIFTEEN

"And then Alec said, 'Welcome to the Brithlean League.'" Bryanna told Seara fifteen minutes later.

She'd debated not saying anything at first. The Brithlean League was a secret, covert entity, after all, and as a new member, it was her duty to ensure it stayed that way. But Seara already knew about the League, so it wasn't as though she was technically breaking any rules. Besides, it had been due to Seara that she'd been prepared—or as prepared as she could've been—when the League had approached her.

She was still struggling to believe it was all real.

That Lady Auberagh, of all people, could've been watching her for the League without her ever suspecting it. Of course, she'd sometimes sensed herself being followed, but she'd always assumed it had been her father's sentinels, trailing her at his command.

"You need to tell the League about me, Bryanna," Seara said, standing up from where she'd been perched on Bryanna's bed, the same determined look on her face as she'd had when they'd faced the wyvern earlier that summer. "I want to join too."

"I will," Bryanna assured her, not at all surprised by her

demand. She would've been, too, had their places been reversed, and she knew there was something she could do to get one step closer to avenging Aveline. Though she didn't think the Brithlean League would consider initiating the young sidhe. After all, *her* age had been one of the factors in the League resisting her induction, and *she* was almost eighteen.

"When will you see them next?" Seara pressed. "I'll come with you."

Bryanna hesitated. "I don't think it works that way."

"Then you need to figure out what *is* the way it works. I'm not going to spend years waiting for an induction. I have half a mind to go down to the cellar right now—"

"You do that, and they'll just take away all the memories you have of the League's existence," Bryanna said at once. "Just leave it with me."

Seara bunched her fists at her sides. "Fine. But don't let too much time pass, Bryanna. I need to be part of their fight. They owe it to me," she said, her voice cracking slightly. "For what happened to my mother."

Bryanna reached for her hands and squeezed them gently. "I will," she promised. "Soon."

***

Somehow, Bryanna fell back asleep.

When she woke the next day, she couldn't wait for night to fall so she and Obelia could return to the cellar. She got dressed, mindful of the soreness in her back—thanks to Alec knocking her to the ground the night before—and headed down to breakfast, eager to start her day.

But she was halfway down the final staircase when she was forced to a standstill.

Weylin was in the kitchen, bustling about as he cooked breakfast.

She hadn't hit her head the night before when she'd faced Alec, had she?

"What are you doing in here?" she blurted, taking the last steps slowly.

Weylin pressed his lips together. "What's it look like, Ms. Nicholls?"

Bryanna moved closer, her brows rising as the smell of baked goods hit her. "Are you making *bread*?" She wasn't sure if she was more surprised by the fact that he'd finally turned up to one of his shifts, or if it was just that he knew how to cook. Extremely well, too, judging by the smell coming from the oven.

"I am." Weylin took a wooden spoon and stirred the large pot of porridge over the flame. Then he bent down and opened the oven door, letting the fresh smell of baking bread waft toward Bryanna, making her mouth water.

"Are you all right?" she hedged, clasping her hands in front of her. There was something off about him. Whatever it was, she got the distinct impression that he was cooking to keep whatever he was obviously trying to avoid at bay. "You couldn't sleep again last night, could you?" she guessed, her voice softening.

Weylin gritted his teeth and closed the oven door. "No."

She moved forward. "Do you need any help?"

"No."

"I can set the table—"

"Ms. Nicholls?" Weylin said curtly, his hard smoky-blue eyes meeting hers for the first time since she'd stepped into the kitchen. "If I'd wanted help, I would've waited until Bain was up."

Bryanna stiffened at his harsh tone. It was hard to believe that something had almost passed between them when they'd been in the forest the day before. Perhaps she'd imagined he'd felt the same pull she had toward him.

"Right," she said, straining to keep her voice level. "I'll leave you to it then."

She made to leave, but before she'd taken more than a few paces, Weylin's voice stopped her.

"I'm sorry," he said, the frustration on his face softening to regret. His gaze dropped to her bare arm, lingering on the healing gash she'd gotten from facing Alec the night before, then he let out a slow breath. "I'm just concerned."

Bryanna moved closer, the twinge of hurt that had gripped her stomach easing. "About your daughter?"

He shrugged and didn't respond.

"Is there anything I can do?"

"No." Weylin lifted the lid of the second pot on the wood-burning stove, checking the mixed berry compote before taking it off the heat and setting it on the trestle table. "Apparently, I just have to accept that I can't control other people's choices. No matter how daft they might be."

He turned back to the bubbling porridge.

"I'm sure your father will come around," she said bracingly. "He wouldn't have been here if he didn't care about you."

Weylin made a low sound of discontent in the back of his throat and replaced the lid onto the saucepan. Then he opened the wood-burning stove's door that held the burning embers and dampened it with an ash shovel. Bryanna watched as he took out the breads and set them near the window to cool.

"I'll be in the forest," he said. "Tell Bain breakfast's ready."

Bryanna opened her mouth to stop him, but he was already out the back door, his shoulders tense, as though whatever was bothering him had settled over him like an extra burden.

Bryanna threw herself into her chores after breakfast, sorting through her aunt's mail and preparing the spare bedchambers for new boarders who'd undoubtedly walk through the tower's double doors as the day wore on. Despite keeping busy, her thoughts kept straying to Weylin. She'd seen him in a poor mood before, but there'd been something different about him that morning. More than the broody wariness that usually followed him around like a dark shadow.

By midafternoon, she'd finished all her chores and headed to the library to find a few volumes that might be useful later that night, when she would hopefully be training with Alec. She would've gone to Obelia and asked for something else to while away the time, but her aunt had left for the village earlier in the afternoon to purchase the supplies they couldn't get from the forest or the tower's grounds.

Before she'd gotten halfway there, though, terrified shouts came from outside, stopping her in her tracks. She rushed to the nearest window in time to see a massive bird-like creature the size of a steed diving with spear-headed precision for Iodhna, who was sprinting for the pond. The rest of the boarders were beside themselves, ducking for cover under the clothes wringer and courtyard tables.

"Bollocks," she muttered, pushing off from the window ledge and racing down the stairs, taking them two at a time.

Of all the days her aunt had to choose to leave her in charge of the tower ...

As she went, she couldn't help but appreciate the irony of Iodhna's predicament. After all her talk of embracing the nature of the predator, she was finally getting a taste of what it felt like to be the prey.

"Bryanna!" Seara shouted as soon as she'd made it outside. "It's an *adar llwch gwin*. What are we going to do?"

"I'll handle it!" Bryanna called to her.

"But there's a—"

The unmistakable sound of rushing water drowned out the rest of Seara's words. A great waterspout had burst forth from the middle of the pond. It had to be one of Iodhna's creations because Bryanna couldn't catch the slightest trace of wind in the air. It spun rapidly, edging ever closer to the adar llwch gwin, whose beady eyes were locked on Iodhna's quavering form beneath the surface.

"Get back!" Bryanna yelled as the force of the waterspout sent her hair flying over her face.

The boarders scattered—all except for Seara, who dug her nails into Bryanna's arm. "Listen to me! There's a girl—"

But Bryanna didn't need to hear any more. She knew exactly what Seara was trying to tell her. She'd just seen the harness strapped to the creature—and the girl in it struggling to regain control of the beast.

"Iodhna, no!" she yelled, sprinting for the pond as the waterspout curved, ensnaring the adar llwch gwin and its passenger in its grip. "There's a girl in the harness!"

"She can't hear you," cried Seara. "Besides, even if she could, when has that ever stopped her?"

Bryanna plunged her hand into her skirt pocket, pulling out the enchanted watch her aunt had given her the night before. Taking a deep breath and hoping she wasn't about to get into trouble for using the League's method of communication for sanctuary-related emergencies, she tapped the pocket watch's face twice. Immediately, the watch vibrated in her palm, sending a pulse up her arm. She placed it back into her pocket and brought her attention back to the chaos unraveling before them. Until her aunt returned, it was up to her ...

"We need to tear the waterspout down," she told Seara, her gaze glued to the adar llwch gwin's mingled blur behind the revolving wall. It was fighting tooth and nail to get out of the waterspout, pitching itself at the magically imbued coursing water. But the current was so strong, it kept getting knocked back. Iodhna wasn't going to let it go easily. Bryanna could feel her magic in the air, so intense that it made the Belfire rite she'd performed for the boarders on Beltane Eve look like child's play.

"How exactly are we going to do that?" cried Seara. "This isn't some low-level spell, Bryanna!"

"Aim for the left side. If we both focus on the same spot, the waterspout might lose enough momentum for the adar llwch gwin to fly through it."

They worked together, siphoning great bucketfuls of water back into the pond. But it was like trying to take sand from a shore; it was easily replaced as soon as a new wave crashed into it. Still, they persevered. Bryanna's hands shook from the amount of magic her spell was taking, but she didn't falter. Not when there were two lives at stake.

Finally, after what felt like an hour, a gaping hole formed on the side of the waterspout. At once, the water's rotating speed fell, and the adar llwch gwin plunged through the opening with the gusto of a starved man, cawing angrily.

Bryanna lowered her hands, cutting off her magic, and raced after the creature and its rider.

"Are you all right?" she asked the damp, out-of-breath girl as soon as she reached her.

The girl pushed her wet strands of blond hair back and threw Bryanna a withering look. "Of course not! Where's Obelia Nicholls?"

"We're expecting her shortly," Bryanna assured her. "Why don't you come in—"

"I'm not staying here with that deranged creature around," the girl snapped, her sharp, angled face splotched red. "That vile creature has it in for Gossel. He was only trying to defend himself."

Bryanna glared in Iodhna's direction, her contempt for the morgen mounting.

"Get me the calming draught I'm here for. It's under Grace Watson. And don't even think about charging me for it—*Gossel, no!*"

Bryanna barely had time to duck as the adar llwch gwin's wings sliced through the air, glaring at the spot where Iodhna's head had just surfaced. Cawing furiously, he launched into the air, diving straight for where Iodhna had submerged herself once more.

Horrified screams rent the air as both the creature and Grace disappeared below the pond's surface with a resounding splash. Bryanna didn't think twice. She plunged headfirst into the bitter-cold water, forgetting that she wasn't a strong swimmer, that she hated the inescapable gurgle pushing against her ears. Her thoughts were singularly bent on saving the girl.

Iodhna wouldn't be taking another child's life if she had anything to do with it.

She swam toward the center of the pond, where she'd last seen the adar llwch gwin. There, she found a sight she hadn't expected. Rather than a gradual deepening of the pond bed was a pit so deep that it could've fit her five-story Castlereagh home comfortably. A single thatched cottage lay at the bottom. Iodhna was perched on the roof, watching the adar llwch gwin swim toward her with a vengeful smile.

Bryanna kicked hard for the surface and drew in a deep lungful of air. Then she pulled on her magic, casting a spell to sustain her breath while she was underwater. She'd need it if she were going to have any chance of saving the oversized bird and his passenger without drowning.

Before she dove back down, at least ten voices accosted her, including a husky one that she was pretty sure was Weylin's.

"Bryanna, don't—"

"Is she—"

"What are—"

"Someone get—"

But Bryanna paid them no attention. She kicked off, diving into the depths of the pond, swimming deeper than she'd ever gone before, ignoring how heavy her head felt as she descended lower and lower. The adar llwch gwin was more than halfway to the cottage where Iodhna still sat, patiently waiting for him to reach her.

And he wasn't alone.

Bryanna almost lost her breath as she saw Weylin swimming toward the creature. What in all of Castlereagh was he doing in the water?

She pulled on a little magic to propel her toward the girl and beast faster, reaching them at the same time as Weylin.

Grace's eyes were wide and bulging. She was struggling to unbuckle the straps keeping her tethered to the adar llwch gwin. But they wouldn't give. The engorged leather was too waterlogged to come undone.

Bryanna wrapped her fingers around the harness, adding her strength to pull it apart, while Weylin locked his arms around the creature's neck, trying to stop him from getting to the cottage and pulling the rest of them along with him. But the adar llwch gwin's will was so bent on getting to Iodhna, Weylin's efforts did little to stall him.

Bryanna pulled on her magic, ready to tear the harness apart with a spell, but before she could, Weylin's hands moved hers aside and, with a powerful tug, the buckles ripped clean off.

The girl kicked loose from the harness and scrambled for the surface. Bryanna followed, but she'd only made it a few paces up when she realized Weylin was swimming in the opposite direction, toward Iodhna and the adar llwch gwin.

She stopped, treading water until Grace broke the surface, then dove once more, going after Weylin. She couldn't leave him to face Iodhna alone.

But she didn't make it far before what felt like thick ropes looped around her chest. Bryanna looked down—and a scream caught in her throat. It wasn't ropes, but the thin, scaly coils of an acid-green sea serpent with a lion-like face. The creature glared at her, a predatory gleam in its eyes, and opened its mouth wide to reveal sharp, pointed fangs.

Fangs that were closing in on her throat.

Bryanna tried to pull free, but the creature tightened its hold around her, constricting her rib cage and squeezing the air out of her lungs.

Her breathing spell broke—she'd needed to keep her breath for it to hold.

Piercing pain erupted along her ribs. It was worse than when she'd been poisoned. At least then, the venom had addled her mind, dulling her discomfort.

The pressure around her eased suddenly.

Weylin was there, a silver dagger clenched in his fist as his fingers dug into the sea serpent's coils, wrenching them from around her middle. But with a savage hiss, the creature rounded on him and lunged, sinking its fangs into Weylin's waist.

No!

Weylin's hold on his dagger slipped as his face twisted in a grimace.

The creature's hold on Bryanna slackened, and she reacted at once, pulling on her magic and retrieving the dagger slowly sinking to the bottom of the pond. She sent the blade hurtling back, and with deadly precision, sank it deep into the sea serpent's scaly flanks. It jerked, releasing Weylin, and floated lifelessly toward the surface.

"Silver!" Iodhna shrieked. She was no longer reclined on the cottage roof but on her feet, an ugly, unforgiving expression contorting her features.

"How dare you!" she screeched, pushing off the cottage roof. "You killed Silver!"

Weylin's arm came around Bryanna's waist, tugging her in the direction of the surface with an urgency she could sense despite the pain she was in. They rose through the water, passing the boundary where the shallows started. Behind them, Iodhna's magic unfurled, charged with a fury that made Bryanna's blood ice in her veins.

"You're never leaving this water!"

Bryanna's lungs burned. Pinpricks of light flickered in the corners of her eyes. If she didn't take a lungful of air soon, she'd lose consciousness.

Bryanna could see the tranquil water rippling above them, the sun's rays beckoning them forward. Before they could reach it, though, a harsh current surged into them, wrenching them backward with brutal force. Bryanna kicked harder, her legs screaming, desperate to keep her panic at bay as the water's surface got farther and farther away.

She turned desperately toward Weylin, and her heart jerked as she found him unnaturally still. For a moment, Bryanna thought he'd passed out. He'd been down a lot longer than she had.

But he was still conscious.

He had an odd, dreamy look on his face. The sort of look Bryanna had seen many times before ... on the salmon lying over Iodhna's plate every morning at breakfast.

Panic gripped her stomach.

Somehow, Iodhna had put Weylin under her thrall.

CHAPTER

SIXTEEN

Bryanna forgot about the pain in her ribs.

She forgot about her need to breathe.

All she could think about was how unnaturally still Weylin was as he watched Iodhna rise from the pond bed to meet them. The suppressed contempt and distrust that so often darkened his face were gone, replaced with a longing Bryanna had only glimpsed once before, as he'd held the Brodericks' newborn in his arms.

She kicked off toward Weylin, pulling on her magic to reinforce the mind-shielding spell she'd been maintaining for weeks. And it was a good thing she did, because she could feel Iodhna's influence pressing against it, trying to wheedle its way past her mental barrier and take over her mind the way she had Weylin's.

As soon as she reached him, Bryanna spun, keeping her body between Weylin and the morgen as the same volley spell she'd used against Alec pulsed at her palms.

Iodhna's eyes narrowed on her, hatred blending with cold mirth. "You can't save him, you know," she goaded, her words distorted as they echoed through the water. "I have you both exactly where I want you."

Bryanna glared back at her, putting as much loathing into the look as she could muster. She'd kill Iodhna. What did she care if the morgen was one of Obelia's boarders? She wouldn't hold herself back. Not when Weylin's air supply was gone, and he was drowning mere feet away.

Except he wasn't the only one out of air …

Already, her vision was clouding over. Even if she managed to incapacitate the morgen, they'd still be down there, neither of them in any state to save the other.

Unless …

Bryanna's hand snaked out, clasping a bunch of Weylin's shirt as tightly as she could.

"No!" Iodhna screamed.

But it was too late. Bryanna had already redirected the spell that had been meant for her into her own stomach. Her spell hit her with the same unforgiving impact as a small boulder, sending pain lancing through her already cracked ribs. They went careening through the water at mind-boggling speed, too fast for the powerful undercurrent that had been holding them prisoner to keep them in its deadly grip.

"Bryanna!" Liadan screamed from somewhere behind her as she and Weylin hit the pond's shallows. "What's going on?"

"Weylin," Bryanna managed, fighting past the excruciating pain in her chest as she expelled water from her lungs in huge, rasping gasps. "He's—"

The sound of Weylin retching water beside her had her sagging against Liadan.

He was alive.

Everything hurt.

Her lungs.

Her throat.

Her head.

"Gossel!" Grace shouted from the other side of the pond. "Where is he—"

Crash!

Bryanna and Liadan reared back as the adar llwch gwin exploded out of the water, screeching terribly. Iodhna hung between its gigantic sharp talons, her teeth bared as she called upon the water to rise with them. But before she could conjure up another waterspout, Seara's magic tinged the air. The morgen slammed into an invisible force, as though a thick wall of glass had been raised between them, and fell back into the water.

The adar llwch gwin screeched indignantly, but the barrier Seara had raised kept him from doubling back for the morgen.

"Gossel, come here!" Grace cried.

Seara stepped forward, her eyes narrowed to slits as she glared at Iodhna, who was advancing on them, water surging forward with her every step. Weylin rose unsteadily to his feet and placed himself in front of Bryanna and Liadan.

"I'm going to—" Iodhna slammed into Seara's barrier and toppled back several paces.

"You're not going to do *anything* until Obelia gets back," Seara growled.

The glower Iodhna sent her was murderous.

Weylin turned to Bain, suppressing another coughing fit. "Get the girl whatever she needs so that she and her incessant bird will get out of here before it tries to go after that wretched morgen again."

"What about Bryanna—" Liadan started.

"I've got her." Weylin's boots squelched as he closed the distance between them. He bent down, one of his arms coming around her back, the other behind her knees, and lifted her easily against his chest.

Bryanna tried to keep from crying out, but the sound

escaped her anyway. Whatever damage she'd sustained in Iodhna's attack, it was bad. She couldn't take deep breaths, and it was more than because of her broken ribs or how long she'd been deprived of air. She couldn't expand one of her lungs properly. Each time she did, a sharp wave of agony flooded her chest, coupled with a wet gurgle.

"Go," Liadan said quietly as she and Bain joined Seara. "We'll stay with Seara."

"Obelia shouldn't be too much longer," Weylin told them grimly. "Tyffin would've already relayed what's happened."

Bryanna's fingernails dug into Weylin's wet shirt as he carried her over to the tower. She would've asked him to let her go, except she didn't think she'd be able to get herself inside. Not when her chest was getting increasingly painful with every passing moment, the shock and adrenaline of having escaped Iodhna fading now that neither of them was in danger anymore.

Inside, Weylin kicked the door to the medical chamber open and carried her to the bed.

"I don't know what you were thinking," Weylin grumbled as he set her down. "Going into that water knowing what Iodhna is."

"You—did—" Bryanna started, each word sending a sharp jab through her.

"Don't speak," he said, though the harshness had left his tone as he lowered himself in front of her. "You can tell me all about your nonsensical reasons for jumping into the pond once you're healed. I'm not sure how much longer your aunt will be, and I need to see how hurt you are."

Bryanna's face twisted. "A few broken—ribs, I think."

"Broken ribs are painful, but they don't leave you gasping the way you are, Ms. Nicholls." He bent his head, tilting one ear toward her chest before sighing. "Your lung's punctured." His hand hovered over her ribcage, hesitating. "I need to check if there's any more damage we should be worried about. It shouldn't take me long."

Bryanna gritted her teeth. She would've checked herself, but she was in too much pain. Besides, she knew what Weylin was going to do. Not just check for broken ribs, but if any of them were still in the lung that was punctured. She couldn't bring herself to check it on her own. She felt queasy as it was.

"All right."

Bryanna started to undo the buttons of her blouse, but Weylin's hand came over hers, stopped her.

"What are you doing, Ms. Nicholls?" he said, and Bryanna couldn't help but notice his cheeks reddening. "I can feel your ribs through the material of your drenched clothes just fine."

Bryanna's hands stilled. She was in so much pain, she wasn't thinking straight. "Maybe you should get Liadan."

"Why? Didn't I just prove I can be a gentleman?"

Bryanna gritted her teeth. "It's my—brassiere," she winced. "It's too—tight over my ribs—and I can't ..."

"Right." There was a pause before Weylin spoke again. "I'll go get Liadan—"

"Wait." Bryanna clenched her jaw as a new sharp wave of agony jabbed through her. "Can you—do it?"

She did *not* want to wait for Weylin to get Liadan.

"I just—need it—untied."

Weylin straightened. "I'll help you up."

He moved behind her, placing his arms along her back and supporting her into a seated position. "Tell me when you've untied the front of your blouse and I'll reach underneath and get it for you."

Bryanna undid her buttons, her hands trembling slightly. She wanted to think it was from the adrenaline of everything that had happened, but part of it was because of how close she and Weylin were.

And how alone.

She pushed those thoughts aside. She was injured, and he was helping her. That was all.

"Done," she said as soon as she'd finished.

Weylin tugged the back of her blouse from her skirt and reached underneath it. His knuckles brushed along her goosebumped skin lightly, and the breath stalled in her lungs for a millisecond before she forced herself to take a calm, measured breath.

He cleared his throat as though there was something caught there. "Got it."

The relief that came as soon as her brassiere was no longer hugging her pain-wrecked ribs was so instantaneous that Bryanna couldn't help the sigh that passed her lips.

Weylin stepped back. "Better?"

"Yes."

He moved again, toward the shelf of potions at the end of the small chamber.

"What are you doing?" she asked.

"Getting you some numbing potion. It'll be easier for you when I check you over."

He returned a minute later with a phial. "I'm not sure how much to measure out—"

Bryanna took it from him and downed half the lot. She would deal with any adverse effects if it meant she could think straight through the pain.

"Thanks," she said, handing the phial back to Weylin.

He glanced at it, then back at her. "Are you sure that was safe?"

"I'll be fine." The pain was already ebbing, her mind clearing with it. "I've seen—patients take more—in one go."

"Lie back down," said Weylin. "The amount you had is going to have your head spinning in a few minutes. You don't want to give yourself more injuries than you already have."

But instead of listening, Bryanna pulled on her magic and hovered her hand over the spot where one of her ribs was making her lung feel as though it was nothing more than a leaking waterskin. Immediately, the pressure in her chest lessened, and she sucked in as deep a breath as she could with the broken ribs that had not yet been mended.

"Where did you learn to heal?" he asked as Bryanna moved to one of the lower cracked ribs so she could heal it. "I thought you had to go study at a tertiary institute to do that."

"My mentor, Lady Auberagh, taught me," she said. "I worked under her at an apothecary while I was still in school."

Weylin leaned against the edge of her bed, far enough away to let her maneuver as she worked, but close enough that he'd be able to catch her if she felt suddenly faint. "I thought apothecaries dealt in potions and tinctures."

"They do. Lady Auberagh was a healer before she decided to open her own apothecary. It's how she knows my aunt. They used to work together, back when she and my aunt were at the Castlereagh Healer Hospital."

"I didn't realize that being a healer in the past qualified one to teach novice magic-weavers to do so, too."

"She didn't teach me how to heal others." Bryanna moved on to her other side, wincing as she tackled a rib higher than the others. "I figured that part out for myself."

"Is the numbing potion's effect fading already?" he asked at once, seeing her reaction.

"No. But the muscles around the broken bones are getting aggravated the more I move. Let's just say that if they don't get healed up before the numbing potion wears off, I'm going to be wishing I'd just stayed put until my aunt got here."

"That you will." Weylin placed the phial of numbing potion into his shirt pocket, out of her sight. "I may not be able to heal any wounds using magic the way you are, but I know my share of potions and how to administer them. In fact, I think I just might impress you with my knowledge, Ms. Nicholls."

Bryanna rolled her eyes. "I doubt that. I've been taught by one of the best in the healer profession."

He smirked. "Funny. So was I."

"Speaking of healing wounds, how is yours going?" she asked, lowering her eyes to his wounded side. His shirt was black and still dripping wet, and she couldn't tell what was water and what was blood. Though with Weylin being a faoladh, the sea serpent's fang marks might've been completely healed.

"I should probably make sure there's no venom in your wound. Would you unbutton your shirt, please?"

"Aren't you being a bit forward today, Ms. Nicholls?" Weylin quipped, the corner of his lip lifting. "First, you ask me to help loosen your brassiere, now you want my shirt off?"

Heat wafted over Bryanna's neck and cheeks. "Just do it."

"So pushy. You know, if you wanted to see me with my shirt off, all you had to do was ask."

"You're incorrigible."

"There you go, using those big words again."

Bryanna lowered her hands. She could still feel a few of her injuries, but they could wait until she'd made sure her aunt's insolent boarder was all right. If the sea serpent really was venomous, he might need her magic more than she did.

"Go on, then."

Some of the humor left his face. "Your aunt will be here any moment. I'm fine, honestly."

She gave him a pointed look. "Then you won't mind if I look."

It wasn't a question.

"Won't take no for an answer, huh?" Weylin sighed. "Your upbringing is showing, Ms. Nicholls."

"Not my upbringing, my healer instincts," she said, meeting his gaze steadily. "It's a family trait, and I'm afraid I'd rather you not start presenting with venom intoxication while you are in my care."

"I thought you were in *my* care until your aunt gets here."

"Enough stalling, Weylin," she snapped. "Unbutton your shirt so I can make sure your wound is clean."

Weylin gave her a long-suffering sigh and undid the first button of his sodden shirt.

Bryanna leaned forward, suppressing a grimace as her muscles stiffened over the broken bones around her ribs.

But then her breath caught for a different reason. Weylin had unbuttoned his shirt enough for her to see the scars over his chest. She reached out, almost touching the old wound scars that looked as though they'd been made with claws before catching herself.

"What happened to you?" she breathed.

"I dove after you into a pond filled with violent sea-dwellers, remember?" he said lightly.

"That's not what I meant, and you know it. Where did you get these scars?"

Weylin hesitated, his eyes searching hers as though weighing whether he could trust her with the truth. "My father has enemies," he said at last. "Let's just say it's not the best time to be a faoladh, particularly one related to a natural chieftain."

"Isn't there only one of those left?" Bryanna asked, remembering what he'd said about his father being the last one on the day that he and the rest of his family had turned up unannounced.

"Yes. And there are some who'd have him be the last."

Bryanna straightened, rage coiling in her stomach. "So they tried to *kill* you?"

Weylin looked down at his chest, where the largest scar was. "Some of these were meant for my father. I just got in the way."

Bryanna's eyes widened. He'd taken a blade to the chest for his father, and yet he'd still banished him. Still kept him from his own child.

The injustice of it had her digging her nails into her palms.

No wonder he was in such a prickly mood sometimes.

Weylin cleared his throat and unbuttoned the rest of his shirt, revealing a hard, defined chest. He looked as though he'd spent years training, which in retrospect, he probably had. And a good thing, too, otherwise the scars on his chest wouldn't have been scars at all, but fatal wounds.

Bryanna shuddered at the thought.

Swallowing, she forced her gaze away from the sculptured lines of his torso and focused on the area she was actually meant to be examining.

"See?" he said, lifting the side where he'd been bitten. The fang marks that had been left by the sea serpent had almost faded, leaving the rest of his skin unblemished. "Told you I was fine. Now, stop fussing about me and get the rest of your ribs sorted."

Bryanna settled back into the seat, but instead of continuing to heal herself, she paused and turned to him again. "Weylin?"

He stopped buttoning his shirt to look at her. "Hmm?"

"Thank you. For coming after me."

"Just doing my part," he said with a shrug.

Bryanna shook her head. "No, you weren't."

"Actually, it is." Weylin took a deep breath and slipped his hand into his pocket, his fingers closing around something she couldn't see. "I—"

But whatever he was going to say died on his lips as Obelia burst into the medical chamber.

"What in all of Castlereagh happened?" she demanded, out of breath.

Weylin got to his feet, the unguarded warmth that she'd glimpsed evaporating as he turned to her aunt, his expression hardening.

"Oh, you know," he said in a tone that Bryanna knew all too well, "that dear morgen boarder of yours tried to kill your niece and me."

Obelia blanched. "Weylin—"

"You should heal your niece," he said before she could finish. "And don't let her have any more numbing potion." He reached into his pocket, grabbed the phial he'd stored there for safekeeping and gave it to Obelia. "She's already overdosed on the stuff. I'll be upstairs."

It took Obelia several minutes to set Bryanna right again. Although she'd taken care of the punctured lung and a few ribs, Obelia had to heal the rest of them, as well as three vertebrae that the sea serpent had fractured. "You need to tell me what happened," Obelia said once she'd finished.

Bryanna did, starting with how she'd raced out after hearing the boarders screaming, and how Iodhna had forced the adar llwch gwin to attack her once she was deep in the pond and in her element. When she moved on to how she'd turned on her and Weylin, Obelia shot to her feet.

"I can't believe Iodhna did this," she managed.

Bryanna tried to snort but hiccoughed instead, the numbing potion threatening to climb back up her throat. She wasn't sure why her aunt was so shocked by the news. Hadn't she and

Weylin been warning her about the morgen for moon cycles? "You're getting rid of her now, right?"

Obelia's lip curled in disgust. "You have no idea how much I want to. But she's under the Brithlean League's protection."

Bryanna sat bolt upright. *"What?"*

Obelia sat back down, weariness lining every inch of her face. "It's why she escaped the noose in Coral Cove. Her gift of premonition is strong. She's the closest thing we have to a spy in the Brotherhood of Sìorraidh's ranks right now."

Anger flared in Bryanna's chest. She couldn't believe the League was *protecting* Iodhna. Castlereagh knew how many beings she'd already killed. Why was she even allowed to roam the tower's grounds? If the League wanted to keep her close, why not lock her up in the cellar and weaken her so that she couldn't use her thrall to get herself released by whoever was guarding her?

"Can't we find another morgen?" Bryanna demanded.

"Don't think I haven't been looking." Obelia rose to her feet. "I promise, if she does anything like this again, I'll hand her over to the authorities. Let the League try to stop me."

SEVENTEEN

"Show me your defensive stance," Alec said later that night.

He and Bryanna were down in the secret cellar. She'd had to wait to sneak down to meet him until after midnight. Several boarders had lingered in the library until late and had only retired to their chambers when Weylin stormed in, growling that he couldn't sleep with the ruckus they were making.

"Like this?" Bryanna asked, bringing her fists up the way her brothers had taught her. Hands over her face, thumbs tucked in, knuckles facing up. It was a stance she was quite proud of. At least until Alec grabbed her fists and pushed, sending her back several steps and almost knocking her off her feet.

"Why was I able to do that?" he asked.

"Because you're strong?" she guessed, trying to keep the irritation out of her voice as she regained her balance.

"No. Because your stance is weak. Look at the position of my feet. How are they different from yours?"

Bryanna looked down. Alec's right leg was behind his left,

back foot angled so that his toes faced the wall. She did the same with hers.

He nodded. "We might make a warrior of you yet. Bend your knees a bit ... no, not that much ... good. Let's try again."

Bryanna was much more prepared for the pressure Alec put into her fists that time. She braced herself, and when he pushed, held her ground despite the crushing weight in her heels.

"Now we can begin."

Bryanna had been looking forward to learning how to wield weapons, but Alec had other ideas. A regime that he called "strength training". Or as Bryanna would refer to it privately by the end of their session, "disguised torture". He had her lifting weights that she could've sworn were enchanted to become heavier with each repetition. Alec made her lift them over her head, from her knees to her belly, and—the worst one—resting on her shoulders while she squatted and lunged.

Bryanna hated every minute of it.

"When will we begin weapons?" she asked when Alec finally brought their session to a close.

"Weapons?" He gave a booming laugh and handed her a goblet of water. "If you can't keep a light weight above your head for more than a minute, what makes you think you can hold a sword for more than five seconds?"

Bryanna brought the goblet to her lips, her arms shaking. She tried to lock her elbows in, but it didn't help. "I *can* keep a light weight above my head," she muttered. "Just not after training for an hour without pause."

He chuckled. "An hour? You've barely been in here thirty minutes."

Bryanna's jaw dropped. "Are you sure?"

It felt as though she'd been down there for *hours*.

He picked up his pocket watch from the fence surrounding the sparring grounds and showed her.

Bryanna's shoulders slumped. He was right.

"Take a jog along the perimeter of the sparring grounds," he said, returning the pocket watch to its perch. "It will help loosen up your muscles."

"My muscles are already loose, trust me," Bryanna returned. In fact, they felt boneless, as though they could barely keep her weight.

"Trust me, you'll thank me for it tomorrow."

Bryanna lowered her goblet and stretched her legs, wincing at how her muscles pulled as though she were trying to stretch a bread dough that had not yet rested. Then she did as Alec bade, though her jog was more of a bouncy power walk.

"Keep stretching tomorrow," Alec said when she'd finished. "You're going to be sore."

"See you tomorrow night?"

"Only if you can make it here undetected," Alec said, grabbing the weights she'd abandoned as easily as though they were hollow logs.

The next morning, Bryanna awoke in terrible pain.

Not the pain of broken ribs.

Or poisoning.

Or drowning.

But the kind of pain that made it impossible to stretch a single muscle without agony. The shakiness in her limbs from the night before was gone, replaced by a tearing sensation, as though her muscles were being stretched to their snapping point. Attached to the pain was a gnawing hunger. Dimly, she recalled Seara knocking on her door earlier that morning but couldn't remember what excuse—or threat—she'd made to get her to leave. Whatever it was, it had stopped Seara from calling her a second time.

Bryanna got up and cringed. She smelled most unladylike. Hobbling to the privy, she ran herself a hot bath, then dressed and made the slow, torturous way down to Obelia's floor.

When she entered her aunt's office, Obelia took one look at Bryanna's state and pushed away the letter she'd been reading. "I could kill him," she said through gritted teeth.

Beside her, Tyffin made what sounded suspiciously like a snicker.

"It's not Alec's fault," Bryanna said half-heartedly.

Obelia stood and grabbed a balm from the glass cabinet against the wall. "Here, this should help with the soreness. I'll tell Alec not to expect you tonight."

Bryanna straightened. "What? No, I *have* to train."

There was no way she'd miss her next session. The last thing she wanted was for tongues to start wagging about how she was already taking time off when she'd barely started with the League. She'd prove to them all that she had what it took to be amongst them, regardless of who her family was.

Even if it meant having to push past her body's physical limits.

"Are you certain?" her aunt asked, frowning.

"Definitely."

<hr>

Bryanna's training sessions got easier.

Alec started each one with a ten-minute lap of the cellar and twenty minutes of weights before moving on to the strenuous portion of their sessions—weapons.

They began with daggers and short swords, followed by the

bow and arrow and crossbow. Bryanna much preferred the latter. She might've been getting stronger thanks to Alec's training, but she didn't think she'd ever be able to beat someone of his stature in hand-to-hand combat or with a close-range weapon.

Obelia, too, had started training Bryanna. Mostly using the ancient magic volumes she'd brought down for her, but every once in a while, when Alec wasn't using the sparring ground, she and Bryanna would train in defensive magic, too.

Bryanna enjoyed these sessions more than Alec's, though they usually left her equally exhausted. The sessions took just as long for her magical store to recover as her muscles, but left her feeling much more restless. She'd come to rely on a ready and bountiful source of power thrumming beneath her skin, ready at her command, particularly since her ascension to sorceress. Not being at her full power was something she was still struggling to get used to.

One night, after Bryanna and Obelia came down from the uppermost floor after a particularly grueling magical training session, they found Seara in the kitchen, cooking supper.

Bryanna averted her gaze as the young sidhe looked between her and Obelia, hope lighting her features. She'd mentioned Seara to Obelia, but the latter had reacted in the same way she'd known she would: by telling her that Seara was far too young to be inducted into the League.

"Wow, Seara, did you do this all on your own?" Bryanna asked, staring at the bench, where Seara had prepared a buffet of chocolate cakes, puddings, and mousses.

Seara nodded. "Figured we could all use something sweet."

"Well, then I'm afraid you've wasted your time," said Iodhna, strutting into the kitchen on her barnacled heels. "I can't have any of it."

Iodhna's presence had an immediate effect on the boarders.

Many stopped talking, while others edged as far away from her as they could.

Bryanna forced herself to look at the morgen, her loathing for her surpassing anything she'd ever felt for any other being.

"So go and catch your own fish," Seara snapped. "From now on, you can forget one of us going anywhere near that pond as long as you're in it."

"Why, little sidhe? Are you afraid of me?"

Seara's nostrils flared. "I could make you forget who you are in an instant. You could be groveling before us like one of your sailors if I wanted it. Just try me."

"That won't be necessary, Seara," Cayde interjected, coming in behind the morgen. "Iodhna's sorry for what happened with the adar llwch gwin incident. *Aren't you,* Iodhna?"

Iodhna's thin, navy lips forced themselves into an unconvincing smile. "Of course. Even though they were in my territory, came between me and the thing that tried to kill me, and murdered Silver right in front of me, *I'm* the one who's sorry."

"We were trying to save the girl," Bryanna snapped. "That thing attacked *us*."

Iodhna looked ready to eject venom. "Silver wasn't a *thing*!"

Cayde stepped between them. "Come on, Iodhna. Let's find our seats."

The rest of supper was a tense affair. No one bothered to keep their voices down as they speculated why Iodhna was still there. Weylin was the worst. Between spoonfuls of chocolate mousse, he asked the boarders if they knew what a morgen's dried flanks would sell for, whether morgens would suffocate if their air supply was cut off, and what would happen if they weren't in contact with water for a few days.

Bryanna had been surprised to see Weylin join them for

supper. She could count the number of times he'd sat at the table with them during mealtimes on both hands.

"Are you feeling all right, Ms. Nicholls?" he asked, lowering himself in the seat Liadan had vacated beside her.

Bryanna ignored how her pulse spiked at his nearness. They hadn't been so close to each other since he'd lifted the back of her blouse and untied her brassiere in the medical chamber. "Why wouldn't I be?"

"You looked like you were having trouble reaching for that bowl of boiled peas earlier," he said, his eyes glinting with what looked suspiciously like amusement.

"I'm fine," she lied.

She wasn't.

The muscles along her arms and upper back were in agony. Alec had upped her weights, even though she'd only just started to complete her reps without wanting to crumple afterwards.

"I thought Obelia healed you all up after everything that happened with that wretched creature."

"She did."

"Then why are you moving as though another one of that morgen's beasts attacked you?"

"Quit being so insensitive, Conveil," Cayde snapped from the seat opposite them, scowling. "That poor creature was just trying to defend Iodhna."

"Is that what Iodhna told you happened?" Weylin asked, draping an arm along the back of Bryanna's chair and sending a shockwave of awareness coursing through her. "It might interest you to know, Garnet, that Iodhna's pet sea serpent would've killed Ms. Nicholls here if I hadn't been there."

Cayde looked as though he were only half-listening, his eyes narrowed on the arm Weylin had resting across Bryanna's seat.

"And that it tried to take a good chunk out of me, too," Weylin added. "Though I don't suppose you'd mind that last bit, would you? Not when it would've succeeded in getting me out of your way."

Bryanna froze, her cheeks flushing on Cayde's behalf at what he was insinuating.

Before she could protest, though, Cayde leaned forward, meeting Weylin's gaze coolly. "You're not in my way, Conveil."

"Aren't I?" Weylin interjected, arching his brows as he edged close enough to Bryanna that she could smell his woodsy scent radiating from him.

Cayde's expression hardened. "Not with your track record."

Weylin's whole body tensed. "What's that supposed to mean?" he asked, his voice so deadly, the temperature around them seemed to drop.

"Weylin," Bryanna said softly, placing her hand on his arm. "Don't."

Weylin's jaw unclenched slightly at her touch, though his furious gaze remained locked on Cayde, daring him to say whatever he was going to.

And Cayde, it seemed, had no qualms about doing just that. He leaned forward until the two of them were nose to nose and said, "Only that you can't seem to keep your women from falling into the arms of other men."

Bryanna stared at him, gobsmacked. "Cayde—"

Before she could say any more, Weylin reached across the table, grabbed the top of Cayde's clump of black hair, and slammed his head down onto the table, hard enough that a crunch resounded around the kitchen.

"Weylin!" Bryanna cried, leaping to her feet.

"Be grateful it's not your teeth, Garnet," Weylin growled as Bryanna pulled him away from Cayde.

What was the matter with the two of them? If she didn't know better, she might've thought *she* was the cause of the conflict, though that couldn't be possible.

"Cayde, are you all right?" she asked as Iodhna handed him a tea towel, her lips pressed together to hide the gleeful smile spreading across her face. It shouldn't have surprised her that the morgen's compassion didn't even extend to the closest person she had to a friend in the whole tower.

"Fine," he said, though blood gushed from his broken nose. Accusation burned in his eyes as he looked at her, a mixture of hurt and betrayal flickering across his face.

"Weylin, go and wait for me in my office," Obelia growled, marching over to them, her tone crisp as her piercing gaze leveled on Weylin. "You and I are going to have words."

"Can't wait," Weylin said, his voice dripping sarcasm.

"Cayde, come into the medical chamber," her aunt continued, her voice softening. "I'll get you sorted out."

Bryanna didn't take her eyes off Weylin as he pushed his chair in and started for the stairs.

"Weylin, wait," she called, rushing after him and grabbing his arm. "I don't know what's going on between you and Cayde—"

"Don't you?" Weylin bit out. "Well then, allow me to spell it out for you. Cayde's drawn to you, and so long as he is, you're not safe."

"No, he isn't—"

"And what's worse, your aunt's been convincing him that he can control what he is, when that's not possible for his kind."

"I don't believe that," Bryanna argued. Sure, she knew what Cayde battled with his new instincts each day, but her instincts told her that, despite the behavior he'd exhibited that evening, Cayde wasn't the monster Weylin believed him to be. "He's not a bad person, Weylin."

"That's where you're wrong, Ms. Nicholls," Weylin said, his tone clipped. "He's no longer a person. And until you understand that, you're in danger."

"I can tell who is and who isn't dangerous for myself," Bryanna said between clenched teeth.

"In most cases, I'd probably say you were right," he said, his jaw locking. "But in this case, you're wrong, Ms. Nicholls. And the sooner he realizes that and leaves, the sooner everyone will be safer for it."

"Everyone deserves a chance to be good, Weylin, no matter what their nature appears to be," she insisted.

Weylin shook his head. "You are too much like your aunt. And it's going to get you hurt."

And with those words, he continued up the stairs.

———

Bryanna dreamed she was in Aveline's bedchamber again that night. It'd been a while since she'd been there. So much had changed for her in the last moon cycle that she almost expected Aveline's bedchamber to have changed too. But it was the same as always. Her bed was made without a single crease, crocheted pillows propped up against the white headboard like they usually were. Even the dressing table looked the same, the bottles, jars, and powder containers in the exact spot they'd always been.

Aveline stood behind her, combing out the knots in Bryanna's hair with a heavy, gilded comb, humming as she pinned tufts in place. "You're getting stronger," she said.

Bryanna's gaze remained fixed on her entwined fingers. "What makes you say that?"

"The strands of your hair have changed at the roots." Aveline pulled at a clump. "Not as easy to break as they once were."

Bryanna shifted in her seat. "That's good. I'll need to be strong for what's coming."

"Not if you stop this now, Bree. Forget about the Brotherhood of Sìorraidh."

"I can't," Bryanna said softly.

Aveline yanked Bryanna's hair back, forcing her to meet her eyes for the first time in five years. Bryanna sucked in a breath. Aveline hadn't changed. Her hair was braided from the crown of her head down to the middle of her back, like when she'd been alive. She wore the same white dress as the day she'd died, only it looked freshly pressed, not dirty like it had been in the alleyway.

"You can't?" Aveline murmured, her gaze piercing. "Or you don't want to?"

"Both," Bryanna admitted. Her vengeance may have started because of Aveline, but it was no longer the only reason she was after the Brotherhood. What the Brithlean League stood for was noble, a cause she wanted to be a part of.

Footsteps approached from the other side of the chamber's door.

Aveline dropped her comb, her face ashen. "You need to go. Quick!"

"What—"

But the chamber faded.

Bryanna awoke with the witchscript volume she'd been studying over her face, the scent of old, musty pages wrinkling her nose. Putting it aside, she sat up, pushing the unsettling dream from her mind. She didn't have time for her thoughts to linger on them. Not if she was going to make it to her training session with Alec. She reached for her pocket watch, checking the time against the oil lamp on her bedside table. It was still lit, though only a small flame flickered.

Two o'clock.

Obelia had promised to fetch her when Alec was ready for their training session, but that should've been hours ago. Had she forgotten?

She pushed her counterpane aside, adjusted the shirt and breeches she'd picked out for what was sure to be a grueling training session with Alec, pulled on her boots, and headed downstairs, trying to forget the painful image in her mind of Aveline in her white dress.

The kitchen was deserted when she got there, though her aunt had left the entrance to the secret cellar open. She climbed into the window seat's hollow opening and descended the jagged, uneven steps. Halfway down, the sound of clashing blades below reached her, and she paused, straining to hear what was happening in the cellar. Were her aunt and Alec training?

She took the remaining steps as quietly and swiftly as she could, eager to see her aunt in action.

But it wasn't her aunt crossing swords with Alec.

Someone else was.

Someone who moved so fast—faster than a regular human —that she couldn't make out his features. Whoever he was, he wasn't as heavyset as Alec, though his agility more than made up for it. Alec barely had time to parry each blow for how quickly the next one rained down on him.

Bryanna sank onto the closest stool, watching in awe. She'd seen her share of professional swordplay, but it'd never been anything like what she was seeing before her. Alec and his opponent were using their swords as though they were extensions of themselves, just like she did with magic.

Their blades clashed again, swifter than before. Alec redoubled his efforts to remain on the defensive. But with a muttered oath, his sword whirred into the air and clanged onto the long table across the cellar.

"Show-off," Alec muttered as his combatant pressed the tip of his sword to his throat. "I let you win."

His opponent withdrew his blade with a low, husky laugh. "You've been doing that a lot lately."

Bryanna's breath lodged in her throat.

She recognized that voice.

How could she not, when it sent her pulse racing each time she heard it?

Weylin.

EIGHTEEN

"What are *you* doing here?" Bryanna managed, though even as she voiced her question, she knew the answer. There could only be one logical reason for Weylin being in the cellar, training with Alec as though they'd been doing it for moon cycles.

She gripped the edge of the stool, glad she was sitting. Her knees were so weak, she was certain she would've sunk to the floor if she'd been standing as all the signs she'd missed slid into place. Weylin's late nights, all the time he spent in the forest, his appearance when the wyvern attacked, and again after she'd activated her pocket watch when the adar llwch gwin had attacked Iodhna ...

Weylin was a member of the Brithlean League.

"You have got to be jesting," she said under her breath.

Alec's brows knitted together as he glanced between them. "Bryanna, did nobody tell you Weylin was in the League?"

"No." Bryanna sent a withering glower in Weylin's direction. "No one."

Weylin's expression turned unconvincingly innocent as Alec

pierced him with an exasperated look. "What? I thought she knew."

"We'd best hope you're never captured by the Brotherhood, Weylin," Alec muttered, shaking his head. "You're such a poor liar, you wouldn't make it through five minutes of interrogation in their hands. They wouldn't even need to torture you."

Weylin scoffed. "I'd last longer than you would, old man. You couldn't even beat an underage sorceress. Though maybe you were just going easy on her."

"Trust me, he didn't go easy on me," Bryanna snapped, drawing herself up. She would've bet anything Weylin was one of the members who'd opposed her induction. "Perhaps he's been going easy on you, though. Inflating your ego so he can knock it down when you least expect it."

Weylin's smoky-blue eyes became impenetrable. "I'm not trying to offend you, Ms. Nicholls. But you don't have any extraordinary physical, magical, or intellectual merit. A minimum of at least one is usually needed to be inducted into the League. Not to mention you're not of age."

Bryanna crossed her arms. "*You're* barely of age."

"Aye, but I know how to track, I have elevated senses, and I can handle myself against most creatures."

"I can, too."

"Can you really?" He turned to Alec, rolling the cuffs of his shirt up to his elbows. "Why don't you let me take over training tonight? I'd love to see what our newest recruit has to offer."

"*What?*" Bryanna forced herself to shift her gaze away from the corded forearms he'd exposed. She did *not* want Weylin training her. Not when she could barely focus whenever he was around. Besides, she could just imagine the sort of training session he'd have in store for her.

Alec looked between them. "I'm not sure about that, Weylin—"

"It's fine," Weylin interrupted. "Besides, I think Obelia would appreciate your company. Don't you, Ms. Nicholls?"

Bryanna squared her shoulders. She might not have wanted him training her, but she wouldn't give him the satisfaction of admitting as much. "It's fine by me, too."

Alec still looked hesitant to leave. "Go easy on her, Weylin," he said at last. "She's new to this."

"Going easy on her is only going to get her killed faster," Weylin retorted.

Without responding, Alec headed upstairs.

"Warm up," Weylin said, turning back to Bryanna.

She did as he bade, finishing her laps in record time. If he was looking to make a point that she wasn't ready to be in the League, she wouldn't make it easy for him.

"Ready?" he asked when she'd joined him on the sparring ground.

"Yes—"

But she'd barely finished responding when Weylin spun around. His leg hit the backs of her knees, sending her tumbling onto the pressed dirt floor.

"Hey!" Bryanna growled, glaring up at him. "What was that?"

"I thought you said you were ready," he replied, deadpan.

"Not for that, and you know it," she growled. "Alec and I were due to start on the quarterstaff."

"Not tonight. I'm teaching you how to use your body in combat instead. Something you needed to learn before you started weapons, in my opinion."

Bryanna clenched her fists. "Or, you can just forego the pretence of training me and get what you really want to say off your chest: That you don't want me to be in the League."

Weylin sighed. "I never said I didn't want you in the League, Ms. Nicholls. I just don't think you're ready. I meant what I said. You have no significant abilities to offer the League."

Bryanna scoffed. "I beat Alec single-handedly."

"You did," he allowed, albeit reluctantly. "I know you're a strong magic-weaver, but once that power is spent, what will you do if you're facing the Brotherhood?"

"The same could be said for Lady Auberagh," she argued, pushing to her feet.

"Which is why her role in the League is intel and healing. Something tells me you wouldn't be content sitting here, crafting weapons imbued with clever magical enchantments for those of us on the field to wield."

Bryanna's eyes narrowed. He was right about that.

"That's why I'm being trained," she returned. "It's two in the morning, and I'm down here with you, aren't I?"

"It's not enough. Obelia is too busy running the sanctuary to train you properly, and an hour with Alec here and there won't get you to where you need to be, either. You heard Deagon Broderick. Ten ex-boarders have been attacked this year, and anyone who's associated with Obelia and this tower could be next."

"I understand that," Bryanna said tersely. "Why else do you think Alec and I have been working with long-range weapons until I'm strong enough to fight at close quarters?"

"Long-range weapons aren't the answer, Ms. Nicholls. I hate to break it to you, but you can't wait to be 'strong enough'."

"What else can I do?" Bryanna demanded.

"You need to learn to fight smart. I meant what I said. There are things you should've been trained in before weapons. You're small, but that doesn't mean you can't use it to your advantage. Take my sister, for example. She's only ten, but that didn't stop me from training her ever since I got these." He pointed to the scars she knew were under his shirt. "I would not have her defenseless if I could do anything about it. And I won't have you defenseless either."

Something warm and unexpected unfurled in Bryanna's chest at his words. "What are you saying?"

He shrugged. "I'm perfectly positioned to train you. You wouldn't need to wait to get down here. We could go into the forest or use one of the unoccupied chambers during the day. Admit it, Ms. Nicholls. You need me."

"That remains to be seen," Bryanna said, though she knew he was right. Her aunt and Alec weren't available as often as she needed, and she'd seen Weylin fight. He was more than capable of training her. And she needed training, especially when it came to hand-to-hand combat.

"We can talk about this later." Weylin stepped forward, closing the space between them. "Ready to begin?"

Bryanna nodded.

He grabbed her wrists, his grip tight, but not painful. "Try to get out of my hold."

Bryanna yanked at her wrists, pulling them toward her. But Weylin's grip didn't waver. "Is that all you've got?"

"Well, no, I can do this ..." She pulled on her magic, conjuring a spell that sent static crackling across his skin.

Weylin let her go immediately, shaking his hand. "Ingenious," he said, his voice dripping with sarcasm. "But let's leave your magic out of this."

Bryanna let him take her wrists again, struggling to quench the unwanted thrill that passed over her at his touch. But no matter what she tried, she couldn't break free.

"You've made your point," she grumbled after multiple unsuccessful attempts, giving one last brutal tug that almost dislocated her wrist. "I can't get out of your hold."

"That's where you're wrong," Weylin said, letting her go and extending his own wrist. "Take it."

Bryanna did, her grip as tight as his had been on her.

"Watch carefully." With a quick, flawless twist, Weylin slipped his hand from her grasp as easily as if it had been a wet bar of soap. "The thumb is the weakest point of most hands. Twisting your wrist toward it will usually allow your hand to slip free. You try."

Weylin's fingers came around her wrist. Bryanna swiveled her hand toward his thumb like he'd shown her and was pleasantly surprised when her wrist came free.

"Good. This time, do it as fast as you can. Don't give your opponent time to regain their hold."

They practiced until Bryanna could do it reflexively, then moved on to a new maneuver.

"This," said Weylin, his fingertip tracing the groove between her thumb and forefinger, "is the most sensitive part of the hand for most creatures."

"I thought you said the thumb was," Bryanna countered, forcing herself to focus on what he was teaching her and not the way her skin tingled from his touch.

"No, it's just the *weakest*. Using the side of your hand, you want to push it in the groove's center. The more force you use, the more effective. It should give you a few moments' advantage as they won't be able to grasp much in their grip without considerable pain." He pulled a training glove out of his trousers' back pocket and slipped it on. "When you're ready."

Bryanna aimed at the spot Weylin had just instructed. The impact sent a dull pain shooting up her arm.

"You wouldn't happen to have a spare training glove for me, would you?" she asked, massaging the part of her hand that was aching dully from the impact.

"Try it a few more times. You need to be familiar with how it feels without protective gear."

Bryanna gritted her teeth and took care not to hit him as hard over the next few rounds before he let her stop and found her a glove of her own.

They continued for several more minutes before Weylin brought their session to an end.

Bryanna couldn't help her disappointment. She was loath to admit it, but she'd actually enjoyed the training session.

"When are we doing this again?" she asked as she stretched her arm.

"Tomorrow," he said, putting the training glove away. "I'll come find you once I figure out somewhere we can train without anyone catching us."

Bryanna could barely focus on the supper preparations she and Liadan were working on a week later. Her mind kept drifting back to the session she and Weylin had finished not an hour ago, where he'd pinned her against one of the forest trees. The exercise had been simple enough in theory. All she'd had to do was break free of his hold. But it hadn't been as easy as she'd thought. Not when Weylin's body had been so close to hers, his forearm setting her skin ablaze as he'd pressed it to her collarbone.

For one wild moment, Bryanna had considered pressing her lips to his, to see if he'd let her go, or abandon their training altogether and kiss her back. And she could've sworn his eyes had darkened, too, as if he'd been thinking along the same lines.

She shook herself.

She was in dangerous territory, and the sooner she stopped thinking about him in that way, the better.

"Are you all right, Bryanna?" Liadan asked, pulling her from her thoughts as they waited for the jackalope and root vegetable stew they were cooking to tenderize. "You look flushed."

"It's the heat coming from the stove," Bryanna lied, pushing off from the bench.

"It should be done soon," she said. "But before that, can we talk?"

"It's not about Cayde, is it?"

All week, boarders had taken her aside to caution her against Cayde. Even though she knew they did it with good intentions, it was becoming irritating.

"Well ..."

Bryanna sighed. "Oh, Liadan, not you too."

"Look, I know you don't want to hear this, but you need to be careful where Cayde is concerned. You didn't see his face that night he and Weylin fought."

Bryanna shook her head in exasperation. "Liadan, Cayde was just annoyed that I got between him and Weylin."

"No, Bryanna, it was more than that," Liadan said, taking an onion out and slicing into it. "He looked as though you chose Weylin over him or something. Cayde's made it very obvious he has feelings for you."

Bryanna scoffed. "Oh, come on, just because we talk doesn't mean we're attracted to each other."

"In Cayde's case, it does," Liadan insisted. "And now he thinks you like Weylin."

Bryanna's face grew hot despite herself. "*What*? That's ridiculous."

"No, it's not, and—" Liadan stopped slicing her onion, spotting Bryanna's pink cheeks. "Oh my goodness, you *like* him."

"Don't be daft," Bryanna said, so fast, her words came out sharp.

"Not Cayde. Weylin."

"Shhh." What was Liadan thinking, saying that out loud? Had she forgotten that Weylin had preternatural senses and could hear things the rest of them couldn't? "No, I don't."

Though even as the words left her mouth, she knew they weren't true.

"You know, now that I think about it," Liadan mused as if she hadn't heard her. "I think he fancies you too. It explains why we've seen so much of him lately."

"Liadan, Weylin doesn't fancy me. If he did, he'd know exactly how to go about courting me. Ignoring me and criticizing my cooking is no way to gain my favor."

To her relief, they called supper a few minutes later.

Bryanna didn't need to look up to know when Weylin finally walked in—late, as usual. Her whole body hummed as though lightning had charged the air between them.

She chose a seat as far from him as she could, hoping the distance would slow her racing heart, and spent the rest of supper trying to ignore him. Cayde attempted to make conversation with her several times, but Bryanna couldn't focus on what he was saying. She was too busy pretending not to notice Weylin's disapproving glare each time she nodded at something Cayde said.

As soon as supper was over, Bryanna excused herself and headed out to the apothecary workstation in the barn. Liadan hadn't been able to stop talking about Weylin as they'd cleared the table, asking question after question that made it impossible for Bryanna to keep the feelings she'd been trying to ignore for moon cycles from surfacing. Eventually, she'd had to pretend Obelia needed her to finish a re-energizing potion for Elgar to get away from Liadan and her prying.

She spent the rest of the night up in the barn until she was certain Liadan had retired for the night. Only then did she dampen the fire in the grate, lock up, and head toward the tower, eager to train with Alec and then get some sleep. She was hoping that, come morning, she'd wake with the feelings Liadan had brought up back in the deep recesses of her mind, where they belonged.

But as she left the barn, the hairs along the back of her neck prickled, the same way they had the night she and Gawain were in the forest.

She stopped dead in her tracks and reached into the pocket of her breeches for the League watch. But just as she gripped it, the creature leaped off its bough, its large, bat-like wings expanding as it glided into the forest.

No.

Bryanna sprang after it. There was no way she could take the time to alert the others. She needed to go after the creature now, before she lost track of it. Her feet carried her into the forest as if of their own accord, following the gigantic creature as it led her away from the tower.

Somehow, despite the ever-encroaching darkness of the trees, Bryanna kept up with it. It was almost as if the creature was keeping a leisurely pace on purpose, making it possible for her to keep it in sight.

She wasn't sure how long she'd been following it when she made up her mind to check on her mental barrier spell. Although she felt more like herself than she had the night she and Gawain had been ensnared by the creature, she still didn't feel quite right. The second she pulled on her magic, the unctuous presence she'd sensed moon cycles before returned. Its influence was pressed up against her barrier, oozing into any weak spots it could find. Immediately, Bryanna wrenched at her magic, using every force of her will to purge the malevolent presence from her mind.

At once, the sharp focus she'd had when she'd left the barn returned. She took a sharp intake of breath, her grip on the oil lamp tightening as she willed herself not to panic, and scanned her surroundings. But it was too dark, even with her oil lamp, for her to recognize how far into the forest she was.

Above her, the creature paused, as though it could sense that she was no longer under its mind-weaving grasp. Bryanna pulled on her magic, preparing to face off against it, her heart racing at double speed, but instead of swooping down on her the way he had that first night, it rounded a large trunk and disappeared.

Bryanna's breath caught in her throat. For a moment, she didn't dare move, afraid that doing so would give the creature the opening it needed to strike. But she could no longer feel its presence. It was as though it had teleported. Except only ovates could do that, and the creature had definitely not been one.

Then, up ahead, a rustling of leaves and the sound of heavy footfalls made her whole body stiffen.

Another being was in the forest with her.

Cold beads of sweat formed on her brow. Was this new being the reason why the green-blooded creature had fled?

"Who's there?" she called, unable to disguise the quaver in her voice.

Bryanna moved forward, squinting at the dark patch of branches until she caught sight of a tall, gangly being prowling toward her, his form coming into sharp relief as he stepped into the light emanating from her oil lamp.

"Cayde?" She almost laughed in relief. She'd been so sure she was about to come face-to-face with some unknown, perilous forest denizen. "For the love of Castlereagh. You scared me."

He continued to close the distance between them, looking paler than she'd ever seen him, more like the creature who'd wanted to inflict pain on Weylin over Beltane than the young man with the quick smiles and easy banter.

The urge to put space between them was paramount, though Bryanna held her ground. "Cayde, what are you doing here? Did you see that strange creature?"

"No."

She swallowed, fighting back the dread coursing through her. "We should get back to the tower before it comes back."

It was the wrong thing to say. Cayde's eyes narrowed to slits. "You mean get back to *him*?"

Liadan's words reverberated in her head.

Cayde's made it very obvious he has feelings for you.

"I thought you saw Conveil for what he really was," he said, rage lacing his voice. "You've seen how he treats me. Do you know what it's like to hear your heart pick up every time he comes close to you? To watch your gaze linger in his direction when he isn't looking? It's sickening to watch. I thought it would pass, but you're just getting worse."

Cayde was shaking.

He wanted to attack her; she could see it in his eyes.

He was barely containing himself.

"I can't fight this," he whispered.

"Cayde, don't say that," Bryanna said softly.

But Cayde was beyond the point of reasoning. He lunged for her, his fingers clamping around her arms, pushing her up against a tree. The impact jostled the oil lamp from Bryanna's grasp. It fell to the floor, splintering the glass case into a hundred pieces and extinguishing the flame, leaving them in inky darkness.

"Cayde, stop!" Bryanna cried, struggling to free herself from his grip. "This isn't you."

"Don't you understand?" Cayde murmured as a wet, squelching noise sounded in the vicinity of his forehead. Two slimy feelers emerged, glistening in the moonlight. "It *is* me. And I'm tired of pretending it isn't."

"Cayde, *no*."

Bryanna reached for her magic, but Cayde's feelers latched onto the space between her brows. She tried to wrench them off, but he was too fast, and with a sickening pull, pain erupted through her skull, searing and inescapable.

"Cayde, stop!" Bryanna screamed, trying to twist free. But it was like fighting against iron shackles. The feelers only dug deeper, and the pressure intensified as though something was burrowing into her brain. "You're hurting me!"

But there was no restraint or recognition in his crazed eyes. His nails dug deeper into her arms, drawing blood as he forced her still. She scrambled desperately for her magic again, but his feelers were draining her of her strength too fast. The sucking became unbearable, as though he were trying to draw her brain out through the incision his feelers had made in her forehead.

Bryanna couldn't scream anymore, couldn't focus on her magic. The pain was no longer just physical. Cayde's assault had gone deeper, bringing her an agony of a different, more vulnerable sort. He was no longer feeding off her body, but the part of her soul that all beings needed to survive—comfort, strength, and the will to live.

A keening pierced the air, infiltrating the forest. The sound was strong and unnatural, filled with sorrow. It reverberated through the trees at a deafening octave. Nisienne's lament—for that, she knew, was what it had to be—was leading her out of the living world and into the next, where she was sure Aveline would be waiting.

CHAPTER

NINETEEN

Nisienne's keening became a dull, muted ringing in Bryanna's ears, fading in the same manner as the other forest sounds around her. She could no longer hear the wind brushing through the branches above her, or the scurrying of nocturnal creatures flitting across the treetops. Soon, unconsciousness would come. Then death. Bryanna welcomed it. She didn't have any will to go on. If it weren't for Cayde holding her up, she would've sagged, boneless, to the floor. The physical pain was leaving her, replaced by a strange numbness that left her limbs feeling so heavy, she didn't have the strength to move them.

She'd been naive to think her existence, everything she'd done—becoming the youngest sorceress of her time, training to vanquish the Brotherhood of Sìorraidh—had been for something. In the great scheme of things, she was no more than one of the billions of extraneous life forms that came and went in an extraordinary, immortal, ever-changing world. She would be remembered only by those who'd mourn her until they, too, passed on.

No.

She wouldn't think of herself as dead.

Not while she could still draw breath.

Bryanna's magic surged, and she grasped onto it, sending a repelling spell over herself and forcing Cayde's hold, which in his frenzied state had become so unyielding, to loosen until he could no longer maintain his grip on her.

"What are you doing?" he snarled as Bryanna fell through his slackened fingers. She crumpled to the ground instead with an involuntary whimper. "Stop it!"

He crouched over her, his wet, glistening feelers suctioning uselessly as he tried to reattach them to the wounds on her forehead. But they kept sliding off her skin, unable to regain their grasp.

From somewhere behind them came a great, resounding *neigh*.

Bryanna blinked, her gaze falling on the lithe, snowy-white unicorn she'd healed in the forest as it came charging through the trees and barreled into Cayde. He went hurtling away from them, crashing into the thick underbrush several paces away with a heavy thud.

Run, she tried to shout at her valiant defender. Cayde wouldn't think twice about attacking him in his predatory state.

But her mouth was too slack to form the words.

The unicorn ambled forward, placing himself between her and the neach-ithe anam, the silver horn on his forehead glinting as he glowered at Cayde's crumpled form, his nostrils flared.

"*What have you done?*" shouted a husky voice as Cayde staggered to his feet, his feelers askew as he stared at the unicorn with wide, startled incomprehension.

Bryanna's heart staggered against her ribcage as a fresh

wave of horror encased her. She'd recognize the voice anywhere.

Weylin.

What in all of Castlereagh was he doing there, and not safe behind the tower's walls?

Pulling on the last dredges of strength she had left, Bryanna tried to shout at Weylin to get out of there, to get to her aunt, but all that she could manage was a feeble, distorted whisper. "Go."

Weylin didn't even bother looking in Cayde's direction as he rushed to her side, sucking in a breath as he took in the condition she was in. His fingers came gently to her forehead, touching the edges of the wounds made by Cayde's feelers before lowering to her neck, his strong, sure fingers trembling slightly as he felt for her pulse.

Bryanna's brows furrowed. Why were they trembling?

Leaves crunched under Cayde's feet as he neared them. Before he could, though, a deep growl erupted from Weylin, the possessive kind wolves made when uninvited creatures neared their den. "Don't even think about coming any closer, Garnet," he snarled, his voice quivering with rage. "If she wasn't on the brink of death, I'd be choking you by your feelers right now."

His words drifted to her as though through a thickening fog.

If she wasn't on the brink of death.

Was she dying? Because if she was, it wasn't as painful as she'd thought it would be. The only thing she felt was an exhausting tiredness.

"C-Conveil?" Cayde murmured, sounding more like his usual self. His feelers were gone, retracted behind a creased forehead. He looked like the Cayde who'd been her friend for the last few moon cycles. "Conveil, listen. I don't know what came over me—"

"Don't lie!" Weylin shouted, his voice raw with fury. "I knew it was only a matter of time before you did this!"

"Conveil—"

Cayde tried to get closer, but the same protective growl that he'd made when he'd first seen Bryanna's prone form erupted from Weylin's chest, thick with a menace directly leveled at him.

"I never meant—"

But before he could say another word, the unicorn neighed in warning, setting himself between them, his horn pointed threateningly.

"Save it," Weylin barked. "You're exactly what I told Obelia you'd be. You should've never come here. If I were you, I'd start running, Garnet. Because if she doesn't make it, I'm coming after you."

The violence behind his promise made Bryanna still.

"Please. I didn't mean to do this—"

Weylin rounded on the unicorn. "Get rid of him."

The unicorn strode forward, herding Cayde away from her and Weylin by the tip of his horn.

"I'm sorry," Cayde whispered, his voice wretched as he backed away from them. "This was never meant to happen."

Weylin waited until his footfalls had receded before letting out a shaky breath. "Bryanna?" he said, the ferocity that had been in his voice softening to a bare whisper. "Can you hear me?"

Bryanna was too tired to nod. Her head ached dully. She wanted to sleep. There was no need to stay awake anymore. Cayde was gone, and Weylin was safe.

"Keep your eyes open, Bryanna," Weylin said, his hand coming around the back of her neck and tilting it forward so that she had no choice but to look at him. "I need you to stay with me. You're going to be all right." The fingers of his other hand came up, touching the edges of the wounds Cayde had left on her forehead. They came away wet with blood. Weylin swallowed hard and drew her to him, pressing her into his chest so that she could hear the hard, fast beating of his heart against her ear. He took a deep, determined breath, his grip on her tightening as he came to some sort of decision. "Bryanna, I'm going to do something. It will help, I swear. Just ... stay with me."

He eased her back to the ground, his movements careful so as not to jostle her head.

"Keep your eyes open," he reminded her, though Bryanna could feel herself slipping, the haze that had been dancing at the corners of her vision welcoming her into its depths.

She wasn't sure how long she'd sunk into a semi-conscious state when the sound of Weylin's labored breath pulled her back. Wet popping noises were coming from all over his body, as though his bones were being pulled out of their joints. He was bent forward so that she could see the top of his head. Instead of his usual mahogany hair, though, was something thicker, shorter ...

Fur.

Bryanna had seen Alec shift several times during their training, but his transformation had been seamless. He certainly hadn't been making the sort of pain-filled sounds Weylin was, as though morphing into his faoladh form was causing him physical distress.

She needed to stop him. She wouldn't have him hurting himself on her account. Not when, as he'd said, she was already on the brink of death.

Bryanna tried to reach for him, but her arms were too heavy. Claw-like hands pressed over her heart and forehead, and Bryanna found herself looking up at lupine, smoky-blue eyes.

The rest of Weylin's face was covered by fur, but there was something about his wolfish features that was still uniquely Weylin's.

A strange sensation came over her, enveloping her in a tangible aura. It warmed her soul, made her want to curl up in its embrace, and never relinquish it.

At least until the pain returned.

"No." She tried to push Weylin away. Whatever he was doing, it was making the pain sharper, both in her mind and in her body. "Stop."

It is all right, child, said a disembodied voice. *He is helping you.*

It was the last thing Bryanna heard before oblivion wrapped around her like a heavy winter blanket.

Bryanna stood in her bedchamber in Castlereagh—or a version of it. The drapes across the windows were a subtle rose rather than the burgundy brocade she'd changed them to years ago. The four-poster bed was hung with white lace, the walls covered in soft, pastel-pink wallpaper instead of the present-day cream stripes, and the frilly counterpane was weighed down with her mother's treasured collection of smooth-faced, rosy-cheeked porcelain dolls. It was exactly what her bedchamber used to look like before Aveline died.

"Hello, Bree."

Bryanna turned, her chest tightening with a familiar, bittersweet ache, the same way it always did when she heard her late cousin's voice. Aveline sat in front of the old dollhouse they'd spent hours playing with as children. She was in a satin dress that had been so big for her, Bryanna's aunt used to have to pin it back so it would fit. Only it wasn't pinned back anymore. Aveline had grown into it so that the waist hugged her body snugly.

"Am I dead?" she asked.

Aveline shook her head. "Not quite. You're in the In-Between plane."

Bryanna forgot how to breathe. There were only two ways to get to the plane she was allegedly in: as a dead spirit or a soul whose physical body was hanging on to the last dredges of life. From what Bryanna knew, the In-Between plane was unsafe for the living. Hardly anyone who crossed over returned.

"So I'm dying?"

She supposed she shouldn't have been surprised. She'd known that was her fate as she'd lain in the Sheidlow Forest's underbrush with Weylin at her side. But it didn't stop the sadness and disappointment that came with knowing the life she'd been building was no longer within her reach.

"Don't worry. We'll keep you safe until you can go back."

Bryanna didn't miss her use of the plural. "We?"

"Mistress Nichollson and I."

"*Who?*"

As if summoned, the doorknob twisted, and the scrawny, unkempt woman who'd been haunting Bryanna's dreams since the night she'd been poisoned entered.

Bryanna took a hasty step back, knocking into the dressing table and sending the little bottles and jars askew.

"About time," the woman said, her tone clipped as her gaze raked over Bryanna with cold calculation. "I was beginning to think I would not get to you until it was too late. Your cousin was my last hope."

Bryanna stared at Aveline, betrayal stinging worse than lemon juice on an open wound. Aveline had never been vindictive when they'd been children. Had death changed her so much that she'd led the frightful woman to Bryanna to get back at her for abandoning her all those years ago?

Hurt crossed Aveline's young features. "Bree, it's not what you think. Mistress Nichollson is here to help, I promise. I haven't let her come near you before, but I can see now that you really aren't going to stop what you're doing, and she's the only one who can help."

"Help how?"

Mistress Nichollson extended her hand. "There is something you need to see."

Bryanna didn't move. She didn't trust the woman before her. Not when she'd been featuring in her dreams for weeks, speaking in a nonsense tongue she couldn't decipher.

"It's all right, Bree," Aveline said bracingly. "You can trust her. Go."

"We do not have time for this," Mistress Nichollson growled.

She seized Bryanna's arm, and with a swift and violent surge of magic, Bryanna's old bedchamber and Aveline disappeared as she and Mistress Nichollson plunged down, down, down into a shadowless vortex. Bryanna's heart felt as though it was jammed in her throat, keeping her from screaming as she clawed at the rushing cool air whipping around them.

Frightful thoughts chased each other in Bryanna's mind, each more harrowing than the next. Was she going to remain in the darkness forever, falling through a timeless black hole?

But then the abyss fell away, and she landed unceremoniously on an uneven forest floor, her skirts a tangled mess. Bryanna rushed to her feet, staring around her. They stood on the edge of a valley hedged in by a towering rock face.

Bryanna didn't recognize the landscape, though she could tell they were still in Otherworld. The layered hills, green meadows, and misty mountains couldn't belong to any other realm.

"Where are we?" she demanded, glaring daggers at Mistress Nichollson.

"Where it all started," her unwelcome companion replied.

Before Bryanna could retort, footfalls came from behind them. Bryanna turned to see who was coming and froze. She was staring at Mistress Nichollson. Or at least, the living version of her. Unlike the ragged, unkempt specter beside her, her living counterpart was striking, with dark hair that fell thickly past her shoulders and sharp, angled features.

The woman didn't show any signs of seeing Bryanna or Mistress Nicholls as she passed them, her attention focused on a crop of trees up ahead. They had to be in some kind of vision, one only accessible through the In-Between plane.

"Come," said Mistress Nichollson. "What happened next is important."

"I'm not going anywhere until you tell me what's going on," Bryanna said, planting her feet. "Where are we?"

"Like I said, where it all—"

"Started?" Bryanna interrupted. "I heard you. Where *what* started?"

"Follow, and you will see." Without another word, Mistress Nichollson turned and followed the young woman down a dirt path that led to a thick, ominous forest with a canopy so dense that it kept sunlight from coming through.

Bryanna clenched her teeth. She had half a mind to refuse to do what Mistress Nichollson wanted. But then she remembered what Aveline had told her about the churlish woman being the only one who could help her, and made after them.

Aveline had better be right, or the next time they saw each other, they'd have words.

Darkness surrounded them as they entered the trees, their only company the strangled, croaked cries of unseen birds. Bryanna's hair stood on end as they moved deeper into its heart. Something didn't feel right. The forest didn't have the same inviting ambiance as the Sheidlow Forest. Instead, there was an ominousness to it, as though a malignant entity imbued every trunk, branch, and leaf.

They didn't stop until they reached a small cave. The woman stalled for a moment, catching her breath. A lot of their trek had been uphill. Bryanna was certain she would've been struggling for air, too, were she not in the In-Between plane, her current form not corporeal. At least, not the tangible kind.

The cave, when they entered it, was poorly lit. Inside was a huddle of pale-faced, disheveled humans and a cast of dark creatures. Bryanna stopped in her tracks, recognizing some from her basilisk hallucination, like the ogres and will-o'-the-wisps, but there were other, more formidable beings as well, including a pair of nuckelavees, who looked like black steeds, but with the upper bodies of rotted humans.

A man appeared from the shadows of the cave. He was handsome enough, with well-defined muscles and healthy, glowing skin. Unlike the other humans, who looked pale, gaunt, and emaciated, he looked more like a lord. His hard face narrowed momentarily as he caught sight of the woman, before it melted away into an expression of mild—and in Bryanna's opinion, insincere—concern. "You seem upset, Brithlean," he said, drawing her attention to him. "Was it your brother?"

Brithlean? Bryanna glanced at Mistress Nichollson. Surely her name didn't have anything to do with the Brithlean League?

Brithlean's head rose defiantly. "I no longer have a brother, Agron."

The man's lips pulled up in a tight smile. "I am pleased. You do not need him. You have us now. And after tonight, we will never need anyone again." He gazed at the sliver of sunlight slowly extending into the cave. "It is almost time. Are you ready?"

"I am," said Brithlean. "Are you? You know what to do once I complete the ritual. You must be fast, for I will be weak. This branch of magic has been hidden for centuries for a reason. Even the highest ovates fear its potency."

"Have faith, my love," he said, caressing her face.

Brithlean kissed his palm. "You know I do."

"Good. Everything will be fine. You shall see. After tonight, no one will ever part us again. I promise. Now, all is prepared. The only thing left is for us to take our positions."

"Positions for what?" Bryanna asked Mistress Nichollson as she watched the man take Brithlean's hand and lead her to a deep pit at the end of the cave.

"The ritual I performed," the robed woman rasped in reply. "That was Agron Vortigern. He and I were going to take charge of our lives and rule the world."

Bryanna's brows rose. "*Rule* the world?"

"Let's just say we lived in a time where peace between beings wasn't common, especially where the faoladhs and faeries were concerned. Now come, you need to understand what happened here."

Mistress Nichollson tugged her forward, toward the pit Vortigern and Brithlean were standing on the edge of. Bryanna took one look at the content inside, and a horrified gasp escaped her lips. It contained some of the most atrocious items known to magic-weavers. Giant snake heads, long unicorn horns, acid-green dragon hearts, and worst of all, the dead, naked body of a Tuatha Dé Danann infant whose cheeks were still red from crying. The sacrificial use of a child in a ritual had been outlawed for many centuries, and for good reason. It invoked the most dangerous and abominable forms of magic.

"What did you do?" she asked in a harsh whisper.

"This was the evening of the summer solstice," Mistress Nichollson said as the thin line of sunlight that had been slowly crawling toward the repulsive contents spilled into the pit. There was a great *whoosh!* and the pit burst into flames like well-oiled kindling, casting shadows over the cave walls. They crackled menacingly, as though protesting against the nature of the magic being evoked, and turned blue. "It was when the ritual had to be performed. We'd planned it for moon cycles."

Around them, Brithlean's voice enveloped the cave as she chanted in an ancient language Bryanna found mildly familiar. It sounded a lot like what she kept hearing each time Mistress Brithlean featured in her dreams. Despite not understanding the words, Bryanna could tell she was invoking an extremely powerful spell, one that, in Bryanna's time, would've required multiple magic-weavers.

What was Brithlean doing, performing such a high-level spell on her own? She *had* to know the risks of overexerting her magical stores. And yet, there was a determined gleam in Brithlean's eyes. She didn't flinch, not even when the magic she wielded weakened her down to her knees, the ritual feeding on more than her magic. She pushed through like a woman in labor who knew her perseverance would reap a priceless reward.

A black, putrid smoke formed above the fire, billowing toward Vortigern, who stood stoically, breathing it in as if it were a healing mist. As it engulfed him, though, he grunted, clenching his jaw to keep from crying out. But the pain overcame him until his gut-wrenching screams reverberated around the cave.

Bryanna itched to pull him out of the acrid smoke, to stop the agonizing wails hurting her ears. But she was the only one affected by the sight before them. The other humans stood around the fire, staring vacantly as though they'd been overdosed with calming draughts. The creatures, too, watched on, their faces alight with glee each time a new bellow forced its way out of Vortigern's mouth.

Bryanna wasn't sure how much time passed before the smoke dissipated and Vortigern fell still, taking deep, heavy breaths.

Several pregnant minutes dragged by before he pushed to his feet, sweat dripping down his face. He didn't look any different from before the ritual, though Bryanna could tell something was off about him. Something that made every fiber of her being stand on end.

"Agron," Brithlean gasped, crawling to him, her sunken eyes glassy.

Vortigern bent down until they were eye to eye, his lips curved in a cool smile. "My love, I am surprised you are conscious. It would have been better if you were not."

Bryanna stared at Vortigern, more horrified than she'd been when she'd seen the contents of the pit.

"I am afraid I will have to renege on our pact. Power is a corrupting business. It should never be shared, not even between lovers. It causes havoc. And I do not want havoc while I reign."

Tears spilled down Brithlean's cheeks.

Bryanna turned away, her eyes prickling with injustice. "Take me back," she told Mistress Nichollson. "I've seen enough."

"Not yet," said Mistress Nichollson, her gaze filled with hate and contempt as she glared at Vortigern.

A shuffle sounded nearby, drawing Bryanna's attention. A nuckelavee was dragging a scrawny, bedraggled villager toward them.

"Let me go," the man bellowed, trying to twist free.

But the creature pulled him the rest of the way to Vortigern and threw him bodily at his feet.

"Be careful," Vortigern snapped. "I need his body unharmed."

The man whimpered, shaking worse than Bryanna. "Please," he begged, his voice quivering with fear, "don't do this, Vortigern."

Bryanna knew what would come next. She'd seen it once before. She averted her gaze, bile rising in her stomach. She had no inclination to see it again. But Mistress Nichollson grabbed her chin with her sharp, brittle fingers and forced her back to face Vortigern. His eyes had rolled to the back of his skull. As she watched, his body crumpled to the ground, coming to rest beside his fallen lover.

A milky-white creature with Vortigern's dulled features stood in his place. "Shhh," it murmured.

The man sniffled, his eyes beseeching as Vortigern's hand moved from his neck, over his collarbone, and stopped at his torso. Then he drove his vapor-like hand into his rib cage.

The man screamed, staring down at the wrist wedged in his chest. The sound reverberated around the cave, forcing Bryanna to clap her hands to her ears as she tried to block out the horror. But his cries filtered through, filled with deep-seated agony and terror.

And then, as suddenly as they'd started, the man's wails cut off. Vortigern had twisted all the way into him, leaving a deafening silence in the cave.

No one moved.

Their sights remained singularly glued to the motionless figure in their midst until, at last, his eyes flew open and a wide grin that didn't match the man's face stretched across his lips.

Bryanna's stomach churned. Was this what Mistress Nichollson had wanted her to see? Because if it was, she'd already seen it before, right alongside her when they'd been behind the cascading waterfall several weeks back.

"Now," said Mistress Nichollson, "we can go."

In a whirlwind of magic, Bryanna was pulled back into the black vortex.

CHAPTER

TWENTY

"It was you," Bryanna seethed, pushing away the counterpane she was under. "You started it all."

She grabbed the front of Mistress Nichollson's blouse ... only it wasn't Mistress Nichollson who looked back at her, concern heavy in her exhausted, solemn face.

It was her aunt.

Bryanna snatched her hand back, recognizing the familiar scents of eucalyptus and talcum powder. She was no longer in the In-Between plane, but in Obelia's medical chamber.

No.

She couldn't be back in the land of the living. Not yet. She needed to get back to Aveline. To warn her to stay away from Mistress Nichollson. The woman couldn't be trusted. Not when *she* was the reason Aveline and so many others were dead.

"Bryanna, you need to calm down," said Obelia, pushing her into her pillows. "You're all right."

"No. I'm not." Bryanna dug her fingers into her aunt's arm. "I need to go back!"

"Oh no, not if I have anything to do with it. I've been working for hours to reverse what Cayde did to you."

"Aunt Obelia, please. I have to warn my cousin. She doesn't know what Brithlean did!"

"You're *not* going back there, Bryanna," Obelia said firmly.

"But Aveline—"

"Is *safe*. And she'd already know. The souls in the In-Between plane are privy to more than what we see or hear." She took a seat on the edge of Bryanna's bed. "Now, tell me what you saw in the In-Between plane that has you in such a state."

Bryanna told her everything, from seeing Aveline to how Brithlean Nichollson had taken her back in time, to show her what she'd done and how the Brotherhood of Sìorraidh had come to be. By the time she'd finished, Obelia looked ashen.

"Foolish woman," Obelia muttered, shaking her head.

"Was Brithlean a common name?" Bryanna asked. It seemed a little too coincidental that the League was named after the magic-weaver who'd created the Brotherhood of Sìorraidh.

"No. The League is named after her because she was believed to be their first reported victim. She and her lover, Agron Vortigern. Except now, thanks to you, we know he wasn't a victim at all."

"Why does she come to me? Why not someone else? Surely she doesn't think *I* can reverse whatever she did."

Obelia's brows knitted together. "It must be easier for her to reach out to you. We are, as it happens, loosely related."

"We're *what*?" It was as though her aunt had swept a rug out from under her feet. Bryanna would've never thought she and her family were in any way connected to the formation of the Brotherhood. Just the thought of such a thing made Bryanna's stomach turn.

"Yes. Her brother, Victor Nichollson, grew up to become our very great-grandfather."

A strange emptiness began to weigh heavily on Bryanna. She touched her forehead, the memory of just how she'd ended up in the In-Between plane returning to her. The skin there felt whole and unblemished, if a little tender. She swallowed. She never would've thought Cayde capable of betraying her the way he had.

As if sensing her thoughts, Obelia's face grew taut. Learning what Cayde had done to Bryanna had to have come as a deep betrayal, especially after how many times she'd vouched for him despite her boarders' protests.

"Where's Weylin?" Bryanna asked as the rest of what had happened slowly returned to her, including his part in saving her.

"He went after Cayde, we're assuming," she said, handing Bryanna a goblet of orange potion. "This is for you. It will help regenerate what Cayde took from you."

Bryanna accepted the goblet but didn't drink from it immediately. "Did anyone go after him?"

"Two of the League members did. I'm sure they'll return with him soon." Obelia nodded at the goblet. "Now drink."

Bryanna took a sip and almost gagged. It tasted like expired mustard seeds and caviar soaked in squid ink.

"Get some rest." Obelia extinguished her oil lamp. "You're going to need to recover faster."

"But Weylin—"

"I'll wake you once he's back," Obelia promised her. "Now sleep, before I make you take a sleeping tonic."

"Fine," Bryanna grumbled.

But it was a while before she fell back asleep.

The sound of rustling pages brought Bryanna out of a restless sleep a few hours later. She sat up, expecting to see Weylin beside her, but as her eyes adjusted to the dim lighting coming off the oil lamp, she found Liadan sitting at the other end of her bed, squinting furiously as she read a tattered volume.

Bryanna leaned back against her pillow, her disappointment palpable. "Liadan?"

Liadan dropped the volume onto her lap and moved closer to Bryanna. "How are you feeling?" she asked gently. "When Nisienne started keening, we thought perhaps the Brotherhood had gotten to you. Poor Seara was beside herself."

Bryanna pushed herself into a sitting position once more, letting the counterpane pool in her lap. "Liadan, why would you think it had anything to do with the Brotherhood?"

"Don't think I haven't noticed you leaving your chamber every night and not returning until the wee morning hours," she said indignantly. "If I didn't know better, I would've thought the rumors of you working against the Brotherhood were true. And if that's what you're doing, then you need to be careful. Believe me. After they took Drystan—"

"Liadan, Drystan wasn't taken by the Brotherhood," Bryanna interrupted. She'd know too. She'd memorized the name of every being who'd met their demise at the hand of the Brotherhood, and the young man who'd been with Liadan the day she'd been attacked by the questing beast wasn't one of them.

"He was," Liadan assured her. "But his family kept it quiet. They told people he'd died from an aggressive case of faerie-stroke. But I know it was them. The day we went to Quarry Cliff Woodlands, Drystan sensed something was wrong. He told me to wait in the carriage while he checked the area, but I went after him. At least, I thought it was him ..."

Liadan's gaze fell on the counterpane, her fingers poking

between the weaves. "Drystan found me just before the questing beast could finish me off. What was left of me, that is. He got me back to the carriage, but before he could take me to a healer, we were attacked."

Bryanna leaned against the bed frame, speechless.

"I don't know exactly what happened. My wounds were so extensive, I passed out." Liadan took an unsteady breath, her pink irises flashing like a cat's in the lamplight. "When I awoke several days later, the healers told me I'd hallucinated the struggle outside our carriage. That Drystan was the one who'd brought me in. I can't tell you how relieved I was to hear that. For days, I waited for him to visit me, and when he finally did, it wasn't my Drystan."

Bryanna clapped a hand to her mouth. "He'd been compromised?"

Liadan nodded. "Drystan and I were together for years. I would've recognized him with a mask over his head. And the thing that sat in the parlor in front of me wasn't him. He was more fascinated with my wounds than my well-being. When I told him my scars felt strange, as though they were spreading rather than healing, he told me it was normal and not to bother anyone about it. That's when I knew it wasn't my Drystan. He'd always had an obsession with questing beasts. He's the one who told me that when a wound made by a questing beast didn't fade, it meant its victim was turning into a questing beast too.

"That night, I begged my brothers to take me to the Mage's Sanctuary. I told them not to tell anyone, especially Drystan. Not that they needed much convincing. To this day, they still blame him for what happened to me. The entire carriage ride over, I was petrified the Brotherhood would take me and force me to turn into a questing beast. But they didn't. Perhaps I wasn't a priority. Or maybe they were afraid of Obelia. I don't know. A few days later, I received news that Drystan was dead."

"I'm so sorry," Bryanna whispered, squeezing Liadan's hand. She knew exactly what it was like to receive such devastating news. She had, after all, gone through the exact same thing when she'd lost Aveline.

"He died because of me." Great big tears rolled down Liadan's cheeks. "He'd wanted to go to a new tea shop that had opened in town. If I hadn't convinced him to take me to the Woodlands, he'd still be alive."

Bryanna wrapped her arms around her. "Don't say that, Liadan. You couldn't have known what would happen."

They were silent for a moment, each lost in their own forlorn thoughts.

"Does Bain know about Drystan?" Bryanna asked at last.

Liadan blushed. "Yes. He was there when I got the letter that he'd passed."

"Are you two ..."

"No. I can't ... It wouldn't be fair to Drystan."

Bryanna's chest tightened. She couldn't imagine what it must've been like for Liadan, unable to forge a new life when the last person she'd pledged herself to had died trying to save her. The guilt had to be crushing, especially when she felt to blame for what had befallen him.

And Bain ... He couldn't be in the same chamber as Liadan without gravitating toward her. Any being who spent two minutes with him could tell how smitten he was. Yet, he'd never acted on his feelings. Bryanna didn't think he would until Liadan was ready.

The question was, would she ever be?

There was a standing ovation for Bryanna the next morning when she and Liadan entered the kitchen. Everyone had heard about what happened to her and how it had led to Cayde fleeing Sheidlow Ridge. Although Bryanna didn't wholeheartedly approve of the underlying cause for their elation, she appreciated their warm reception nonetheless.

Nisienne was the first to reach her and wrapped her arms around her. "I've never prevented a death with my gift before."

Bryanna's throat clogged, something that was most unlike her. It usually took a lot for her emotions to overwhelm her. She blamed the abundance of essence Cayde had taken from her, though her aunt had told her the side effects wouldn't be permanent.

"You have to stop doing this to us, Bryanna," Seara cried, throwing her arms around her. "We thought you were dead—*again*. When we saw Weylin carry you in ... You should've seen his face. I've seen Weylin angry before, but last night ..."

Bryanna's heart gave a sweet flutter. "Is he back?"

"Not yet," said a familiar voice. "But don't worry, he will be. Hopefully with Cayde's head on a spike."

Bryanna nearly tripped over her feet. Alec sat at the breakfast table, looking familiar in the boarders' midst. He stood and shook her hand, squeezing it gently in warning. "You must be Bryanna. I'm Alec."

Alec is an old friend of Obelia's, Bain told her.

"You gave us quite a scare last night," said Alec. "I'm glad to see you back on your feet. You have your aunt's spirit."

"I wouldn't call what she has spirit," said Iodhna mulishly from the other side of the kitchen. She sat on her own, friendless now that Cayde was no longer around.

Alec turned to her. "You must be Iodhna Finn. The one who killed that boy in the tide last year?"

"That's her," said Bryanna.

"Huh." Alec took a sip of his tea and turned away from her. "I didn't expect her to look like a plucked chicken with cursed lungs."

Iodhna's pale complexion exploded into dark splotches. Bryanna didn't think the morgen had ever been so insulted in her life.

It did more for her recovery than Obelia's monstrosity of a potion.

***

Weylin didn't return until after supper.

Bryanna hadn't been able to focus on anything as she waited for him, her stomach a bundle of nerves. Not even training with Obelia, where they'd practiced a bone-breaking spell using old candelabras, had helped take her mind off him. Disastrous scenarios kept plaguing her thoughts, of Cayde losing control of himself again and attacking Weylin, sucking him dry of his essence the way he'd almost done with her.

But when he finally rode down the ironstone path on his steed, he was unharmed. Cayde's head start must've given him the time he'd needed to evade Weylin's pursuit. Despite how angry Bryanna was with the neach-ithe anam, a small part of her was glad Weylin hadn't found him.

Excusing herself from where she sat with Seara, Liadan, and Bain in the library, she headed up to the floor Weylin shared with Bain to wait for him, her palms sweating. She would've met him downstairs, except she didn't want an audience when she saw him again. Besides, she didn't think he would've been happy if anyone overheard her thanking him for the "tethering" he'd performed to save her. Alec hadn't been happy when he'd learned what he'd done. According to him, a tethering was dangerous to perform and almost never invoked. Had her way back to the living been severed after she'd slipped into the In-Between plane, she would've died and pulled Weylin along with her.

Bryanna had been gobsmacked when he'd told her. Weylin would've known what he was risking by forging the tethering, yet he'd done it anyway. Why he'd risked his life to keep her alive when she was little more than a stranger, Bryanna didn't know. But she was deeply grateful that he had, or she wouldn't have been standing there otherwise.

"You're back," she said as soon as he emerged from the staircase landing, straightening.

Weylin's steps faltered for a moment as he saw her standing in front of his door. Dark bags had settled under his blue-gray eyes. "What do you want, Ms. Nicholls?" he asked, his voice carefully controlled as his gaze swept over her, lingering on her pale skin before striding toward his door once more.

"I wanted to thank you," she said quietly, clasping her hands behind her back.

She wasn't sure if it was just exhaustion, but she thought she detected a coolness to him as he reached her. She couldn't see any trace of the Weylin who'd entreated her to stay awake and risked his life to keep her alive.

Weylin gritted his teeth and pulled her into his bedchamber, shutting it behind him. Bryanna barely registered the unmade bed or sparse oak furniture before he rounded on her. "You think I want you to thank me?" he growled, his voice low. "We told you not to trust Garnet, and you went ahead and did it anyway."

Bryanna paled. "I know, but Weylin, something wasn't right with him—"

"Stop trying to defend him," he cried, his voice dripping with fury. "He *attacked* you. Do you understand that if I hadn't reached you in time, you wouldn't be here?"

"I know," Bryanna whispered, her voice catching.

His expression softened slightly. "What were you even doing in the forest?"

Bryanna swallowed. She had a feeling that telling him she'd followed the creature into the trees wouldn't go as well with him as it had with her aunt. "I saw the green-blooded creature—"

Weylin's jaw worked as he fought to keep his temper in check.

"I wanted to tell you and my aunt," she said in a rush. "But it compelled me to follow it. Weylin, I swear, I wouldn't have gone after it alone if I'd had my own mind."

Weylin shook his head, though some of the animosity on his face disappeared at the earnestness in her tone. In that moment, Bryanna realized something: she'd thought the anger and fury she'd sensed coming from him had been because he was mad at her, but that wasn't it. At least, not completely. There was another emotion there. One he'd been doggedly trying to hide.

Worry.

Was it possible that he'd been afraid for her?

The more Bryanna thought about it, the more certain she was that she was right. Weylin had left himself exposed when he'd seen how close to death she'd been. His concern for her had overpowered his own self-preservation.

"You shouldn't have been out in the barn so late," he said. "If you'd told one of us you were out there, we would've kept watch."

"And likely ended up in the forest alongside me," Bryanna reasoned. "We would've both been dead by now, or worse."

"Don't tell me you'd care if something happened to me?"

"Of course I would!" she growled, the words coming out before she could stop them.

Weylin's lips twitched, as though to hide a pleased smirk.

"I mean—" Her cheeks burned. Why in all of Castlereagh had she said that? What had she been thinking? "If something happened to you, we'd have to get another sentinel. It would be a huge imposition on my aunt."

Weylin moved closer until she could smell the scent of pine coming off his skin. "Right ..."

"Though perhaps it wouldn't be so bad," she continued, completely aware that she was rambling and unable to stop herself. "I might actually like whoever replaces you."

Weylin's lips twitched. "Really?"

They were so close, Bryanna could feel the heat coming off him. It was making her knees weak and stirring things in regions of her body that had never stirred before. "They'd probably be half the knave you are."

Weylin's laughter filled the chamber. The sound was so unexpected, the action so unprecedented, that it transformed his face. The heavy burden that usually weighed down his features fell away. The difference it made left Bryanna short of breath. She'd always found him grudgingly handsome, but he was even more so when he was lost in true, unguarded mirth. The feelings for him she'd tried so hard to jam away into the recesses of her mind burst forth once more, and this time, she didn't think she'd be able to wrestle them down.

Weylin's eyes met hers, and something shifted in his expression. For a moment, neither of them moved. It was as though the air between them had stilled.

"You're welcome, by the way," he said at last, becoming serious once more. "For the tethering. I'd never done one before. Though, truth be told, I had a feeling I was going to need to eventually, what with the number of times I've had to save you."

Bryanna's mouth opened in protest. "Wha—I've saved you …"

Weylin leaned closer, his face hovering over hers. Bryanna caught her breath. She could no longer remember what she'd been about to say, not with Weylin so close. She waited, her heart fluttering against her chest as Weylin moved forward, closed the distance between them, and touched his lips to hers.

His kiss was light, almost hesitant, as though he was waiting for Bryanna to recoil from him. When he pulled back, Bryanna's hand snaked out, finding purchase at the base of his neck, keeping him from moving any farther.

Weylin's eyes locked on hers, and Bryanna saw something raw within their smoky-blue depths, a deep vulnerability that he was helpless to hide.

Her hand slid down the collar of his shirt and pulled him back to her, closing the distance between them once more. She parted her lips, surrendering to his pull. Weylin responded with a soft groan, pressing her up against his door. His lips moved over hers hungrily, as though he'd been waiting moon cycles to have her in his arms.

Was that always how it felt to be kissed? Because if it were, Bryanna couldn't believe she hadn't started doing it sooner. She couldn't get enough of Weylin's touch. It warmed her better than a blazing hearth in the middle of winter.

She wasn't sure how much time passed before Weylin broke off. It could've been seconds or minutes or even hours. They were both breathless by that point, their cheeks flushed.

Weylin traced a finger along the edge of Bryanna's cheek, a wry smile tugging at the corners of his mouth. "Alec's going to kill me."

"Alec?" Bryanna repeated. *What did Alec have to do with anything?*

"He threatened to have me transferred to the uninhabitable Faerie Kingdom of Falias if I ever tried anything with you."

"Oh."

"Don't worry, I don't think he'll actually do it." He gave her an impish grin. "After all, who'd save you if I wasn't around?"

Bryanna tried to look affronted, but the effect was ruined by the twitch of her lips. "Err, *I* would."

He snickered and kissed the tip of her nose. "I'd still better stick around. Just in case."

TWENTY-ONE

With Lammas—the day when all of Otherworld stopped what they were doing to acknowledge the wheel of time—on the way, Bryanna, Obelia, and the boarders were inundated with work as the days rolled by. There was plenty to do around the tower. The last of the wheat had to be reaped, the summer vegetable patches had to be picked, and new seedlings for the autumn crops had to be sown. There were also fruits to be harvested before the birds and worms got to them, and livestock to be culled, their meat salted and preserved for the colder moon cycles.

Most of the boarders, like Bryanna, had never worked on a farm before, and despite Obelia's patient instructions, there were accidents. Annabele and Shay, Obelia's newest boarders, were found prostrate in front of a freshly hanging dun cow they'd been gutting in the barn, Fergus pulled a tendon in his back trying to lift a crate of pumpkins, and Seara's ribs had to be nursed after she tried to sweep down the stable with Weylin's steed, Epona, still in it.

The approach of Lammas meant that winter was beginning to whisper in the wind. Nights grew colder, and although most of the trees in the forest were evergreen, the ones Obelia had planted around the tower and in her vegetable garden weren't. Leaves drifted over the lawn in varying degrees of decay, turning the ground around them into blankets of tawny brown and rusty orange.

Despite the chill in the air and the rise of activity, Bryanna wasn't given a reprieve from training. In fact, Alec had been intensifying her training, believing, as many others had started to whisper, that it wouldn't be long before the Brotherhood closed in on them. He wanted her to be as ready as she could be.

The cellar was becoming uncomfortably full with more Brithlean League members joining their ranks every day, many of whom brought it upon themselves to yell well-meaning advice while Alec or Weylin trained her. Bryanna wouldn't have minded, except that their advice kept contradicting everyone else's and led to arguments, which made it hard for her to focus.

"I can't believe you still haven't told the League about me," Seara seethed one day while they worked in the wheat field. "If it had been me, I would've mentioned you immediately."

"It's not that simple," Bryanna ground out, tightening her grip on the scythe. The truth was, she hadn't mentioned Seara to any of them since asking her aunt, mainly because she knew there was no way they'd induct her, especially given her age.

"Come on, Bryanna, it's been over a moon cycle. Figure out how to get me inducted before I do it myself."

Bryanna was beyond relieved when the luncheon bell rang and Seara stormed off. She watched her go, guilt pulling in her gut, until she heard footsteps behind her. Weylin's arms came around her shoulders, pulling her back against him and resting his chin on the top of her head. He smelled like freshly rumpled sheets and pine, and Bryanna couldn't help but breathe it in like she couldn't get enough.

"What's wrong with Seara?" he asked into her hair.

Bryanna tilted her head up to look at him. He must've just woken up, judging by the extra husky timbre of his voice. "She wants to join the You-Know-What?"

Weylin's arms around her tensed. Whatever he was expecting her to say, it wasn't that. "How does she even know about that?"

"Her mother was a member," she replied. "She caught some of the *members* in her home a few nights before the Brotherhood attacked."

"Right. Darcell." Weylin sighed, the warmth of his breath skating along the crown of Bryanna's head. "I was there that night, too. I keep forgetting Seara is her daughter."

Bryanna's hands came up, running along his forearms. "I didn't know you knew her."

"I met her a few times, at the meetings we both attended. Poor woman."

Bryanna didn't miss the sadness in his tone. She supposed, in a way, it was lucky that she was stationed at the tower and didn't have as much contact with the others. They'd lost several members since her induction, though it had never been anyone she'd met. It was easier to come to terms with a person's death when you hadn't known them in life.

"Speaking of meetings," she said, trying to lighten the mood. "Why haven't I been to one yet?"

"You won't have to wait too much longer. Obelia sent a memorandum requesting all available members to present themselves to headquarters last night. She wants to make sure everyone knows what you saw when you were in the In-Between plane."

His arms around her tightened, and she didn't need to look at him to know that how she'd gotten to such a dire place still weighed on his mind.

"That's good. Perhaps I can mention Seara there—"

"Don't even think about it," Weylin warned.

"She's stronger than you think," Bryanna argued, turning around to look at him. "You saw how she kept Iodhna trapped within the pond's confines."

His features compressed in a frown. "It's not her magical prowess that worries me. Any more than it had been yours when you'd been put forward for induction, Bryanna. She's only thirteen. A few years older than my sister. I'll admit, I *may* have been wrong about you—"

"May have?" Bryanna arched a brow.

"You've come a long way, magic aside." There was a hint of pride in his eyes as he looked down at her. "But I mean it about Seara. Maybe in a few years ..."

"She's not going to wait that long," Bryanna murmured. "One of these days, she's going to turn up in the cellar. She already knows our headquarters are here."

Weylin pressed his lips together and cut her an exasperated look. "And how does she know that, I wonder?"

"I didn't tell her, if that's what you're insinuating," Bryanna said, poking him in the chest. "She caught me coming back the night I was inducted. Lying would've been pointless."

"Of course it would've." He took the hand still on his chest and clasped it in his own. "I suppose we could have one of the ovates modify her memories."

Bryanna winced. "I wouldn't recommend that. If she catches wind, it may well be them who obtains the memory loss."

He thought about it for a moment. "I wouldn't put it past her either, truth be told."

"So?" she asked, wiggling her brow. "Will you help me convince the others?"

"No."

"Get her on their radar, then? The League watched me for *years*."

"Come on," he said as his stomach made a particularly loud rumble. "Let's go inside. I'm starved."

Bryanna let him lead her toward the kitchen, smiling.

He hadn't said 'No'.

Obelia served her boarders a cup of her early-harvest honey mead with supper that night. She skipped Bryanna, claiming it'd meddle with the potion she was still taking to recover from Cayde's attack, and Elgar, who'd finally been given the all-clear to come down from his chambers. The new potion she and Obelia had been administering seemed to finally be strengthening him.

Bryanna suspected there was something more than honey in the mead because by ten o'clock, the boarders were fast asleep in their bedchambers. All of them, except for Elgar. It turned out he knew about the League, even though he wasn't a member. He and the Tuatha Dé Danann were allies, working together to bring about the Brotherhood of Sìorraidh's end.

At around eleven-thirty, League members began arriving. Bryanna braced herself for a horde of warrior-like individuals, but hardly any of those who turned up fit the description she had in her mind. The first to appear through the trees surrounding the tower was Eremon, the bocanach from her trial. Several gray-bearded men with wine-stained fingernails entered next, followed a few minutes later by a severe-looking woman with her hair held tightly in a bun.

A handful of regal beings who might've been sidhes came next, followed by a squat man who looked half goblin, and a small group of magic-weavers. Lady Auberagh was among the latter and practically dragged Bryanna over to meet her friends.

"I trust you've heard of Bryanna Nicholls?" she said, presenting Bryanna like a treasured granddaughter.

A middle-aged woman with more gray than black hair rolled her eyes. "Of course we have, Jane."

Bryanna colored slightly.

"It is a pleasure to meet you at last, my dear," said a tall, elderly man, taking Bryanna's hands gently in his wizened ones.

Bryanna's mouth fell open. "You're Master Taliesen, the Overseer of the Magic-Weavers."

Master Taliesen's eyes misted. "I am."

Bryanna had known there would be some formidable beings in the Brithlean League, but she would've never expected to see Master Taliesen among them. He was considered the most powerful magic-weaver of their time, and was so wise that even the High Courts and researchers at the prestigious Avalon Institute consulted with him when they needed counsel.

"Sit, Bryanna," said Lady Auberagh, pulling her onto the wooden bench. "We're about to start."

Bryanna glanced around. Other members were taking their seats as well, staring expectantly at a woman far past her centennial birthday who stood on a platform. Wafts of magic radiated from her, and an assortment of necklaces hung from her neck, set with precious stones and rare herbs.

"Who's that?" Bryanna whispered to Lady Auberagh.

"Lady Oona," her old mentor replied. "The leader of the Brithlean League. She's the one who trained your aunt all those years ago."

Bryanna stared at the majestic woman with renewed interest. So *she* was the seer who'd foretold the Brotherhood of

Sìorraidh's end when her aunt had struck out on her own. Bryanna would've loved to know if she'd had any more premonitions since the day she'd saved her aunt. Had she, perhaps, seen *her* fighting in the final battle?

"We're ready," said Lady Oona as Alec and Weylin ambled out from behind the bookshelf concealing the secret entrance.

Bryanna's heart skipped a beat at Weylin's appearance. He and Alec had left to greet those who'd be accessing the tower through the cellar earlier that afternoon.

Weylin scanned the chamber. When his gaze found her, he smiled and crossed the cellar to join her at her table, forcing Lady Auberagh to shuffle aside so that he could sit beside her.

His warmth sent a thrill through Bryanna's body as he pressed his thigh to hers. His hand reached beneath the table and entwined his fingers with hers.

"As you may be aware," Lady Oona's voice infiltrated the cellar, "we have several new members here tonight. Bryanna Nicholls, as most of you know, has already made quite a name for herself as the youngest sorceress of the century."

Bryanna went red as every eye in the cellar fell on her.

"We also welcome Seamus Dunlop, a retired historian, Mary Turnbar, an arithmetic schoolmistress from Hagslea, and Cyleste Timewarmer, who graduated top of her year at the Otherworld School of Magical Arts several years ago."

There was polite applause.

Weylin squeezed her hand and smiled at her.

Lady Oona called upon the first speaker, a faoladh named Fergin Toviele, to speak about his team's progress tracking Finch, the wyvern who'd attacked Bryanna and Seara thanks to the tracking spell Obelia had placed on him. Bryanna tried to focus, but Weylin leaned close to her ear and whispered, "Alec knows there's something between us. He spent all afternoon threatening to have me reassigned if I 'make any misstep' where it comes to you."

"Shhh," Lady Auberagh hissed like an angry snake as Fergin finished his report and another speaker stepped up.

They were quiet as the next member told them about new measures to safeguard towns and villagers from Brotherhood attacks, and the one after him about the weapons and magical solutions they were working on to benefit the League.

Obelia went next, updating everyone on the comings and goings of members at headquarters before moving on to the evasive creature in the forest. "Weylin has been tracking it for weeks. We haven't identified it yet, though we believe it's been able to access the tower without detection."

"What about the sensory spells?" asked a man in a loose-fitted shirt who looked like he might've been a Law Keeper. "Are they not active?"

"They are, Darius, but it can evade them. My niece followed the creature into the forest several nights ago, but it disappeared before she could get close. Bryanna?"

Bryanna pulled herself upright. She'd only been half-listening, too distracted by Weylin, who'd been drawing lazy circles over her palm.

Alec stalked over to them, glowering at Weylin like an overprotective uncle.

"My aunt's right," she said, forcing herself to focus on the matter at hand. "One second it was there, the next I was staring at empty air."

"It could've traveled through an old portal," said Master Taliesen. "Sheidlow Forest was a site for portal travel centuries ago."

Lady Oona frowned. "Perhaps we should station more sentinels around the forest. Until it is caught."

Obelia nodded. "I have already done so."

"Excellent." Lady Oona turned back to the chamber at large. "Now, for the main reason I've risked gathering so many of us here."

Bryanna wasn't sure if it was her imagination, but she thought several Brithlean League members straightened in their seats at her words.

"Recently, Ms. Nicholls was cast into the In-Between plane—"

She recounted what Bryanna had seen there, from Brithlean Nichollson taking her back in time to her witnessing the ritual that had given Agron Vortigern the power to become what he was.

No one asked how Bryanna had ended up in the In-Between plane, too horrified by what she'd seen while she was there. Instead, their questions, when they came, centered on Vortigern and the beings he'd amassed.

"What sort of creatures were there exactly, Ms. Nicholls?" asked a brawny woman who could've taken Alec on in the sparring arena.

"Oh—um—there were nuckelavees and—"

"What about Vortigern's family? Were they part of the ritual?"

Bryanna shook her head. "No. They looked as though they'd been overdosed on calming draughts. Probably to keep them from interfering with the spell."

"What about the ritual?" asked one of the magic-weavers. "Do you remember the incantation?"

There were so many voices echoing around the cellar that Bryanna could barely hear herself speak. "I don't know—"

"Members of the Brithlean League, please," Lady Oona called over the din.

Quiet descended once more.

"Now, we don't know what abilities someone who has

undergone such a dangerous magical transfiguration might possess. That is what we must focus on. Master Chadbury at the Castlereagh Ancient Archives is currently searching for information on the dark ritual Ms. Nicholls witnessed. I will be going to assist him shortly."

"I can help too," said a swarthy, middle-aged man Bryanna thought she'd seen at a ball once. "My family has donated much to the Archives over the centuries. I can get access to the restricted scrolls."

"That will be useful, thank you, Master Lyndon. I'd also like several volunteers to work on pinpointing where Brithlean's ritual was performed. There could be spell remains present that may help us find a way to reverse Agron's transmogrification."

"Bryanna and I can do that," Obelia volunteered.

"I can stay until the location is confirmed," said Cyleste. "Then scout the site."

"I shall too," said Lady Auberagh.

"As will I—" Bryanna started.

"No, you won't," said Obelia before she could finish. "You're still in training."

Bryanna bristled. "So is Cyleste."

"Cyleste has been a member for a while," Weylin corrected her, his tone making it clear he was on her aunt's side. "This is just her first meeting."

Bryanna glared at him. Of course he'd side with Obelia. Between the two of them, she'd be hard-pressed to do anything useful against the Brotherhood.

"It's not that I don't think you're capable," Weylin whispered, sensing her line of thought. "But I'd feel much better if you had at least a few moon cycles' worth of training before you're out on active duty. It's League protocol, anyway—"

Alec cuffed him upside the head before he could say any more.

"Excellent," said Lady Oona. "Let's adjourn. You may return to your stations. As always, discuss nothing of what you've heard today unless you've taken the secure measures."

"I'll be back." Weylin brushed a kiss to her temple before standing. "Alec and I are seeing everyone safely to the watermill."

Bryanna nodded. "I can come, too."

But she'd barely gotten out of her seat when Lady Auberagh stopped her. "Lady Oona wants a word, Bryanna," she said, inclining her head to where the venerable magic-weaver stood, a small smile tugging on her lips.

"She does?" She turned to Weylin, sure her shock and apprehension had to be on her face. What did the ovate want to speak to her for?

"I'll be back soon," Weylin told her.

Bryanna nodded and stumbled over her skirt as she made for Lady Oona.

"No need to be shy, Ms. Nicholls," said Lady Oona when Bryanna reached her. She placed an arm around Bryanna's shoulders and tucked her into her side. Bryanna was so surprised, her eyes almost bulged to the size of dragon eggs. "I've heard a lot about you."

"From the Brithlean League's spies?" Bryanna guessed.

Lady Oona chuckled. "Not just our spies. The newspapers too."

Bryanna's face fell. "Oh."

There had been many articles in the papers about her since she'd become a sorceress, which was surprising considering she'd never given an interview.

"Tell me, what made you join the Brithlean League?"

Bryanna hesitated. Would the League's leader care if she

told her that she hadn't had altruistic motives when she'd first been inducted? That all she'd cared about was learning what she could to avenge Aveline?

"I assume it had something to do with your young cousin?" Lady Oona prompted.

Bryanna nodded solemnly.

"Aveline Whilholme. Such a young, innocent life taken in such a cruel way. Destiny is a funny thing. Every action we take or don't take, every word we speak or don't speak, is weighed by it. There is life beyond our world. You should know. You've seen the In-Between plane. Aveline has a great destiny ahead of her. One she wouldn't have had if she hadn't been forced out of our world."

Bryanna stopped in her tracks. "What do you mean?"

"I've already said more than you're ready to hear. It's been a pleasure talking to you."

"Wait—"

But Lady Oona patted her shoulder and moved on to Master Lyndon, leaving Bryanna brimming with unanswered questions about Aveline and her supposed destiny.

Bryanna was still in the cellar when Weylin returned an hour later, sitting in the exact same spot she'd occupied during the League meeting. All of the others had gone off on assignments Lady Oona had given them, leaving Bryanna alone to process what she'd said about Aveline.

Weylin took one look at her, and the playfulness that had surrounded him while they'd been in the meeting dissipated. "What's wrong?" he asked, sinking down onto the seat next to her, his eyes creased with concern.

Bryanna shrugged and told him what Lady Oona had said.

"Do you think she's right?" she asked when she'd finished. "That there's a higher purpose for my cousin that she was destined for?"

Weylin was quiet, considering his words, before he spoke. "I think we have just as much of a role to play when we pass on as we do here. I mean, the In-Between plane wouldn't exist if there weren't."

Bryanna swallowed. "I guess I just hoped that wherever my cousin was, she was at peace."

Weylin placed a hand gently over hers. "I'm sure she is. Or at least, as much peace as anyone who's left loved ones behind." He hesitated for a moment, his gaze fixed on their hands. "My grandmother died a few years ago. My father's mother, that is. But I can still sense her sometimes, even if I can't see her. Particularly when things have been ..." He looked down, and Bryanna didn't need to ask to know he was thinking about his daughter, and everything that had happened to him since discovering he was going to be a father.

Something in Bryanna's heart expanded as she watched the valiant, selfless faoladh before her. It was funny how, despite their different backgrounds, their heritage, and their upbringing, there was something between them that went beyond just how drawn she was to him. A connection that she'd never experienced with anyone else.

Tentatively, she closed the distance between them, pressing her lips to his in a searing kiss she'd been hungering for since he'd left the tower to join Alec at the watermill. Her hands slid into his silky-soft hair, the need to pull him closer overwhelming. Gone were all thoughts of what Lady Oona had told her. They'd all fallen away as their lips came together, as though they were nothing more than distant memories that no longer held any power over them.

Weylin kissed her back feverishly, his hands sliding down to her waist, raising her off the seat and onto his lap, wrapping her legs around his hips. Bryanna hooked her arms behind his neck, bringing them closer still—

Then, quite abruptly, the droning of Obelia's sensors erupted, deafening against Bryanna's ears.

Weylin launched them to the ground with inhuman speed, barely getting them out of the way in time before the wall behind them exploded, sending stone and mortar flying in all directions.

Blood drained from Bryanna's face as a familiar figure strode into the cellar, his three tiers of sharp, jagged teeth bared.

Finch, the wyvern, had returned.

And he'd brought friends.

TWENTY-TWO

At Finch's side stood a wyvern who looked, if possible, even fiercer and larger than Finch. His tail was raised over his head, the tip of a paralysis-inducing spike sticking out the end. And they weren't alone. Behind them, their faces alight with malicious glee, hovered two squat, sharp-taloned winged trolls.

Bryanna had to suppress the urge to bolt as they stared straight at her, as though she were a prized white hart they'd been tasked to hunt and kill.

Unbidden, Weylin's words to Obelia from the last time Finch had shown his true colors returned to her: *That wyvern was after your niece.*

Finch crept forward, his malicious gaze trained on her. "Our master is most eager to meet you again, girl."

Chills climbed up Bryanna's back. There was only one master she could imagine his kind taking orders from.

Agron Vortigern.

Ice flooded Bryanna's veins as the cellar tilted. Why would Vortigern want her? There were members of the Brithlean League who were far more perilous to his reign than she was.

A low growl rumbled from the back of Weylin's throat. He pushed to his feet, tugging Bryanna behind him. "You're not taking her anywhere."

The winged troll on Finch's right gave a ghastly chuckle. "You think you could stop us?"

"I've faced worse." Weylin took a calculated step back, forcing Bryanna to do the same. "I have to say, Finch, I wouldn't have taken you for a creature who'd take orders from someone with no regard for your life."

Finch hissed. "Our master has shown more than regard for our lives, boy."

Bryanna's eyes darted frantically around the chamber, searching for something, *anything*, they could use to defend themselves.

"And yet he sends you to your deaths?"

Her gaze lingered on the swords lined up against a rack in the armory. But they were too far. There was no way they'd get to them in time, not with how fast the wyverns could shoot their spikes.

"An unseasoned faoladh and a teenage magic-weaver are no match for us," the second wyvern returned.

Before Weylin could reply, Bryanna raised her hands and pulled on her magic. The swords tore from their holders, launching themselves at their foes. Weylin dived, catching a sword in midair. He spun and, in one fluid motion, hurled it at the nearest winged troll.

It sank deep into her chest.

"Go!" he shouted as an onslaught of spikes flew at them.

Bryanna raced for the armory, pulling up a magical shield to block any oncoming spikes as she went. She cleared the metal door just as five spikes ripped through it and wedged themselves deep within the armory door. Black pus oozed from their ends, the smell of rusted metal coming off them making

Bryanna's tongue roll on itself. She snatched the first crossbow she could find, swung a sheaf of bolts over her shoulder, slotted one into place, and sprang back out.

Weylin hadn't followed her. He'd remained behind, keeping the creatures at bay to give her time to arm herself. He'd managed to get another sword and was using it to deflect the spikes the largest wyvern was launching at him. Behind it, the surviving flying troll trembled with anticipation as it waited for the wyvern's spikes to stop flying so it could join the fight.

Bryanna made for them. Before she'd taken more than a few paces, though, she halted in her tracks. She'd been expecting to see both wyverns facing Weylin, but one of them was missing.

Finch.

Her stomach plummeted. Had he gone after the boarders?

She charged for the stairs, crossbow at the ready, but skidded to a stop when she was halfway there as she spotted Finch standing in front of the armory, methodically scanning the shelves and cabinets against the walls as though taking a mental inventory.

Bryanna sucked in a breath as understanding hit her. The wyverns and flying trolls weren't there for her ... at least, not entirely. They'd been sent as scouts, to inspect the Sheidlow Tower's defenses.

From outside came the unmistakable howl of a faoladh.

Help was on the way.

The remaining winged troll's head snapped up at the sound. With a savage grin, it unfurled its wings and flew out into the night, claws drawn.

Bryanna closed in on Finch, tightening her grip on the crossbow. She couldn't let him return to the Brotherhood of Sìorraidh. Vortigern and his brethren needed to believe the tower was impenetrable.

She took careful aim and pulled the lever, letting the bolt

shoot out at breakneck speed. It flew straight for the center of his back, its aim true. But rather than penetrate the wyvern's tough hide, it ricocheted off like a blade hitting a boulder.

It must've still hurt, though, because Finch whirled around, snarling.

Bryanna reloaded, her fingers slick with sweat, fumbling slightly as she aimed her next shot at the crease in his neck, the only place Finch's hide showed any vulnerability. But before she could pull the lever, a fresh onslaught of spikes shot out the end of his tail, forcing Bryanna to dive under the table and use her magic to upend it, stopping the spikes from hitting her.

The ground vibrated as he changed course, closing the distance between them. Bryanna scrambled to ready the crossbow, cringing each time a new crunch in the table announced another spike had been launched her way. Yet, her finger on the trigger remained steady.

Taking a deep breath, she pulled on her magic, pouring it through the crossbow and into the arrow. When Finch reached her, she was ready. She released the bolt and it sliced through the air, shooting straight for him. With a sickening squelch, it embedded itself into the soft hide at the base of his throat.

Finch's beady eyes widened. His front claws reached up, trying to pull the arrow from his throat, but the damage was already done. Blood spurted from his mouth as he gave a low, mournful gurgle and crumpled to the floor.

Not a second later, Weylin's breathless, pain-filled cry tore through the cellar. Bryanna spun on her heels, her heart launching into her throat.

"Weylin!"

He was on the dirt floor, two spikes lodged in his back, blood spreading darkly across his shirt.

And he wasn't moving.

Panic clawed at her chest, but she forced it down. She

couldn't afford to let it overtake her. Not when she was the only thing standing between Weylin and their foes.

Bryanna dug her hand into her sheath, rummaging for a bolt, but it came away empty. She'd lost them all when she'd dived under the table. She threw the crossbow aside, picked up the first thing she could use as a close-range weapon, and charged for the wyvern with a strangled cry, thrusting it straight into his flank.

A manlike howl escaped the wyvern's lips as he clutched at the thing she'd driven into his side—one of Finch's spikes. Already, the venom was slowing his movements. He slumped to the floor with a whimper, twitched once, twice, and went still.

Bryanna rushed to Weylin's side, her hands shaking. The metallic tang of blood hit her nostrils as she pulled the spikes out of his torso and pressed her palms against the wounds, staunching them.

Blood soaked through her fingers, warm and sticky.

So much blood.

It was coming away *black*.

"You're going to be all right," she said, fighting the panic that threatened to overwhelm her.

More than the inky blood flowing from his wounds were the wet, ragged wheezes forcing their way out of his mouth. One of the spikes was lodged between his ribs, leaving him gasping for each breath.

"I can heal this," she said, her voice heavy with determination as she met his pain-filled gaze. "Just ... stay with me."

"Bryanna!" Obelia yelled as she leaped over the rubble. "Is he—*Oomph*."

Surprise forced Obelia's eyes to bulge. She keeled over, a wyvern spike protruding from her shoulder.

Bryanna jumped up with a mangled scream. The second

wyvern was back on its feet. His paralysis had barely lasted more than a moment. She reacted at once, reaching for her magic, but before she could cast a spell, a whizzing sounded behind her, and a silver halberd plunged through the wyvern's eye, cramming itself deep into its skull.

The wyvern fell to the ground, dead.

Seara stood over the debris, a second halberd in her hand. "Save Weylin and Obelia!" she cried. "I'll help Alec get the last one!"

Without another word, she spun and raced to where Alec was fending off the last winged troll.

TWENTY-THREE

Weylin hadn't regained consciousness by the next morning.

Although Obelia had assured her that he'd wake as soon as he was ready, Bryanna couldn't help but pace up and down the end of his bed, struggling to stay calm. What was taking him so long? Obelia had come to hours ago, and had regained most of her mobility. Sure, he'd been hit with twice the spikes her aunt had, but he was a faoladh. He should've healed several times faster than ordinary humans.

She'd worked well into the night, extracting the wyvern venom from her aunt's and Weylin's bloodstream and suturing Weylin's punctured lung. Elgar hadn't left her side, assisting her where he could. He might not have had his full powers back, but his knowledge of the healing arts had been a great help.

Despite their efforts, though, Weylin hadn't moved a single muscle.

Those first few hours had been excruciating. Bryanna had contemplated sending one of the League members who'd returned after learning what had happened to fetch the nearest healer, but part of her knew, deep down, that he was out of harm's way. Still, it didn't keep her from watching Weylin's chest rise and fall, hating how vulnerable he looked in his prone state.

Heaving a sigh, Bryanna settled back down in the chair by his bed, taking his limp hand in hers. It was cool to the touch, though not as cold as it had been when Alec had helped her get him and her aunt into the medical chamber.

Outside, she could hear Alec readying the tower for the influx of boarders' families who'd be coming soon. There'd been no use hiding what had happened. Not when Obelia's magical security alarm had propelled everyone out of bed so deep in the night. It had taken some coaxing to get everyone back into bed. Once they had, Alec had returned to the cellar, Seara in tow, to rebuild the wall their foes had blasted apart—a feat made easy thanks to Seara's sidhe magic. It'd been imperative that the wall be intact as soon as possible. They did *not* want the boarders or their families and friends to see the contents of the cellar where the Brithlean League operated.

Bryanna would've been out there with them, but she'd been too busy healing Weylin and her aunt.

But that had been hours ago.

Already, she could hear the first visitors trundle along the ironstone path.

At eleven o'clock, Alec entered the chamber, frowning at her dirt-riddled, bloodstained clothes.

"You need to go and make yourself presentable. We don't want any of the visitors seeing you in such a state."

Bryanna looked down at her soiled shirt and breeches. She'd yet to return to her bedchamber to change, not wanting to be away from Weylin just in case his condition regressed.

"Go on," said Alec, setting a piece of cloth, a matchbox, and an old, stubbed candle on the bedside table. "I'll stay with Weylin."

Bryanna rose out of her chair, her brow raised. "What's all that for?"

Alec cracked his knuckles. "Waking up Weylin. I thought I'd start by flushing out his ears."

Bryanna's mouth dropped open. "You wouldn't."

But Alec lugged her out of the chamber with a gruff, "Off you go," and locked the door for good measure.

<hr>

Bryanna bathed in record time, donned a respectable long skirt and matching blouse, and headed downstairs to greet the boarders' guests. Several guests were already in the kitchen when she got there, including a bulky middle-aged man who sat beside Bain. His adoptive father. He had skin the color of cinnamon sticks and a kind, weathered face. Beside them was a man who looked like a younger version of Bain's father. Bain's brother, Mattheen. Bain had mentioned him several times. He towered over the other kitchen occupants and was so sturdily built that the group of farm boys who'd scuffled with Weylin and Deagon weeks back wouldn't have dared pick a fight.

"How much longer do you think you'll be here, Bain?" asked Mattheen. "You can communicate with everyone now. Wasn't that the whole point of your remaining here?"

Bain shrugged, unable to meet his eyes. *There are still some things I'm working on.*

Mattheen glanced knowingly over at Liadan, who was helping Nisienne with a tray of oatcakes. "Some *things*? Or some*one*?"

Bain didn't respond.

Bryanna excused herself and made her way outside to greet those sitting in the courtyard, but she didn't remain long— their guests hadn't come to the Sheidlow Tower to see her, after all. Instead, as soon as she could, she headed back to Weylin to make sure Alec hadn't resorted to torture in order to rouse him.

When she got there, she found Weylin sitting up, the left side of his head and shirt soaked.

The weight that had settled heavily on her shoulders from the moment she'd rushed to his side in the cellar lifted as she took him in. His skin was still ashen, his movements stiff, and he looked like he could've used a few more hours of sleep, but at least he no longer resembled a comatose patient.

"How are you feeling?" she asked, closing the door behind her and making her way over to him.

A scowl marked his face. "Let's just say if I were at full strength, Alec wouldn't be standing right now. The coward fled before I could properly avenge myself. Didn't even get a chance to ask about what happened last night after I was hit with ruddy spikes."

Bryanna dropped into the chair beside him and filled him in on everything that had happened after he'd passed out, making sure to highlight Seara's involvement. When she approached the Brithlean League about her—and she was going to have to now, especially after how admirably she'd performed the night before—she didn't want him trying to oppose her induction.

"So ... you saved my life," he said when she'd finished, a reluctant smile forming on his lips.

Bryanna raised a brow. "Why do you sound surprised?"

"Well ..." His fingers found hers, squeezing gently as the ghost of a teasing half-smile she was becoming all too familiar with raised its head. "... it's just usually the other way around."

Bryanna started to protest, but before she could get more than an affronted gasp out, Weylin tugged her out of her seat and onto the narrow bed, fusing his lips to hers. She melted into his touch, savoring the heady sensation of his hands threading through her hair. His mouth worked slowly, softly, as his fingers traveled down her spine, leaving her skin sizzling, wanting more—

"For the love of Castlereagh, *no!*"

Bryanna and Weylin sprang apart.

Gawain stood in the doorway, his face flushed with rage as he glowered between them.

"*Gawain!*" Bryanna shot up at once. "What are you doing here?"

"I thought I would come and surprise you, but I think *I'm* the one who's surprised." He pointed an accusing finger at Weylin. "I told you to stay away from this—"

"Get out, Nicholls," Weylin growled, shooting Gawain a sharp glare, "before I kick your arse all the way to the village square."

Gawain scoffed, taking in Weylin's haggard form. "By the looks of you, I don't think you could kick a bucket, much less my arse."

"Gawain—" Bryanna started.

"Aunt Obelia wants to see you in her office," he snapped before she could finish.

Bryanna exchanged an uneasy look with Weylin. Why would her aunt want to see her when the tower was inundated with visitors? Had something serious happened? Something that needed Bryanna's urgent attention?

Weylin got unsteadily to his feet, but he'd barely managed a couple of paces before Gawain stepped in front of him, barring him from exiting the medical chamber. "Where do you think you're limping off to? My aunt didn't ask to see you."

The look Weylin gave him would've made most boarders quake at the knees. Gawain just smirked.

"You're not extraordinarily attached to this brother, are you, Bryanna?" Weylin asked between clenched teeth.

Bryanna thumped him in the chest. "Hush, you. I'll be back as soon as I can."

She marched out of the medical chamber, making sure Gawain was behind her before heading through the kitchen where Nisienne was serving luncheon, and up to Obelia's office, greeting guests politely along the way.

"Gawain!" said Obelia as soon as she saw him, her face lighting up with delight. "This is a surprise. What are you doing here?"

Bryanna rounded on her brother, shooting daggers at him with her eyes. She should've guessed he'd lied to her. Her aunt hadn't even known he was *there*.

"We finished the semester at the Avalon Institute," said Gawain, shutting the door behind them. "I thought I'd come and stay with you until Lammas, and I walk in to find *this one* with that faoladh all over her!"

For a moment, it was so quiet that they could hear conversations flowing up to them from the courtyard. Bryanna's face flamed. She'd yet to tell her aunt that she and Weylin were an item, unsure of how her aunt would react. She was afraid to see the same disapproval she was sure to get from her mother. Mrs. Nicholls held a very clear idea of who she thought a suitable match for her daughter was, and it wasn't a banished faoladh, even *if* his father was the last natural faoladh chieftain.

Then Obelia threw her head back and laughed. "Oh, Gawain, you can be so much like your father sometimes."

"This isn't funny!" Gawain thundered, pinning her with a disapproving glare. "I happen to know Conveil from the Annual Otherworld Senior Student Intellectual competition. And you should, too, Bree. He came first! Beat me by one meager point!"

Bryanna's jaw almost dropped. Sure, she'd been more focused on drawing plausible escape routes out of Castlereagh at the time than on the overzealous schoolboys battling over a trophy, but she was sure she would've noticed Weylin if he'd been there. He was hard to miss.

"That can't have been him," she said weakly.

"Oh yes, it was! Do you know why I remember? Because the way he looked at you during the presentation ceremony would've made any brother want to knock his teeth out."

Bryanna's ears turned pink. Had Weylin really noticed her, even back then? Because if he had, why hadn't he ever mentioned it?

"And now here you are," Gawain continued, "letting him make a fool out of you!"

"I'm not—"

"He's a boarder, Bree. Do you really think you'll see him again once he leaves Sheidlow Ridge?"

"Gawain," Obelia said with a warning look, "do you mind stepping outside? I'd like to have a word alone with Bryanna."

Gawain's expression turned smug as he nodded and left their aunt's office, a bounce in his step. "I'll be downstairs."

"Stay away from the medical chamber," Bryanna yelled after him.

But he shut the door smartly without replying.

Obelia sighed and lowered herself into her seat, looking at Bryanna closely. "You and Weylin?"

Bryanna nodded and clasped her hands together, taking a seat on the wing chair opposite her.

"I see." Obelia took a deep breath, her gaze shifting to Tyffin before returning to her, a crease etched between her brows. "Weylin has many admirable qualities. You can do far worse. But I'd be remiss if I didn't say what I'm about to."

Bryanna stiffened. Was her aunt really going to warn her against being with a faoladh after she'd been betrothed to one? Or how close she was to Alec? She wouldn't have been surprised if there was something more than they let on between them. The two acted as though they were an old, wedded couple. She'd even caught him sneaking into her bedchamber one night when she'd gone to check on Elgar.

"I'm not sure how much Weylin has told you about his circumstances, but there are things about him that you don't know."

Bryanna almost sagged in relief. "Aunt Obelia, I know more than you think."

Her aunt's brows furrowed deeper. "I used to think that too when I was a little older than you. Believe me, Bryanna, I've been where you are. The faoladhs may look like us in their human skins, but they have their own ways, and some are more set in them than others. Weylin's pull to his tribe is stronger than any other faoladh alive today, especially given who his father is. There may come a day when he will have to choose between them, or his daughter, and you. I don't want to see you get hurt."

"I know what I'm doing, Aunt Obelia," Bryanna assured her, though even as the words left her lips, a sliver of doubt reared its head in the back of her mind. Because the more time she spent with Weylin, the more he was becoming someone she wasn't sure she wanted to live without. And she wasn't sure if she'd ever be the same if they were ever to part ways.

Obelia studied her for a long moment before nodding. "For your sake, I hope you do."

TWENTY-FOUR

Bryanna and Weylin spent the rest of the afternoon on the library's mezzanine, watching the soft rain shower over the pond from their vantage point. The wet weather had forced the boarders and their families indoors, filling the lower floor to capacity and forcing others to venture to other parts of the tower in order to spend some quality time alone together. Bryanna would've much preferred the privacy of her chamber or Weylin's, though she knew that would only result in Gawain bursting in on them a second time.

In fact, she would've been content to remain in the library and not see him again until after Lammas.

But at around four o'clock, Weylin stilled underneath her fingers. Bryanna raised her head from the comfortable spot she'd found between his chin and collarbone and lowered the volume on ancient magic she'd been reading. "What is it?" she asked at once.

Weylin sighed, his features stiff and wary. "My family is arriving."

Bryanna glanced out the window, but she could only see the

pond from their vantage point, not the ironstone path. "How do you know?"

"It's a faoladh ability," he explained, running the hand that wasn't around her waist through his hair. "I can sense my immediate family when they're near or in pain. Sometimes when their emotions are extremely heightened, too."

"You don't think they sensed it when you were attacked last night, do you?" she asked.

"They must've," he said grimly. Then he heaved another deep sigh, as though he were about to walk himself to the gallows, and got to his feet, tugging her up with him. "Come on."

Bryanna hesitated, her cheeks flushing. "You want me to meet your family?"

"Why not? I mean, I've already met some of yours."

He offered her his hand, and she took it. Together, they made their way down to the entrance hall. His family was already there, looking out of place as the other visitors stared at them, recognizing Mr. Conveil for what he truly was.

"Weylin!" his sister cried as soon as she saw him. She extricated herself from between their parents and ran to him, wrapping her arms around his waist. "Thank goodness you're all right."

Weylin ruffled her hair affectionately. "Of course I am, Elspie. Why wouldn't I be?"

"We felt you in trouble."

Weylin's face sobered as his gaze met Bryanna's. "Right." He turned back to Elspie, forcing a smile on his lips. "Honestly, it was nothing. Just some wild beasts in the forest. But I'm glad you're here. There's someone I want you to meet." He tugged Bryanna forward. "Do you know who this is?"

Elspie's face lit up as though she were meeting her favorite celebrity. "It's Bryanna Nicholls."

Weylin winked at her. "She really likes me."

Bryanna swatted his arm, her cheeks heating. "Weylin!"

Elspie and Weylin laughed.

"He really likes you, too," Elspie said as Weylin folded Bryanna into his side and kissed her temple. "I can tell. He never smiled with Tavia."

"No?" Bryanna asked, her gaze locked on Weylin's face as his smile became rather fixed.

"She was always angry about something—"

"Elspie," Mrs. Conveil said quietly, "I don't think Ms. Nicholls wants to hear about Tavia."

"It's all right, Mrs. Conveil," Bryanna said, turning to the older woman. Her breath caught as she saw the yellowing bruise on her cheek.

Weylin must've just seen the bruise, too, because his grip on her hand loosened as his eyes narrowed coolly on his father.

"Please, call me Bryanna, Mrs. Conveil," Bryanna said, keeping her voice light. "And it's lovely to meet you all."

"Pack your things," Mr. Conveil barked at Weylin as though Bryanna hadn't spoken, his sharp, chiseled jaw a shadow away from being a scowl. "You're coming home."

The smile on Weylin's face dropped completely. He stood stock-still, the arm around Bryanna dropping in surprise. "I beg your pardon?"

Bryanna looked over at him. Learning he could return home, to be closer to his newborn daughter, was something he'd wanted from the moment his father had banished him. She'd known that about him, been prepared for him to go back one day to claim her, so why did it feel as though her stomach had suddenly dropped?

"You heard me," Mr. Conveil said coolly.

Weylin swallowed, glancing between Bryanna and his mother and back again. "You're lifting the banishment?"

"There's been unrest in the tribe," Mr. Conveil replied, his lip curling. "Your return will serve to quash some rumors that have been circulating. Now, what are you waiting for?"

Weylin hesitated, glancing in the direction of the kitchen's window seat before turning back to his father and raising his shoulders. "I can't come back straight away. I need some time to sort out a few things here—"

"You will return with us *now*, boy," Mr. Conveil commanded, his tone brooking no argument.

"Lubos, please," said Mrs. Conveil, hovering behind him anxiously as several of the boarders and their visitors glanced in their direction. "Not here."

But Mr. Conveil ignored her. "I smell Alec Marrock all over you, boy. Is that what you want to become? An outcast like him?"

"Who's to say I'd be an outcast?" Weylin returned, quiet enough that only Bryanna and his family could hear.

Mr. Conveil's deep burgundy eyes—eyes his son had inherited—flashed in a way Weylin's couldn't. "What else would you be? A chieftain? You aren't of full blood."

"I'm still a natural chieftain's successor, banishment or not."

Mr. Conveil's eyes turned to slits. "Perhaps I'll rectify that."

The hair on the back of Bryanna's neck stood on end. If she didn't know better, she might've thought Mr. Conveil had just threatened his son.

Beside him, Weylin's mother paled. "Lubos, please, you're talking nonsense."

Mr. Conveil's hand flexed. Bryanna could practically feel his desire to strike her. She pulled on her magic, her gaze narrowing steadily on Mr. Conveil, more than ready to intervene if she needed to.

"I came to Sheidlow Ridge willing to lift your banishment

and bring you home," Mr. Conveil growled, his voice low and menacing. "But I can see Alec and the scheming magic-weavers hold your loyalty more steadfastly than our tribe."

Weylin bunched his hands into fists. "This isn't about them."

"Let's go," Mr. Conveil snarled at his wife. "The boy doesn't want to come with us. You've cost me a wasted trip."

Without waiting for his wife or daughter, he marched out the front double doors.

Mrs. Conveil cast a nervous glance in her husband's direction before turning to her son. "Weylin, please, come home. There is unrest in the tribe. You need to be at your father's side."

But Weylin shook his head. "Not yet, Mother. Go. Don't keep him waiting. He's in a dangerous mood."

"Can I ask you something?" Bryanna asked quietly after supper that night.

She and Weylin were back in the library's mezzanine, though the light, blissful bubble they'd been in earlier that afternoon had long since burst. Weylin had been quiet all evening. Several times, Bryanna had teetered on broaching the subject of his father. But each time she'd tried to, she'd caught sight of the remote look on Weylin's face and wavered.

"You want to know why I was banished," Weylin guessed without taking his gaze off the window.

"Yes."

"Let's just say there's a lot brewing in the faoladh tribes. For a while now, there have been whispers of removing my father— permanently—so that no other like him can exist. Natural chieftains' powers can't be transferred, you see. Even if a faoladh were to challenge my father and win, they wouldn't become what my father is. His powers can only pass on to the full-blooded offspring of a natural chieftain."

"What's that got to do with your banishment?" Bryanna asked.

"Over the years, my father has become paranoid, especially since the other natural chieftains died without heirs. And there are many who don't like how my father runs Dalvin's Pound. For a while now, there have been whispers of my tribe's faoladhs preferring someone else."

Bryanna's stomach clenched. "Someone like … you?"

"Or my daughter. Her mother, Tavia, is a full-blooded faoladh. She'd be much more likely to inherit my father's abilities, if they were to be passed on. When my father found out Tavia was with child, he was furious. He became convinced that I was trying to overthrow him and take the chiefdom until my daughter was of age."

"Is that why he banished you?"

Weylin's lips pressed into a grim line. "No, I was banished after an assassination attempt on his life."

Bryanna's mouth went dry.

"It happened while I was away. Someone planted evidence to make it look like I was involved. Alec tried to help, but my father had made his decision. I've been here ever since, waiting for him to see sense."

"And Tavia?" Bryanna asked, though she thought she already knew the answer.

"She wanted nothing to do with me from the day of my banishment. I think she was only with me because of my father's position in our tribe. Once she realized that being with child didn't put her in higher esteem with him, she was no longer interested in me. She wedded another faoladh before I'd been gone a moon cycle."

Bryanna entwined her fingers with his, her heart aching at the injustice he'd had to endure. "I'm so sorry."

Weylin brought their joined hands to his mouth, kissing the skin on her knuckles and sending butterflies flying in her stomach.

"At least you know your father no longer suspects you," she said. "If he did, he wouldn't have lifted your banishment."

An unnatural cawing outside made them both stir. A murder of skeletal scavenger birds flew past the windows, heading for a patch of forest some distance away. Weylin was up at once, his sentinel instincts taking over. He moved closer to the window, and Bryanna followed suit. It had turned dark outside, the perpetual rain making it hard to see beyond the first line of trees, where the birds were gathering.

Child? A disembodied voice sounded in Bryanna's mind, making her start.

It was the same one she'd heard the night Cayde had attacked her.

She glanced over at the adjacent trees and caught sight of the unicorn glowing in the forest's surrounding darkness.

You need to keep everyone inside, the unicorn's voice cautioned in her mind. *Something has happened in the forest.*

Fear prickled at the back of Bryanna's mind as she sensed the unicorn's distress. It was so visceral, it felt as though she were experiencing it herself.

"What's wrong?" Weylin asked as the unicorn galloped back into the trees and out of sight.

"I don't know," she murmured.

Though the unicorn's sudden warning, paired with the strange skeletal birds that had passed through, left Bryanna with an ominous feeling she couldn't shake.

Obelia refused to let anyone leave the tower after Bryanna told her about the unicorn's warning. She set Weylin and the few Brithlean League members parading as boarders to patrol the tower, but nothing out of the ordinary happened all night. The misty wall didn't rise, the atypical birds didn't return, nor did the unicorn reemerge.

Yet, Bryanna sensed something unnatural in the forest.

She tossed and turned all night, barely able to drift off into a light sleep. When she did, she kept having fitful, recurring nightmares that left her shaken and drenched in sweat. Sometimes they were of Mistress Nichollson, babbling in her ancient tongue. But more often than not, they were of an aggressive, great black mare surrounded by flames. The creature would chase her through the forest with Agron Vortigern astride it, shouting, "We shall meet very soon, little sorceress."

Eventually, she pushed her counterpane aside and headed to Weylin's chamber.

But when she reached his floor, she found Bain's door open, the light from various oil lamps illuminating his chamber. She'd been stunned to hear he'd decided to return to his hometown after all. She hadn't thought he'd ever go without Liadan in tow.

"So ... you're really leaving?" she asked, leaning against his door. Most of the chamber had been packed away, though there were a few art supplies still piled atop the chest of drawers.

Bain looked up from the easels he was folding. *I don't have any reason to stay, apparently,* he said, bitterness coating his voice.

Bryanna pushed off from the door, standing upright. "What do you mean?"

Bain's shoulders fell. *I told Liadan I loved her.*

Bryanna stepped into the chamber, unease clenching her stomach. "What … err … did she say?"

That she'd never be what I want, he said, his face downcast. *Which is crazy, because she's already everything I want.* He threw a box of charcoals into his trunk.

"Maybe she needs time …"

I can't stay here anymore. My family needs me at home. They've done so much for me, sending me here for all these years. I can't let them down.

He grabbed the canvas he'd set to dry in front of the window and propped it against the wall. Lines and shadings of black and maroon chased each other across the canvas, converging to create a landscape of scraggy woods with gnarled, leafless branches and a withered, barren canopy.

"Quarry Cliff Woodlands?" Bryanna asked, stepping forward for a closer look.

Bain hesitated. *You know it?*

"It's where Liadan was attacked."

I went there. He pointed to a sliver along a gap in the canopy. *It's a ray of light, to symbolize that good things can come from bad experiences. I'd never have met Liadan if it weren't for this wretched place.*

Bryanna's throat tightened. "Bain—"

I should keep packing, he said, running a hand through his hair.

Bryanna stood, feeling politely dismissed. "I'll see you at breakfast."

She left his bedchamber, an intense sadness descending over her. She couldn't imagine the Mage's Sanctuary without Bain any more than she could without Obelia.

Halfway down the hall, she stopped in front of the door that belonged to Gawain. Obelia had put him next to Weylin, perhaps in the hopes they'd become friends. Bryanna privately thought she'd have a better chance of becoming an ovate before the night was through.

Lamplight flickered underneath Gawain's door. It seemed he hadn't been able to sleep either.

Bryanna sighed softly and knocked. She was done not talking to him. They'd never been able to stay mad at each other for long. After their older brothers had moved out, it had just been the two of them, what with their father always working long hours at Nicholls & Sons and their mother too busy maintaining her social engagements to spend time with them.

"Go away, Bree," Gawain called through the door.

Bryanna turned the knob. Having grown up with four overbearing brothers, she'd learned the art of stubbornness earlier than most children.

Gawain was lying on his bed, staring up at the ceiling. He let out a long-winded exhale at her entrance. "Thanks for listening."

Bryanna ignored his jab. "What are you doing in Sheidlow Ridge, Gawain?" She didn't believe he was there just to visit. Three Visitors' Days had passed prior, and he hadn't been to see her at *any* of them.

"I wanted to see if you'd listened to me and stayed away from Conveil."

"No, that's not it. Tell me the truth."

"Fine." He snatched the bunched newspaper on his bedside table and handed it to her. "There are rumors the Brotherhood of Sìorraidh is getting closer to Sheidlow Ridge."

Bryanna didn't need to look at the newspaper to know what he was talking about. She'd seen the article reporting the Brotherhood attack in Elphinestone earlier that morning.

"Bain's got it right, leaving," he said. "I have half a mind to take you back to Avalon with me. Aunt Obelia, too, if I can manage it."

Bryanna sat on the edge of his bed, her face set. "You're not taking me anywhere, Gawain."

"What should I do, then? I won't lose you to them the way we lost Aveline."

Bryanna's chest tightened. It had been years since Gawain had spoken about Aveline. He usually walked out of a chamber when anyone brought her up.

"You'll never lose me, Gawain."

Gawain ground his teeth. "Won't I? Because sometimes it doesn't feel that way. Aveline didn't have a choice, but you … ever since she died, you've been so hard to reach, always hiding in the school library with volumes I don't even know how you got hold of, ready to lay down your life for something that won't even bring Aveline back."

"I know it won't," said Bryanna in a small voice.

Gawain made a sound of dissent, unable to meet her eye. Bryanna was so used to the cocky, obnoxious exterior he'd projected for so long, she'd almost forgotten the vulnerable, insecure boy he'd been when they were younger. She'd thought that little boy was gone, but he was still there. She could see him in the sadness etched on his face, and the way he tried to hide it by avoiding her gaze.

She did something then that she hadn't done in years. She wrapped her arms around him and didn't feel the urge to writhe away when his arms wrapped around her, too. "I love you, Gawain."

Gawain sighed. "I love you too."

They remained that way for a minute before Gawain pulled away. "Go on, then."

"Hmm?"

"You can apologize now."

Bryanna raised her brows. "*Apologize*? For what?"

"Take your pick. Ignoring me all these years—"

"But I haven't—"

"—or getting with that faoladh when I specifically told you to stay away from him. Come on, it's just a little S-word."

"Not going to happen."

"Just once."

"No."

"Don't make me tickle you."

But she did.

And when she finally choked out the word "sorry," it was through a fit of giggles she hadn't emitted in five years.

CHAPTER

TWENTY-FIVE

The unicorn didn't return until early the next morning. Bryanna felt his presence in the trees before he stepped into view, his glowing, lithe coat shimmering in the moonlight.

Child, he greeted her, his voice echoing in her mind.

Bryanna's relief was palpable as she stepped out onto the balcony. He'd been gone so long, she'd started to worry that he'd been harmed by whatever was out in the forest. *What was out there?* she asked, somehow knowing he'd hear her as she projected the thought out to him.

The same unnatural being I fought last time. My kind call it the mallaichte. *The Cursed. They're beings formed of dark magic that can read and control minds, even compel entire armies to turn on fellow soldiers. I have been trying to rid the forest of the abomination for many moon cycles, but it has been difficult. You saw what it did to me the last time I faced him. Please inform the mistress of this tower of the danger the being poses.* He turned and trotted back into the trees. *I shall return tonight.*

Wait! Bryanna called after him. If the creature was as cunning as he said, what was he doing, going after it alone?

Do not fear for me, child, the unicorn said as though he'd heard her thoughts. *He is not my first* mallaichte.

He was out of sight in the millisecond it took Bryanna to blink. She rushed back into her bedchamber, her heart racing in her chest. After moon cycles, they finally knew what the creature was. With any luck, they'd figure out how to rid themselves of it before the luncheon bell rang. Quick as she could, she pulled on her slippers and raced for the staircase. The sooner she told her aunt, the sooner they could start researching what a *mallaichte* was and how to defeat it.

"Let's get these patrol schedules to Darius," Obelia's voice came from her office when Bryanna reached her floor. "Until we know what the creature is—"

"It's a *mallaichte*," Bryanna told her, pushing the door open and stepping inside.

Obelia, Alec, and Weylin were leaning over a patrol schedule unfurled across Obelia's desk. At her entrance, Weylin straightened, concern flickering across his face. In her haste to get there, she'd forgotten to drape her dressing gown over her nightdress.

"A *mallaichte*?" Alec asked, stricken, pushing away from the desk. "Are you sure?"

Bryanna nodded. "That's what the unicorn called it."

Alec and Obelia exchanged a grim look. Clearly, they'd both heard of the creature, and from the expressions on their faces, whatever it was wouldn't bode well for them.

"What is it exactly?" asked Weylin. He'd obviously never heard of it either.

"An amplified mind-weaver," said Alec, setting the schedule on the desk. "If your familiar is right—"

"The unicorn's *not* my familiar," Bryanna corrected him. His suggestion that such a creature could be one was absurd. Unicorns were free creatures, unbound by anything or anyone.

"It must be," said Weylin. "It's rare to see the same one twice, and you've seen him several times now."

"So have you," Bryanna pointed out.

"Yes, but you're the one he talks to, funnily enough."

"Why is it funny?" Bryanna asked, nonplussed.

Weylin smirked, a teasing glint in his eyes. "Well, because unicorns are meant to be intelligent creatures. Yet here this one is, attaching himself to you."

Bryanna gave him a sound shove that, thanks to all her training, made him stumble backward.

"We're going to need something to block its influence over us," said Alec to Obelia, a frown forming between his brows. "If it ensnares someone from the League …"

"I know," said Obelia grimly. "Leave it to me."

***

That evening, when Bryanna headed down to train with Alec, she found Weylin in his place again. She wouldn't have thought anything of it, but there was something off about Weylin. He was unusually preoccupied as he went through the motions of training her.

"What's going on?" she asked quietly when they'd finished and were out of earshot of the others.

"Alec headed out about an hour ago," he said, his voice laden with tension. "Wouldn't say why, but he wasn't himself."

Bryanna's brows furrowed. "Has he ever done such a thing before?"

"No. At least, not without telling me where he was going or why. I don't know what got into him. He was his usual self one moment, joking around with Eremon, and the next, his entire face leeched of color, and he streaked for the secret entrance to the edge of the village."

Weylin's concern over Alec's unexpected departure had Bryanna worried, too.

They kept watch for Alec together for the rest of the night, taking turns to allow the other to sleep, but by the time breakfast was called, he still wasn't back.

Obelia looked as though she'd gotten even less sleep than her and Weylin as she sat at the end of the table, her breakfast untouched, if the dark circles cast shadows under her eyes were anything to go by.

"Aunt Obelia, do you know where Alec went?" Bryanna hedged when the others had left the kitchen.

"No," her aunt replied, looking out the window, as though hoping to see Alec turn up between the trees. "I'm sure he'll be back soon, though."

Bryanna wasn't sure if her aunt was trying to convince her of that, or herself.

"Should we be concerned?"

Obelia pushed her chair back and stood. "Of course not."

Bryanna grabbed her forearm, keeping her from leaving. "Then what's got you so worried?"

Obelia tugged at a stray wisp of hair that had fallen out of her tight bun. "Elgar had another episode last night."

Bryanna's stomach plummeted. If Elgar had experienced another fit, then the Brotherhood would've attacked again. Elphinestone had been three hours away. Were they perhaps only an hour or two from Sheidlow Ridge? Or closer still?

She couldn't wait for Deagon to arrive with their daily mail so that they could learn where the last attack had been. But for the first time since the birth of his son, Deagon still hadn't arrived by afternoon tea.

"I'm going into the village," Bryanna told Obelia when the grandfather clock in the kitchen struck four. She couldn't sit still anymore. If the Brotherhood of Sìorraidh had attacked a town or village close by, they needed to know. She couldn't stay huddled inside the secluded tower another minute.

Obelia looked up from the memorandum she was writing. "No. It's too dangerous to go into the forest with the mallaichte there."

"Fine, then I'll take the secret passage to the watermill and make my way to the Brodericks from there."

But Obelia shook her head. "I'm not opening the cellar entrance with my boarders milling around everywhere."

Bryanna's jaw tightened. "Come on, Aunt Obelia. We've had people turning up all day. If the mallaichte was out there, don't you think we'd know? Honestly, I'll be forty minutes at most."

"*We'll* be forty minutes," Weylin corrected, resting his hand on the small of Bryanna's back. "I'll go too."

"You're going to the Brodericks?" asked Liadan. She was halfway down the stairs, her eyes drawn. Gelert was pressed against her leg. The wolfhound hadn't left her side since Bain's departure the day before.

Obelia had tried to convince the Lintons to remain a few extra days until they caught the mallaichte, but they'd been adamant about leaving. Mr. Linton had hired some local dairy hands to look after his farm, but they'd only been contracted to remain for the day he and his son had left to visit Bain, and he hadn't been willing to leave his farm unattended any longer.

"Do you mind if I come?" Liadan asked.

Bryanna stared at her in surprise. Liadan had barricaded herself in her bedchamber and refused to leave despite Bryanna's best efforts to coax her out. "You want to come with us?"

"We haven't heard from Bain yet," she said. "He should've written by now. Perhaps the Brodericks have his letter."

Obelia tapped the tips of her fingers on the dining table, her instinct to keep Bryanna and the others safe warring with her desire to make sure Bain had made it home. "All right," she said at last. "But take Tyffin. And come back immediately. No detours, no matter what you might hear."

***

Bryanna couldn't believe her luck as she, Weylin, Liadan, Tyffin, and Gelert settled into the carriage, Mr. Ahearn up front with the steeds. Both she and Weylin were on the alert as they jostled to and fro on the uneven ironstone path, keeping their senses peeled for any danger, just in case the mallaichte descended on them once they left the relative safety of the Sheidlow Tower.

But they'd barely passed the first line of trees when a *thump* on the side of the carriage had them all jumping out of their seats.

"Mr. Ahearn, stop the carriage!" Gawain shouted.

Bryanna groaned. She'd really been hoping for some respite from Gawain's company. He'd barely left her side since they'd made up, staring out every window she did, picking up every volume she put down, and joining every conversation she started. What was worse, he wouldn't leave her and Weylin's side, wedging himself between them at mealtimes and tagging along behind them wherever they went. It was getting annoying, particularly since Weylin and Gawain couldn't be near one another without bickering like old men.

"Phew," Gawain puffed, wrenching the carriage door open. "I didn't think I'd make it—" He caught sight of Weylin and glowered. "What are *you* doing here?"

Weylin heaved an exaggerated sigh. "Making sure Bryanna and Liadan get to the village and back safely. What are *you* doing here?"

"*I'm* making sure they get to the village and back safely,"

Gawain retorted, taking the seat beside Liadan. "As if I'd trust you around my sister and her friend. Which reminds me, how's that willowy brunette you were all over two years ago?"

A flash of jealousy hit Bryanna at the mention of Weylin's ex, but she pushed it aside. She refused to let herself be bothered by his past relationships. Especially when, from what his sister had implied, he hadn't been happy.

"She's married to someone else," Weylin said in a steely tone.

Gawain snickered. "I thought she looked too clever for you."

Liadan leaned over as the carriage took off again and whispered in Bryanna's ear, "Do they know each other?"

Bryanna nodded. "They competed in the Annual Otherworld Senior Student Intellectual competition two years ago."

"I won," Weylin added.

"By a point," Gawain interjected.

"It was two, actually."

Gawain's ears turned pink. "*Anyway*. Where did you go once you graduated? I never heard."

Weylin's hands balled into fists. "I didn't."

"What do you mean?" Gawain's hostility evaporated in academic outrage. "You would've had offers from *everywhere*."

Bryanna glanced at Weylin. He must've wanted to further his education if he'd participated in the A.O.S.S.I. competition. No one took part in that rigorous contest unless they were serious about their academic future. But if that was the case, what had stopped Weylin from pursuing his studies?

Weylin shrugged, shifting in his seat. Bryanna had never seen him look so uncomfortable. "That's none of your concern."

Gawain's eyes narrowed. "What about your intentions toward my sister? Is that none of my concern either?"

Bryanna's foot swung out and connected with Gawain's shin.

"Ouch!" Gawain clutched the spot where she'd kicked him. "It was an innocent question! What sort of brother would I be if I didn't ask?"

"He's right," Weylin allowed, entwining his fingers with hers. "I imagine I'd be far less civil if it were my sister."

Gawain shot her a pointed look. "See, Bree? He doesn't mind."

Weylin might not have minded, but *she* did. They hadn't discussed where their relationship was heading, and she would've preferred to have that conversation in private, not in front of her brother and Liadan.

"I'm going to tell you something I haven't told your sister yet, Nicholls," said Weylin, running his thumb lightly over Bryanna's skin and sending a thrill coursing through her. "You see, when I first heard she was coming to Sheidlow Ridge, I didn't want her here."

Gawain looked affronted, as though he couldn't believe anyone wouldn't like Bryanna. "And why is that?"

"For one, I knew she was related to you."

Gawain half rose from his seat. "*Meaning?*"

"Nicholls, most of Otherworld has heard of you and your family. You've always had people waiting on you, attended the best schools ... I figured your sister would be just as shallow as the rest of your sort. Add to that the fact that she'd become a sorceress at sixteen, and I thought for sure the attention would've gone to her head." Weylin glanced at Bryanna, his eyes softening. "But then, that first night, she almost had me on my backside with a single spell, and I knew I'd misjudged her."

Bryanna warmed all over. She was sure her face was the color of a ripe tomato.

Beside her, Gawain made a gagging sound.

"Hush, you," she whispered sharply.

They cleared the Sheidlow Ruins a few moments later. A few strides in, though, they found their way blocked by several worn carriages and wagons, each packed high with tottering piles of trunks, cases, and odd bits of furniture.

"Yeh!" one of the village women screeched, casting Bryanna a mutinous look. Around her, older children were helping their harried, determined parents carry large trunks out. "I knew from the moment yeh and that fool of an aunt of yers stepped foot in Sheidlow Ridge that yeh'd be the death of us!"

The other villagers stopped what they were doing to glare at her. Bryanna stared back at them, gobsmacked. What in all of Otherworld did she and her aunt have to do with them leaving Sheidlow Ridge?

"Let's get to the Brodericks," she murmured as Tyffin shook his head at the villagers' hostility. "They'll know what's going on."

But Mr. Ahearn couldn't get past the carriages and wagons, leaving them with no choice but to walk the rest of the way.

Just like the first afternoon Bryanna had arrived, the villagers shrank away as she passed, many of them muttering under their breath. She gritted her teeth and tried to ignore them as best she could.

When they arrived, though, they were met with a scene even more unusual than the one they'd left behind.

"If yeh want ter go ter yer mother's, Valentine, then go!" They heard Deagon yell as they arrived at the Brodericks'. "I won't stop yeh. But Reith is staying here with me!"

"Like I'd leave him with you after what you did!" she yelled back.

"Putting a wee drop of whisky in a baby's bottle ter help 'em sleep has been a remedy in me family fer generations! How else do yeh think we've been able ter sleep the night through fer an entire moon cycle?"

"*You're a monster!*"

"And yeh will be, too, if yeh put Reith on the path the Brotherhood of Sìorraidh will be on!"

Bryanna's heart sank. No wonder the villagers were abandoning their homes in such haste. If there were rumors that the Brotherhood was in their area, she didn't blame them for trying to evacuate. Though why they were blaming her and her aunt was beyond her.

"What's going on, Deagon?" Weylin called without preamble, pushing the Brodericks' door open.

Both Valentine and Deagon froze.

"How long have yeh been here?" Deagon asked, running a hand through his unshaven beard.

"Never mind that," said Bryanna. "Why are the villagers fleeing?"

He glanced over at Valentine before sighing. "There's been another attack in Koah's Pocket, not far from here. The villagers think the Brotherhood of Sìorraidh will come to Sheidlow Ridge next."

Gawain snorted. "I wouldn't worry about it. I doubt they've ever heard of Sheidlow Ridge before. Did you really give your baby whisky?"

Deagon's lips thinned. "It was less than a drop."

"The villagers aren't the only ones worried about the Brotherhood coming here," Valentine told them. "I am, too. The attack has never been so close in these parts."

"I told yeh," Deagon maintained with an exasperated look at his wife, "if they're on their way, we'd just end up in their path."

"Well, we can't stay here."

"And where are we supposed ter go?"

Valentine's gaze fell on Bryanna, her eyes lighting up. "To the Sheidlow Tower."

Bryanna shared a glance with Weylin. She could just imagine how her aunt would react to having even more people to find beds for. The tower was already so crammed, Obelia was complaining about not having enough space for her boarders and the new League members who'd begun residing in the free chambers, masquerading as new patients.

"Yeh can't be serious," said Deagon, rounding on Valentine.

"Oh, yes, I can! You won't let us leave Sheidlow Ridge, and I'm not staying here. The tower's our only choice."

Deagon gave a long-winded sigh. "Fine. Let me just get a few things in order."

"Before you do that, Deagon, have you been to the post office?" Liadan asked.

"Aye, but it wasn't open this morning. Why?"

"We haven't heard from Bain yet."

Deagon's brows knitted together. "Alec told me the same thing las' night."

Weylin's ears perked. "Alec was here?"

"He wanted ter know if we'd seen Bain. Didn't he tell yeh?"

"No. He never came back to the tower."

"I'm sure Bain's fine," Deagon said as Liadan paled and clutched Bryanna's arm. "The attack only happened las' night. He'd have had plenty of time ter pass Koah's Pocket before the Brotherhood arrived."

"Then why hasn't he sent us a letter letting us know he's back home?" Liadan asked.

"Perhaps it's still in Koah's Pocket," Deagon guessed, running a hand through his hair. "Would not surprise me if they shut down their post office, too."

Weylin glanced at the timepiece on the cottage wall, his lips pressed in a tight line. "How long will it take you to be ready, Deagon?"

"Not long."

But it was a while before they were able to depart, even with Liadan, Bryanna, Gawain, and Weylin helping the Brodericks lock and bar every door and window. Deagon wouldn't leave until he'd carried the bales of hay from the barn to the paddock so the cattle would fare on their own for the interim and had Bryanna charm the hen pen so the chicken feed refilled itself. While they worked, Valentine packed away what looked like half of Reith's nursery.

At last, laden with the Brodericks' things, they set off.

The ride back was squished and filled with Reith's wails. He'd woken up the moment the carriage started its jolting way into the forest. Liadan was quiet the entire time, biting her nails. Bryanna wished she'd stop. It was putting her on edge.

As soon as they reached the tower, Bryanna and Weylin raced to the front double doors—

—and found Seara running toward them.

"Bryanna!" she cried, her cheeks leeched of color. "Have you heard?"

Bryanna blinked. "Have we—how did *you* hear?"

"Orlagh told us. She's just flown in from Gorias."

"Orlagh?"

But their conversation was cut short as the unmistakable sound of rushing water came from the back of the tower. Bryanna raced for the pond, Weylin, Tyffin, and Seara close behind.

When they got there, they found Iodhna floating prostrate, immobile around swirls of deep, thundering whirlpools. She must've been having another one of her premonitions.

Fear gnawed at Bryanna's insides as she watched Obelia in

the water, swimming against the gigantic, relentless waves the morgen was conjuring in her petrified state, trying to reach her.

Bryanna moved forward, pulling on her magic. She wouldn't put it past Iodhna to attack her aunt while she was in such a state.

"No!" Iodhna cried as Obelia pulled her toward the bank.

"Shhh," said Obelia soothingly. "It's all right, Iodhna."

Weylin plunged into the water, helping Obelia bring Iodhna to shore. It wasn't easy. The morgen kept thrashing about, as though trying to keep whatever she was seeing from reaching her. Bryanna waded into the water, too, helping Obelia and Weylin carry the morgen onto the grassy edge of the pond.

"There are so many of them," Iodhna whispered, her voice cracking. Her eyes were wide and bulbous, just like they had been the last time she'd had a premonition. "Th-They're everywhere."

"Who are?" Obelia demanded.

"The Brotherhood of Sìorraidh." Iodhna gulped, her words no more than a whisper. "They're ... they're coming to the Sheidlow Tower."

CHAPTER

TWENTY-SIX

Bryanna took several unsteady steps back, struggling to comprehend what Iodhna had just said.

They're coming to the Sheidlow Tower.

The Brotherhood of Sìorraidh couldn't possibly be on their way to them. Her mind didn't want to accept it. Although she'd been wanting to face the Brotherhood from the moment they'd taken Aveline's life, she'd never thought that when the time came, it would be in the middle of the Sheidlow Forest, surrounded by innocents with no way of escaping their deadly foes.

There was no relish, no vengeful fire smoldering in Bryanna's chest, only an overriding sense of foreboding. Lady Oona, Master Taliesen, and many of the other League members were stationed across Otherworld. How would they get to Sheidlow Ridge in time, when the Brotherhood was already in Koah's Pocket, if not closer?

"What are we going to do?" asked Seara.

They'd been so focused on Iodhna's revelation, none of them had noticed Seara, Orlagh, Gawain, Liadan, and several

309

League members masquerading as boarders had joined them on the pond's bank. Others leaned out of their windows, anxiously awaiting the answer to Seara's question.

Obelia cleared her throat, her apprehension melting under a guise of collected calm. "Seara, Orlagh, gather the boarders and meet me in the kitchen in five minutes. I have an important announcement."

Seara and Orlagh sprinted off, leaving Bryanna and her aunt with Gawain and the remaining League members.

Gawain looked from Bryanna and Obelia to the others, taking in the weapons they were no longer concealing before a dry chuckle escaped his lips. "You really fell in with your crowd these last few weeks, didn't you, Bree?"

Bryanna smiled faintly.

"Mr. Lazuri," said Obelia, addressing a short, swarthy League member who'd been posing as a healer apprentice, "send word to Lady Oona and the others."

"What about Iodhna?" asked Weylin.

They glanced down at the morgen still in his arms. In all the commotion her premonition had wrought, Bryanna hadn't realized she'd fainted.

"Take her up to the fifth floor and put her in the second chamber to the left," Obelia told him before turning to the others. "The rest of you, come with me."

Bryanna and Gawain followed Obelia to the kitchen. Everyone was already there, the tension in the air palpable. Obelia took in her boarders one by one, from Fergus, who'd just started to control his newest power, to Nisienne, who looked like she was swallowing a keening wail, to Liadan, who hadn't had a nightmare about the questing beast for weeks. Lastly, her gaze fell on Bryanna, and she swelled with pride and rose to her full height.

"There's something you all need to know," Obelia said into the deathly quiet chamber. "As some of you may have overheard, we have reason to believe the Brotherhood of Sìorraidh is coming to the Sheidlow Tower."

An array of shocked gasps and high, confused chatter erupted.

"What we need to do right now is try not to panic," Obelia said, raising her voice to be heard over the din. She waited until everyone had settled enough before speaking again. "As of tonight, the Mage's Sanctuary will be closed."

A string of protests broke out from every direction.

"I'm sorry," Obelia continued, "but given the severity of what's happening, it's in your best interests to leave the tower until it's safe for you to return. There's an uncharted path in the Sheidlow Forest that will get you to Gorias."

Orlagh puffed out her chest. "I can lead them there. It is the faerie kingdom where I reside, after all."

Obelia nodded. "Thank you, Orlagh. Pack lightly. It's a long way to Gorias on foot, and you'll need to make haste."

"What about those of us staying behind?" asked Seara.

Bryanna doubted being bedridden with faerie-stroke would've kept her from fighting the Brotherhood of Sìorraidh. But she wasn't the only one looking at Obelia expectantly. Liadan, Nisienne, Fergus, Deagon, and Gawain did too. Bryanna could suddenly empathize with her parents for all the times they'd tried to keep her from going after the Brotherhood.

"Seara, think about what you're doing," said Orlagh, her brows drawing tight. "You can't win against the Brotherhood."

"You don't know that," Seara retorted, lifting her chin.

"Seara's right, Orlagh," said Liadan, a determined steel in her voice. "We have to stand against them. They've taken too much from us."

"Too true," said Gawain, resolve burning behind his eyes. "We're staying and fighting alongside you."

Weylin rolled his eyes, coming down the stairs. "What will you do against the Brotherhood of Sìorraidh, Nicholls? Spout facts at them?"

"I'll have you know I'm a member of the Knights of King Arthur's Round Table."

"The *what*?"

"It's the Avalon Institute's combat club." Gawain drew himself up. "I'm one of the top fighters."

"Well, then we're lucky to have you," said Weylin, deadpan.

"Just tell us what we need to do, Obelia," said Liadan.

But Bryanna shook her head. "You're not staying, any of you. You don't know what you're up against."

"Why should *you* be allowed to stay and not us?" Liadan snapped.

"Exactly," said Seara, rounding on Bryanna.

Obelia glanced helplessly at Bryanna. "We can't force them to leave …"

"Aunt Obelia, you can't be serious."

"What would you have me do? Knock them out?"

"Well …"

"Try it, and it'll be you who's unconscious and on their merry way to Gorias," Seara said without a hint of hesitation.

Bryanna gritted her teeth. She wouldn't put it past her to do just that.

"We need you in the kitchen," said Obelia. "Put together what rations you can for those leaving the Sheidlow Tower."

Leaving Seara and Liadan to organize everything for those who'd soon be fleeing, Obelia made for the stairs, motioning for Weylin and Mr. Lazuri to follow her. Bryanna went with them up to the fifth floor, where Weylin had set Iodhna before joining them downstairs. The chamber, which had once belonged to Cayde, was the only one in the tower that had a confining enchantment over it. There, they found Iodhna pacing up and down the chamber, her expression murderous.

"You wait until I tell my father you're holding me prisoner," she spat, glowering at Obelia. "You'll have every morgen in Otherworld's Eastern Seas on your doorstep."

Obelia ignored her. "Iodhna, I'd like you to answer a few questions."

Iodhna raised a hairless brow. "Why would I answer anything you ask when you've had me incarcerated here for moon cycles?"

"What if I could offer you a way back home?"

Bryanna almost cracked her neck as she swiveled to stare at Obelia. She could just imagine what a rampage Iodhna would go on if she were ever released.

Iodhna snorted. "Let me guess, you're curious about what I know about the Brotherhood of Sìorraidh. Well, all I can say about them is that you could've kept them from coming here. I told you before Beltane that your niece traveling to Sheidlow Ridge would bring darkness upon us all. You should've listened."

Bryanna stared at the morgen. Surely Iodhna didn't think *she* was the reason the Brotherhood was headed to Sheidlow Ridge? She was hardly Vortigern's greatest threat. Even Iodhna was more of a threat to them than she was, with her ability to foretell their whereabouts and warn their enemies.

Iodhna strutted to the door. "I *knew* this was coming. My visions always come to pass, no matter what I do." She leaned forward as much as the invisible, quivering shield on the threshold would let her, standing so close, Bryanna could smell her briny breath on her face. "And believe me, I tried to do *a lot*."

Bryanna reared back as though Iodhna had struck her. She'd always suspected the morgen was behind the basilisk poisoning, but it suddenly occurred to her that it wasn't the only thing that she'd been behind. Hadn't her pet sea serpent tried to kill her when she'd dived into the pond after the adar llwch gwin? Hadn't she overheard her trying to persuade Cayde to embrace what he was, to become the predator and give in to his cravings? Cayde hadn't been himself the night he'd attacked her, and Bryanna was willing to bet everything she'd brought to the tower that Iodhna had put him under her thrall, using compulsion to make him attack her the night she'd been in the forest.

"*You're* the one who's been trying to kill me all summer," she breathed.

Bryanna wasn't conscious of her next actions. One second, she'd been standing beside Weylin, the next, she'd launched herself across the threshold and swung at Iodhna, catching her squarely in the jaw. The sound of the flat of her hand hitting Iodhna's scaly flesh rebounded around the chamber. It was almost as satisfying as seeing the shock and pain cross the morgen's face.

Iodhna's eyes turned to slits. It was an unsettling sight, though Bryanna didn't think so for long. Her fury dulled suddenly until all that was left was nothing but an unparalleled awe for the ethereal morgen in front of her. No wonder so many sailors were enticed by her.

She would've done anything for her, no matter how questionable.

Even take her own life …

Jump, came an incorporeal whisper.

Bryanna strode to the window closest to her and climbed onto the window ledge. She glanced down at the beautiful view of the calm pond, marveling at the shallow ripples on its surface as a light wind swept over it.

Jump, the whisper came again, almost like a caress against her mind.

Bryanna tilted her head. *Why not?* she mused. It would rid the pesky voices in the chamber trying to get her attention. Perhaps then she'd be able to embrace the scenery before her in peace.

She released a breath, braced her hands on either side of the window, and pulled herself up onto the ledge.

"Bryanna, stop!" cried a familiar, husky voice behind her.

She hesitated.

She knew that voice.

Knew it in the same way she knew her own heartbeat.

She wanted to turn around.

To see what had caused the strangled urgency in that voice.

But the pull of water beneath her, of her will to let go and give in to her urge to step off the ledge, was too strong.

She stepped off the edge, wind whisking past her ears as she free-fell in a way she'd never had the nerve to do before. But her millisecond of euphoria was short-lived. Strong hands caught her upper arm, almost pulling it out of its socket. She went slamming against the tower's gigantic sandstone bricks with unforgiving force. Pain exploded all down her front, coupled with the searing agony from her shoulder. It laced through her body, shattering the fog in her mind she hadn't even realized was there. For a moment, Bryanna could do no more than gape down at the five floors' worth of open air beneath her feet.

Then her senses rejoined her sanity.

"Weylin!" she screamed, scrambling for purchase on the sandstone walls, chipping the ends of her nails as she did.

"I've got you," Weylin grunted above her.

It was his hands around her arm, keeping her from plunging to her death.

Bryanna clutched any bit of him she could grab as he tugged harder, heaving her up and back through the window.

"You're all right," Weylin said, setting her on her feet as she continued to cling to him, her limbs shaking as though she'd just scaled the summit of Otherworld's tallest mountain in the middle of winter. "Breathe."

Bryanna did as he bade, sucking in a breath and holding it as long as she could before releasing it. The simple action helped the rational part of her brain regain control of herself ... at least until she saw Iodhna smirk at her.

White-hot rage flooded through Bryanna, making her blood roar in her ears. She pushed Weylin away and made for Iodhna once more. If the morgen thought her slap was painful, she was going to find what she did next absolutely torturous.

But Weylin caught her before she could reach Iodhna and pinned her against the wall.

"Let me go!" Bryanna screamed, her voice muffled by the wallpaper pressed against her cheek.

"Under any other circumstances, I would," Weylin said against her ear, sounding as though he, too, was fighting to remain restrained. "But we need her."

His words had Bryanna seething. "No, we don't!" She reared her head back, hoping to catch Weylin's nose, but he was too fast and moved out of her trajectory.

"Get her out of here," Obelia ordered.

"No!" Bryanna stilled, sucking in a deep breath and forcing her fury down. There was no way she was going to give Iodhna the satisfaction of watching Weylin wrestle her out of the chamber. When she spoke again, her voice was carefully level. "I'm not going anywhere."

"Bryanna—"

"I've got her," said Weylin, his grip tightening. "If she tries to get to Iodhna again, I'll remove her."

Obelia looked like she wanted to argue with him, but then she caught the look on Weylin's face and changed her mind. Instead, she turned back to Iodhna. There were far more important things to get to the bottom of than forcing Bryanna out of the chamber.

"Why have you been trying to take my niece's life?" Obelia asked the morgen.

"I have no idea what you're talking about," Iodhna snapped.

There was an angry smudge on the corner of her pale cheek where Bryanna had slapped her. Bryanna wished Obelia would move a fraction to the side so Iodhna could see the smug smile on her face.

"I'm afraid you're not leaving me a choice, then." Obelia nodded to Mr. Lazuri, who raised his hands.

Magic infiltrated the chamber. It wasn't as strong as Bryanna's or Obelia's, yet there was a strange quality to it that Bryanna had never felt. A quality that made her want to blurt out all her secrets.

Her eyes widened.

He was a *truth-weaver*.

"What are you doing?" Iodhna demanded, staring at Mr. Lazuri. "Stop it now, or I'll have your entrails for dessert."

"Have you been trying to harm Ms. Nicholls?" he asked, ignoring her threat.

"Yes." The word came out before Iodhna could clap a hand to her mouth.

"Where did you get the basilisk venom?" asked Obelia.

Iodhna clenched her teeth, but the words worked their way out, anyway. "The mallaichte gave it to me."

"And when it didn't work, you used Cayde?" Obelia guessed.

Iodhna glared at Mr. Lazuri. "I figured I wouldn't have another chance to make it look like an accident."

Bryanna's whole body went rigid. Poor Cayde. He'd been making such progress, both as a neach-ithe anam and with the boarders. Some of them had even warmed to him. Hadn't they stood to defend him when Weylin's friends had targeted him?

Obelia's lips formed a compressed line. "Why?"

"To prove my allegiance wasn't with you."

The chamber fell into a deadly silence.

"You're working with the Brotherhood of Sìorraidh?" Bryanna asked, her voice barely audible in the stillness of the chamber. She didn't need the morgen to answer to know she was right. A wave of nausea washed over her. How long had she been working against them, passing information about her and Obelia?

"It's a shame *their* allegiance isn't with you," Weylin sneered, his hold on Bryanna loosening. "The Brotherhood of Sìorraidh is marching for us right now and yet, you're still here."

"They're not here for me," said Iodhna waspishly. "Once they're done with you, I'll be free. *He's* assured me personally."

Bryanna's heart skidded. "*He?*"

The morgen's lips lifted in a superior leer.

The magic in the air intensified. Iodhna's eyes went hazy, as though she'd been sedated.

"Who's assured you immunity, Iodhna?" Mr. Lazuri asked, his voice soft, hypnotic.

Sweat condensed into droplets on the morgen's forehead as she fought to keep what she knew from them. "The leader of the Brotherhood of Sìorraidh. He's ..." Iodhna growled low in her throat as her words were wrenched from her. "He's taken possession of one of the boarders."

Liadan gasped.

Bryanna hadn't heard her enter the chamber, but she was standing in front of the window she'd jumped out of, staring in abject horror at something below them.

Bryanna disentangled herself from Weylin and rushed to the window.

"No," she whispered as her knees buckled.

In the middle of the ironstone path, looking up at them with dull, vacant eyes, was Bain.

TWENTY-SEVEN

Bryanna stared down at Bain's pale, haggard shell—so similar to what Aveline had looked like in that cold, dark alleyway five years ago—and experienced the same mind-numbing horror as she had then. She wanted to cry, to rage, to assuage the anger inside her that demanded retribution. Not only because the Brotherhood of Sìorraidh had taken yet another person she'd cared about, but because she'd been just as powerless to stop them as she was the first time.

"Bain," Obelia breathed, coming up beside her. Bryanna could practically feel her aunt's despair as she stared down at him.

Her reaction had Bryanna tearing from the chamber. They couldn't remain immobile. It was precisely what Vortigern wanted, and it would lead to their downfall. They were the only ones who knew the Brotherhood of Sìorraidh's leader was literally on their doorstep.

She hurtled into the kitchen, where Deagon and several boarders who'd already finished packing were filling sacks of fruit for those who'd soon be evacuating.

"Everyone, get upstairs! Now!"

Deagon dropped the jar of berries he'd been about to thrust into his sack. "Bryanna, what's wrong?"

"It's Bain," she said, struggling to keep her voice level. "He's been compromised. He's—*it's*—standing outside."

Her words sent the boarders into a frenzy. They scampered around the kitchen, screeching and yelling like mice who'd been dropped into a cage of felines. Which, Bryanna thought, was exactly what they were. Except the feline was outside, waiting to be let in.

Obelia appeared on the staircase. She looked as though she'd aged fifteen years. "Deagon, I need you to get the others to safety. Weylin and I will give you as much time as we can. Go with Bryanna—"

"No," Bryanna said, rounding on her aunt. "I'm not leaving."

She spun on her heels and marched straight for the entrance hall. There was no way she'd miss a confrontation with the vile monster who'd murdered Aveline.

"Bryanna, stop!" Obelia called after her. "Bain wouldn't have wanted you to see him like that."

"Too late," Bryanna ground out.

She headed straight for the front double doors, bracing herself for what she was about to face. Weylin met her there. He'd morphed into his faoladh form. His lupine gaze met hers, smoky-blue eyes flashing with determination. Gone was any sorrow he'd felt when they'd seen Bain's animated body. Only a cold, unwavering gleam remained.

"Bryanna, wait," Obelia said, catching up to her. "You have to understand, that won't be Bain out there."

"I *know*." Bryanna wasn't worried she'd hesitate—she was worried *Obelia* would. Vortigern couldn't have chosen a better boarder to impersonate; he'd taken possession of the one Obelia had been most attached to.

Bryanna pulled on her magic, allowing it to tingle over her skin. She had a few spells in mind from the ancient magic volume she was keen to unleash on Vortigern. She no longer had any reservations about invoking those spells.

Obelia's hands hovered over the oak door handles. She took a deep, determined breath, then looked over at them. "Ready?"

Bryanna nodded, her heart threatening to burst in her chest.

The double doors flung open, giving them an unhindered view of the tall, dark-haired figure before them. He hadn't moved from the spot he'd been when they'd first seen him on the fifth floor, but as Bryanna, Weylin, and Obelia stepped out onto the portico, he shuffled forward, a distinctive limp in his left leg.

Obelia jerked forward, but stopped herself from rushing to his side, though it looked like it cost her to do so.

Obelia, Bain's voice flooded their minds. *The Brotherhood of Sìorraidh is closing in. You need to get everyone out of here.*

Bile rose thickly on Bryanna's tongue. Vortigern's portrayal of Bain was flawless. She could understand just how he'd managed to fool his victims' families and friends over the centuries into believing he wasn't an impostor. Beside her, Obelia and Weylin remained rooted to the spot, both of them searching his face as though desperate for any hint that it was still their Bain.

Bryanna steeled herself. Unlike them, Bain wasn't the first loved one she'd seen taken over by Vortigern. The shock wasn't as paralyzing the second time around. She raised her hand, hatred fueling her magic, and let a white-hot bolt of lightning erupt from her palms, straight for him.

Bain threw himself out of its projection faster than any speed a human could replicate. If anyone needed confirmation that it wasn't Bain in front of them, Bryanna had just given it to them.

Bain straightened, a mixture of bewilderment and trepidation flooding his handsome face. *Bryanna, what are you doing?*

"Stop pretending you're Bain," she snarled, taking careful aim once more. "You can't fool me now any more than you could five years ago."

Bain took a step toward her. At the same time, Weylin bounded forward with a deep growl, closing the distance between them. He was nearly on Bain when a tall, burly figure burst from the trees and barreled into Weylin. They went rolling toward the courtyard tables and out of sight.

"No!" Bryanna rushed forward, a new lightning spell ready to erupt from her palm.

"Obelia, stop her!" Alec's voice boomed from the courtyard.

Bryanna forced herself to ignore him. She couldn't afford to be distracted. Alec would understand, once she'd explained that it wasn't really Bain.

She unleashed her spell, the blinding trail of light careening toward Bain. But before it reached him, Obelia's magic joined hers, redirecting the spell so that it hit a tree lining the tower's perimeter instead, forcing a resounding crack to rebound throughout the courtyard.

"Aunt Obelia, are you mad? That's not Bain! You saw the way he moved! Bain couldn't have moved that fast!"

But Obelia stood her ground. "Yes, he could. He's part-faoladh."

Bryanna's blood turned to ice. Her aunt must've been under the mallaichte's influence. Why else was she standing between her and the abomination trying to kill them?

"She's telling you the truth," Alec cried from the courtyard. He had one of his knees between Weylin's lupine shoulders, trying to restrain him while Weylin bucked and twisted, fighting to dislodge himself. "I don't know what's going on here, but trust me, Bryanna, Bain's no impostor—Oomph!"

Weylin had twisted free and aimed a well-executed uppercut at Alec's jaw, throwing him off. He straightened and launched himself at Bain once more, moving so fast that their foe didn't have time to react. They went tumbling to the floor, Weylin's clawed hand wrapping around Bain's throat.

"Weylin, no!" Alec shouted.

Bryanna rushed forward, but Obelia knocked her to the ground, holding her down with the vigor of a mother keeping prey away from her child.

"No!"

What was wrong with them? Didn't they understand that it wasn't Bain? That at any second, Vortigern would jump out of Bain's body, straight into Weylin's? Bryanna redoubled her efforts to escape her aunt's clutches. She couldn't let what happened to Aveline happen to Weylin, too.

"Weylin, listen to me!" The next words that streamed from his mouth were a string of Faoladhian that Bryanna didn't understand. Whatever he said had Weylin stopping in his tracks. He lifted his head, the fight that had been vibrating around him, making his fur stand on end, receding.

Bryanna tugged fruitlessly at Obelia's hold on her, her heart pounding. What was happening? Why had Weylin stopped?

Weylin, it's me, the creature whispered. *I'm not an impostor.*

"It's true," Alec ground out. "It wasn't Bain who the Brotherhood of Sìorraidh took in Koah's Pocket."

"You don't know what you're talking about!" Bryanna seethed.

He's not lying, Bryanna, Bain said in a hollow voice.

He blinked back tears.

Actual tears.

Vortigern couldn't have perfected his act if he'd had another century of practice.

"Listen to me," Alec cried. "Yes, the Lintons were attacked. But it wasn't Bain who became compromised. It was his brother, Mattheen."

"Why would they take Mattheen?" she demanded. "Bain's the one with connections to the Mage's Sanctuary."

"Because they left Bain for dead," said Alec, his gaze meeting Obelia's as something unspoken passed between them. "They thought he wouldn't survive his injuries. They didn't realize what he was."

Bryanna was still not convinced. "Bain never mentioned he was part-faoladh."

I didn't know I was, said Bain. *My adoptive parents never told me.*

"His faoladh side had been suppressed. It must've been released when he almost died. I saw Agron take Mattheen with my own eyes, Bryanna. But he was seriously injured. Vortigern would've needed to find another host immediately. By now, he could be *anyone*."

Movement sounded between the trees, startling them. Alec raised his sword just as the unicorn emerged from the forest, shimmering silvery-white in the darkening sky.

Child, there's an impostor in your midst.

Bryanna's gaze swiveled to Bain, but before she could so much as point an accusatory finger in his direction, the unicorn spoke again.

Not this boy. Someone else.

Blood rushed to Bryanna's ears as a deep-seated horror threatened to engulf her. There'd been no doubt in her mind that Bain was Vortigern. She'd been so certain, she'd almost killed him.

"Vortigern's here," she told the others, her voice strained. "But he isn't Bain—"

Liadan's scream pierced the air.

It came from the tree house Finch had favored during his stay. Bryanna sprinted toward the back of the tower, wind howling against her ears, barely conscious of the others following close behind her.

"Liadan!"

As they got closer, they saw Orlagh's frame in the window, her languid smile at odds with her petite face.

Bryanna faltered, stumbling back several steps as realization set in with an overwhelming degree of shock.

Orlagh hadn't been the one who'd come back to the Sheidlow Tower.

Bile rose in her throat. Had the poor pixie been in his clutches the whole time?

"How—" Obelia croaked, her face ghostly-pale as she stared up at her old boarder.

"How am I Orlagh?" asked Vortigern in dulcet tones. "A dear mallaichte friend of mine found the young pixie in the Sheidlow Forest several weeks ago. She was very resourceful, I must say. And speaking of resources ..." His gaze lingered on Liadan, Fergus, and Seara, who Bryanna could see trapped in the treehouse behind him. "Your boarders are quite the impressive specimens, Mistress Nicholls. It's a shame they aligned themselves with you, and alas, against me."

He reached behind him, dragging Liadan to the ledge.

"Don't touch her!" Bryanna cried. She raised her hand, calling forth one of the gruesome spells from her aunt's ancient magic volume, but Obelia snatched it back down.

"Don't. You don't have a clean shot."

"You would've been magnificent, you know?" Vortigern said to Liadan, caressing her cheek. "As a questing beast."

For a heartbeat, Liadan blanched. Then fury flashed across her face, and she swung, her fist connecting with his nose. "That's for Drystan, you—"

But with a move tiny Orlagh wouldn't have managed, Vortigern sent her rushing toward the rough, uneven ground with a backhand strike.

Bryanna raised her hands instinctively, throwing up a cushioning spell.

But before Liadan reached it, Bain leaped into the air and caught her, sending them both tumbling into the underbrush. The second they were clear, Obelia's hand shot up with a mighty jerk.

Vortigern gave a strangled cry, though it was quickly followed by a dry, highly amused laugh. He climbed out the window, flapping Orlagh's wings, keeping himself airborne. "You think a blood-poisoning spell will stop me? You have no idea of the pain I have endured."

"It won't stop you, no," replied Obelia. "But by the end of tonight, you'll wish you'd never come near Sheidlow Ridge."

"No, Mistress Nicholls. By the end of the night, I'll have finally eliminated the last of the Nichollsons' magical bloodline."

A human-like, winged creature with a long, thin tail appeared behind him. Bryanna had just enough time to recognize the mallaichte before it wrapped its bandy legs around Orlagh's body and the two disappeared.

An hour later, Obelia, Bryanna, Gawain, Deagon, the Brithlean League members at headquarters, and the boarders who'd refused to leave for Gorias stood around the secret cellar. Obelia had sent most of their sentinels with the evacuating boarders,

Valentine, and baby Reith, just in case they were set upon by the Brotherhood's creatures.

"Vortigern is familiar with the tower and its grounds," she said. "He's been parading as Orlagh for hours. And he's had her in his clutches for moon cycles. Who knows what he extracted from her while she was in his captivity?"

Bryanna stifled a shudder, trying not to think about what the poor pixie must've suffered at his hands.

Beside her, Seara dabbed at her eyes.

"I propose we don't wait for them to make their way to us, but meet them halfway."

"We're still at an advantage here," Alec argued as he sharpened his sword with a whetstone. "We can fall back inside the tower."

"And be surrounded from every angle?" asked Bryanna.

"Where else would we meet them?"

Bryanna didn't respond straightaway. There was one place she could think of. Somewhere that wouldn't give them an advantage but would at least set them on equal ground. "What about the Sheidlow Ruins?"

A frown tugged at Alec's brows. "You want us out in the open?"

"It's better than being barricaded in here. Besides, Vortigern could've found the passages in and out of the tower. We could be breached from the inside."

Alec grunted. "The Ruins do have the open ground, I suppose."

"It's settled then," said Obelia.

Bryanna made for the crossbow cabinet. She'd become quite attached to the weapon. She pulled out two sheaths of arrows and belted a holster to her waist, adding her dragon-venom-tipped daggers. Obelia had finally returned them to her, along with her other weapons. She also added two short swords, though she had a feeling she'd be using magic for the majority of the battle.

"Here," said Weylin, holding up his fist.

Bryanna extended her palm, expecting a small object to drop into her hand. Instead, her fingers met an invisible curtain of thick, metal-like fibers. "What's this?"

"Undetectable armor. It's a faoladh heirloom that's been passed down through my family. Put it on."

Bryanna blinked up at him. "Me? What about you?"

"I'm not planning to fight what will be the most legendary battle in Otherworld in my human skin. Besides, you need it more than I do. You heard Vortigern. He's coming for *you*."

Still, Bryanna shook her head. "I can't wear it. Not if it means you're left vulnerable."

"Please," he ground out. "It's my way of knowing I've done everything I can to protect you."

"And who'll protect you?"

"You will. You may have a lot to learn, but I've yet to face a foe with you at my side without prevailing."

Bryanna's lips broke into a smile, something she hadn't thought would ever happen again. She let him lift the armor over her, belting it in all the right places.

"Oh, wait," she said, catching sight of her weapons underneath the featherlight armor. "My holsters—"

Weylin slid his hand through the material and unsheathed one of the daggers, handing it to her, hilt first. "It will only work as armor against those who'd wish you harm."

"Oh."

Weylin's hand came to rest on her cheek. Their eyes met, and despite them being in a cellar teeming with beings, the others fell away until it felt as though they were the only ones there. Bryanna opened her mouth, but anything she wanted to say got lodged in her throat. She didn't want to voice her fears.

How petrified she was, knowing he'd be on the battleground, even with her beside him, how scared she was that something would happen to him. They may not have known each other for long, but in that short time, he'd still come to feel as integral to her as any member of her family.

As if he could sense her thoughts, Weylin's hands moved to cup her face, tilting her head up to his. His lips met hers with unwavering tenderness.

Silence descended around the chamber.

They both looked around to see what had drawn everyone's attention and saw Liadan on the sparring ground, rotating a sword through the air with a force and precision she hadn't thought possible. Though it didn't quench the stab of anxiety at the thought of her warm, sweet-tempered friend going up against the most powerful, despicable beings in existence, Bryanna couldn't help but feel relieved knowing Liadan knew how to wield a sword.

Fear, nerves, and resolve warmed Bryanna's chest as the others finished getting ready. It was hard to believe that only hours before, she'd been fixated on keeping Weylin and Gawain apart so they'd stop bickering. But there they were, side by side, united in their objective to protect those around them.

Obelia led the way up the stairs once they were ready. They followed her into the entrance hall and out into the forest. Bryanna wasn't sure if her eyes were deceiving her, but as they left the tower grounds, she thought she saw the silhouettes of three people by the front portico: a bearded, thick-haired man, a slim young woman, and an infant tucked between them.

You're ready, child, said the unicorn.

Bryanna didn't need to search the trees to know he was close. Their fight had become his, too.

She kept her gaze up front, not wanting anyone to see how nervous she was.

"Can you believe we're doing this?" asked Seara. "To think, a couple of moon cycles ago, we were making wagers about why you'd come to Sheidlow Ridge."

"What wagers?" asked Bryanna, welcoming the distraction.

"Seara, I don't think this is the time," said Liadan, amused.

"Of course it is," said Gawain, adjusting the sword in his scabbard. "We could be marching to our deaths. What did people say?"

"I said she was working to defeat the Brotherhood of Sìorraidh," said Seara.

"I said she was here to train to become a mage," said Fergus.

Gawain turned to Weylin. "What did you say, Conveil?"

Weylin shrugged. "I don't remember. It was a long time ago."

"I do," said Seara, her eyes dancing with mirth. "You said you thought Bryanna was being hidden by her family because she was with child."

Bryanna thumped Weylin's shoulder as their entourage laughed. Even Gawain. It seemed to release some of the tension they'd all been feeling, and the rest of their trek toward the village became more bearable, though Bryanna still couldn't shake the nerves gnawing at her.

They were several paces away from the Sheidlow Ruins when Nisienne's crows began cawing shrewdly.

"There's something up ahead," the banshee said in her somber cadence.

Bryanna drew her short sword, a deep unease forming in the pit of her stomach.

Around her, the others did the same.

An ominous silence settled over the field. It was as if the wind stopped blowing, the grass stopped rustling.

Four human-like beings came into moonlit view, their bodies brittle, dry, and blackened under a thick, prestigious armor. Bryanna sucked in a breath, recognizing them from the memory she'd seen when she'd been in the In-Between plane. Agron Vortigern's family's expressions were as vacant as they'd been the fateful afternoon Mistress Nichollson had performed her disastrous ritual.

More creatures appeared behind them: flying trolls, wyverns, ogres, nuckelavees, and other vile beings Bryanna had only ever read about in extensive cryptozoology volumes or seen in her nightmares—and others not even the latter could've conjured. One of them, a tall, black-swathed being who could've easily been mistaken for human, except for the aberrant, distorted magic rippling from him, had her recoiling. She'd never felt such potent magic from a single being before.

"Where's their leader?" asked Deagon, twisting the hilt of his sword in his hands.

"He's approaching," said Alec.

Bryanna sensed Vortigern before she saw him. He felt like winter descending—cold, malicious, and impenetrable. How she'd not noticed it when he'd impersonated Orlagh in the tower was beyond her. He must've been able to suppress his powers, to keep them from alerting those around him to his foul presence.

She stifled a gasp when she got her first unhindered view of him. Vortigern had found himself a new victim. One with short whiskers of hair on his head, seedy eyes, and a paunchy belly.

Mr. Doherty.

The familiar twinge in the pit of her stomach gripped her at the sight of the stolen life. She'd never liked the Sheidlow Ridge banker, but that didn't mean she'd wanted him to end up in Vortigern's possession.

No one deserved that.

A crack rent the air, as though a whip had been struck

against the floor. The tall, dry grass surrounding the ruins sparked, alighting with flames. Bryanna lifted her hand to shield her eyes. It wasn't the usual orange blaze rising from the grounds around them, but a bright yellow that looked almost white.

"There was no need to meet us here," Mr. Doherty's voice called over the field. "We were coming to you."

"We were eager to meet you and your friends," Obelia called back.

"I'm sure you were," said Vortigern with a belittling laugh that quickly rumbled through his followers. "I must say, we've heard a lot about the Brithlean League. We were, however, expecting fewer of your boarders."

Bryanna's jaw clenched. They were hardly the formidable army they could've been. If only they'd had more time to call upon the rest of the League. Maybe then, Vortigern wouldn't have sounded so certain of his upcoming victory.

A gasp behind Bryanna made her look back. A great rustling came from overhead, growing louder and louder as dozens of adar llwch gwins landed between them and the forest trees. Bryanna's relief was palpable as she saw Lady Auberagh dismount along with other beings she'd glimpsed at League meetings. Lady Oona was among them, dressed in a flowing cloak that glowed like starlight in the night.

Master Taliesen teleported behind her. His face was grave as he stared at the Brotherhood of Sìorraidh's forces lined up in front of them.

They weren't the only ones to appear. More beings materialized behind them, too tall to be human. Most had blue-tinged skin and hair pale as ivory. Elgar and his brother, Prince Resli, were at the forefront. They'd brought a small army of Tuatha Dé Danann with them that hadn't been seen in Otherworld for millennia.

"You didn't think we'd leave you to face the Brotherhood alone, did you?" Elgar called to Obelia.

Euphoria filled Bryanna's chest as Vortigern's face tightened. They were no longer outnumbered. In fact, with the Tuatha on their side, they were evenly matched.

"Go," Vortigern's voice carried over to them as he ordered his brethren. "You know what is at stake if they succeed."

A corrupt magic infiltrated the air, leaving a sour taste in Bryanna's mouth. The ground gave an almighty lurch, and she and those around her fell forward, crashing to the heaving earth.

On the other side of the field, their enemy advanced.

TWENTY-EIGHT

Bryanna scanned the charging army, trying to locate the source of the shifting ground. A dark, distorted magic hummed beneath her hands, but it was impossible to figure out who was behind the perpetual earthquake when she and those around her were being jostled back and forth, unable to find purchase.

Then a new, formidable magic laced the air, countering their enemy's spell. The ground steadied enough for Bryanna to scramble to her feet, pulling Weylin up as she went. Ahead of them, Lady Oona and Master Taliesen hovered over the grass, their faces strained with concentration as they worked to stabilize the ground beneath them.

"Bryanna, look out!" Seara screamed.

Bryanna ducked as a wyvern spike sailed past her, wedging itself in the grass where she'd been splayed seconds before. Black pus oozed into the soil, the acrid smell of rusted metal burning her nostrils. She looked up, meeting the gaze of its snarling owner. A new spike was already poking out of the wyvern's drawn tail.

Bryanna raised her hand. But before she could aim a spell at the creature's exposed neck, a dull sting pricked the tip of her ear, just as an arrow hissed past her and lodged itself into the wyvern's eye.

"Sorry, Bryanna, did I get you?" Elgar called behind her.

Bryanna felt the edge of her ear, where Elgar's arrow had nicked her. It came away wet, though Bryanna barely felt the pain with the adrenaline pumping through her veins.

"It's all right," she yelled as Elgar loaded a new arrow into his quiver.

She turned her attention to the horde of Brotherhood members closing in, their battle roars reaching them like a tidal wave. Beside her, Seara gave a great bellow, halberd aloft, and charged at the oncoming creatures. Bryanna tightened her hold on her short sword and sped after her, closely followed by Weylin, Bain, Liadan, and Gawain.

The first creature they met was a winged troll who tried to wrap his talons around Bryanna's shoulders. Bryanna swung up, catching his torso with her dragon-venom dagger, and watched him shriek and flap his wings harder, rising into the sky, away from the ensuing battle and out of sight.

Liadan wasn't as lucky. Three of the vile creatures had descended on her and lifted her off the ground.

"Liadan!"

But they hadn't gotten far before Bain brought his sword down on one of them. The flying troll screeched and fell limply to the ground, leaving the remaining two floundering as they struggled to keep Liadan airborne between them. Unable to bear her weight, they landed unceremoniously in a spray of dirt and feathers. Liadan twisted free at once and stabbed the closest creature with her sword. "Take that!"

Weylin launched himself at the last one, making quick work of him. Their tussle was over in less than a minute.

"Come on!" Seara yelled, halberd in hand.

Ahead of them, Cyleste Timewarmer, the magic-weaver who'd been inducted into the League at around the same time as Bryanna, was fending off a dark magic-weaver whose face was stained with black streaks. Her hand was vibrating violently, as though she was struggling to lift it high enough to aim a spell at her assailant. Seara's magic hurtled through the air, delivering a well-aimed spell that caused the magic-weaver's head to rear back as though he'd been punched in the face.

He rounded on Seara, his teeth bared. Bryanna felt his dark magic just as Seara gasped, hands clasping her throat.

"Get him," she rasped, already reversing the spell that was crushing her windpipe.

Bryanna rushed forward, conjuring ropes out of thin air, and wrapped them around the magic-weaver's neck. She squeezed, blocking his airway the same way he'd done to Seara. But the magic-weaver was far more accomplished at offensive magic than she was. With a wave of his hand, the ropes thinned and fell to the ground like old, loose ribbon.

Bryanna pulled on a new spell, but before she could unleash it, Seara's halberd flew past her and stabbed the magic-weaver squarely in the chest. He keeled over, his blackened hands wrapping around the weapon for a few seconds before falling limply to the ground.

"Are you all right?" Bryanna asked Seara, though even as she spoke, she couldn't help but notice their side was falling, much faster than their enemy.

"I'm fine," Seara rasped, her hand massaging her throat.

Bryanna's gaze fell on the center of the Sheidlow Ruins, where the heart of the battle was underway. Brithlean League and Tuatha Dé Danann alike were clashing to the death in a way that had never been seen in Otherworld.

They raced toward the huddle, but before they got too close, a deep, amplified howling erupted from the direction of the village. Bryanna's breath caught in her chest as a pack of huge, spectral dogs with glowing red eyes streaked onto the Sheidlow Ruins' grounds.

Hellhounds.

Bryanna may have never seen them before, but she knew what they were straightaway: the creatures who resided in the darkest pits of the Celtic Underworld. There was only one way they could've crossed over into their living plane: Lammas. The veil between their world was thinning, the way it only could during a sabbat.

The creatures weaved around the Brotherhood of Sìorraidh, streaking straight for Master Taliesen and Lady Oona. Whoever had unleashed them had set them on the most powerful magic-weavers on their side.

Bryanna charged at the creatures. They couldn't afford for the ovates to be incapacitated, not when they were keeping the heaving ground from activating once more. Weylin headed for them, too, his strides far outstripping hers. The hellhounds saw them too. Three of them changed course, bounding for Weylin.

Bryanna added an extra spurt to her steps, but she was still too far when they descended on Weylin, sinking their jowls into his flesh.

"Get off him!" Bryanna screamed, pulling on her magic. She aimed a spell at one of the creatures, sending it careening through the air.

It growled as it hit the ground and changed course, bounding for her instead. Bryanna unsheathed her dragon-venom dagger, but before she could swing, it bit her arm, sharp teeth digging through skin and sinew. The pain had Bryanna gasping, but she pushed through it, plunging her dagger into the hellhound's side.

The creature released her at once, howling as the venom's effects took immediate effect.

Two others made for her, but Bryanna pulled on her magic and pushed them into a heap of flaming rubble. They collided and turned on each other as easily as they had her.

"Get to Master Taliesen!" Gawain yelled behind them.

Bryanna spun. At least seven hellhounds had reached the ovates. A cry of horror lodged itself in her throat as one of them clamped its jaw to the side of Master Taliesen's neck and yanked, forcing him back onto the ground. Even from her vantage point, Bryanna could see a large chunk missing from the old magic-weaver's throat.

Master Taliesen raised his hand, and with a flash of light, the hellhound fell, its muzzle wet and bloodied. Bryanna sped toward him. But she'd barely taken a few paces when he shook his head, pointing in the direction of Gawain and Deagon, who were fighting a creature with five snake heads and a raptor body. Bryanna hesitated, torn between joining her brother or racing to the aid of the magic-weaver powerful enough to single-handedly tip the odds of the battle in their favor. But then she saw the state of Master Taliesen's neck. It was healing before her eyes, the skin around his neck knitting together seamlessly.

She changed course and raced toward Gawain and Deagon.

"Get its other heads!" Gawain was shouting as she reached them.

Bryanna raised her short sword and cleaved two of the creature's heads with a single blow, while Deagon made quick sport of the fourth and final one, spearing it with the tip of his poker.

"That creature must've been an interbred," Gawain panted, doubling over. "I've never seen anything like it."

His face blanched as he caught sight of something behind

her. Bryanna turned in the direction he was facing and froze. A group of ogres was emerging onto the thoroughfare, heading straight for their side of the battlefield. Bile burned at the back of her throat. There was something off about the way they moved, as though they were under some sort of heavy thrall. A thrall so strong, they didn't seem to register where they were.

A shower of arrows, courtesy of the Tuatha Dé Danann, rained over the ogres, plunging into their bellies, their chests, their limbs. And still, not one of them flinched. They continued marching toward the Sheidlow Ruins, oblivious to the pain from their wounds.

Bryanna pushed to her feet and pulled on her magic, setting the path in front of the ogres aflame. But they kept coming, their faces blank even as their flesh caught fire.

The ogres' appearance seemed to embolden the Brotherhood. They congregated around Master Taliesen and Lady Oona, attacking them with renewed fervor. Bryanna and her friends made for them. And they weren't the only ones. From the other side of the field, Lady Auberagh, dressed in old chain mail and a visor, scuttled for them too.

But before they'd made it a few steps, Lady Oona was plucked from the air and disappeared into a fray of goblin-like creatures with red caps. The ground around them gave a mighty lurch and heaved once more.

Bryanna toppled to the ground, slicing her hand open on one of her short swords. She scrambled onto all fours, fighting to remain steady—

—and then she saw him.

On the opposite side of the Sheidlow Ruins stood a figure as still as a tree on a windless summer night. She would've bet all the coins in her bedchamber that he was the one causing the ground's havoc.

A single, unyielding thought took hold as Bryanna grappled

for stability; she needed to stop the being before he became the death of them all.

Gripping the tall grass to keep herself balanced, as well as hidden from her enemy's sight, Bryanna began making her painstaking way to the other side of the field. Several times, she came across a dead combatant, though she never looked too close for fear that it was someone she knew. On she went, keeping her focus singularly fixed on the world-weaver, and not the raging chaos erupting around her until she reached the burning remains of an ancient wall halfway down the field. There, she crouched and peered around.

She was only a few paces away from the being. She pulled the crossbow from the holster on her back and fished out a bolt, slotting it into place. Before she could move on him, though, giant paw-like hands grabbed her. Bryanna reacted instinctively, swinging her crossbow like a sword. But it was knocked out of her grasp by massive clawed fingers. She thrust her hand through her armor, reaching for one of her dragon-venom daggers, but the creature's clawed fingers phased through the armor, too, keeping her from drawing one.

Bryanna glanced up into a familiar wolfish face, relief coursing through her.

Weylin.

Somehow, in all the tussle, he'd morphed into his faoladh skin.

"I could've killed you," she breathed.

He dropped beside her, his eyes narrowed on the cloak-swathed being who'd drawn Bryanna's attention. Then he froze, his hackles rising.

Bryanna whipped around.

The spot where the being had stood was empty.

"Where did it go?"

Weylin pointed to the spot she'd last seen it. She looked

again, but unless he could see something she couldn't, there was nothing there …

And then it happened.

The air where Weylin pointed bristled as though it were sitting over a boiling cauldron, becoming denser and denser until the being flickered back into corporeal view.

Bryanna wasn't sure if the trembling ground came to a stop, or if it just felt like it to her numbed, shocked brain.

The being was a world-weaver.

She'd read about them. They were from parallel worlds and could draw magic from one dimension to another. No wonder he'd been able to keep the spell on the Sheidlow Ruins going so long, despite Lady Oona's and Master Taliesen's best efforts. He was being fed by the magic from his secondary dimension.

Bryanna's nails dug into the stone bricks. How in all of Castlereagh were they supposed to sever the world-weaver's connection to his other realm? Lady Oona and Master Taliesen, or one of the Tuatha Dé Danann, might've stood a chance against such a strong magic-weaver, but none of them were available.

"We need to get closer," she whispered, retrieving the crossbow.

Weylin nodded, and together they crept toward the dark magic-weaver, using the decrepit ruins to conceal themselves. Bryanna's heart thumped painfully against her chest the closer they got to the being, sure they'd be set upon any second.

And yet, no one attacked them.

The lack of protection around Vortigern's most prized fighter unnerved her. He couldn't have possibly been arrogant enough to believe the world-weaver wouldn't need protection.

But then they reached the slab of stone close to the world-weaver, and it became clear to Bryanna just why Vortigern hadn't set several of his vile creatures around him.

He didn't need to.

The mallaichte was there, prowling the plot of earth, unaffected by the quake that rendered the rest of the ruins asunder.

Weylin's eyes narrowed, a plan forming in the depths of his mind. A determined glint gleamed in his eyes as he pointed at himself, then the mallaichte. Bryanna shook her head furiously. Surely he wasn't suggesting that he distract the mallaichte and leave her to deal with the world-weaver?

He must've, though, because before she could stop him, Weylin launched out from behind the stone and lunged straight at the mallaichte. They collided with bone-crushing force, their growls thundering in the night as they tumbled into a pile of burning embers and out of sight.

Muttering expletives under her breath, Bryanna raised her crossbow and took careful aim at the center of the world-weaver's heart. But even as she pulled the lever and her bolt hurtled through the air at blinding speed, she knew it wasn't going to work.

The bolt stopped about three paces from the being's chest, wedging itself in a clear, shimmering shield that reminded Bryanna of the thick mist that formed around the Sheidlow Tower in times of peril.

"Bollocks."

There was a magical shield around the being. The sort, she was certain, that wouldn't be penetrated by any meager weapon she possessed. If she wanted to get past it, she was going to have to remove it the same way it had been made: by magic.

Bryanna discarded her crossbow. She knew a spell that might work. It was one she'd read about in Lady Auberagh's volumes several years ago. There'd been a footnote at the bottom of the page, warning the magic-weaver of the dire risks associated with the disintegrating spell she was thinking of performing. Once it was cast on an item—in this case, the blade of her short sword—it would crumble everything it touched. If there was ever a time for such magic, though, it was that moment.

She hesitated for only a heartbeat before springing out from behind the rubble, unsheathing her short sword as she went, and raced for the spot where the world-weaver had just disappeared. She wouldn't have much time before the being flickered back into corporeal form. Conjuring the spell in record time, she swung out at it, and was rewarded as the shield shimmered into moonlit view briefly before returning to its invisible state. Over and over, Bryanna stabbed into it, ignoring the sharp pain that increased up her forearms with every blow until finally, with a weak flash, the shield shattered—

—just as the world-weaver reappeared.

Bryanna took an involuntary step back, a strangled scream escaping her lips. She'd just caught sight of what was underneath the being's hood: *nothing*.

No face.

No nose.

No eye sockets.

Only darkness.

She swung out haphazardly, but before she could make contact, something slammed into her side, sending her rolling over a jagged pile of flaming rubble.

Her exposed skin blistered immediately as it made contact with the embers, forcing a sharp cry from her lips. She pushed to her feet, Alec's reminders to never let an opponent get to her on the ground rebounding in her head. Gripping her short sword, she faced her assailant ... and almost stumbled backwards.

Vortigern's mother stood before her, staring at Bryanna

vacantly. It was a disarming sight. For the second time that night, Bryanna couldn't shake the sense that the woman wasn't of her own mind.

The woman bent down, picked up a section of flaming wall, and tossed it at Bryanna as easily as if it were a handful of mud.

Bryanna was forced to dive behind an overgrown standing bit of ruin to avoid its projection. Her thoughts raced. How was she going to stop the withered, unresponsive woman? Was there even anyone sentient inside her anymore?

Bryanna chanced another look at the woman, peering around the toppled, decrepit wall, and found her picking up a new section of burning debris. The crumbling ruin she'd taken shelter behind may have withstood the first assault, but it wouldn't survive another. She dropped to her knees, her stomach roiling. She didn't want to hurt the woman. But she wasn't giving her much choice. She wouldn't spend the rest of the night huddled behind walls, avoiding the woman as she launched debris at her.

Bryanna hastened to her feet, but before she could so much as think about her next move, a sickening crack split the air. The debris in the woman's hands fell to the mud with a resounding *splat,* her limp body following without a single sound of protest.

Behind her, looking sallower than Bryanna had ever seen him, stood Cayde.

"Get to Conveil!" he shouted, bounding off to meet a nuckelavee charging toward them. "Hurry!"

Bryanna glanced around. In the chaos between the world-weaver and Vortigern's mother, she'd lost sight of Weylin and the mallaichte.

They weren't on the field or between the flaming blocks of rubble.

In fact, she realized with a sickening jolt, they weren't in the Sheidlow Ruins at all.

TWENTY-NINE

Bryanna dashed toward the forest, the only place the mallaichte could've taken Weylin. She didn't want to think about how they'd ended up there. She'd have thought the mallaichte would've preferred to remain close to Vortigern and his dark brethren, especially when Weylin was armed and in his faoladhian skin, but he must've figured he'd gain the upper hand by getting him away from the others, cutting him off from anyone who could come to his aid.

She reached the first lot of trees in record time, but before she could race in after them, a large equine figure stepped out from behind a trunk, blocking her path into the forest.

And from Weylin.

Bryanna's breath hitched as she took in the beast's red-rimmed eyes and mane of wild, roaring flames. More of them surrounded his hooves, so that it looked as though he was wearing boots of fire.

A nightmare.

She'd seen the creature before. Its kind was known to haunt the dreams of their enemies, generating crippling fear before they met in battle. Bryanna had dreamed about it several times that week, she just hadn't realized what it was until that moment.

The malevolence rolling off the nightmare was tangible, as though it were a freak storm in the deepest ocean, merciless and catastrophic to behold. It whickered, the sound more menacing than anything the wyverns ever made, and reared, forcing Bryanna to take several hasty steps back.

Bryanna had grown up around steeds. Her father had a stable behind their family home where he bred them. She'd visited it frequently, particularly when she wanted to get away from her mother's nagging. She was used to their dilating nostrils, their impulsive neighing, their stamping hooves. But despite her steed-like build, the nightmare was no steed.

Which was why Bryanna felt no guilt as she charged it, dragon-venom dagger aloft.

The nightmare bent its overlarge head and cantered for her with just as much vigor. Bryanna pivoted at the last moment, driving her dagger into the creature's flanks with all the force she could muster. But the blade snapped clean off its rock-hard flesh as though its hide were made of granite.

She hadn't even left a scratch.

The nightmare neighed menacingly, its eyes flashing, and cantered for Bryanna again.

Before it could reach her, though, a great white blur whipped in front of Bryanna, setting itself between them.

Go, the unicorn urged, tossing his mane. *Leave this abomination to me.*

Be careful, she beseeched him before racing into the forest.

Bryanna kept her eyes and ears peeled for any sign of Weylin or the mallaichte as she sprinted past the dense forest trees, stopping only to pick up a branch and set its end aflame to light the way for her. She knew it wasn't ideal, not if she wanted to catch the mallaichte by surprise, but without it, she could see nothing in the darkness.

She rushed past ferns and shrubs, earning the occasional scrape against her calves from a stray branch, hoping she was going in the right direction. Before long, she found herself so deep in the trees that she couldn't hear the cries of the battlefield anymore, only the wind whistling through leaves and the creaking of dead branches under her feet.

And then she heard a soft voice up ahead.

"Among us," the mallaichte purred, "we can retrieve all that is yours. No one can stop you."

Bryanna impaled her makeshift torch into the ground, extinguishing it. There was more than enough light coming from the bonfire in the clearing she was on the edge of for her to see the mallaichte ... and Weylin.

The latter was back in his human form, resting against a large fallen tree. Gone was the fierce conviction that had coursed through him when they'd left the Sheidlow Tower. In its place was a thoughtful expression, as though he was actually considering the mallaichte's offer.

Bryanna stepped toward them. She had to reach Weylin before the mallaichte warped his mind further.

"Weylin—"

But then she stopped, her mind clouding over.

She glanced around the clearing and paused. What was she doing there? Weylin and the mallaichte were fine. Better than fine, really. He didn't need her there. She needed to return to Sheidlow Ridge, to fight alongside her family and friends.

The latter were the ones who needed her.

Bryanna spun on her heels, adding an extra spurt of speed to her steps as she ran back the way she'd come. What had she been thinking, abandoning the others to the Brotherhood of Sìorraidh to go chasing after Weylin?

"Oomph!"

Pain erupted at her scraped knees as she tripped over something cold and unyielding on the forest floor, collecting dirt under her fingernails as she fell onto the rough, bark-strewn ground. The haze she hadn't realized had enveloped her mind fell away as though it had been doused with ice-cold water. Bryanna gasped and pushed herself up, her gaze falling on the naked hilt of Weylin's sword as a deep-seated dread engulfed her.

The mallaichte.

It must've ensnared her mind again, compelling her to leave the clearing so he could finish coercing Weylin into joining the Brotherhood and turning against the rest of them.

"Bollocks!"

She had to get back to Weylin.

A hiss at the back of her neck was her only warning that she was no longer alone. She stilled, her stomach churning as thick, pointed claws descended upon her, splitting the tendrils of weightless armor at her throat into jagged strips.

Bryanna's hand went up, stemming the stinging, shallow pools of blood steadily flowing from the gash in her neck. She would've been choking on her own blood if Weylin hadn't insisted she wear his armor.

"Weylin!" she screamed as a fierce terror gripped her.

Before she could move, her feet were swept out from under her. Bryanna flung out her legs, but the mallaichte was too fast and evaded her easily. Its claws came around her head, digging into her forehead and forcing her to stare up at the slivers of inky sky above them. Bryanna's hands flew to the creature's wrists, trying to unravel herself, or at the very least, bring her head forward so that her throat wasn't so exposed. But it was no use. The creature's strength far surpassed hers. She was

entirely at his mercy, unable to stop what she knew was coming
...

She scrambled for her magic, but although it gathered at her palms, she couldn't think of a single spell to stop him. He was keeping her from accessing the part of her brain that controlled her magic, leaving her completely vulnerable to him.

She shut her eyes, moving her hands to the skin over her jugular, as though it would lessen the damage the mallaichte was about to inflict there. She could sense its relish as its claws tore through the air, aiming for her neck with deadly precision.

But it never reached her.

Bryanna staggered backward as the mallaichte was snatched from her. She opened her eyes, barely making out Weylin in the soft moonlight, and her knees nearly buckled. He was himself again. A low growl tore from his throat, so menacing that it sent shivers coursing down her spine. Even the mallaichte looked unnerved. His wings flexed, as though tempted to take flight, but Weylin launched himself at the creature before he could. They collided in a flurry of claws and wings, moving so fast that Bryanna couldn't discern whose limbs were whose as they traded blow after merciless blow.

Fear worse than she'd felt seconds before engulfed her as she watched on, a silent cry threatening to rip from her chest. She wanted to help, to give Weylin some sort of leverage on the mallaichte, but she was afraid her efforts would do more damage than good. Instead, she teetered on the edge, her magic tingling at the tips of her quaking fingers, ready to intervene if Weylin needed her.

She wasn't sure how long it was before their grappling ceased.

Seconds?

Moments?

It felt like hours.

But when they stopped, Weylin's hands were wrapped around the mallaichte's neck. The creature's wings beat erratically behind him, trying to thrust Weylin off. Weylin leaned forward, his mouth set in a grim line as he gave a powerful twist of his hands and snapped the creature's neck. The sound it made echoed among the trees around them, like the tightening of a noose when a trapdoor beneath the criminal's feet was released.

Nausea crawled up Bryanna's throat as the mallaichte's wings twitched and fell limply at his side.

"Are you all right?" Weylin asked, rushing to her side. He traced his fingers over the bleeding line at her neck.

"I'm fine," she whispered, grasping his warm, sure fingers in hers, needing to feel the steady calm and safety that washed over her whenever they touched.

Weylin pressed his lips to the top of her head, dropping a gentle kiss there and lingering a moment, as though he needed her touch just as much as she did. "We need to get back to the others."

"I know."

He pressed one more kiss into her hair before moving back. "Come on."

More prone bodies littered the grounds between the tall beds of grass and rubble when they reached the Sheidlow Ruins. Alec was single-handedly fighting off two wyverns, while a pair of nuckelavees careened into Brithlean League members like stampeding bulls. A dark-haired magic-weaver she hadn't seen before was still on his feet, fending off the remaining members of Vortigern's family. Bryanna scanned the ruins for Gawain and her friends, but before she could locate them, the ground in front of them exploded into clumps of fire and ash. Bryanna gasped as blistering-hot embers burned her exposed flesh. Before she could look up, the ends of two fiery whips coiled around her wrists like flaming shackles, digging deep into her skin.

Bryanna pulled on her magic, unwinding the ropes so that they dropped to the ground, their flames catching on the dry patches of grass, and turned to face her new opponent: Vortigern's younger sister. The woman's gaze was filled with hatred as she leered at Bryanna. Whatever spell Vortigern had on the others to keep them in a mindless haze, he hadn't extended it to her.

In her hands were two fiery whips, the same ones that had lit the hay bales around the ruins before the battle had begun. With a sneer, the woman cracked her whips once more, winding them around Bryanna's middle and burning through the protection of her armor. Instinctively, Bryanna jerked at the fiery strands, trying to pull herself free. But all it did was scorch through the final layer of armor, blistering her skin.

Bryanna cried out as all-consuming agony threatened to overtake her. She needed to get the fiery coils off herself before the pain became too much. She pulled on her magic, sucking the heat from the whips just as Weylin wrapped his arms around Vortigern's sister's middle, squeezing the unnaturally long life from her ancient lungs until she was nothing more than a desiccated heap in his clutches.

The fiery whips cooled to black and fell to the ground.

"Bryanna—" he cried, throwing the decrepit remains of the woman aside.

"I'm fine," she said breathlessly. "Thanks."

She cast a quick healing spell over herself, alleviating the severity of her burns, and raced headlong toward Gawain, Deagon, and Seara, whom she'd just spotted near the edge of the forest. They were fighting a long-fanged, cloven-footed creature that was behaving most peculiarly. It was lumbering along as though under a subduing spell.

Seara stood behind it, her hands raised and face scrunched up in concentration as she struggled to keep it under her control. Beside her, Gawain charged, his blade brandished in front of him like a lance. But at the last moment, the creature slumped back, and the blade that should've speared its throat pierced its shoulder instead. The impact brought the creature back to itself with a ferocious roar. It swung out, its beefy fist crunching against the back of Seara's skull, sending her tumbling to the rubble.

Bryanna tore for them. "Seara!"

A silver arrow whizzed past her, lodging itself in the creature's chest. Bryanna spun on her heels and saw Elgar nod in her direction before fetching another arrow from his quiver, his eyes narrowed on a nuckelavee galloping toward them with Cayde, caked in mud and blood, hanging on to its back.

Bryanna threw herself down next to Seara, turning her onto her back.

"Seara!"

Blood trickled from a wound at the back of her head. Bryanna's fingers trailed down her neck, searching for her pulse. It was there, beating steadily.

"Get her into the trees," she shouted to Gawain and Deagon.

Then she set off for Liadan and Bain, who were trying to stave off a pack of small, spike-headed creatures. One of them hung from Liadan's leg by its teeth. They were so preoccupied fighting the fiends, they hadn't noticed something glimmering in the shadows, heading stealthily toward them.

"Bain, behind you!" Bryanna screamed.

She streaked for them, determined to get to them before the being did. But she was still several paces away when a familiar pair of strong arms engulfed her and threw her to the ground, cushioning the brunt of her fall with his powerful body.

"I thought you took care of that thing," Weylin growled.

"What thing—"

The world-weaver flickered into view in front of them. Elgar and Prince Resli saw him too. They fired arrows in his direction, but before any of them could reach their target, the world-weaver vanished, and the arrows, which had been meant for the world-weaver, shot for Bryanna and Weylin instead.

With a mangled curse, Weylin leaped over Bryanna, covering her body with his.

"Weylin!" Bryanna screamed shrilly as the arrows hit his back, their feathery ends mocking her as they swayed in the evening breeze.

He fell forward, a low, short, guttural sound escaping him as he used the last of his strength to heave himself off her.

White-hot rage coursed through Bryanna. She was on her feet before she had any awareness of it, charging for the spot where she could sense the world-weaver's dark, coagulating energy. Magic vibrated around her, flowing out of her pores and surrounding her in a boiling shield.

When he reappeared, she was ready for him. Her hands clamped around the area where his neck should've been. Her fingers came away empty. The magic she emanated, however, met with an odd resistance, as though the air where his body should've been was stiff, tangible to her power alone. She wrapped her magic around it and heaved. A crack sounded, like a snapping branch, and the dark, distorted magic that had been assailing her senses all night disappeared.

The being's cloak fell to the ground in a heap.

Bryanna dropped to her knees with it, fighting the urge to retch. It didn't matter that the world-weaver had brought so much destruction on the Sheidlow Ruins grounds and all those who'd stood on it, or that she'd done what she had to save those she loved. The act of taking another life, of feeling the pulse snuff out between her hands, still made her stomach turn in a way that nothing ever had—or ever would.

She made her way back to Weylin, needing something, *anything*, to get her mind off what she'd done.

"I'm all right," he ground out as she threw herself down beside him. "Just take the arrows out and go. The others need you."

"But—"

"Just do it, Bryanna."

Bryanna swallowed hard, her hand shaking as she gripped the first arrow and pulled it out with a nauseating squelch.

Weylin grunted, digging his nails into the ground.

"Weylin?"

He nodded, his eyes squeezed tight as the wound knitted together before her eyes. "I'm fine. Get the other one, please."

Bryanna's hand wrapped around the second arrow. She wrenched it out, grimacing as though the arrow were being pulled from her own back.

Bryanna glanced up. The malignant being she'd seen nearing Liadan and Bain was almost upon them. Bain had finally seen it. He quickly dispatched the last spiked creature and pulled Liadan behind him, shielding her with his body.

"Go," said Weylin.

This time, she did.

"What is it?" Liadan yelled as Bryanna headed for them.

A lich! Bain replied, shoving her back farther.

Bryanna had heard of lichs. They were beings who'd placed dark spells on themselves, connecting their life forces to an object so they could lead immortal lives. There was only one way to destroy them—

"We have to find its phylactery!" she yelled as she reached them.

"His *what*?" cried Liadan.

A chest or box where he keeps his power, Bain answered. *It's the only way to kill it.*

"And where are we supposed to—"

But the lich had reached them. It wrenched Bain up by the throat, lifting him several paces into the air.

"Bain!"

Liadan threw herself at the lich, trying to force its arm down low enough for Bain's feet to touch the ground. His face was turning bright red, his eyes popping. But the lich lifted her off her feet, too.

"Let them go!" Bryanna screeched, grabbing the creature's other side.

But they were still no match for the being's strength. At least, not until Alec threw himself onto the lich from behind. Their combined weight was too much for the creature, and they toppled to the ground, their limbs tangled in a disarrayed mess.

"Liadan, the phylactery!" Bryanna yelled, helping Alec and Bain hold the lich down.

Liadan worked quickly, digging her hands into the being's cloak until she found a small, intricately carved box. She threw it into the closest burning ruins, stamping on it for good measure until it crumbled like old paper.

The lich gave a strangled cry. Before their eyes, its body lost its gray tinge, its hair darkened from silver-white to dirty blond. A soft, final, relieved sigh issued from the being's lips as it stared up at them, unseeing.

Bryanna dropped back, breathless.

And then a sound that curdled her blood sounded; Nisienne's mournful keening ripped through the air. The sorrow in it penetrated Bryanna's heart.

Somewhere, someone close to them was dying.

CHAPTER

THIRTY

Cold. Deep, impenetrable cold.

That was all Bryanna could register.

Not the fiery ruins, the shouting, grunting, moaning, triumphant cries, slashing swords, snapping bowstrings, galloping hooves, or rustling feet. Not even Nisienne's keening.

The Sheidlow Ruins were strewn with the prone bodies of familiar faces, though she fought to see past them to the individuals she was most desperate to find. Deagon and Seara were still in the trees, the latter clutching her head and wincing. Gawain and Fergus weren't far from them, facing a lone red-capped fiend. Nisienne sat huddled in the confines of a nearby ruin, nursing one of her crows against her chest, her head bent as the unnatural keening erupted from her lungs.

Bryanna's legs felt as though they couldn't hold her weight anymore. It must've been her aunt who Nisienne was sensing close to death. But where was she?

"Bryanna, breathe," Weylin implored, tilting her head up so she had no choice but to look into his pale, determined face.

How long had he been standing in front of her?

She forced herself to suck in a breath. Her lungs burned as though they'd been deprived of air for a while.

"My aunt ..." she whispered.

It isn't over yet, child, the unicorn's voice came to her. He stood on the edge of the forest, his white mane spoiled with blood and blackened tufts of hair. At his hooves were the ashen remains of the nightmare.

Weylin's grip on her tightened. "Nisienne's been wrong before."

But Bryanna knew she wasn't wrong this time. The same foreboding sense she'd had the last time she and Aveline had played together was there, its presence like an icy knot she couldn't shake.

Thinking of Aveline twisted her stomach to the point of pain. There'd been such faith in her eyes when she'd seen her in the In-Between plane. Aveline had truly believed Bryanna could beat the Brotherhood. She'd gone so far as to enlist Mistress Nichollson's assistance once she'd realized Bryanna wasn't backing down on her vow to avenge her.

And yet, Bryanna found herself failing her all over again.

Her gaze fell on the boarders, her heart lurching. Even if they survived the night, Vortigern would never let them walk away. Once he was done in Sheidlow Ridge, he'd pick them off one by one.

How long would it be before the Brotherhood turned up at the homes of her parents, brothers, sisters-in-law, and nephews?

Bryanna straightened at the unwelcome thought. There was no way Vortigern or the Brotherhood of Sìorraidh would *ever* touch another member of her family while she still breathed.

She pulled herself out of Weylin's grasp, resolution burning to the core of her soul. "I'm going after him."

Weylin nodded, his face set, as though he didn't expect any less. "I'm coming with you."

But Bryanna shook her head. "You're injured, Weylin. You're in no state to face him. Besides, this all started because of my family. It's why Brithlean Nichollson sought me out. It has to be me."

Weylin gripped her shoulders, his eyes intense as they bored into hers. "You don't need to do this alone."

"Yes. I do."

Bryanna fused her lips to his, needing the strength and warmth he could provide her unlike any other being.

"I'll be back," she whispered.

The unicorn trotted to her side. *I will take you to them.*

With Weylin's help, Bryanna mounted his back, clutching his mane to keep herself steady.

Then they were off, plunging into the forest.

Riding a unicorn was vastly different from riding any other steed. He moved so fast that Bryanna couldn't see more than a blur as they raced through the trees. He seemed to know where Vortigern and her aunt were, because he galloped deeper into the forest with precision, weaving through the thick trees and underbrush until Bryanna could no longer see where the forest started.

How had Obelia and Vortigern ended up so far from the Sheidlow Ruins?

Through there, child, the unicorn said when they stopped, tilting his head toward a sparse, unsettlingly quiet clearing ahead of them.

Bryanna slid off his back, her fingers stiff from how hard she'd been holding on to his mane. Her gaze darted around, noting the telltale signs of a vicious fight. Blood was splattered over branches, ferns uprooted from the ground. Daggers were stuck hilt-deep in tree trunks. She stepped gingerly over the bracken, treading as silently as she could. At the bottom of a small pine, she caught sight of something that made tears spring to her eyes. Tyffin's prone form was curled up on himself, huddled against the trunk, his vacant gray eyes staring up at the stars.

Bryanna's throat clogged as she forced herself to move forward. She didn't want to stop. Not until she'd made sure Vortigern *never* did such a thing to another living creature again.

On she went, using the cover of trees to conceal herself until she heard Vortigern's triumphant voice carry over to her—

"I have to admit, Mistress Nicholls, I was expecting so much more from you."

"I'm sorry to disappoint, Vortigern," Obelia's response came between labored breaths from where she lay, prone, on the forest floor.

A sinking feeling settled in Bryanna's chest. Although she'd been steeling herself to find her aunt in bad shape—bad enough for Nisienne's banshee senses to detect—she was unprepared to see her aunt looking so pale and sickly, a shell of her former self, as though she'd been facing faerie-stroke for years.

"It's quite all right, my dear. I'm sure you tried your best. Perhaps your niece will prove worthy of the fight I've been anticipating." He paused. "Do come out, little sorceress."

Bryanna froze.

She'd been so careful not to make any noise. How had he known she was there?

Pushing the thought aside, she balled her sweaty hands into fists, squared her shoulders, and stepped into the clearing, her gaze unflinching as she stared back at Vortigern. There was no way she'd huddle behind a tree trunk, letting him think she was afraid of him.

"Well, haven't you grown?" he said, looking at her as though he were a doting uncle taking her in after a long time apart.

Bryanna moved closer, her eyes narrowing to slits. "Remember me, do you?"

"Of course I do. And your cousin. Such a foolish young thing, telling me she was you."

Bryanna's stomach dropped, the way it always did at the mention of Aveline. Vortigern's words rebounded painfully in her mind. He had to be lying. Because if he were, then Aveline had died because of her. She couldn't bear for that to be true.

"That's a lie," she said.

Vortigern laughed. "Hardly. Isn't it precious, how one small act of defiance can change the course of so many lives? Had your cousin told me the truth, she would've been spared. Would you like to hear why we were in Castlereagh five years ago, little sorceress?"

"Sure," said Bryanna, her voice filled with contempt. "I want to know everything before I kill you."

Vortigern's guffaw echoed among the trees. "So courageous."

Bryanna arched a brow. "Are you stalling?"

"Can a man not pay you one last compliment?"

"You're not a man."

Vortigern threw his head back, his cold, cruel laugh echoing around the clearing. "No, you're right. I'm far more exalted than that."

His gaze flickered to Obelia. "Mistress Nicholls, I understand if you can't sit up, but do try to listen closely. I've a little tale about your strapping Fillian Conveil that may just help you manage your pain until your reunion."

Obelia's jaw clenched, her eyes becoming transfixed on

Vortigern, hungry to learn after so many years, the mystery behind her late betrothed's passing.

Bryanna rushed to her aunt. There was no way Vortigern would attack her just yet. He'd put too much time and effort getting them where he wanted to not gloat first.

She cast a perfunctory healing spell over Obelia, assessing her injuries. There weren't many. Besides a few scrapes and bruises, there was only a slight cut at Obelia's waist. A cut that should've been superficial. But if it was, why did her aunt look so close to death? Bryanna pulled on a little more magic, the way Lady Auberagh had taught her.

And then she felt it.

Dark magic.

It was coursing through her aunt, shutting her body down one organ at a time.

Bryanna's blood turned cold. She knew a little healing magic, but definitely not enough to restore the magnitude of destruction wreaking havoc on Obelia's system. They needed a strong healer, one who specialized in malignant magical wounds.

Still, Bryanna tried to purge as much of the spell's effects as she could. But it was no use. Whatever was flowing through Obelia was blocking her magic, keeping Bryanna from repairing the damage that had been inflicted on her organs.

"I met Fillian Conveil only once," said Vortigern. "He was so much like my younger self. Determined. Stubborn. He had a thirst to protect his family and all those who would come after him. I admired that."

Obelia made a sound of disgust. Despite her severe injuries, she was taking in his every word.

"I confess, I wanted him to join my brethren. I even offered him a place at my side. His loyalties, however, were not transferable. He retaliated by taking the lives of both my brothers. I know you may not think it, but I do know the pain of losing a loved one. And for what he did … his death was not enough."

Bryanna scoffed. She could tell by the expression on his face that he had no idea what the pain of losing a loved one was. The loss of his brothers had been merely a blow to his ego.

It wasn't vengeance that had made him seek retribution.

It was spite.

"As he lay taking his last breath through those overlarge canines, I swore to him that I would find all those he loved and destroy them as surely as he had my brothers. He died repenting the day he decided to come after me.

"It didn't take long to trace him back to Castlereagh. All I had to do was wait for his body to be identified by the authorities. I stood at the forefront of his funeral as he was laid to rest. That's when I saw you for the first time, Mistress Nicholls. A vision so like my own Brithlean that initially, I thought my eyes deceived me. You were all anyone could speak of: Obelia Nicholls, the woman who was burying her betrothed on the morning she should've wed him."

Obelia's grip tightened on Bryanna's hand, her gaze hardening as she continued to stare at Vortigern.

"I stayed my hand, delaying what I knew was inevitable, especially after I learned that you were not only an unusually gifted magic-weaver, but the very great-niece of my first love, the woman who made me what I am. But as the moon cycles went by, you began to prove yourself resourceful—too resourceful. I decided it was time we had that confrontation you so desperately sought. I let you capture me, put that knife to my throat … and then you disappeared.

"For moon cycles, I waited to hear word of what happened to you. No one knew where you'd disappeared to, not even that besotted ally of yours, Alec Marrock, and he was combing all of

Otherworld for you. Then, a year later, news came to me of a mage who'd opened a sanctuary for paranormal beings and ailments. And who should be the proprietor of the establishment but the very magic-weaver who intrigued me like no other in centuries? I would've come for you then, except that I liked knowing you were still around. That in your blood flowed the magic I might one day need again."

Vortigern turned, his gaze locking on Bryanna. "But five years ago, we learned of a possible new threat to me. That's where you come in, little sorceress. One of my spies reported known members of the Brithlean League following you. You were twelve years old and already showing promising signs of magic. One magic-weaver from the Nichollson bloodline was a risk. Two was a threat. So I decided to travel to Castlereagh personally. One of you needed to be eliminated."

"That's why you took Aveline," Bryanna whispered, her stomach churning.

Vortigern inclined his head. "I took the wrong child. By the time I realized, it was too late. I couldn't get to you a second time. Not with the protective spells your aunt and Myrrdin Taliesen placed over you and your family.

"But when we heard you'd become the youngest sorceress of the century, I knew I had to act. Too many whispers were traveling around Otherworld. Whispers of the Nicholls magic-weavers someday being my undoing. And so, here we are."

"You do realize that by coming to Sheidlow Ridge, you've decimated your army," said Bryanna tartly.

Vortigern laughed. "Foolish girl. I can build an army just as formidable as the one in the Sheidlow Ruins before your family has you resting alongside your cousin."

Bryanna jumped to her feet. "I won't let that happen."

Vortigern let the cloak about his shoulders billow to the floor. "Sweet, deluded child, don't you understand? Your aunt had to die because she's always been a threat to me. But you? Your death is merely a precaution."

"Bryanna, run!" Obelia cried.

But Bryanna couldn't move. Her feet were rooted to the spot, unable to tear her gaze away from Vortigern as his remains slumped to the ground, leaving behind a distorted, hunchbacked figure with translucent skin the color of aged parchment, a skull clear of hair, and eyes as black as soot.

Bryanna pulled up the strongest magical shield she could muster, but Vortigern breezed through it as though it were made of smoke and slammed into her with the force of a carthorse. She steeled herself against his penetration, but it was no use. His foreign presence coursed into her, weighing her down as though she were being filled to the brim with clay.

Vortigern was taking over her body, his essence overpowering hers one cell at a time. In a matter of seconds, she'd be nothing more than another one of his victims. Fate had played her a cruel hand, granting her reprieve after reprieve, only to fail her when she'd counted on it most.

Child? The unicorn's voice came to her from far away. *Remember, your magic is a part of you. It wants to survive as much as you do.*

As if in accordance with his words, her magic rushed forward, wrapping itself around her like a cocoon, or perhaps it was Bryanna wrapping herself around it.

Vortigern may have taken control of her body, but she was still tethered to her mind—and her magic.

She pulled on it, using it as a shield to fight back against his grip. Almost immediately, Vortigern's grip, which had felt so unmalleable, became brittle, like old, decaying wood. She pulled on more of her magic, purging his gluttonous presence from every fiber of her being.

The clearing came back into view, as did the feeling of loose, dense soil beneath her feet, and the tang of fear and determination on her tongue.

"Bryanna," Obelia cried, her voice coarse. "How?"

"An excellent question," a deep, deadly voice said to Bryanna's left.

Vortigern's hideously deformed figure stood before them. Bryanna was surprised he hadn't jumped into her aunt's body—but perhaps he'd maimed it beyond the capacity for possession.

She didn't think twice, throwing the same blood-poisoning spell Obelia had used on him when he'd taken possession of Orlagh.

But Vortigern didn't flinch as her spell took hold. Instead, he laughed, the sound sending chills over her skin. "Silly girl, I have ruled kingdoms, occupied the most sumptuous homes, and lived the most lavish lifestyles in existence. Did you really think no one had ever tried to take it from me? That I haven't modified this form to survive anything that could be used against it?"

Vortigern raised his arms, unleashing a bout of magic so powerful that the trees around them crackled ominously.

"Don't you see, little sorceress? You can't defeat me. No one can!"

Bryanna's breath hitched, though not for the reason Vortigern intended. There was something uncanny about the magic he was employing. She'd felt it before, weeks back, when Mistress Nichollson had taken her through time to show her how she'd performed her abominable ritual. Bryanna had assumed she'd brought her back to show her what she'd done, but that wasn't the only reason. She'd been trying to show her *how* she'd done it. Brithlean hadn't just turned Vortigern into a body-weaver, she'd transferred her magic to him. It was the only way he could've survived such a devastating magical transfiguration.

She'd wanted Bryanna to understand the spell so she could figure out how to free him from it.

And Bryanna knew exactly how to do that. The spell didn't need to be *reversed*; Vortigern simply needed to be *released* from it. And there was one sure way to ensure that happened—by using the same element that created him.

Fire.

Bryanna unleashed her magic into the ground, setting the perimeter surrounding them ablaze with the same flame she'd conjured on Beltane Eve.

"Foolish girl," Vortigern flung at her as the flames rose up high, enclosing them in a wall of burning orange and red. "It will take more than that to destroy me."

"Yes, it will," said a raspy voice.

Mistress Nichollson had materialized beside Bryanna, as clear and corporeal as Bryanna had been the night she'd crossed into the In-Between plane.

Shock filled Vortigern's features, though he was quick to mask it. "Brithlean. How I had hoped you would have found peace by now."

"I will soon enough," Mistress Nichollson sneered before turning to Bryanna. "Hurry, girl. The veil has dropped for Lammas, but it won't stay down for long. Invoke the incantation. It's the only way to stop him."

The words Mistress Nichollson had constantly repeated in Bryanna's dreams came back to her, the foreign words as familiar as those of the latest ballads sung around Castlereagh. Bryanna's mouth moved, forming the words of the *olde* tongue that would unmake what Vortigern was. The words streamed out of her, the power it carried thrumming in her blood. Never had she conjured such power, and in that moment, she didn't care about the consequences that wielding such strong ancient magic would have on her, not if it meant the end of Vortigern's reign.

"What are you doing?" Vortigern bellowed, an ugly look crossing his face. "Stop her, Brithlean! You know what will happen if she succeeds."

But Mistress Nichollson sent him a smile to match the cold, cruel one he'd bestowed upon her centuries ago as she'd lain dying at his feet.

"You fool!" Vortigern lunged for Bryanna, but she pulled on an extra spurt of magic, raising a wall of fire between them, keeping him from reaching her. "I'm not the worst thing out there! Otherworld needs me!"

"No, it doesn't," Bryanna said, momentarily breaking off mid-chant. "You've cost good people their lives. People who were meant to have had more than the unfinished existence you forced upon them."

"You're making a mistake!"

Licks of flames surrounded Vortigern, catching easily on his skin. He screamed in agony, trying to snuff them out, but the fire wouldn't extinguish.

Bryanna wouldn't let it.

She watched in a detached, almost indifferent way, as his body crippled before her eyes. Darkness hedged at the corners of her vision, but Bryanna continued to feed the flames, continued her chant, fighting to remain conscious, even as the exertion took its toll. Her heart pounded dully against her chest, but she didn't stop, didn't care how much her body protested from the copious outpouring of magic she was channeling.

"Bryanna, enough!" Obelia cried as Vortigern fell forward, no more than crumbled ashes.

It was the last thing Bryanna heard before her vision faded to black.

CHAPTER

THIRTY-ONE

Bryanna stood in front of a familiar tall building with mauve stone walls that glistened in the afternoon sun. An arched alcove with four stone steps led up to soaring oak double doors. She would've sworn it was the Sheidlow Tower, except there were slight differences. Its walls were festooned with crawling gardens that didn't exist at the Sheidlow Tower she knew, and a massive sundial sat on the right side of the front lawn. Four small cottages stood on either side of the ironstone path, near where the forest started, each surrounded by garden beds and connecting pebbled tracks.

A group of children, younger than any Obelia had ever taken in, ran out the front doors. Bryanna followed them over to the courtyard, where six adults sat, poring over an ancient map. The one closest to her was Bain, though he looked much older. Late thirties, if she had to guess. Lines she'd only ever glimpsed around his eyes when he laughed had turned into permanent creases. He sat next to Liadan, whose red hair was graying at the temples. Her scars were still prominent along her skin, but unlike her teenage self, who'd always hidden them, she wore a short-sleeved blouse that displayed them proudly.

Elgar was there too. His body had filled out, and there was a healthy glow about him. Opposite him was Weylin, who looked the most changed out of all of them. The Weylin she knew wasn't lanky by any means, but he was nowhere near as well-built as the man in front of her. He was chiseled and hard-muscled, his linen shirt clinging to his biceps, threatening to burst at the seams. A sense of danger emanated from him, though that could've been because of the faded scar running over his jawline, down the base of his throat, and past the collar of his shirt.

A stunningly beautiful young woman sat beside him. She had a heart-shaped face, dark, smoky-blue eyes, and thick, dark hair that barely stayed pinned at the back of her head due to its sheer volume. She had to be Weylin's daughter, grown up.

Sitting next to her was a woman who looked a lot like Obelia but could only be herself. Her hair was pulled back in a Celtic bun, her cheekbones defined thanks to the translucency of her skin. An air of authority and accomplishment surrounded her, the likes of which Bryanna had never felt in her life before.

"Hello, Bree."

Aveline stood by her side. Except it wasn't Aveline as she'd ever seen her. She looked like a young woman, resplendent in a long, shimmering white dress, her hair dressed in thick curls over her shoulders.

"Let me guess," Bryanna said in a flat tone. "I'm in the In-Between plane again?"

Aveline shook her head. "Just dreaming ... sort of."

"Sort of?"

Aveline shrugged. "They wanted to give you a glimpse of your future."

"Who did?"

"I can't tell you."

Bryanna rolled her eyes. "Tell me this, then. Did you really tell Vortigern you were me when you ... when he took you?"

"You would've done the same for me," Aveline said without a hint of regret.

"Aveline ... you were only twelve."

"Everything happened the way it was supposed to. I was meant to be the one the Brotherhood of Sìorraidh took, just like you were meant to defeat them. That wouldn't have happened if it had been you who'd died that day. We're all where we should be ... or will be soon. That's why I'm here. To say goodbye."

It was as though the floor had given out beneath Bryanna. "What do you mean?"

"You did what you set out to do. Now you can make your peace with my passing. And I can move on, too, knowing you're safe."

"Move on to where?" Bryanna asked, her voice catching on the lump in her throat.

"Somewhere they wouldn't let me go while I haunted you. But now ... now we can let each other go."

Bryanna swallowed the sting of tears tightening the back of her throat. "I can't do that."

Aveline smiled. "Not completely, no. I think that regardless of where we are, we'll always feel a pull toward each other. It's what will allow us to meet again one day. Now, you need to go. They need you back."

Bryanna wanted to protest, but she was too choked up to form words.

Aveline's arms came around her, squeezing her tight. "I'll check in on you when I can. Gawain too."

Then Bryanna was rising up into darkness with blinding speed.

She came to lying over a white mane that reeked of acrid, burned hair. Wind swept across her face with biting ferocity. She opened her eyes, catching sight of the blur of trees on either side of her and the Sheidlow Tower looming in the distance.

Somehow, she'd ended up astride the unicorn again.

Behind her came a husky, relieved sigh, and the smell of faint pine mixed with the tangy scent of metal reached her nostrils.

"Weylin?" she said through a paper-dry mouth, pushing herself up.

"I'm here." His arms, which had been encircled around her middle, keeping her astride the unicorn, tightened. "The battle's over. Vortigern's dead."

His words were like a cool balm on a severe bout of sunburn.

They'd done it.

They'd won.

But if that was the case, why did Weylin's voice sound so constricted?

And then, with a sinking feeling deep in the pit of her chest, she remembered—

"My aunt. Is she—"

Weylin swallowed hard, as though he'd gulped down a whole apple without chewing it. "She's at the tower. Lady Auberagh and Elgar were going to do what they could ..."

I'm sorry, Child, said the unicorn.

Bryanna didn't respond. They had to be wrong. Sure, Obelia had been severely wounded, but Lady Auberagh had brought patients out of death's baleful grip before. She would do the same with her aunt.

They reached the tower a moment later. Bryanna slid off the unicorn and hurried past the Brithlean League members illuminated by the glowing lamplight of the front steps, who were laying blankets over those who'd perished on the battlefield. Others were huddled together on the courtyard tables, curved in on themselves.

She swept past them and raced up the stairs, barely noticing the makeshift healing center that had been erected in the cavernous kitchen. On her aunt's floor, she found Liadan limping from Obelia's door to Elgar's and back again, her eyes red-rimmed. She threw her arms around Bryanna as soon as she saw her. Neither of them spoke. They didn't need to. The sorrow, horror, and desolation of everything they'd been through that night—were still going through—couldn't be articulated by mere words.

"Go," Liadan sniffed, releasing her. "Obelia has been asking for you."

Bryanna swept past her into Obelia's bedchamber. Lady Auberagh, Alec, Gawain, Master Taliesen, and Bain were there, standing around Obelia's bed. The latter was kneeling at her side, his head bent as Obelia whispered something to him. His shoulders shook silently as he nodded at whatever she said. Bryanna's heart went out to him. He'd lost his adoptive father, brother, and the closest thing he'd had to a mother figure, all in the space of a couple of days.

"Bryanna's here," said Master Taliesen softly.

Bain slid over as far as he could without letting go of Obelia's hand, giving Bryanna an unhindered view of her aunt. It was all she could do not to take an involuntary step back. Dark maroon splotches marred her face, and her skin was so blue, she reminded Bryanna of Elgar. Any hope she'd harbored that Lady Auberagh and the others could heal her vanished. If only she'd gotten to her aunt sooner. If she had, she could've kept Vortigern from doing what he had. Could've prevented what was happening to her.

"Bryanna?" Obelia rasped, lifting her head from the bed.

"I'm here." Bryanna moved until she was kneeling at her side.

Obelia sank back against her pillows. "You were wonderful."

Bryanna's throat clogged with suppressed emotion.

"I need you to understand, this ... isn't your fault." Obelia swallowed, a wet, guttural sound. "After I'm gone, I want you to go to my desk. There are a few things there you'll need." Obelia's free hand touched Bryanna's cheek. "You're going to be an extraordinary woman."

Bryanna's eyes welled, though she tried to keep her tears at bay. She wanted Obelia to see her as the strong, remarkable woman she thought she'd become, even if such a thing felt so out of reach at that moment.

Obelia's gaze shifted to the window, as though she'd heard her name. Her lips tugged up in a tender smile, seeing someone none of the others could. She took one more deep, labored breath, and the hand over Bryanna's cheek fell to the counterpane.

She remained that way until Bain reached over and closed her lids for the last time.

***

Obelia's funeral was held a few days later in a small grove, a short walking distance from the Sheidlow Tower. People from all over Otherworld journeyed to Sheidlow Ridge to pay their last respects. Among them were many of Obelia's ex-boarders, as well as a myriad of people Obelia had helped throughout her life. Several Sheidlow Ridge villagers turned up, too, as well as the few surviving Brithlean League members who'd opted to remain behind to see Obelia off.

Bryanna's family was there as well, except for her eldest brother, Aedàn, and his wife, Ainslie, who hadn't been able to make the journey. Upon arrival, Mr. Nicholls had locked himself in his sister's bedchamber and hadn't come out for two days, leaving Bryanna and her mother to make the funeral arrangements. Mrs. Nicholls had been in her element, arranging everything, which was just as well because Bryanna hadn't felt like talking to the flower suppliers or gravediggers.

Nor had she had time. The morning after the Brotherhood's defeat, Bryanna, Lady Auberagh, Master Taliesen, and Lady Oona—who was recovering from her own injuries—had been kept busy with Bain, who'd woken up with his telepathic barriers shattered. By the time they'd subdued him, they were all nursing migraines.

The funeral itself lasted well into the evening.

Mr. Nicholls had been the first to stand before the congregation. He spoke of Obelia's affinity for helping those less fortunate than herself, even from an early age, as well as her love for her boarders and how she'd regarded them as an extension of herself. By the time he'd stepped down, his cheeks were wet, and he'd stopped trying to wipe the tears away.

Gawain had gone next, opening with an anecdote that made them all laugh and cry at the same time. As he shared details of his antics with Obelia, it was as though she were alive and with them again.

Bryanna went next. She'd prepared a few words, but as she stood in front of everyone gathered, she'd scrunched her paper up in her stiff, clammy palms. The words she'd written didn't encompass what she was feeling. Instead, she forced herself to look away from the sea of faces whose gazes were trained on her, cleared her clogged throat, and began her eulogy, speaking from the heart.

"There isn't a lot I can say about my aunt that hasn't

already been said. Growing up, I didn't spend much time with her. She was always here in Sheidlow Ridge, caring for her boarders. But even then, I knew a lot about her. I think all of Otherworld did. That she was a gifted healer, generous and brave. What I didn't know until I came to stay with her these last few moon cycles, though, was how compassionate she really was. My aunt refused to turn anyone away, regardless of who or what they were or what people said against them."

Up in one of the tree boughs, Cayde lowered his head, tears streaming down his cheeks.

"She dedicated her life to helping anyone who needed it, regardless of whether it was acknowledged or appreciated. It's why her passing is such a tragedy, not just for my family and her friends, but to every being in Otherworld. My aunt knew the risks involved in facing what we did, and still, she sacrificed her life for it because that's who she was. It's thanks to her that we face a new age, free from the fear of a silent, slippery enemy stealing our loved ones away. And although I will miss her, I know that wherever she is, she's with those she loved and lost, and that one day we will meet again."

The congregation clapped as Bryanna bowed her head. Unlike with the other speakers, though, the applause didn't stop once she'd sat down beside her father. It grew louder until those who'd been sitting stood, and there wasn't a single person whose hands were still.

If Bryanna thought her feelings of loss would fade a few days after Obelia's funeral, she was wrong. Obelia's absence continued to weigh heavily on her the more time passed. There wasn't a day she didn't yearn for just a few more moments with her.

A week passed before Bryanna could bring herself to enter Obelia's office. In there, she found two envelopes. The first held the deeds to the Sheidlow Tower and the Mage's Sanctuary, all of which were to be transferred to Bryanna in the event of Obelia's death. The second was a letter addressed to her. She unfolded it with shaky fingers and read it.

Dearest Bryanna,

If you're reading this, then it can only mean I'm no longer in your world. By now, you would've no doubt seen the deeds to the Sheidlow Tower and the Mage's Sanctuary. Both are yours to do with as you please.

If by chance you do decide to keep the Mage's Sanctuary running, there are a few things I wish someone had told me when I first started. You'll make mistakes, and giving up will be easier than trying. But you are persistent and highly intuitive, and I know you have what is needed to ensure the Mage's Sanctuary endures.

To help you, here are a few tips:

1. Make sure you know what allergies your boarders have. This was the first blunder I ever made, after I cooked Lochiel Blackburn a supper of wolfsbane-marinated beef. He was writhing on the floor after his first bite.

2. Don't administer under-matured sleeping tonics. I accidentally swapped the wrong phials one night, and several of my charges slept for a week, even with the strongest smelling salts under their noses. Don't tell Lady Auberagh.

3. Don't forget to recharge the protection spells around the livestock and vegetable patches. This needs to happen every few weeks, or they weaken.

There are many more, but you'll figure them out. And believe me, you won't make the same mistake twice.

There is another reason I am writing to you. Even if you decide to leave Sheidlow Ridge, and Vortigern and the Brotherhood of Sìorraidh are defeated, the danger has not passed. In fact, things will only get worse. There are many nameless, faceless dangers in our realm. They've been kept subdued, thanks to the Brotherhood, but with them gone, these threats will be eager to rise. Stay vigilant and keep your allies close.

Until we see each other again, I remain yours sincerely,
Aunt Obelia

P.S.: If you can, look out for Bain. He was never just a boarder.

A knock on the office door made Bryanna look up. Weylin stood at the threshold, a smile that didn't quite reach his eyes on his lips. He came around to the back of her chair, rested his hands on her stiff shoulders, and leaned down, his lips pressing warm kisses down her face until he was nuzzled in the crook of her neck.

"You reading your aunt's letter again?" he asked, his breath warm against her ear.

Bryanna nodded, her cheek grazing the short stubs of his regrowth as she moved her head up and down.

"Do you know what you're going to do? Where you're going from here?"

"I have an idea," she said, the snippet of future Aveline had shown her clear in her mind: the Mage's Sanctuary thriving once more, children playing around the tower, Weylin sitting in the courtyard with Bain, Liadan, and the others, his daughter beside him. That image was imprinted in her memory. It would be the driving force that kept her strong, whatever the future brought.

A lot needed to be done before she could adequately restore

the Mage's Sanctuary to what it once was. Already, most of the boarders had left. Only Liadan, Bain, Elgar, and Seara remained, the latter having nowhere else to go—at least not for another two days, after which Bryanna would be eighteen and legally eligible to claim her as a ward.

She put Obelia's envelopes on the desk and placed her hands over Weylin's, giving them a small squeeze as she steeled herself to start the conversation they'd both known was inevitable for days.

"Are you going back to Dalvin's Pound?"

It was his turn to nod. "Now that the Brithlean League has fulfilled its purpose and Iodhna has been handed over to the authorities, I need to go home. There are things I have to take care of."

Bryanna tried to swallow the lump forming in her throat. She'd known he wouldn't have remained at the Sheidlow Tower much longer, but that didn't make the fact that he was leaving any easier to hear. Nor did the fact that she was worried about who he was going back to, or more accurately, *what*. There was still a lot Weylin hadn't told her about his father and the faoladh tribes around Otherworld. She couldn't shake the sense that he was heading into danger. One much more insidious than what they'd been up against with Vortigern and the Brotherhood.

She knew that she wouldn't be able to change his mind, though. Especially when he was returning for his newborn daughter. So instead of trying to convince him to remain at the Sheidlow Tower to help her rebuild what her aunt had created, she molded her lips to his, channeling everything she felt for him into it, as though it would help keep him safe while they were apart.

He kissed her back just as intently, and Bryanna tried to block out how her heart panged against her chest as she wondered how much time would pass before they'd be together again.

That night, Bryanna dreamed of Obelia standing on the ironstone path, wearing a glorious bridal gown, looking young and bright and happy. Bryanna waved to her from the oak double doors. Obelia's smile was radiant as she waved back. Then she turned to where Fillian Conveil was waiting for her at the tree line, handsomely dressed in a tailored black tailcoat and fur-trimmed cloak. She walked over to him, the train of her dress trailing behind her yet never overturning a single ironstone, and took the arm he offered. Together, they set off down the path.

Bryanna recalled a similar dream. Unlike that one, though, Obelia disappeared down the ironstone path and never returned.

BRYANNA & WEYLIN'S STORY WILL CONTINUE...

Purchase your preorder of *The Mage's Successor* now and have your copy sent straight to you as soon as it releases in Mid-2026.

You can preorder your copy by visiting S. A. Caddell's website here: www.sacaddellbooks.com

JOIN S. A. CADDELL'S NEWSLETTER

Want FREE bonus scenes and the latest updates on S. A. Caddell?

Join S. A. Caddell's newsletter and you'll receive a FREE short story, as well as be the first to know about the latest news on her books, exclusive sneak peeks, giveaways and more!

You can sign up at www.sacaddellbooks.com.

FROM THE AUTHOR

Thank you for reading *The Mage's Sanctuary*. I hope you enjoyed reading this book as much as I did writing it. If you could, I would be incredibly grateful if you could take a few moments to leave a review. Your support would help my books find more readers and continue to bring magical stories like mine to life.

Acknowledgments

The Mage's Sanctuary has been many years in the making, and in that time there have been many ups and downs. I spent years believing I'd finished my final draft, only to set it aside for a few weeks and come back to it and being compelled to make a change ... or ten. Each time, I convinced myself that I was making the story that much better (and I still believe I did!). If it wasn't for the following people convincing me it was finally time to get Bryanna's story out into the world, I don't think this book would've ever made it into your hands:

My sister, Rosie. Thank you for reading the first hundred variations of The Mage's Sanctuary, even though you could no longer distinguish between versions. Your constant belief in this story and my abilities as a writer is one of the reasons I never gave up on my dream to be an author.

My mother, father, brother, and grandparents. Thank you for supporting me when I finished high school and decided to not apply for an Arts/Science degree like I originally wanted and instead put forth an application for a Professional Writing & Editing Advanced Diploma (and getting in the first time around, despite being told by the university that they didn't usually take in high school graduates!). And then following it up with an Art Degree in Creative Writing a few years later.

To Donna, for being my first official beta reader. Thank you for your patience as I tried to figure out how to use Google Docs so that you could comment/make changes to my manuscript.

You have no idea how nerve-racking it was to send my manuscript to you and wait for your feedback. Thank you for all your kind words and encouragement, and for helping me elevate this book to a whole new level.

To my critique partners, Shab and Hope, thank you for picking up on all the repetitions and typos, for pointing out which sections didn't work or make sense, and best of all, for all the "LOL" and "LMAO" comments. Also, for your love and enthusiasm for my characters. I promise you will be seeing much more of Gawain Nicholls!

To my developmental/copyeditor, Jennifer Sommersby. I was so nervous when I first approached you. Being so new to the publishing world, I didn't know who to approach to edit my baby. I remember finding your name listed at the front of one of my favorite author's books and looking you up online. When I saw you offered one-on-one consultations, I remember spending at least an hour compositing the message I sent and praying that you wouldn't see it, roll your eyes, and delete it without contacting me. Instead, your response was immediate, and we met virtually a few days later. I remember losing all feeling in my legs when I got your email. And when we met and I told you about the manuscripts I had written, one of the first things you did was welcome me to the author community.

By the time I sent you Bryanna's first book, I knew I had something that I could be proud to put forth into the world. But with your help, I was able to craft a book well beyond anything I could've done on my own. Thank you for all the hours you have spent converting my manuscript into US spelling, correcting all my grammatical errors (I know there were a TON), pointing out all my misuse of words, and nudging me to delve further into my characters and their situations.

And lastly, I would like to thank you, my reader. However

my book came to you, I am so grateful that you have taken the time to read it, and get to this page. I hope you have enjoyed this book and that it is something you will come back to from time to time, just like I have.

ABOUT THE AUTHOR

S. A. Caddell writes captivating romantic fantasy stories with strong Celtic and British Folklore elements. She is a bookworm at heart and would love nothing more than to spend the rest of her life curled up on a sofa (or in bed if it's winter), getting lost in a book she is reading or writing.

A perfectionist at heart, she writes stories that are a labor of love and will hopefully teach her readers something. She hopes to write characters that become as unforgettable to them as they have been to her, who will offer them the comfort and solace getting lost in her characters' world has provided her. When she isn't reading or writing, she can be found watching documentaries on Celtic mythology, 18th-century living, or funny cat videos.

The Mage's Sanctuary is her first book and she is excited about finally releasing it into the world.

You can find out more about S. A. Caddell and her books at www.sacaddellbooks.com.

facebook.com/s.a.caddell

instagram.com/s.a.caddell.author

tiktok.com/@s.a.caddell_author